The Paths
of Marriage

The Paths
of Marriage

A NOVEL

Mala Kumar

Bedazzled Ink Publishing Company • Fairfield, California

978-1-939562-58-6 paperback
978-1-939562-59-3 ebook

Cover Design
by

TreeHouseStudio

BInk
a division of
Bedazzled Ink Publishing Company
Fairfield, California
http://www.bedazzledink.com

To my amazing mother and father—Latha and Ashok Kumar. Thank you for having the strength and courage for letting me grow into the person I am.

To Kiran Kumar—the best brother one could hope to have. Thank you for your unconditional support.

To my resilient grandparents—Lalitha and Sri Rama, and to my aunts, uncles, and cousins around the world. Thank you for showing me true wisdom takes generations to contextualize.

To my insightful development editor—Mya Spalter. Thank you for your guidance. To my line editor—Keidi Keating. Thank you for your attention to the details.

To my inspiring friends—APS, AKF, AE, LV, ES, PB, JS, VSK, KP, NG, SA, KLW, AI, EAE, FBK, FC, JC, MM, HWGF, ZH, GS, MV, MTC, MLC, ST, JV, KAH, AEW, MJW, and LT. Thank you for your ever-present encouragement. This book would not have happened without your help.

Finally, to my 11th grade English teacher—Bear O'Bryan. You gave me one of the most important pieces of advice in my life: "Mala, you really need to work on your writing skills."

Definitions of Commonly Used Terms

1. Amma—he Telugu (see below) word for 'mother'
2. Nana—the Telugu word for 'father'
3. Avva—the Telugu word for 'grandmother'
4. Pinni—the Telugu word for 'mother's younger sister'
5. Shudra *—the fourth of the Varna caste system, often known as the servant caste
6. Caste *—a social structure in India that divides the population into traditional labor roles
7. Chennai—a city in south India and the capital of the Indian state, Tamil Nadu. The former British colonialist name for Chennai was Madras
8. Bangalore **—a city in south India and the capital of the Indian state, Karnataka
9. Telugu—a south Indian language spoken in parts of Chennai and Bangalore, among other places
10. Tamil—a south Indian language spoken in Chennai, among other places
11. Kannada—a south Indian language spoken in Bangalore
12. Beta—a word in Hindi that literally means 'son' that is used more generically to mean 'dear'
13. Standard (use: second standard)—a grade level in school

* These terms have historically, economically, and socially complicated definitions that can vary greatly according to the defining source. Definitions provided here are simplified for the sole purpose to aid in reading *The Paths of Marriage*.

** Bangalore is the British colonialist name for the city of Bengaluru; it is used in The *Paths* of Marriage as it today remains the most commonly used name for the city.

Ekam sat vipraha bahudha vadanti

Truth is one, the wise call It by various names

—Rig Veda 1.164.46

Part I

Lakshmi

Chapter 1

I AWOKE TO a crash loud enough to disturb the Gods. As my blurred vision came into focus, I saw my mother standing a few feet away from me, swearing under her breath as she bent over the contents of a small Tiffin container that bled streams of *sambhar* down its side. She cursed her clumsiness and began cleaning the mess off of the small plastic runner that served as our kitchen floor.

Trying not to make too much noise, I shifted in my cot to peer out of the door. A few warm sunrays lent enough light to show the first signs of life in our Chennai village. On the other half of my cot, my baby sister was curled up, resting peacefully. I pulled myself up so as not to disturb her.

"Morning, amma," I said to my mother.

"Good morning, my dear." Her voice was strained.

"Can I help you, amma?"

"No, don't worry. You go get ready for school."

I lingered for a few seconds, hoping she would follow with the most anticipated words that anyone in our village could hope to hear. On some lucky mornings, I ate before preparing for school. Amma telling me to go and get ready meant this was not one of those mornings.

At the other end of our dirt-packed six-meter house was my school uniform. Quietly changing, I heard my mother in the background stifling her cries. The sound of strain in her voice always sent a chill down my spine. I hated hearing amma cry.

Dressed in my sweat-stained uniform, I walked outside and saw our village was already abuzz at that early morning hour. The toils of preparing for the day had begun: walk half a kilometer, collect the water, build a fire, prepare the vegetables, cook the food. I saw one of the villagers twisting his body in his dancelike bathing ritual a few one-room houses down. He was the only person I had ever met who could coat his entire body with less than two cups of water.

I made my way to our outhouse; it was a simple structure of scrap wood and a half-buried plastic bucket, though it took us two months to scrounge the village for the materials. It was worth every painstaking minute. Our neighbors looked at us with envy for having a place to defecate so close to our house. Most of them were forced to walk a kilometer to the nearest public lavatory or cover their droppings like dogs in the wild.

I used the last of the soap in the tin cup hanging on the door. We were taught in the second standard the importance of washing. I still remember the absolute pride I had in standing up and informing the other students that I already knew this fact because my amma was the most intelligent woman in our village.

Back inside, I saw amma had cleaned up the mess, salvaging the bits of food that weren't completely coated in village grime. She was an excellent cook. I was sure the vegetables tasted like little treats from the Heavens, even with the dirt. Amma did not offer me any of the food; I knew she was not saving it for herself.

I softly called out to her that I was leaving. She turned around and gave me her usual radiant smile, which always lit up the village far better than the sun did.

"Look at my daughter. You are the smartest person I know, my dear."

"Look at my amma. You are the wisest person I know."

"Make nana and I proud, okay?"

I told her I would. Making my parents proud was the motivating factor that unlocked my every passion and desire for a better life. As I turned to walk out the door, my stomach growled. Spilling food was not something we could afford to do.

1950S INDIA DID not provide me with electricity, running water, adequate nutrition, or public transport. In fact, it barely provided a roof over my head. The one thing 1950s India did provide me with was an education.

For ten years, I walked three kilometers each way to get to school. At the age of eight, I had my first terrifying glimpse of the world beyond the boundaries of my village. At age twelve, the walk was a familiar playing ground to relieve tension before a long day of studying. At age sixteen, it was a stressful addition to my already busy life. At age eighteen, that walk had become a stepping-stone to achieving the unimaginable. An education would bring a better life.

"Lakshmi. Lakshmi. Lakshmi!" I heard someone shouting.

As I approached the final steps, I turned around and saw my best friend running toward me. Her parents had chosen her name, Alpa, meaning "small," in the hopes that their daughter would grow up to be a tiny, fair-skinned princess. Much to their dismay, Alpa used her parents' relative wealth to stuff herself with candy. The extra weight slowed her down, prolonging her exposure to the sun.

We had nothing in common. She dreamed of an easy and tranquil life, whereas I dreamed of having enough work to support my family. She was at the bottom of our class, and I did everything in my power to ensure I stayed at the top. But Alpa had the kindest heart of anyone I had ever met.

While the other students threw dirt in my face, stole my pencils, and called me a peasant girl, Alpa stood by me.

"Chee. What did you get on your uniform?" I asked as she waddled up to me.

Alpa peered down at the dark stain on her stomach before looking back up at me with a smile. Of course the stain was chocolate, and of course Alpa did not worry that it ruined her uniform. For Alpa, life was much too fun to worry about such small problems.

I shook my head to demonstrate my disapproval of her habits. Secretly, I was just trying to distract myself from my growling hunger. Sometimes I was envious of Alpa and her carefree attitude about the world. Carefree was not something I could afford.

Alpa sheepishly looked down at the floor. She meant no harm. I apologized for being so mean.

"I'm just nervous about final exams next week. Come on, let's go inside."

Made of a mix of mud, cement, sweat and tears, our school stood three stories high. Its sand-colored exterior matched the outside ground so perfectly that it was not unusual to hear someone had walked straight into the walls after the sunset. Eventually, our headmaster made the same mistake and decided to use the government tuition money to have life-sized portraits of himself painted on the walls.

"The colorful exterior is a safety measure for the students," he said.

No one could question him—what could a villager say to rebuke the powerful headmaster? We could not complain even though the tuition money was supposed to be for books. Village children lived with what headmaster wanted, and headmaster wanted giant portraits of his face.

Our humble school hosted all twelve standards for the surrounding population of nearly one million people. Even as a poor village girl, I prayed that the building would not collapse under the pressure of the students' constant worry for their futures.

When villagers petitioned the local government to build another school, the official government response was always the same. "Stop complaining. There is very little demand past the second standard."

Very few families could surpass the limitations of poverty to keep their children in school past the second standard, beyond the age of eight. We could not argue either way.

My parents' childhoods had been no different. My father, my nana, had been pulled out of school in the first standard so he could help support the family. Amma had only attended school twice before her father dragged out by her hair and beat her for trying. When Amma was eight years old, she decided to break that cycle with her daughter. She endured constant heckling from the villagers to have me married. In three weeks, I would be the first person on either side of our family to graduate from higher secondary standards. I was already the most educated person in the family—man or woman.

The rooms were crowded, we were four to a book, and had few other supplies. I knew no different. This building had allowed me to see the wonders of the world that no one else in my family had ever had the privilege of knowing. The Pyramids of Egypt, Darwin's theory of evolution, the czars before the USSR . . . Whatever the subject, I found everything fascinating.

In 1950s India, a desire to learn was rarely met with praise. Being a girl, being poor, and just being was never easy in India. Your character was the least important measure of your worth. Most people in school regularly put me in my place.

"Scheduled caste is the only reason you are here, Lakshmi. You don't deserve to go to school." the other students except Alpa would taunt.

Despite the constant reminders of my place in society, I enjoyed every minute of my education . . . until this year. Even in our common Chennai village school, most of the teachers desired to impart knowledge on their students. They did not approve of my caste, they did not approve of my poverty, but they allowed me the privilege of learning without insulting me. That year, however, our teacher had dedicated her life to tormenting children.

Her favorite object in the world was the giant wooden stick she used as a cane, as a pointer, and above all, as a weapon to beat students. Questions aren't allowed in Indian schools, which was the reason she had a job. She did not know anything about most of the subjects she was required to teach. Unless the question was about M.K. Bhagavathar, her favorite film actor, teacher would not know the answer.

But teacher had the one quality all schools valued: a high caste. Her father had been a priest; her mother had come from one of the highest Brahmin families in all of Chennai. No one understood how she fell from grace and landed in the slums, though she never let us "heathens" forget where she came from. She told us how lucky we were to have such a highly respected person as our teacher. She told me how lucky I was to even be allowed to stand in the same room as her, or to breathe the same air.

Teacher loved to torment the few impoverished students who had managed to survive until the last standard. While we ignored the hunger eating away at our stomachs, we had to hear about all of the lavish vacations and the endless quantities of food she had consumed while seeing the grand landmarks of *south* India.

"The beaches of Goa, the palace of Mysore, the . . . Taj Mahal."

Teacher was an idiot, but teacher could not be questioned. "Lakshmi," she shouted, hovering right above my desk.

"Yes, Madam?" I said as I stood up attentively.

I was poor, I did not speak Tamil at home, I was of an inferior caste, and I was smart. Teacher hated me.

"What is the date of Indian independence, Lakshmi?"

Teacher's breath stank of stale onions. Teacher's brain stank of unearned privilege.

"Fifteen August 1947, Madam."

"Incorrect."

She gathered a fistful of my hair and pulled me to the front of the class. Demonstrating to my classmates how to properly point and laugh, she hit me five times in the back with her beloved wooden stick for a correct answer.

Chapter 2

THE BEATING TEACHER gave me burned beneath my uniform; I left without waiting for Alpa, who came waddling down the path, screaming my name.

"Lakshmi. Lakshmi. Lakshmi. Let's go to the cinema. They are playing a new America film."

"America*n* film. I can't, Alpa, I have to go to work now."

Even on my days off, I never went to the cinema. I could buy ten pencils—enough for the entire year—with that money. The disappointed look on Alpa's face made me feel guilty every time. I asked her to meet me after work so we could study together. Her face lit up at the suggestion, and she gave me a quick handshake before bouncing off. The handshake gesture was new. She probably learned it from watching American films at the cinema.

Two days a week I would tend a field of vegetables for our local village farmer. I had to pull out the weeds by hand, dig out holes for the new seeds, kill bugs that infested the plants, and chase away animals that tried to burrow in the soil. Already, I had a bad back, calluses on my feet, and more scars on my hands than I could count.

My second job was slightly more manageable. Four days a week, I assisted the seamstress in the next village over. We were all poor, but most of the customers were still far richer than me. For five to seven hours a day, I measured uptight mothers, fathers who tried to grope me, and spoiled children for new sari blouses, work shirts, or school uniforms.

Everyone watched their weight before coming to get measured, yet as soon as we recorded their measurements, they would stuff their faces with ghee, wada, idly, and dosa. I was the one who heard their screaming when none of their new clothes fit.

Most days I didn't care. Without the work, I would have to drop out of school. Really, I was lucky, I told myself. How many people in India can go to school until the last standard and still be able to eat a meal every day? By my age, amma had a child and nana had a family to support. Out of 207 children in my first standard class, 120 had not made it as far as I had in school.

That was the attitude I coached my mind into every day before work, even on a particularly exhausting day such as this one. An official from the municipal government had been given a bribe from a north Indian cotton salesman. As a result, the official forced the parents of the students in the primary standards to buy new uniforms less than a month before the holidays. My boss received much of the fitting business. After six hours of measuring hyper boys and girls and listening to parents scream about how they could not afford the cost, I finally made my way home after the sun had retired for the night.

In the distance, I could see nana. He was one of the tallest and strongest people our village had ever seen, though he used his physical stature solely to carry the most grain at his job in the fields. Other men might have used such power to control the weaker villagers or to threaten physical violence.

"Hello, my princess," he called out to me.

The sound of his melodic voice always brought a huge smile to my face, and I ran to give him a hug. Though his leather-worn face always told me the answer, I asked how his day in the fields had proceeded.

"A special gift from God," he would always reply.

Amma and baby sister came outside to greet us. As I peered inside, my heart jumped at the sight of four brilliant green banana leaves arranged around two small steel containers. The smell of fresh vegetables and spices wafted through the house, and I sat down with great anticipation. Nana pulled the lid off of the containers and divided the food into four equal portions. I looked down at my leaf—a full cup of rice and a half-cup of vegetables. It was the biggest meal we had eaten in days.

Alpa came over after dinner so we could study for our final exams, which would start the next week. Her chubby little legs moved slowly as she peddled her bike down the path that led to our section of shanty houses. Completely out of breath, she walked over to baby sister for their usual exchange. It was understood that I would help Alpa study if she let baby sister use her bike.

My mind was clouded with a hard day's work, and Alpa had gone to the cinema after all. Instead of studying, she spent the night describing every detail of life in America while baby sister whizzed around happily on the bike. I listened to Alpa talk about the high-heeled shoes the women wore, the cigars the men smoked, and the fancy cars everyone drove. Never having seen anything that compared, I had no idea what she meant, though it sounded wonderful.

My stomach was full, Alpa and my family were resting comfortably, and both my mind and body had the rare pleasure of being able to relax at the same time. Nana must have carried me to my cot after I drifted off to sleep. I spent the night dreaming about pearls, diamonds, and a life of luxury that Chennai never offered. Invigorated with hope and rest, I awoke the next morning to start another special gift from God.

AFTER TWO WEEKS of constant studying, my standard of Gandhi Matriculation Primary/Secondary School completed its final set of exams. Today was the most important day of our lives: results announcement.

"Keep quiet," teacher shouted with every angry bone in her body.

She banged her giant wooden stick on the desk. The sound echoed through the crowded room like waves of destruction.

"We are announcing the top and bottom scorers for this year's final exams only. The rest of you will check your rank on the postings outside."

I held my breath. Last year, an official had announced that as part of a new government initiative, the top scorer from our humble school would automatically gain entrance to the local university with all tuitions fees waived. A top score was my only chance at being able to attend higher education.

Teacher cleared her throat and spat on the floor. Still bubbling with her foul odor, it absorbed into the ground before she had a chance to humiliate the lowest scorer. I prayed that it was not my dear Alpa.

"This year's *lowest* score goes to . . . Alpa."

Teacher threatened to beat anyone who did not participate in her pointing humiliation ritual. I turned to look at my kind friend. Behind the safety of her desk, Alpa snuck a piece of candy into her mouth before silently bursting into tears. She would never admit anything, though I knew she tried to do well in school. Her brain simply could not hold the information.

"And this year's top score goes to . . . Lakshmi."

Time slowed down as teacher spat my name. At the conclusion of the last syllable, I felt all the blood in my body go straight to my head. I must have been glowing, I was so elated. Before I even had the chance to thank God for the results, teacher slammed her wooden stick millimeters from my hand.

"Shut up," she screamed at me. "Get out," she screamed at the rest of the class.

No one needed to be told twice. Alpa patted me on the back as she walked by. To that, teacher slammed Alpa's round bottom as hard as possible with the stick. Alpa shrieked and scurried out of the classroom as fast as her little feet could move.

"Stand up."

Teacher circled around me, her beady eyes looking me over. As she inched closer, I did my best to keep focused on the rat rummaging through a trash pile across the room.

"You cheated. How could a peasant girl get such high marks? A girl born to such a lowlife caste—dirty clothes, begs for tuitions money, can't afford a proper eraser for her pencil. You cheater. Your father can't write his own name. Your sister couldn't pass her second standard exams."

After a year of studying me, teacher knew exactly what to say to make me snap. How dare this pathetic, lazy human being who had never known a full day's work talk of nana and baby sister that way?

"And your mother. Your mother, who can't even afford to feed her own daughter . . ."

I silently screamed; I could not stop imagining how satisfying it would have been to snap that horrid wooden stick she cradled in her arms as though it were her baby. With one foul blow, I could break teacher's spirit. With one foul blow, I could destroy my future.

Teacher continued to circle around me. I inhaled, waiting for a beating that would leave scars until my next life. Miraculously, she did not raise her hand or her stick. After having me wait in desperation for what felt like hours, she threw my results paper in my face.

"Get out."

I picked up the filthy green bag amma had given me as a school sack ten years ago and ran to the door.

"Lakshmi."

I stopped, careful not to turn around.

"Lakshmi, you know you have gained entrance to university with your score."

I smiled to myself. Yes, I knew. It was the accomplishment of a lifetime.

"But there are added costs that come with university. Books, supplies, uniform. Your pathetic parents could never afford those. A sad, dirty peasant girl such as you is not meant to go to university."

Chapter 3

I RAN ALL the way back to my village, barely noticing the bushes and thick grasses of the south Indian terrain beating heavily against my legs. Teacher's words echoed in my ears without mercy. She was right. Amma and nana could not afford to pay for the additional costs and there was no way I could work while at university.

For a decade, I had imagined the victory of the esteemed accomplishment in achieving first rank. The naivety of an adolescent brain simply overlooked the harsh realities of the world. So I ran. I ran as though my speeding legs could break the poverty barrier.

My feet pounded on the hard dirt path, making hollow slapping noises as I approached our house. By the time I reached the tip of our sanctuary, dirt covered my uniform, my hair was disheveled, and tears streamed down my face. Amma rushed over to me, catching my tired body as I collapsed in her arms.

"What happened? Why aren't you at work?"

In between my sobs, amma looked down at me with confused sympathy. Finally, I rummaged the results paper out of my nearly disintegrated pocket. She looked down at the paper with embarrassment. The letters on the paper meant nothing to her as an illiterate woman.

"What does it mean?"

I quietly told her.

"Oh my God. You got first rank, Lakishmi. You have gained acceptance to university, full tuitions paid."

I TRIED TO explain the problem of added costs and how I would never be able to go. Amma simply smiled back at me and told me to go rest.

"We will talk when nana gets home."

I wanted to keep telling amma about my problem, about how close I had come to achieving the unthinkable. Amma simply quieted me by singing my favorite children's song. Slowly, I drifted off to sleep, letting the sadness in my brain shut out the cruel world around me.

I must have slept for at least six hours. By the time I awoke, amma and nana were sitting on their cot talking. I tried my best to listen in, but baby sister saw me stir and shouted her song of delight.

"She's awake. Lakshmi lives."

If there was anyone in the world who could make me smile through the pain, it was baby sister. No one in my family had ever seen a hospital or a health clinic. The midwife who helped amma deliver baby sister told us that amma was having a Cesarean child. We did not know what this meant. Amma later told me baby sister was born with the umbilical cord twisted tightly around her neck. As a result, baby sister could not communicate as the rest of us could.

As amma passed me to get baby sister, she told me nana wanted to talk. I sunk back into the cot, trying to figure out what I would say. My parents had worked so hard to put me through school. There were always more students than opportunities in India. Going to university and working hard did not guarantee me a job. It was too much of a risk. That kind of risk could not justify making my parents and baby sister continue to go without proper food.

"Nana, I got first rank of my higher secondary class, but . . ." Nana put up his massive hand, motioning for me to stop. "My child, your mother and I are highly proud of you. First rank is most impressive."

"Thank you," I sheepishly replied.

Society had taught nana to start each conversation with a list of his limitations.

"I am an uneducated man who knows little outside of this village . . ."

"Don't say those things, nana."

I did not believe in what society said of nana. My parents were my heroes, no matter what stigmas were branded on their bodies. He assured me that this time it was relevant.

"The first time I held you in my arms, I knew you were special. I wanted you to find a good man and seek better opportunity. Your amma told me you were capable of far more. Your amma told me how brilliant you are. She made me realize you and your sister are the reasons I get up each morning and work a job that brings me constant pain."

His words washed over me, leaving a thick coat of shame. Nana had been working thirteen hour days, six days a week, every week, for twenty-six years. I knew what was coming. He would tell me it was time I stop burdening the family. It was my time to get mar—

"Growing up, we were taught to spend the money we earned as soon as possible. What if it gets stolen, what if the government takes it away? Your mother wanted to do things differently."

I looked up at nana with eager caution; afraid I had misheard the very likely reality as the impossible ideal.

"For many years, your mother and I have been saving a portion of my wages."

He peered around me to make sure no one was coming and pulled out a small steel can from the far corner of our house. He carefully removed the lid and allowed me one small glimpse of the contents. Inside was a sparkling mountain of unblemished coins—the most money I had ever seen in my entire life.

"You gained entrance into university, full tuitions paid. This will make sure that special gift from God does not go to waste. *You* will bring us a better life."

I was speechless. I was going to university.

Chapter 4

I HAD TWO months holiday before the start of university. The pile of money my parents had saved seemed enormous. After counting it all out, I realized that even if nana continued to set aside the same portion of money during holidays, I would still need to earn nearly Rs. 20 to pay for added costs.

After working twelve hours every day for three straight weeks, I saved up enough money to purchase an old bicycle to make the seven-kilometer journey to the university campus. Universities in Chennai required a uniform, though not like the little girls' uniform I wore through higher secondary school. Buying the material and getting fitted for the required university saris and blouses was expensive, so I continued to work for the seamstress to pay off the cost.

As expected, Alpa did not gain entrance into any university with her marks. She had eaten her way to morbid obesity and allowed herself to become very tanned. She didn't have admission to a university and had the work ethic of a sloth, her parents saw no choice but to get her married as soon as possible. The fact they had even allowed her to go this long without getting married was already a miracle.

She spent the days keeping me company while I measured my boss's customers and listened to their complaints about my "peasant girl measurements" always being too small. Alpa would describe the latest film in the cinema, her newest candy obsession, or the fat, gross men her parents invited over as marriage prospects.

The worst of the prospects was Govind, or Go-wind as the boys called him for his smelly gas. He was crass, he was mean, and had trouble figuring out how to put one foot in front of the other. He looked like a giant monkey—the swinging arms, the stupid expression.

We both knew that she would be able to secure someone better than Go-wind. As much as Alpa's size detracted from her physical beauty, it was a sign to the villagers that her parents had money. In between the numbers I furiously scrawled down at work, Alpa and I had a great time imitating Go-wind's smelly gas-passing sounds and his labored walk. Poor Go-wind. Poor Go-wind's wife.

I KNEW THAT I wouldn't be able to work for months once university started, and decided to earn my final wages on the last day of holidays. With the strange reluctance that comes at the end of a long journey, I gathered my few earthly possessions and began the walk to the seamstress's shop. Amma called out to me as I left.

"You're not going today. I was just at the shop to tell the seamstress."

"What? Is something wrong?"

"You worry too much, Lakshmi. Come with me."

She grabbed my hand and led me to the path into town. In the distance, I saw the outlines of the other two most important people in my life. Baby sister cried out with joy in the midst of jumping up and down in the same spot. Nana let go of her hand, and she ran into my arms.

"Lakshmi. We are going to see Amrika."

"What are you saying, baby sister?"

"We will see Amrika today."

Nana smiled mischievously and said that he and amma had not given me a proper gift for all of my accomplishments. I started to explain that sending me to university was the most precious gift anyone could ever provide.

"Please Lakshmi. Let's just enjoy the cinema together."

"The cinema? We can't afford to go to the cinema."

"We are the parents. We make the decisions, and we are going to the cinema."

He said it with such eagerness that I immediately realized this would also be nana's first trip to the cinema. For a man that worked so hard to provide me with food and shelter, I could not argue. The playful side of me did not even want to argue. This was easily one of the most exciting moments of my entire life. It would be my first moving glimpse of a world outside of India.

At first glance, the cinema looked similar to the other sand-colored buildings in the outskirts of Chennai. As we approached, we saw colorful posters of the latest pirated Tamil and American films the cinema owner had purchased. Just underneath the film posters was a sign.

Tickets—
First class, Rs.5
Second class, Rs.2
Third class, Rs.½

Important-looking women and men stood tall as they bought their tickets. I stared at the poster of the movie we were seeing—*Father of the Bride*. The characters looked so sophisticated.

I knew nana was scared, but he marched straight up to the ticket vendor with a total confidence unusual for his normal demeanor.

"Give me four tickets, third class."

The vendor eyed nana, scanning his worn out, dirty sandals, the tattered *lungi* that hugged nana's hips, and the western style shirt that nana had received from Christian missionaries on one of their mass clothing distributions.

"Rs. 2 per ticket, third class," the vendor replied.

"What? The sign says Rs. ½ per ticket." I cried out.

The vendor smirked at me with the same look of superiority teacher used to torment her students. "Ah, peasant girl thinks she can read."

"I can too read. I am first rank—"

"Rs. 2 per ticket, third class to wipe your filth from the floor on which you sit."

"You fat bastard, how dare y—"

"Lakshmi, please," nana sternly said.

I could tell nana's heart was racing at the sudden appearance of every vein in his arms. Any other man of his stature would have flexed his muscles and threatened to kill the ticket vendor on the spot. Nana simply turned and whispered something to amma. She looked distraught at his words and was about to argue until baby sister came running up to her, pulling on her sari.

"Amma, shall we go and see Amrika?"

Amma turned back to nana and painfully nodded.

"Three tickets."

Nana threw the money on the counter as the vendor handed him the tickets. The vendor deposited Rs 1.5 into the collection bucket, and laughed as he openly stuffed the rest in his pocket. Nana gave the three tickets to amma and silently walked away from the cinema.

"No. Nana. You have to see the film." I tried forcing my ticket into his hand, but he refused.

"Lakshmi, it's okay. An uneducated man like me will not understand. I would rather hear the film from the mouth of my beautiful daughter."

Amma had to drag me inside the building kicking and screaming. I will never forget the mountains of defeat folded into the skin of nana's face. It burned into my brain as though the memory was on fire. In all of the suffering I had endured from the world, nothing hurt more than seeing nana publicly humiliated by that miserable ticket vendor.

I spent the first twenty minutes of the film trying to comfort baby sister and stop myself from crying. The luxury flaunted on the screen served as the same insults of the selfish people sucking the limited wealth of our country. Why should we starve while they drape themselves in pearls? What had we done to deserve this?

It was only when amma drew me to her protective warmth and reminded me what nana had sacrificed that I allowed my mind to absorb the wonder of the dream that danced before me.

"Don't let your anger prevent you from enjoying this opportunity, Lakshmi."

To amma and baby sister, the images before us were the window to America. To me, the words and the order were the window to America. I had only seen that level of equality between men and women, between the lowest and the highest, in my own house. In America, these were the standards that were lauded, not dismissed. I heard the echoes of my society telling me their antiquated views of my hard work.

"Your parents are so obsessed with your education, Lakshmi. It is unnatural."

By the end of the film, I knew why God had created someone like me to be born to parents such as amma and nana: I was going to change what it meant to be a woman in India. Somehow, someway, I would be the one to make India a better place.

After the film was over, I carried baby sister out of the theater with amma following closely behind. As soon as she saw nana, baby sister leapt out of my arms and sped towards him.

"How was it, my little darling?"

"Nana. They don't even speak properly, and their clothes are sooo drab."

Nana chuckled.

"Is that right, Lakshmi?"

"Oh, absolutely. They speak nothing of what we know in India."

Nana nodded happily and motioned for us to start our journey home. A few minutes later, he was chasing baby sister down the path. Amma took my hand and gave it a kiss.

"What did you think?" she asked.

I drew her hand closer and allowed my head to rest on her shoulder. That was the world I wished India to be.

Chapter 5

REGISTERING FOR CLASSES had been a difficult process. Most of the staff laughed to my face when I told them my caste and where I lived. Compared to the journey to reach university, however, their taunts did not discourage me. Still, by the first day of classes, I was absolutely petrified of what lay ahead.

Amma sacrificed her portion of food to make sure I had a good breakfast. Normally, I would scarf down every morsel. That morning, even a few bites made my stomach turn. With legs shaking from anxiety, I climbed onto the seat of my bike and peddled off to start a better life.

Riding up to the campus, I saw thousands of bikes leaning against the giant façade of the main building. I was thirty minutes early for the first set of classes; still, every student was rushing as though they had mere seconds to live. The air was charged with an energy and sense of competition that I had never experienced before. It was infectious.

University. What an invigorating word. Everything inside of the campus seemed to move at lightning speed. In two days, we reviewed my entire ten standards of schooling. By the end of the first week, I had taken nearly a hundred pages of notes and had been assigned to read five hundred pages. Total memorization of the material was required.

My professors spoke with precision and without pause. None of them ever slowed down and nothing would be repeated, no matter what the situation. Each of my professors was a leader in academia. Any professor with less than a Ph.D. was considered a joke.

Strangely, I found the volume of work comforting. If there was anything I knew for sure, it was my ability to memorize vast quantities of information, a sought-out skill in the Indian education system. On the rare occasion a professor would stop to ask a question, I always knew the answer.

With so much material to squeeze in, no one had time to stop and dwell on caste. With my new uniforms no one suspected I had impoverished parents, or a learning-disabled baby sister. After a year of being under teacher's wrath, the anonymity of university brought me comfort. University was where I belonged.

THOUGH STUDIES KEPT me busy, Alpa and I saw each other at least once every weekend. Our usual meeting ground was by a small creek where we used to play as children. Alpa and I would find our favorite tree and sit on a patch of grass overlooking the water. She didn't much care for the subjects I studied, so she would do most of the talking—telling me about the latest "America film," while I reviewed my school notes.

One particularly hot Saturday, I arrived at our meeting spot early. The water was crystal clear, the sun was shining bright, and the shade of a tree brought great relief from the heat. After enjoying the serenity for a few minutes, I was startled back to reality when I heard crying behind me. I jumped up and saw Alpa walking toward me with tears streaming down her face.

"Alpa, what's wrong?"

"They . . . they . . . they . . ."

"They what?"

"They are . . . Go-wind . . . next month . . ."

We spoke at different levels, but we always knew what the other one meant. Her stuttered words could mean only one thing: her parents had decided to marry her off to Go-wind. I sighed, trying to find words of comfort for such a terrible prospect. Carefully guiding Alpa over to the tree, I asked her to explain everything.

"Oh Lakshmi. My parents brought many prospects. Some tall, some short, some ugly . . ."

"What happened, Alpa?"

"Every time we met someone, amma would make me wear my best clothes and serve tea. I tried really hard, Lakshmi. I want a good man."

I had rarely seen Alpa express concern about the future. I handed her my handkerchief to staunch the flow of fresh tears.

"Lakshmi, they would never come back. We went over to their houses to deliver sweets, but none of them came back. Only Go-wind."

We sat in silence. To us, Go-wind had only been the joke of the villages. I could not imagine Go-wind as a husband. I could not imagine building a life with someone so despicable.

"Maybe he will get better," I offered.

Alpa blew her nose in my handkerchief. We both knew Go-wind's prime years were now. If this was his prime, we could only imagine his demise.

Alpa told me her parents were having the engagement party next week. The wedding would be at the end of December. Alpa's parents were tired of supporting her and wanted her married into rich Govind's family with children as soon as possible. I tried my best to comfort Alpa by describing how beautiful she would look in an engagement sari.

"Everyone in the village will be so jealous. Think of all the gifts."

For two hours, I set aside my studies and listened to her describe the details of his stupidity. Alpa wanted healthy, happy children who would be smarter than she. She wanted a husband who understood her jokes and who wanted to try new foods. Go-wind could barely function. He would not bring her joy.

We both knew the terrible prospect would soon become a reality. Doing my best to do what I did worst—keep the mood light—I wrapped my arms around the shoulders of my frightened friend and walked her all the way home before parting ways. I left her in her room and told her everything would be okay.

Chapter 6

THERE WERE TWO kinds of people at university: those who were admitted on merit and those who paid bribes. Sahana fell into the latter category. Her father had been a businessman in Malaysia for a number of years. Being raised in Kuala Lampur made Sahana the worldliest person I had ever met. She was also the most arrogant. She had been placed in three out of four of my first semester courses so I saw her five times a week, six hours a day.

I idolized our professors. They had dedicated their lives to the total comprehension of a subject of merit. Ask them anything related, and they could give you the history of some of the most fascinating topics on earth. To Sahana, they were old sacks with strong body odor that spoke with a lisp. If any other student dared to interrupt a professor during their lecture, that student would most certainly be kicked out of the class. With connections like Sahana's, she could mock the professors openly and not receive any punishment.

There was no end to her insults—the way professors dressed, the thickness of their glasses, their salaries, the quality of the food they brought to lunch, where they were born, who their parents were, caste, religion, language, everything. Honestly, if she had spent half as much time studying as she did giving insults, she would have made a fine student.

Sahana made it a policy to publicly torment anyone who crossed her path. Needless to say, if the professors and the students of a higher caste were not good enough for her, neither was I. Avoiding Sahana became my first rule of university survival. Three months into the term, I had successfully failed to make my presence known to her—a hard trick to balance with demonstrating my knowledge of our subjects.

One afternoon toward the end of our term, we arrived to our Principles of Accounting class and took our seats as usual. Professor Gopal was running late, so the majority of the students took the opportunity to review their notes from previous sessions. Twenty minutes after the start of normal class time, one of the assistant deans walked in to make an announcement.

"I have some bad news. Professor Gopal passed away last night."

"Ha! Finally died from the smell of his own body odor?" Sahana said.

The dean looked over at Sahana. Realizing who she was, he kept his mouth shut. As we only had two weeks before our final examinations, he assigned us the rest of the material to cover on our own. We were to write a summary of the material with the members of our groups, which had already been determined.

"You are to report here for your examination at one p.m. exactly two weeks from today. Is that clear?"

Sahana scoffed aloud and commented on the dean's cheap polyester shirt. The rest of us simply nodded.

After the dean laid the stack of papers with the assignments out on Professor Gopal's table, a mad rush of students raced to the bottom to unearth the groupings. In an Indian university, working as a team was a rare luxury—only the death of a professor allowed it to happen.

There were four people to each group. Mine consisted of two I knew to be friendly. Together, we looked down at the sheet and silently panicked. Sahana was our fourth. The rest of us knew dealing with her would be far harder than completing the assignment.

Fortunately, she decided that without a professor to openly humiliate, she had no need to stay for the rest of accounting class. My two project partners, Nallini and Jayesh, and I debated a host of strategies to get rid of the evil queen. We decided to approach her the following day and gently ask how to proceed.

After classes, I somberly rode my bike home, debating whether to tell amma and nana my bad luck. Five kilometers from the house, I decided to keep quiet. Three kilometers away, I decided to tell them. One kilometer away, I decided I did not know what to do. Indecisiveness was not a typical attribute of mine. Striking a balance between being open with my parents and burdening them with my problems was the one exception.

By the time I got home, amma was already perched on the floor, preparing the little food we would have for dinner that night.

"Hello my darling, how were classes today?"

"My accounting professor died."

It was not a typical response, and she did not know how to react. I rarely spoke of my emotions. She asked if I was okay. I told her I was sad to see such a respected person pass. Seeing she was not satisfied with my vacant response, I followed with the news of who I would be forced to work with on the report.

Amma snapped her head up and looked at me with alarm. "You must work with Sahana?"

"Yes. Why, you do not like her either?"

I knew Amma's answer before I finished the question. No one liked Sahana. Amma did not care for long lectures. She conveyed her complex thoughts in very few words.

"Lakshmi, be careful. Sahana's father's money knows no bounds. They are powerful people. Don't get in her way, no matter how terrible she becomes."

Amma told me from when I was a very young age, I was capable of doing anything in the world. Staying out of the way of powerful, important people was the one limitation on life she truly believed. I assured her I would be careful. She examined my face to make sure I understood the message. She had no need to repeat herself.

Nana came home early from the fields that evening. After we all finished dinner, baby sister and I spent a few hours playing outside. She would run as fast as she could to tire herself out, take a break, tire herself again, take another break, and so on. Her methods suited me well as I could study while she sprinted into the night.

While we were outside, amma told nana about my bad luck in being placed with Sahana. With a look of equal concern, nana made me assure him I would be extra careful around her. I told him I would, and that if necessary, I would do everything and put her name on the report. He nodded his approval of my plan.

"It is hard, Lakshmi. They are born to privilege, yet we must do their work. Just be careful."

"I know, nana, I know."

Satisfied I understood the depths of Sahana's control, he asked me to tell him about what I had learned in university that day. He fell asleep to the soothing powers of the knowledge his daughter had acquired. The business principles, the chemistry, the English poetry, the world.

TO IMPRESS GO-WIND'S rich family, Alpa's parents borrowed money from a loan shark to cover the cost of the clothes she wore for the engagement. Normally villagers would be very careful in letting others wear their jewelry, but everyone knew that Alpa was the one person who could be trusted. Villagers helped cover up her pimples, scars, and tan with whatever makeup they could gather and under mountains of gold and precious stones. By the end of their fussing, Alpa wore four meters of cloth, enough jewelry to weigh down a ship, and enough makeup to paint the village.

I thought Alpa looked like a clown, especially with fat Go-wind by her side. He had become so large that the local tailor had to use twice the normal amount of cloth to sew clothes that fit over his giant belly. Alpa constantly complained they were wider than they were tall when standing side by side. She might have been right.

By comparison, engagements are simpler than weddings. The priest says a few chants, the puja lasts less than two hours, and everything is done in one day. Still, the stimulus was too much for Go-wind. On three separate occasions, he got so frustrated that he tried hitting the priest, hitting his father, or stamping on Alpa's feet. I was sitting close enough to know he passed gas each time as well.

After the ceremony had finished and most of the guests had congratulated the newly engaged couple, Alpa waddled her way over to me.

"Lakshmi."

"I know."

"They were sooo smelly, Lakshmi."

She cupped her hands over her mouth and blew a spray of air through the cracks to form the perfect imitation. We doubled over in laughter at the sight of his animal-like shrieks at his aunt for not preparing his favorite sweets. In a mix of disbelief and giggles, Alpa recreated the sound of his gas to the beat of his monkey cries.

"Just think, Lakshmi. In less than a month, that man will be my husband."

Chapter 7

"OKAY, SO WE all agree on the plan?" I asked Jayesh and Nallini.

They nodded somberly. The three of us had decided to carefully approach Sahana and ask how she would like to do the project. We fully expected she would find a way to insult us all. We hoped that she would ask us to do the entire thing and leave her be. The less time we spent with her, the better.

We found Sahana after class sitting in the professor's common area. She made it a point to show the professors she was entitled to use their facilities at her whim. On her nicer days, she would even allow them to sit in her presence. As she thundered her way out of the room, Jayesh tapped her on the shoulder.

"Sorry, madam," he began.

"What do you want, you vermin?"

"I . . . uh . . . I . . ."

His body went rigid in fear. Her eyes could turn someone to stone. Giving the poor soul a break, I stepped in Jayesh's place.

"Hello, Sahana."

"What do you want, peasant girl?"

I cringed. No one had called me peasant girl since teacher.

"Jayesh, Nallini, and I are your project mates for accounting, and—"

"So?"

As she eyed me with disgust, I became increasingly aware that I had not bathed in three days due to lack of water. Somehow I forced out the words to ask how to proceed.

"Well, peasant girl, you will do the work and put my name on the report. *First*."

She walked away without giving us a chance to reply. As soon as she was out of earshot, Nallini pumped her fists and jumped in the air for joy.

The report was much more time consuming than going to class and studying our notes. Jayesh and Nallini would take turns reading the material aloud, and I would write the main points down. The assistant dean assigned us fifty long accounting tables to complete. I finished each in fewer than five minutes. The three of us each reviewed the entirety of the report, making corrections along the way. On completion, we took care in copying Sahana's signature as the first author of the report. Our spirits were diminished in giving her credit, but I had made a promise to my parents.

Before the start of the final examination, the assistant dean came by to collect our reports. I had the report sitting in front me, and was prepared to hand it in myself. Sahana whizzed by and snatched the report from my hands, giving me a paper cut. As I looked at the blood creeping up from beneath my skin, Sahana threw the report pages at the assistant dean. I looked at Nallini and Jayesh, who were both gripping their pencils so hard that their hands turned white.

The final examination was quite easy. In four hours, we were to complete a ten-page essay and a hundred simple accounting problems. I only took two hours to fill in my examination booklet and another half hour to check everything over. I knew I should use the last ninety minutes to ensure everything was perfect, but this was the last of my examinations after a long first term, and I was dying to go help Alpa avoid another clothing disaster for her wedding. With a few final flicks of my pencil, I finished my work and was the first person to turn my paper in. Sahana followed behind me.

"Giving up so soon, peasant girl?"

I did not bother to hear her insults continue. I placed my booklet down on the table first and turned around to go find a true friend.

"WHAT ABOUT THIS one?" Alpa asked as she held up a giant roll of silk fabric.

"No, you'll look like a mango."

"Okay, what about this one?"

"Who wants to wear a black sari for their wedding?"

Alpa sighed and threw the material on the floor, already frustrated with the duties of married life.

"Lakshmi, I hate this."

"Black is not a good color, Alpa."

"No. Not that. Go-wind doesn't understand what is happening. Last night, he asked his amma when our engagement party will be."

I couldn't help but laugh at the thought of monkey Go-wind demanding an engagement party and a banana.

"Lakshmi. It's not funny."

"It is a little funny."

Alpa pouted. She used the same expression when her mother refused to serve her a fifth portion of rice.

"Oh, come on. At least you will be able to do whatever you want. It will be so easy to trick Go-wind. Think of all the chocolate you can buy with his parents' money."

Alpa stood tall like a national soldier at those words. "Speaking of chocolate . . ." She pulled out another bar, which had melted all over her things. "Try it."

The brown half-liquid looked disgusting, and reminded me of the public lavatory.

"No thanks."

"Okay, more for me."

"Chee."

I got up to wipe the chocolate from Alpa's hand, and told her to come find a nice wedding sari.

"Oh Lakshmi, thank you for being my friend. I don't even feel sad when you are with me."

In the reflection of a pool of water that had gathered from the previous night's storm, I saw my dear friend happily licking her chocolate covered fingers. I could not help but stare with a humble appreciation at how easy it was for Alpa to find joy in the throes of such an awful prospect.

Amma and nana were such a guiding force of wisdom and tranquility in my life. Through the shaking reflection, I peered at my friend whose only guidance was a purity that bestowed her heart. She was the one having a lavish wedding. I was the one who was truly grateful for life.

Chapter 8

EXAM RESULTS WERE in, and rankings for the university would be posted tomorrow. I had passed every one of my exams at or near the top of the class. All that stood in my way to first rank was accounting, which was my best subject. The assistant dean walked inside the classroom and heaved the score sheets onto Professor Gopal's desk.

"I need to see Lakshmi and Sahana. The rest of you, come and find your marks."

I looked over at Sahana, and saw for the first time a look of concern on her face. Out of the corner of my eye, I watched Nallini and Jayesh race to the front of the classroom and fight for their score sheets in a crazed fury. Sahana and I walked silently down the hall to the dean's office—a small, dark hole situated in one of the crumbling annex buildings. He closed the door behind us and told us to sit down. For once, Sahana did as she was told.

The dean reached into a drawer of his rotting desk and produced two blank sheets of paper and two pencils. He told us to write our names, dates of birth, and one paragraph about our favorite class. Very timidly, I asked permission to speak. He nodded somberly.

"Sir, I am not positive on my date of birth only. My amma said it was around five March on the Western calendar."

"What a pathetic peasant girl," Sahana mocked.

The dean told me five March was acceptable.

I started writing without hesitation. Sahana demanded to know what was happening. Something gave the dean a new sense of courage, and he stood up to her for the first time.

"Sit down, Sahana."

"I will not be told what to do."

The dean argued no further. He grabbed my sheet of paper from underneath my busy hand and left the room, leaving us in total confusion.

She started pacing around the office. In between her groans and curse words, my mind was reeling with the possibilities of what could be wrong. Within seconds, I convinced myself that I was being convicted of a crime and Sahana was the only other suspect.

While I prepared myself for a mental breakdown, the dean and president entered the room. Accompanying them was an older man who was wearing a three-piece suit complete with a handkerchief and matching cane. He looked like one of the characters in the American film. As soon as Sahana turned to face the three of them, her confidence evaporated into the humid air.

"What the hell are you doing here, papa?"

My eyes widened to the size of coconuts. Why would they call Sahana's father to the university?

"It seems that one of you has purposely failed the exam and one of you has received the highest mark in the class," the president said.

I stopped breathing for a few seconds. Sahana started to scream.

"Well, of course, *I* was the one who got the highest mark. Do you think a lowly *Shudra* girl could beat me? Someone who is practically an *untouchable*?"

I saw the silver arrow of the word "untouchable" pierce through my heart. The pain and anguish that word contained was something Sahana could not possibly understand. Like so many others, she freely used it as a weapon of destruction.

The president cleared his throat. He turned to Sahana's father and said he had collected a fresh sample of my writing.

"It matches the writing on both the top examination and the report. However, the report and the exam list your daughter as its primary author."

I slowly sank into my chair. Nallini, Jayesh, and I had signed Sahana's name thinking it would save us from misery. Now it might ruin my life.

Sahana's father demanded to see the papers, muttering something as the President handed them over. The sound Sahana's father's giant shoes made echoed like canons. He commanded me to stand. I did as I was told.

"I do not believe in this caste nonsense as my daughter does. If you tell me this is your work, I will believe you. I will believe my daughter switched your names on the papers."

"Daddy," Sahana screamed at the top of her lungs.

She charged at him and stopped centimeters from his face. I was sure the fire from her breath could be felt all the way to Sri Lanka. "How can you believe a disgusting peasant over my words?"

Her screams were so loud I temporarily lost my hearing.

Sahana's father ignored the shrieking monster, keeping his attention focused on me. "Did you write these papers?"

I was the most scared I had ever been in my life. My mind flashed back to amma and nana's concerned faces as they begged me to stay out of Sahana's way. Nallini, Jayesh, and I had spent nearly a hundred hours pulling together that final project. We wrote Sahana's name to honor the promise we made to our pleading parents.

As the imposing man with the expensive Western clothes continued to stare down on my tiny frame, I thought about all of the sleepless nights of studying, the countless hours working, and the anguish of hunger amma and nana imparted on our family to save up so much money. My parents wanted me to appease Sahana, but this was different. If I gave Sahana credit once more, I would surely be rusticated from the university. I would be thrown on to the streets to beg like the peasant everyone said I was. There would be no better life.

Barely moving my lips, I whispered one word. "Yes."

Sahana's father nodded. His look of disappointment was one that let us all know it was commonplace. Sahana was her father's living regret. Without another word in my direction, he grabbed Sahana's hand and dragged her out the door. As they passed by the president, her father said one final sentence.

"My daughter will not be returning to university."

The president peered down at his shoes to avoid eye contact with the domineering and conflicting pair. Sahana screamed with an intense vile that she would never let this university live in peace. Halfway down the hall, she kicked her father straight in the groin and managed to break free. She got to an arm's reach from me, caught my eye, and sent me an expression of unearned hatred that every impoverished villager had seen at least once in their life.

"You will pay for this, you peasant girl."

I was awarded first rank that term.

Chapter 9

ALPA'S WEDDING WAS beautiful. Though she was not the prettiest girl in the village, she was the kindest person anyone had ever met. Everyone did whatever possible to make her special day the biggest and brightest celebration of the season. The food stretched out as far as the eye could see, reflecting the rainbow of decorations and ornaments Alpa's father brought from the fanciest stores Chennai proper had to offer.

Amma, nana, and baby sister came with me to the wedding. As a gift to Alpa, we had picked out a book we found in an old colonial-era bookstore; it was about how chocolate was made. Considering the amount of food and sweets we were fed, the book was well worth the money. Baby sister entertained all of the guests with stories about how she rode Alpa's bike. Nana looked happy just to relax. Amma and I spent much of the wedding helping Alpa in and out of her six wedding saris.

A priest was hired from Chennai proper, who executed the puja at a pace even Go-wind could understand. Go-wind managed to survive all the way to the end of the first day before having any major outbursts. All was well until a guest accidentally stepped on his foot. He went crazy knocking over chairs, throwing food at the guests, and punching the air. Fortunately, his father managed to calm him down.

Despite Go-wind's tantrums, the air was generally jovial. By the end of day two, even Alpa seemed happy about the situation. We managed to sneak away from the guests for a few minutes before I had to leave. I brought our family gift along.

"Oh my God. Lakshmi. It's perfect. Now I can make my own chocolate."

"Well, I don't think it is so easy, Alpa. Maybe one day we will go to the real America and see how they do it."

Alpa jumped like a child at the suggestion, telling me she would count the days until our journey. I gave her a kiss on the cheek and congratulated my newly married friend. We agreed to meet at our usual spot next Saturday. After one final hand squeeze, I watched Alpa waddle over to Go-wind, her husband.

MY SECOND TERM of university started soon after Alpa's wedding. Now that the halls were rid of Sahana, a new air of excitement and freedom overcame everyone. Strangely, the examination disaster affirmed my desire to specialize my studies in accounting. There was something satisfying about being in classes where the ultimate goal was to have total equality on both sides of the ledger.

Sahana had forever scared Jayesh out of accounting, but Nallini decided she wanted to continue. We knew we worked well together, and we became close very quickly. She was of the same caste as me, which gave us solace.

As I became increasingly immersed in my studies, I noticed my relationship with Alpa slipping away. Our weekly meetings by the tree lessened to the point that seeing Alpa became the exception, not the standard. I tried a few times to go over to her and Go-wind's house. Every time I walked inside, burly Go-wind would stomp to the door to tell me Alpa was out shopping.

Second term finished without any major events or interruptions. For me, it was a semester of bliss. Nana had found a new employer who was paying double the normal wages, so I could afford to fully concentrate on my studies. Nallini and I had great discussions about all of the things we learned in school. Baby sister and amma kept each other company during the day, and were able to split much of the housework to lessen the load.

After another grueling set of final examinations, Nallini and I decided to wander to the cluster of shops that faced the university campus. Her parents had given her a modest sum of money to buy a new pair of sandals as a gift for finishing her first year at university. A proper cement roof covered the shops in the interior. Knowing the sum of money Nallini had was too small to buy anything from the interior shops, I began walking in the direction of the cheaper stores that were grouped together under a massive piece of blue plastic. Nallini, a wild spirit, stopped me.

"We are in our university saris. No one will know we are poor," she said.

With the confidence of Nallini's boldness, we changed directions for the interior. We stopped in a shop too cheap for the richest that was still too expensive for us. Nallini wasn't sure what kind of sandals she wanted and allowed the shop owner to spend a few minutes describing the different kinds he had in stock.

"What about this one?" Nallini asked me.

"I don't like the red . . ."

Before I had a chance to finish my reply, we heard a scream on the other side of the shop. I gasped when I saw the scene.

"Alpa?"

Trembling like a leaf, Alpa turned her head and slowly picked herself off of the floor. Govind was standing over her. I struggled to catch my breath when I saw her face. Alpa had two black eyes and a giant gash across her forehead. She grabbed her hip and inhaled, revealing a missing front tooth.

"Oh my God, Alpa," I said, rushing toward her. Govind stepped in between the two of us. "You touch not my wife."

He grabbed Alpa's hand and pulled her towards the door. I managed to wedge my way in between them to prevent Alpa from leaving.

"What happened?"

"I just fell on the floor over there, that's all."

The fat bastard dragged my injured friend across the store by her hair. When I tried to go after them, Nallini grabbed my arm and motioned for me to keep quiet. With strength I did not know he possessed, Govind pushed Alpa and disappeared into the crowd. I turned back at Nallini, demanding to know why she held me back.

"My sister went through the same thing. You were going to make it worse for her."

Nallini made sure Alpa and Govind headed west before she let go of my arm to allow me to run east. Through the dizzying balls of light the milling shoppers transformed into, I ran as fast as I could. Above, the false security of the concrete turned into the familiar blue plastic roof before opening into a misleadingly calm sky.

I pushed my bike to its limits and slammed it to the ground with an uncharacteristic force when I reached home. Amma jumped up at the sight of me. Before she even had a chance to ask how my exams had gone, I described the details of the horrible scene I had just witnessed.

"Her face was black and blue, amma. What should we do?"

"Lakshmi . . . I'm so sorry. I don't think there is anything we can do—"

"What do you mean? He's beating her, amma."

Amma nodded empathetically as she peered outside in the direction of her old village. Without her saying anything, I could tell she had gone through this with one of her friends. Afraid to hear the answer, afraid to not hear the answer, I asked what her friend had done.

"She tried to run away."

"What happened to her?"

"He killed her."

I slammed my eyes shut. I had to help Alpa. I had to save her.

Chapter 10

NANA AND AMMA wanted to help, but without uncorrupt law enforcement, a reliable court system, or money, there was nothing they could do.

"How did your sister force her husband to stop?" I asked Nallini.

"She threatened to hire someone to slit his throat at night."

I could never see her making such a threat, even in her angriest state. Govind would not understand, anyway.

After five failed attempts to get past the front door of Alpa and Govind's house, I finally caught a glimpse of her beaten face. Through Govind's best attempt to block Alpa from view, I shouted three key words.

"By the tree."

I only hoped she knew what I meant.

She did. The following Saturday, Alpa managed to sneak out of the house to meet me at the creek. A few boys were playing close by. As Alpa walked down the dirt path, one of the boys cried out at the sight of her.

"Gross. You have something growing on your face."

Alpa looked down at the ground. When she was finally within reach, I stood up and gave her a hug. The something on her face was an open wound from Govind's latest beating. Without proper medical supplies, it looked like a giant leech had spurted from beneath the surface of her skin.

My loving touch opened a dam and Alpa's tears rolled without control. Govind had started beating her as soon as they had moved into the new house. She did not know how to cook like his mother, repair the house like his father, or sing like his aunt. He could not keep a job for more than a few days and took his failures out on her. In the months they had been married, he had beaten her all but eight days. Four of those eight days he had been out of town.

Divorce was out of the question as that meant Alpa and her family would be ostracized from the community. She tried to tell her parents what was happening, but they did not know what to do. Between the dowry, the engagement party, and the wedding, they were in debt and could not afford to help her.

I was distraught, seeing Alpa so broken. We had known each other since we were eight. No matter how many times someone made fun of her weight, told her she was stupid, or announced how ugly she was, Alpa rebounded in minutes. She had a remarkable faith in people. Nothing had ever kept her down, until now.

She was not feeling well, and asked me to fetch her water from the creek. When I came back, she was leaning against the tree, vomiting.

"Alpa. Are you okay?"

"It has been happening for a few months, Lakshmi. I think my stomach can't handle the beatings . . ."

Alpa told me Govind would beat her extra hard tonight for sneaking out. Still, we stayed by the tree for a few more hours. As the sun set on the horizon, we reluctantly picked ourselves off of the cool, soothing grass.

"Don't forget me, Lakshmi."

"How could I ever forget you, Alpa? I will be waiting for you here next Saturday, okay?"

Her once pure and smiling face now carried the emotional and physical scars of a broken spirit. With a heavy heart, I clutched my hands to my chest as she turned and walked back to the injustice.

For the next three Saturdays, I waited for Alpa, but she did not come. Soon after, I started my second year of university. My normal concentration evaded me, as I knew Alpa lived in a constant state of fear. How could anyone be cruel enough to hurt someone so sweet and unassuming?

I would spend hours replaying the terrible scene from the shoe shop— seeing Alpa pick herself up from the floor and defend the man who was making her life a living hell. What would Govind do next? How could Alpa reason with someone who had so much anger and so little compassion?

Nearly a month passed since Alpa and I last met by the tree. The turmoil of not knowing how she was, took my brain hostage. One moment I was sitting quietly by Nallini, the next I found myself outside Alpa's house. After surveying the ground, I spotted a heavy branch and practiced swinging it a few times.

Any other Indian household would allow guests to walk straight inside. I chose to knock on the dark wooden front door. Expecting Govind to answer, I held the branch up, ready to hit him with the strength of every woman, ready to kill the bastard.

Alpa opened the door. Just six months prior, she had the reaction time of an ostrich. Now, she instinctively scurried away like a mouse. Finally realizing who was at the door, Alpa gave me a big a hug and told me to keep quiet. Govind was sleeping. I motioned for her to step outside.

"How are you?" I asked urgently.

"I'm pregnant."

I gasped and looked down at her belly. Due to her size, it was impossible to tell.

"How many months?"

"Almost five, I think. I was scared to tell Govind. He has been a lot better since I did."

I expelled the breath I had been holding in for weeks. I wanted to stay with Alpa longer. I wanted to bring her home with me for safekeeping. She assured me that was not necessary. Govind had barely touched her since she told him about the pregnancy.

"Come back in four months to see my baby."

I told her I would, knowing all I could truly do was pray my friend into safety.

Chapter 11

DESPITE THE GRAVITY of Govind's past behavior, eventually my studies overwhelmed everything else. Doing well in school was a matter of life or death.

Every professor I had ever met made it a point to remind the class how fierce the competition was in India. If we screwed up even one term, we would not get a job. There were literally millions of Lakshmis and Jayeshs and Nallinis in India to replace us.

Nallini and I did not take these warnings lightly. The majority of the students in our university, in every Indian university, were men. Many offices openly declared they would not hire a woman for any position other than a secretary. Whatever the competition was for our male classmates after graduation, it would be exponentially harder for us. Women had to prove much more than mere scholarly achievements.

Nallini and I devised a system of perpetual studying. We would take turns reading aloud the information we had so vigorously written down during class. After going through the entire set of notes, we would pick random pages and ask each other to fill in the blanks. Every time one of us got even one word wrong, we restarted at the beginning. Our brains became walking repositories of all the information presented.

Our hard work paid off. In the third term ranks, I once again placed first, and Nallini came in with a close second. By December of 1958, we were on our way to achieving the unthinkable: claiming the top two slots in the entire school, as women. Together, we felt like we ruled the university. We felt like we ruled the world. I knew if we continued down this path, we would be the women to change India.

I KNOCKED ON the door. Once, twice, thrice. No answer. Peering over to Alpa's room, I saw the window was covered. I walked around the entire building, looking for any sign of life. There was nothing. With a tired sigh, I set down the small dish of sweets amma had sent over. Alpa's mother had stopped by a few days prior to tell us the good news. All toes and fingers in place, responding to sound and light—Alpa gave birth to a healthy baby girl. Her mother was elated.

Her mother asked me to visit Alpa the following weekend. Govind would be out of town visiting relatives in Madurai, leaving Alpa and her mother alone with the baby. So there I was.

Eventually I conceded home. Much to my surprise, Alpa's mother was at our house. By the puffiness of her eyes, I could tell she had been crying for quite some time. Quietly, amma stood up and guided me away. She told me to go to Alpa's parents' house immediately. Alpa was there. She would explain.

"Amma, what is going on?"

"Go to Alpa, Lakshmi. This is something I have no right to tell you."

Not bothering to take off my sandals, I ran through the door and straight to Alpa's old room. She was curled up in a ball at the foot of her cot in the same way baby sister would to block out the world. Except for belabored breaths, there was no sign of life in her body.

The room had the unmistakable stench of despair that was all too common in our lives. I called out to Alpa, hoping my voice would be enough to prompt even the slightest hint of movement. There was nothing. For hours, we sat in total silence. It did not take long for me to notice her baby girl was not in the room.

"He killed her, Lakshmi," Alpa said, without warning. "Girls are worthless, boys are best, Govind said. He screamed when she cried."

Her breathing quickened such that I thought she was hyperventilating.

"First he slapped her on the face. That would make her cry more. Then he put a cover on her nose to stop the noise. That would make her cry still more. I begged him to stop, Lakshmi. He didn't care; he didn't want to hear the baby's cries."

Alpa had stayed awake with her precious baby for two straight days and nights. Govind's cruelties resurfaced as soon as he saw it was a girl that had exited the womb.

"Lakshmi, she was so warm, so nice. But I felt very tired the third day. I fell asleep. When I woke up . . . there was so much blood, Lakshmi. Govind went away. I don't think he's coming back."

Alpa rolled over and fell silent again. I left the room before sinking to the floor and breaking down into tears. In all of the violence I had seen the police inflict on the villagers, in all of the killings employers committed against farmers, in all of the rapes and cases of domestic violence women cried about openly in the streets, nothing hit me as hard as Alpa's words.

That week, I missed class every single day. Alpa's mother and I would take turns staying in the room with her—reading to her, sitting with her, being silent with her. Alpa would not eat, she would not drink, she would not move or talk. Her body had become an empty container.

I begged her to come back to me. All of my love and gratitude for my dear friend did nothing to revive her listless body that had lost the will to live. After five days, Alpa left her bed only twice. The first time I was there to help her vomit the only food she had eaten in three days. The second time was the one hour her mother and I accidentally left her alone.

Alpa walked to her parents' tiny kitchen, found their biggest knife, and slit her own wrists. Her mother found her unconscious minutes later. None of us had the money to bribe the hospital staff to admit her ahead of the other patients.

On the steps of a government hospital, G.R. Alpa Krishnan, my best friend in the whole world, died on 29 January 1959.

Chapter 12

FOOD LOST ITS taste, school seemed meaningless, and the voices of the people I loved were empty and distant. It hurt to touch people, yet it also hurt not to be touched. I could not bear to stay awake for more than a few hours, yet I could not sleep for more than a few minutes. My mind was stuck somewhere between earth and hell. Govind's family bribed the police to not file a report and to make sure the courts would never hear the case. There was no recourse in that world. That was India.

Though she immediately recognized my torment, amma also knew the pain would eventually become tolerable. At some point, she knew I would want to resume living. Despite having attended school for only two days in her life, amma understood there would be major consequences if I continued missing classes. She borrowed my bike one afternoon and rode to the university. After finding Nallini in the massive crowd of students, she explained what had happened. Thanks to amma and Nallini, I received medical leave for the term without having to set foot on school grounds.

Emerging from that bout of depression was like learning how to walk again. Some days I could make it through without help. Other days I was less stable and required constant attention. I would often have a day that made me question the point in living. Why fight so hard when everything that matters is so easily stripped away?

Baby sister did not understand what had happened. She did, however, understand how sad I had become and spent my days of depression singing to me or stroking my hair. Every night on his way home from work, nana would stop by the creek and bring me one single flower from the riverbed.

The collective efforts of my amma, nana, and baby sister ensured I would not let myself die. Slowly but surely, my family resuscitated me from devastation.

One afternoon, nana came home early. I was having one of my better days and offered to prepare him some tea.

"Could we take a walk instead?" he asked.

"Of course, nana, to anywhere you wish." Spending time alone with nana was a rare treasure.

We walked into the fields, continuing as the footpath faded. Nana made a few light remarks about the weather, the crops, and amma's excellent cooking. After nearly forty-five minutes, he turned into the thick brush and led us farther into the countryside than I had ever ventured.

We came upon a small abandoned shack in the middle of the thicket. The roof was a patchwork of ancient metal scraps, straw, and mud. Two of the three walls had fallen, exposing an interior filled with random assortments of cloth, paper, and trash. A family of bush rats had burrowed through a remnant of cloth, leaving the tattered remains of a haven for mold and grime.

After a few moments, I realized the crumbling structure meant something to nana. He stared at the remains with an intense look of contemplation. His massive hand was not enough to shield me from the tears I saw stream down his worn face.

"Lakshmi, this is where I grew up."

Nana never spoke of his childhood. Amma had always been the one to recount his stories to baby sister and me.

"There was once a small river that ran through these woods," nana said.

His father grew up in the heart of the city slums.

"At a young age my father decided to move out here, to return to nature. I would have to walk an hour to find odd chores to save for a school uniform."

The same school I had attended, amma had told me.

"One day, my father returned home early and caught me with my prized clothes. He did not know that I had quit work for an education. He beat me to a pulp and dragged me all the way to the headmaster.

"Don't you *ever* let my son back into this house of lies," he screamed.

"I'm sorry. I didn't know . . ."

"It was a different time, a different life. I do not wish to make you feel guilty. I am so proud of you, Lakshmi."

Simply replying with a "thank you" was insufficient for the power those words carried. I slowly turned my head to gaze at my incredible father, who was lost in the crumbling shack before us.

"Lakshmi, after my father pulled me out of school, I did not want to carry on living. I felt the same way when I lost my two brothers. When Alpa died, a part of you died with her spirit."

He was right. It felt like a piece of my heart was missing.

"What you must remember is that Alpa also gave you a piece of her. One day, someone will live their life with a piece of you."

"What do you mean, nana?"

"Lakshmi, sometimes we do not live this life for our own opportunities. Sometimes, we live this life for the opportunities we bring to others."

Chapter 13

AT THE END of the term, Nallini came by to tell me she made first rank.

"It was easy without you getting in the way."

We spent the next few days catching up on all of the university gossip. The lightness of our conversation felt so natural. Long walks on the beach, exploring different parts of the city, enjoying an occasional snack on the street—spending a carefree month with Nallini was exactly what I needed to start enjoying life again.

Just as quickly as the holidays came, they ended. Nallini had advanced a semester ahead of me, which meant we would not be taking any more classes at the same time. Even though she had given me a thorough explanation of all the upcoming material, I was determined not to become lazy.

Before my first class back started, I reached the classroom early. I sat at a desk in the front and center, closed my eyes, clenched my fists, and did my best to—

"Excuse me," someone interrupted.

A wide-eyed man my age was staring down at me.

"I was wondering what you were doing just now?"

"Clearing my thoughts."

"Ah, I see. Is it okay if I sit down?"

"You already did."

"And you are?" he asked, ignoring my comment.

"Um, Lakshmi."

"I'm Ram. Pleasure to meet you, *um* Lakshmi."

It was strange to be approached by someone of the opposite sex. I looked around and saw a few people staring at me. Rumors would certainly not help my concentration in my first term back. Thankfully, the professor walked in and immediately started the lecture.

After ninety minutes of dutiful note taking, I gathered up my things and ran out of the classroom, hoping Ram would not pursue me.

"Lakshmi," Ram shouted.

I kept walking, hoping to find Nallini. She was nowhere in sight.

"Lakshmi, wait," Ram shouted again. This time, he grabbed my arm.

"What are you doing?"

Realizing he caused a public commotion, Ram put up his hands like a criminal caught robbing a jewelry store. "I'm sorry. I keep forgetting people don't do that here."

"Where is here? Chennai?"

"No, India. I just moved here with my family. I'm from London."

"Oh, I didn't know . . . Your Tamil is really good."

He explained how both of his parents refused to speak to him in English in case his father, an industrial engineer, was ever transferred back to Chennai. The transfer had happened a few months back, and Ram reluctantly followed since he could not afford London, otherwise.

"I am really sorry for grabbing your arm like that."

"No, it's fine. Don't worry," I answered with an unusual air of forgiveness.

"Look . . . I'm new to Chennai. Is there anyone who can show me around?"

My body temperature rose quickly. Ram was handsome, tall and fair, I noticed.

"I could show you around," I said without thinking.

"Great. I'll see you this afternoon? Four o'clock outside the main campus entrance?"

Ram smiled and took off in a gallop. I only managed an incoherent sound before realizing the trouble I had landed myself in.

"ARE YOU CRAZY? You can't go alone with him," Nallini exclaimed.

"Okay, so you'll come then?"

"One day back and already you've found this mischief."

"Great, so it's settled, you'll come with me."

"I missed you, Lakshmi."

Nallini was always excited for an adventure. Ram looked surprised but happy to see us walking arm-in-arm toward him after classes.

"Am I lucky enough to have two tour guides today?"

"Oh my God. He's so handsome," Nallini squealed in my ear.

We spent the afternoon showing Ram around the university. He had only been to India twice before moving back and found everything fascinating. Why do some neighborhoods speak Telugu and not Tamil? Who decided to make Chennai the capital of Tamil Nadu? No one had ever asked us such difficult questions. We were rediscovering our own home through the eyes of a stranger.

We finally parted ways close to dusk. Ram graciously thanked us for showing him around and putting up with all of his questions. Nallini let him give her a quick kiss on the cheek. I settled for one of my dear Alpa's American handshakes.

School in the UK was much less focused on memorization. After a year of studying with Nallini, I realized I worked much better in the company of another person, so Ram became a regular fixture in my study routine. Together, we would spend hours sitting in the small, cramped library, pouring over our lecture notes and copies of the textbooks Ram's father could afford to purchase.

As time passed, I noticed an undeniable physical connection . . . between Ram and Nallini. Though he made a good study partner, and though I had no experience in the matter, I knew Ram and I were not a good match. He needed someone with a better sense of humor, more attitude, and more spontaneity. I needed someone with more security.

"Will you tell anyone about me and Ram?" Nallini asked.

"Of course not."

And so Ram and Nallini commenced a risky "love romance." I did not have a clue what they did behind closed doors. All that mattered was that I had the support of two loyal friends. Together, we formed a perfect triangle of security.

Chapter 14

RAM AND I were in the university library reviewing our exercises from a particularly difficult lecture. Nallini sat next to us studying notes for a more advanced class. Right as I was about to solve the hardest problem from the set, I heard a bang at the other end of the hall. Mukesh, one of the boys in my village, stood up from a pile of books he had knocked over.

"Lakshmi. Lakshmi. Come quickly."

"Mukesh, what's wrong?"

"Just come quickly, Lakshmi."

Not wanting to slow me down, Mukesh gave me directions on where to go, which sounded like the field where nana worked. I was not sure I wanted to see what lay ahead.

After a twenty-minute ride, the dirt paths began to melt away to thick grass. Nana's old house was less than a ten-minute bike ride from where I eventually came to a halt. In the distance, I could hear vacant wails that signified deep sorrow. The voice was unmistakable—it was amma.

Time slowed down and every noise of the Indian terrain was amplified to deafening levels. A huge crowd formed a circle around the wailing that was coming from the center. Hundreds of whispers and clicking tongues rang through my ears as I forced my legs to continue carrying me forward.

"Let me through. I am Lakshmi," I could barely say.

Unable to digest the scene at first, I felt my body crash to the ground as my brain processed what was happening. Amma sat in the middle of the circle, crying and rocking her body in an uncontrolled trance. Her sari was caked in dirt that had mixed with blood to form a death-filled mud. She gently stroked nana's lifeless head, which exposed amma's blood-soaked sari through the gaping hole in the center of the forehead.

My nana, my hero, died on 20 September 1959.

Chapter 15

EVERYONE KNEW THAT nana had been murdered. When the villagers stormed the police station insisting on an investigation, the officers threw them out and demanded nearly a year's wages in bribes before lifting a finger. Having no other choice, two of nana's friends took some twine from a nearby oxcart and strapped nana's body to my bike to wheel him back to our house.

After a two-hour journey, I helped amma into some clean clothes and begged her to take rest. September in Chennai is one of the hottest months of the year, which left me no choice but to work fast. Nana's body would soon start to decompose.

I spent all night properly cleaning our house and washing a fresh set of nana's clothes. At dawn, I grabbed the can that held my parents' life savings and emptied every last coin. I walked into town and suffered the usual taunts and insults of being a poor *Shudra* woman as I made the arrangements to give nana a proper funeral. He deserved to pass into the next world with dignity.

The priest instructed me to remove the bloody shirt nana was wearing and bring the body down to the beach to be prepared for cremation. As I lifted the shirt from his torso, a small piece of paper fluttered out of the breast pocket. I grabbed the paper and threw it on nana's side of the cot. Two of the neighborhood boys helped me carry nana to the beach where the priest was waiting. Amma managed to hold herself up and come with baby sister.

After a humble puja, the priest gathered and placed nana's ashes in a blessed urn.

"Let us spread his ashes in the ocean," amma said.

"No, amma. Nana should be spread elsewhere," I replied.

It did not matter that the river of nana's childhood had been reduced to a tiny stream. Nana had become a man and discovered his purpose in life at the site of his childhood. The piece of nana that I now held within me was telling me he wanted to pass on to the next world there.

Amma needed a few minutes to summon the courage to open the urn. She Slowly poured the last physical remains of my father and collapsed into a heap and cried to the high heavens. The three of us remained with nana through the night, afraid of what lay ahead.

Eight months prior, amma had nursed me back from depression. Now, it was my turn to do the same for her. Taking care of her barely gave me enough time to think, let alone feel sad. Thankfully, the neighbors, and Nallini and Ram spared food, clothing, and water. They gave us enough to allow me to spend every minute by amma's side for the first few months after nana died.

If part of me died with Alpa, half of amma must have died with nana. Her eyes became an empty black, and her hair turned completely gray. She lost a third of her body weight that season. I did my best to feed her, bathe her, and change her clothes. Nallini brought me books from the university library, which I would read to amma every day. But after three months, amma's eyes were as vacant as the day nana died. I did not lose only nana that afternoon. I lost amma, too.

"WHAT DO YOU mean you are quitting school?" Nallini asked.

"What other choice do I have?" I replied.

"Shall I ask my father if you can borrow money?" Ram offered.

Ram was being kind in the gesture, not understanding why I could not accept. Taking loans to stay in school was not an option. Debts in the UK were managed by a bank. In India, debts were managed by a person's whims, and a person's whims were too often brutal. I could not put my family at that kind of risk.

My old jobs at the seamstress' shop and the farm did not pay enough to feed three people every day. Field workers were paid by the amount of grain and rice they carried. There was no way I would make anything close to nana's wages with that job. Besides, I had an education, at least by relative standards.

I went through amma's modest sari collection and picked out the nicest outfit I could find. With a lot of scrubbing and some twine, I was able to patch my only pair of sandals to be passable.

As I pleated my sari, I noticed something on amma and nana's cot. It was the piece of paper that had been in nana's shirt, which I threw in my bag. After lightly whispering to amma and baby sister, I grabbed my bloodstained bike and rode into town.

My first stop was the university. Surely they had to have some kind of administrative job available to former students. I reached the familiar campus entrance, marched upstairs to the offices, and asked for a job application.

The man behind the desk looked me over. "What are your qualifications, madam?"

"Higher secondary, first rank. Three terms here, first rank, sir."

"Why did you drop out?"

"Sir, father passing. I must earn wages to support my family."

He laughed as though I were an imbecile.

"You are not a man. Go get married. It is your husband's duty to take care of you and your family. Next."

He looked right past me and waited to help the next person who shoved their way to the front of the queue. I mentally slapped myself out of the insult.

I waved my hands in front of the man's face. "Give me a job application."

"You are not so ugly; you can find a decent suitor."

"*GIVE ME A job application,!*" I screamed at the top of my lungs.

The man looked startled and embarrassed. Deciding not to question further, he turned and grabbed a form from a giant pile and threw it at my face.

"Place it in the corner box when you're finished," he instructed.

Inside the box lay at least five hundred applications. There were two positions being advertised.

As I left, the man behind the counter whistled at me. I turned to face him, expecting another offense directed at my gender.

"What subject did you study here?"

"Accounting."

"Then why are you wasting your time? Go be an accountant."

He made an obvious point that I had neglected to see. That day, I tried two newspapers, seven shops, and five government offices to see if they had any accounting jobs. The newspapers and government offices laughed me out of the door at the proposition that a woman could handle their precious finances.

The wealthiest and those of the highest caste are often not the same people in India. Though I had amma's best sari on and I spoke intelligently, a lifetime of being a lower caste was not easily disguised. Four of the shops interrogated me about my status as soon as I approached. Only one would let me inside when I finally confessed my background.

"How dare you bring your Shudra filth into the air we breathe?"

In all of my years of schooling, professors and teachers emphasized the nature of a massive population vying for very few work positions. That day was the first I truly understood the gravity of competition.

Chapter 16

I HAD NO choice but to take my old job with the seamstress. Working fourteen hours a day, six days a week barely brought enough money to buy food for the three of us. Eventually, the cries of hunger from baby sister forced amma back to earth. She became a robot that cooked and did the household chores. Nana's death had killed her spirit. The once vivacious and loving woman was reduced to a mere shadow.

As I settled into a routine of poverty without hope, I felt the depression wash over me once again. The mindless work gave me hours to lose myself in thought. My best friend had been driven to suicide and my father had been murdered. Eleven years of hard work in school had not allowed me to progress to the better life nana had hoped I would have.

That November saw the end of a particularly intense monsoon season. The rain flooded nearly half of the village, bringing any activity in the area to a near standstill. The seamstress closed her shop for fear her materials would get blown away or damaged. That meant I could not work. That meant we had even less to eat.

For five straight days, our daily portions were whittled down to a half-cup of rice and a handful of lentils. By the sixth day, the hunger overtook our bodies. I tried to comfort baby sister through the noise of the storm. An unforgiving clap of thunder made baby sister shriek, causing amma to knock the last of our rice into the dirt.

Amma collapsed in a heap, and cried with a pained desperation. I put baby sister down in one of the cots and rushed to her.

"It's okay, amma. It's okay, we'll get more food tomorrow."

We both understood it was a promise I could not keep. Amma spoke her first words in months.

"I am so tired of this life. I am so tired of being defenseless against people who hurt my family. I am so tired of watching my children go hungry."

I wrapped my arms around her; I tried to find the words of comfort I felt I had no place in saying. There was nothing I had to offer.

"Lakshmi, promise me you will leave this village, leave India, leave this life. Promise me, Lakshmi."

She had never spoken such words to me before. She had never suggested I give up on our world. For her to ask me to abandon my dream to change India, her spirit had truly broken. Her words prompted the worst awakening of my life.

"I promise you, amma. I promise."

I finally managed to get amma and baby sister to sleep. The rained pounded heavily well into the night. Before nana had been murdered, the sound brought me comfort for a healthy crop season. Now all it did was remind me how little work I would be able to secure the next day.

Unable to sleep, I found our little kerosene lamp. Reaching into my bag for matches, I rediscovered the small slip of paper that had been in nana's shirt the day he died. Carefully holding it to the light, I read words that made my head explode.

The note was written on the stationary of a company called Malaysian Agrimetrics. It contained one single line: "I said you'd pay."

It was Sahana's handwriting.

Chapter 17

I BEGGED AND pleaded with the police to open an investigation. The deputy said he would not move a muscle unless I had "unequivocal proof" that the sheet of paper had come from my father's shirt, and that Sahana had written the note.

"What if someone stole the paper from her father's office?" he told me.

"And why didn't the police look at the body when your father died?" asked another deputy.

I told him the police wanted too much money. We could not afford to pay. The two deputies nodded their heads. I had my answer.

Our neighbors were sympathetic, but everyone warned me to stop pursuing the matter.

"He will have his daughter rusticated from university, no problem. But he will not let Sahana go to jail," they all said.

"That is a powerful family, Lakshmi. Even if justice finds Sahana, she can have you killed," said Nallini

"I don't care."

"Well . . . she can have your amma and baby sister killed too."

That convinced me to drop the case.

I KNEW IT was time to leave India. Amma and nana had sacrificed their lives to have me educated, to have me walk down a dignified path to self-sufficiency. India told me that path was not possible. Without a proper education, without money, and without connections, there was only one path that would finally lead me to a better life:

Marriage.

One of the newspapers that did not accept job applications from women did accept personal ads for people wanting to marry. The last of our money would only be enough to buy a newspaper, so I prayed with all of my might that someone worthy had taken an ad in that week's edition.

The same clerk who rejected my job inquiry was sitting behind the counter. He gave me a mocking smile when I asked to purchase the personal ads for the week.

"You finally see you are a woman?" he said.

I stepped outside to read through the selection. Most of the ads were trash. Rich families placed many of the ads in the hopes of finding someone for their Govind-like sons. Some of the ads were for foreigners wishing to find someone in India. Amma taught me long ago those ads were code for being sold into slavery.

Tucked away in the far bottom corner, one ad caught my eye.

"Young doctor from Bangalore seeks a new life with intelligent bride. Must speak Telugu."

It was too perfect to be true. Without a moment of hesitation, I ran back inside the newspaper office to leave my reply.

Chapter 18

HE RESPONDED IN less than twenty-four hours. Through a series of messages at the newspaper office, we agreed to meet at the local canteen the following week. He said he would be wearing a bowler hat. I did not know what that was. I told him I would wear a green sari. It was the one amma wore at her wedding.

I arrived at the canteen first. The busboy pointed out a free table, and I sat down to wait . . . and wait . . . and wait. More than an hour after we agreed to meet, Shankar finally arrived, along with two of his cronies.

"Sorry I'm late," Shankar offered.

"Oh, this one is always late, better get used to that," said one of the two. "Just ignore him."

Not two seconds later, his other friend chimed in. "So why do you want to marry this idiot?"

Laughing never came easily to me, and I did not know how to respond. Shankar's friends were distracting and rude. They carried on, not giving Shankar and myself enough time to exchange even a few lines.

"Enough. Get out," Shankar said to the two of them.

"Bad start buddy," one of them replied.

Shankar let out an exasperated sigh and pushed the smaller of the two off of the bench they were sharing.

"Sorry about that," Shankar said once they finally left.

"Why are they your friends?"

I cursed myself at asking such a direct question; assertiveness was not highly regarded by suitors.

Shankar did not seem to mind. "Our fathers are childhood friends. I see them often, whether I want to or not."

"I see. Are you three taking a journey through South India to find a bride only?"

I was serious. He thought it was a joke.

"We just finished our final medical school exams and decided to take a holiday here. They made me place the ad on a dare."

My heart sank.

"So you're not looking to marry someone after all?"

"No, well, I don't know. I'm still trying to decide where I want to work, so it depends on what I want . . . what we . . . would want." His face flushed at the word "we."

Shankar called the busboy to order food. As he brought his hands up from beneath the table to start eating, I noticed how badly he was trembling.

OVER THE NEXT few days, I learned that he came from a middle-class family in Bangalore. His father ran a moderately successful grocery store in the heart of the city, enough to provide Shankar with the comforts of modern life, though not enough to guarantee a life of luxury. His mother was uneducated and kind. His father was uneducated and judgmental.

Most of the girls Shankar had met "made him cry from boredom." Either they only cared about superficial things such as clothes and jewelry, or they only cared about beating everyone in final exams. He had never met a single girl who just liked to learn for the sake of learning.

"That's why I let my idiot friends place the ad in the paper," he explained.

The only thing his parents cared about was elevating their status through his marriage. The only thing Shankar cared about with marriage was being happy.

"I don't care about caste or religion. My kids have to speak Telugu, though," he said.

I told him about the evils poverty had laid on my family. "That's why for many years I was one of those robots you detested."

My motivations were not superficial, though. They were out of the desire to find something better. Yet all of my efforts had only led me down this path of misery and disappointment. In another world, in another life, my education would have solved my problems. In this world, in this life, finding a husband would have to be the answer.

Meeting Shankar made me understand what Nallini and Ram had spoken of in their "love romance." Shankar and I had an obvious connection. On 8 December 1959, G.M. Shankar Deva asked for my hand in marriage. We wed a month later in a small ceremony attended by less than twenty people. Shankar never asked for a dowry, and I never offered one. We found temporary housing just a kilometer away from my childhood home. Six months later, I was pregnant.

Chapter 19

WITH MY PREGNANCY, amma's purpose in life was renewed. The color flushed back to her face, the song in her voice was restored, and the dance she performed with each step resurfaced. If I had not been constantly nauseous, I would have celebrated with her.

Shankar agreed immediately when I suggested we move to the United States or Canada. Ram and his father were very patient in explaining the concepts of "passport," "visa," and "sponsor." I do not think Shankar and I would have made it through the paperwork without their help.

The only place to accept Shankar's application was in a small city outside of Philadelphia called Youngstown. They were in desperate need of new medical residents, and agreed to sponsor Shankar for a temporary visa.

"We can't keep you past your residency, you understand?" they asked him.

We had no choice but to be confident Shankar would find a job after. When we applied for the visas in January 1960, American laws did not grant automatic sponsorship for an immigrant's family. The hospital's advice was to hire a lawyer. But who could afford such legal fees?

I spent half of my daily wages to place a reservation with the international operator. After waiting for hours, sometimes days, my call would be scheduled. With the time difference and general hustle of the hospital, only one in three of my calls would be met with someone on the other line.

No amount of my arguing convinced the hospital to also sponsor my baby and me. They would always reply saying they could not understand what I was saying, or that they had no need for a woman that had not completed a university degree. Finally, Ram offered to use his British accent.

"Hallo, this is Nigel calling from the New York City office of London's finest international law firm. If you don't grant Mr. Shankar Deva's wife and daughter visas, we'll call American immigration services for a thorough sweep of your facilities."

It worked like magic.

There was one condition: I had to wait until after the birth of my child before leaving India. That meant the earliest I could go was December of 1960. Shankar had to start work by August. He was devastated at the idea of missing the birth of his first child, but in the end we decided it was worth the sacrifice.

Shankar's father felt the humiliation of his son marrying a peasant girl would only be cancelled out if Shankar went to America and became a successful doctor. For this sole reason, his father paid for our trip to the New Delhi Indian embassy to collect our passports and visas.

Compared to Chennai, Delhi was a madhouse. Cars, bikes, and auto rickshaws packed the uneven streets, never conceding a single centimeter of space. Child street merchants selling foreign contraband trinkets bombarded anyone who dared take their eyes off the road. Delhi was packed with foreigners, and was by far the most cosmopolitan place I had ever seen. If Delhi was this grand, I wondered what must the United States be like?

Chapter 20

SHANKAR LEFT FOR America on 1 July 1960. He took the train from Chennai to Hyderabad to Mumbai. From Mumbai, he flew to London, then to New York City where he spent the night with a friend of his father's. From New York, he took the train to Philadelphia, where one of the hospital administrators picked him up and dropped him off at the apartment the hospital had arranged for us.

I counted the time of Shankar's journey down to the minute. As soon as he reached our new home, I hired a rickshaw to the calling station where I carefully placed a call with the operator to the number the hospital instructed us to use. After seven hours, the scheduled call went through. More than three days after he departed, I finally spoke to Shankar.

"What is it like? How is the apartment? Where is the calling station? Is it safe?"

He laughed. I imagined the expression on his face as he tried to figure out how to tell me all the details.

"The apartment is large, and the best part, Lakshmi, is that I am talking to you from *inside* the apartment."

"You are speaking from the apartment only?" I asked him in English.

"Yes. The administrator told me everyone in America has their own phone."

It sounded so perfect. I could talk to amma and baby sister with my own private phone.

"And tonight there will be something called fireworks for the American Independence Day."

American Independence Day is July fourth, I noted. I had only seen fireworks once—at the university. I imagined those would be nothing compared to the fireworks of Youngstown.

With the time difference and my growing belly, I was only able to talk to Shankar four more times before December. The first call came a few days after he started work. Though he made everything sound like a dream, I could already hear the strain in his voice. By October, Shankar said the weather had gotten extremely cold.

"Colder than anything we have ever known in India."

In Youngstown, snow fell and stuck to the ground nearly every other day. Shankar slipped a few times, carrying painful bruises to work. I heard the regret in his voice at not being present for the birth our child. It must have been so hard for him being there completely alone.

All of the money Shankar was able to remit back to Chennai went to pay for my expensive train fares and airline tickets. With nothing to spare, private hospitals and clinics for my delivery were not an option. Public facilities were less sterile than our house. I would be giving birth to my child on the same floor on which I slept.

My water broke on the evening of 8 December 1960. Amma sent baby sister to stay with one of the neighbors, and gathered all of the clean material and clean water she could find. Amma's friends took turns staying by my side, singing to me, rubbing my belly, and putting a handkerchief wetted with cool water on my head.

The labor felt like it took an eternity. Amma later told me I gave birth in less than three hours. A midwife was called at the end, and she and four other women sat around me, coaching me through all of the incomprehensibly painful pushing and breathing. With each heave, I held Amma's hand tighter. One year after Shankar asked me to marry him, our little baby girl, Pooja, was born. The midwife stayed to help amma clean Pooja off and to cut the umbilical cord. Amma handed me my precious daughter properly wrapped in a fresh cloth.

"Lakshmi, just think. Soon you will leave this misery behind. Your next child will be born in America," amma said.

Chapter 21

ON 13 JANUARY 1961, Pooja and I landed in America. Pooja had been thankfully quiet for the entire journey. As soon as we entered the New York International Airport terminal, she began to cry. The stimulus was too much for her tiny ears and eyes to handle.

I set down the small bag I had brought with me on the plane and found a seat to readjust her wrapping, hoping it would calm her down. I did not want Shankar's first memory of his daughter to be her sobs. By the time she finally quieted, I realized all of the other passengers had gone ahead. Shankar's instructions had been to follow the flow of people until I saw him. I tried telling myself this was just like discovering another path to school.

My calming tactic did not work. Feeling panicked, I grabbed Pooja a little too forcefully, and she started crying again. I felt thousands of white, black, and brown faces sneering, beckoning me to turn around and fly home. My head started to spin, and I felt my arms go limp. At that precise moment was a tap on my shoulder. Shankar's calm face looked back at me. He brought me close to his chest and bent down to give his daughter the first of many kisses.

Our plan had been to stay with the friend of Shankar's father. At the last minute, they had called Shankar and apologized.

"Our son is sick. We do not wish to risk your baby catching the infection."

Shankar asked what kind of illness their son had contracted. They did not give an answer, and instead hung up the phone. I understood. Even in America, having a peasant girl in your house was undesirable.

Shankar made a reservation at a hotel in Manhattan. The cost was far more than we could afford, but he wanted to impress his wife and daughter. Though the January cold of New York was unbearable, as we crossed the bridge from Queens, Pooja came to life. I held her up so she could see through the glass window and she wrestled her hands out from underneath her coverings and laughed for the first time.

"We are home, amma," she was telling me.

Chapter 22

THE FIRST EIGHTEEN months were difficult. Shankar worked eighty hours a week, leaving me alone to care for Pooja, tend to the apartment, buy the food, and do all of the cooking.

We could only afford to buy one car. In India, one car was a world-class luxury. In America, where everything is spread out great distances, one car was not enough. An Indian community raised a child; in America, childcare was expensive. Without family nearby, caring for Pooja became my full time job.

She grew with each day, and it soon became unreasonably expensive to send for material to make her Indian clothes. Shankar heard a few of the hospital nurses mention a store called "JC Pennies," which was where I would take Pooja to buy American clothes when we felt confident enough to bear the cost.

One lovely spring afternoon, I took Pooja for a walk. She looked pretty in her new white dress. Pooja loved birds. I let go of her hand for a few minutes so she could chase a blue jay. The women in the street would always stare at the two of us. I hadn't grown accustomed to the idea of wearing pants like a man or American skirts that exposed one's legs. Instead, I continued to wear my saris, even though they attracted attention.

That afternoon, one of the staring women decided to approach me. "Um, ma'am?"

"Yes?" I replied, with my best smile.

"Ma'am, your daughter is only wearing a slip."

"A what?"

"Your daughter is only wearing a slip!"

Why did Americans always scream when we did not understand the meaning of their words? I was Indian, not deaf. She saw the confusion on my face and looked as though I was refusing to understand her advice. Frustrated, she walked away.

I decided to take Pooja to the store for an ice cream and pick up a new container of snow. At the time, I did not know that what we Indians knew as "snow," Americans called "facial lotion." As we walked in through the doors, I spotted the new catalogue for JC Pennies.

"Look, Pooja. We will buy you something next month when nana gets paid."

I took the catalogue, but I couldn't find the lotion. "Excuse me, where do you keep the snow?"

"The what?"

"The snow. It is usually near the soap."

The cashier gave me the same look as the other woman as she inspected my clothes. "Lady, what the hell are you talking about?"

"I need snow."

The cashier snorted and turned to another employee.

"Hey, Donna. This woman wants *snow*."

Donna started laughing hysterically and pointing at me in the same way teacher had encouraged the other students to respond to my beatings. "Lady, come back in December if you want snow."

"Oh and by the way," the cashier said, grabbing the catalogue. "Your daughter is only wearing a slip. You brought your daughter out in her *undergarments*."

Both women started cackling so cruelly that I became scared for my safety. Upset at my sudden change in body language, Pooja gripped the ice cream so hard as though it were a shield. I used force I never wished to show my daughter to remove the container from her tiny hands. I picked her up and ran out of the door, leaving my dignity melting alongside my daughter's treat. Was this progress?

MOST DAYS SHANKAR would be so tired, he came home, ate a small plate of food, and went straight to sleep. On the rare occasion we had a chance to talk, I could see the sparkle in his eyes was slowly fading. The closest Indian family lived nearly thirty kilometers away. Very quickly, we grew lonely.

No matter how carefully he spoke, how many times he apologized, or how hard he tried, Shankar would always be blamed if anything went wrong. Doctors would insult Shankar in public, nurses would tell him to find Christ, and patients would spit in his face. The hospital administration refused to pay him for an entire month because they accused him of stealing a bottle of aspirin from the pharmacy. All of the other residents were guaranteed two weeks paid vacation. Shankar was downgraded to three days without explanation.

The worst part was that there was nothing we could do. We did not know the law, we could not afford to hire someone who did, and we did not have an advocate. By the end of the two years in Youngstown, we had reviewed Shankar's contract a hundred times. Being absolutely sure we were safe, we called every hospital in Philadelphia. One rainy day, we got a call back from a private one that would be willing to sponsor all three of our visas. Without telling a soul, we rented a van, packed up the apartment, and left Youngstown the day after Shankar's contract expired.

Chapter 23

I LOVED PHILADELPHIA. Shankar's salary was more than three times what he made before, but the city was not three times the cost. We moved into a spacious apartment in a safe, quiet neighborhood. Soon, I was remitting weekly sums to amma. She used the money to buy a small house near the shops across from the university. Airline tickets and long-stay visas were still very expensive, but amma and I made plans for her and baby sister to come visit us in Philadelphia the following year.

While Pooja played in the park, I sat with my Turkish, Brazilian, and Egyptian friends and listened to stories about their homelands. Everybody I met in Philadelphia wanted to go to India. To them, I had not grown up in a slum. I had grown up in a fascinating world of colors and whimsy. I did not dare crush their idealized dreams of my homeland. It was much too fun to pretend to be someone better than anyone in India told me I was.

Joanne, the mother of Sarah—one of Pooja's friends—quickly became a close confidante. The first day we met, Joanne looked at my sari, though not in the hurtful way the people in Youngstown did.

"Oh my God. What are you wearing? It's so beautiful," Joanne exclaimed.

"Thank you," I said, elated and embarrassed.

"I'm Joanne," she said with a huge smile on her face.

"Lakshmi."

"Lakshmi. That is so pretty. Just like you, Lakshmi."

No one had ever told me I looked pretty.

Joanne taught me so many things. She bought me my first set of make up—a box of lipstick with twenty different shades. She gave me confidence to wear Western fashions and took me to my first beauty parlor to get my hair cut in the style of Jacquelyn Kennedy.

We would buckle Pooja and Sarah in the back of her car and ride all around the city while listening to the radio. She even convinced me to try my first chocolate bar. Oh, how I thought about my dear Alpa as I unwrapped the delicate brick of sweetness. This was certainly a moment that was worth living for someone else.

Joanne and her husband showed Shankar and me the pleasure of hiring a nanny a few nights a week. They took us to the opera, the natural history museum, and even to a baseball game. Shankar and I thought baseball was an easy version of cricket, though we still enjoyed the atmosphere.

Pooja loved the city too. She found everything fascinating. Every dog, flower, child, and building had to be inspected. Thanks to Joanne, I discovered walking to be much easier when wearing pants and closed-toe shoes. On our daily stroll around the neighborhood, Pooja would point out tall buildings, short buildings, and odd-looking buildings. One of the local shopkeepers loved Pooja, and would give her a postcard of a different city every time we passed by.

"That girl is gonna be an architect," he told me.

By December 1962, Shankar, Pooja, and I had firmly settled into Philadelphia. The city provided us with a life of steady food, clean water, proper clothing, and a dignity and respect that we had never been afforded. Together we enjoyed many luxuries of a life that I had once assumed was limited to film stars; the life of stability and happiness spoke far more to the girl I was back in the Indian theater.

That year, one of our neighbors invited us for our first Christmas party. I was not sure what to wear. Joanne advised on the elegant new skirt I had just bought, a red blouse, and a green-and-gold flower brooch. Shankar put on his nicest suit, and I dressed Pooja in a slip *and* a beautiful gold dress. As he looked at the two of us, the sparkle in Shankar's eyes lit up the entire room. He gently pulled us over to a mirror, and the three of us smiled back at our reflection.

Chapter 24

OF COURSE, I dearly missed amma, baby sister, and my friends back in India, but Shankar's work would allow for many reunions, of that, I was sure. With minor exceptions, Philadelphia had been incredibly kind to us. We had become invincible. The problem with a perfect life, however, is that there is nowhere to go but down.

4 August 1963 started out as any normal day would. As usual, Shankar was in the hospital by eight am. Two hours later, a patient came to the hospital with his eye completely swollen shut. Normally, this would be a case for the emergency room doctors. As it was an exceptionally busy day, the nurses dispatched for the best internal medical doctor on staff—Shankar—to help.

"Make sure you take the patient's medical history," Shankar instructed.

According to the chart, the patient had had a minor surgery on his arm a few years back. No allergies, no history of heart problems, nothing wrong with the brain. Shankar looked at the patient's infected eye and determined from the tests run that the patient had a bacterial infection.

"What's the treatment?" the nurse asked Shankar.

"One dose of penicillin."

After being apart from Pooja so much the first few years, Shankar always came home for lunch between noon and two o'clock. When the clock struck two-thirty, I assumed he was simply delayed. As the clock reached three, I began to worry. When I still had not heard from him an hour later, I dressed Pooja and called a taxi to take us to the hospital. I associated American hospitals with strength. In India, any minor injury can cause death. Life in America was not that fragile.

The hospital secretary told me that Shankar was in the medical coordinator's office. After pointing me in the right direction, she shot me a smile. Nearly three years in the country had taught me American smiles could mean many things. I knew this smile was not out of happiness.

Shankar was sitting alone in the office, his face buried in his hands. Pooja shouted happily, startling him out of a daze.

"Nana, lunch?" Pooja asked Shankar.

"No beta, not today," Shankar replied.

"What happened?" I asked.

Shankar shook his head slightly, tears gathering in his eyes.

"Nana, don't cry!" Pooja put her hands up to his eyes to catch the tears as she had done for me so many times in Youngstown.

He called in a nurse. "Can you take our daughter to get a juice box?"

"Orange, nana?" Pooja asked.

"Whatever you wish."

Pooja happily walked off with the nurse, giving us a few minutes alone for Shankar to explain what I felt could only be devastating.

"I told her to take the patient history."

"She forgot?"

"It was incomplete."

Not knowing the patient was allergic, Shankar administered the penicillin and left the room. The hospital had been so overwhelmed it took a few minutes for anyone to notice the patient had a massive seizure.

"He was probably epileptic," Shankar guessed.

The patient died shortly after. The police took a formal report from everyone who had had contact with the patient. Shankar told them he did not know the patient was allergic to penicillin and showed the chart as proof. After questioning the nurse, the police informed the hospital that she denied Shankar tasked her to take the medical history.

"I double checked, he said he'd do it," she claimed.

The hospital administrator knew Shankar was a competent doctor, but said he had to protect the hospital.

"It's a question of liability."

They put Shankar on unpaid leave and advised us to hire a lawyer immediately. Looking at the trauma on Shankar's face, I realized why God had allowed us to find each other as life partners. Many falls from grace ensured I had the strength to gather my family and assure them everything would be okay. My words were enough to convince them, if not myself.

Chapter 25

THE HOSPITAL SENT us a list of the best medical malpractice lawyers in the city. Only one that fell in our price range would take on the challenge of representing an immigrant. Her name was Yael Stein.

"You remind me of my parents. They survived The Holocaust," she said.

Hiring Yael meant sacrificing the money we were saving to bring amma and baby sister over. Breaking the news was nothing short of heartbreaking; by August 1963, it had been nearly three years since we had seen each other. I felt as though I had abandoned my family after all they had done for me.

Shankar's family was more upset that their son might not become a successful doctor than they were about Shankar himself. Whatever happened, they forbade him from returning to Bangalore and further humiliating the family.

"First you marry a peasant girl, now you will go to jail? What did I do to deserve such disappointment in my family?" his father said.

Shankar stopped phoning his household after that conversation.

With Shankar's contract was on hold, Pooja and I would be illegal immigrants after six months. Because criminal charges might be brought against Shankar, he could not leave the country. Six months in misery felt like a lifetime; six months to save one's family felt like an eye blink.

Pooja spent much of the time at Joanne's house while Shankar and I helped Yael in any way we could. Much to our financial dismay, we were forced to hire a second lawyer for our immigration purposes. Though I always favored saving money for future protection, we knew there would be no future without the sacrifice.

Yael's preparation covered our statements on every possible question the judge might ask.

"What did Shankar have to eat that morning? Was he well rested? Was he stressed? Did he get along well with the nurses? How clear is his English?"

We wrote down every piece of information and memorized how best to phrase the answer. The memorization part was easy for me. Knowing how to apply the information was much more difficult.

With the immigration lawyer, we produced copious notes detailing our every move since we landed in America.

"Immigration will leave no detail unnoticed."

What were our intentions in coming to the States? Did we live within our means? Did we have an ulterior motive for coming here? Who, what, where, when, why, and how for every move we made. Day and night, we met with our lawyers. Every little detail, every fond memory, every painful event was relived, dissected, and catalogued.

Yael did her best to obtain records of the hospital staff and administration. We paid for her to fly across the country to bring back copies of the records. Meanwhile, our immigration lawyer spent a week in Youngstown to confirm Shankar's employment record. It was not until then that I realized the gravity of our initial lie to get Pooja and me into the country.

Finally, our big break in the hospital case came with Yael's final trip out of town—to Kansas City, Missouri.

"Our nurse in question went to school there," Yael informed.

"What did you find?"

"Turns out she married last year there and changed her name."

Due to a clerical error, the records under her new last name were filed separately.

"Mrs. Edith Bennett, née Conner, did not pass a require course: medical record keeping. She is an illegally licensed nurse."

The case was dropped against Shankar with a mere ten days to spare.

THE IMMENSE RELIEF that came with dropped charges was temporary. The entire ordeal had proven quite embarrassing for the prestigious hospital. They formed a case against Shankar in violation of the acceptable hospital behavior clause in his contract. Shankar was officially fired a few days later.

"You have the right to appeal," they argued.

But not before we would be required to return back to India.

Working around the clock more out of pity than for the money, our immigration lawyer pursued every possible solution. He spoke with representatives from the American Office of Diplomatic Affairs, he chased down ambassadors, wrote to the United Nations, and appealed to two-dozen members of the US Congress.

"If Kennedy hadn't been shot, I'd even write the President."

With forty-eight hours until deportation, we were unsuccessful. Making one of the hardest decisions of our lives, Shankar and I conceded we would have to return to India. We packed up our most prized possessions and visited our closest friends to say goodbye. Joanne was hysterical. She cried and begged us to not give up.

"They'll take you over my dead body."

"Where are the fucking police? Why can't they do something?" her husband shouted.

My poor Pooja had little understanding of why everyone was so upset.

"Amma, don't be sad. Shall we get ice cream?"

Shankar, Pooja, and I spent our last few hours alone in America in our apartment. We unplugged the phone, drew the curtains tight, and curled up in bed, using the comforter to block out the noise of the outside world. Pooja, unaware of the turmoil that was about to uproot her life, slept peacefully between us.

Humiliated by the situation, Shankar could not bear to make eye contact with me. He rejected my offered hand of support, and I wondered if this rejection would continue in our life back in India. That day was not the first time my world had fallen apart, but with a daughter to care for, it destroyed me more profoundly than anything else.

Chapter 26

THERE WAS A heavy banging on the door. Immigration was early. In our six-month probation period, they had delayed answering each of our questions. On the day we were to be shipped off like criminals, they showed up early.

Shankar still had his arms draped over Pooja. Both were asleep, so I carefully inched my way off the bed to avoid disturbing them in their final moments of peace. I put on my shoes and prepared to let complete strangers invade our house and ruin our lives. I opened the door, and was shocked to see our immigration lawyer staring at me, panting heavily.

"We did it!"

Waving a sheet of paper in his hand like a Wall Street trader, he continued to shout well after I managed to usher him inside.

"We did it. It's over. You're safe, we did it."

Shankar came rushing downstairs. As I unfolded the paper, my heart pounded so heavily that my entire body swayed in motion, like a ship fighting to avoid capsizing in the ocean. The letter was written on gorgeous blue-and-black Congressional stationary. Our lives hung in the balance of five paragraphs.

Dear Dr. and Mrs. Deva,

I was saddened to hear of the unfortunate circumstances surrounding your employment contract termination at the St. Augustine Hospital in Philadelphia earlier this month. Our legal system is in place for the ultimate protection of our citizens and residents; however, it does on occasion result in unfair outcomes, as in your case.

It has come to my attention that your residency status is contingent upon employment with St. Augustine. As such, the US Immigration Services scheduled you to be deported back to your native country of India on February 5, 1964.

I have brought your case to the attention of several of my colleagues, and it was unanimously agreed that there is no legal precedent by which you should be removed. As such, my staff has contacted the US Immigration and Naturalization Services and instructed them to not execute your order of deportation.

The Paths of Marriage

As a US Senator, it is my job to encourage growth for the betterment of my country. Dr. Deva, as a physician, I believe you can serve an important need of our community. Dr. and Mrs. Deva, under a provision afforded to me as a US Congressman, I have put forth a piece of legislation that will allow you and your daughter to secure permanent residency <u>so long as Dr. Deva provides his services as a medical doctor in an underprivileged area of my state of West Virginia for a minimum of ten years.</u>

My staff has been in contact with your lawyer, and will expedite the process to ensure your full protection as soon as possible. It is my pleasure to be at your service.

Sincerely yours,

Robert C. Byrd

United States Senator, West Virginia

Senator Byrd personally drafted a bill allowing for our permanent legal stay and had it passed through the US Congress. Shankar, Pooja, and I were awarded our green cards two months later. In ten years, Shankar and I would be eligible to become citizens. Pooja would be eligible as soon as soon as she turned eighteen.

Chapter 27

WEST VIRGINIA WAS like Youngstown in many ways. Shankar and I, however, were stronger and wiser people. Disillusioned with hospital administration, Shankar took out a small loan and rented a three-room medical office within walking distance of our house.

Though a brilliant doctor, Shankar had neither the time nor the knowledge of how to run a business. In such an unpredictable way, I finally found use of my accounting knowledge, acting as general manager for Shankar's medical practice. University had taught me how to be a master money handler. Life had taught me how to be kind. Shankar's practice served some of the poorest people in the country, and I soon made it a common practice to write off the bills of patients who could not otherwise afford service.

Professionally, Shankar and I found solace. Personally, we were once again alone. Our town in West Virginia had a population of less than twenty-five thousand. We were the only Indian family.

When I found out I was pregnant again, we decided to use our savings to bring amma and baby sister over for a year. Buying airline tickets in a small town of West Virginia became a huge challenge. We took five trips and nearly three months to coordinate the schedules, file the correct paperwork, and make sure amma understood the instructions.

"When shall we have them come?" Shankar asked.

"We can only afford mid-February."

"You're due in early March."

"It will be fine."

I could barely move the last few weeks of my third trimester, so Shankar and Pooja left for New York without me to get amma and baby sister. Shankar gave my large belly a final kiss, then half-walked, half-slid through the snow to the car, and started the four-hour journey to the nearest airport that could connect them to what was now called John F. Kennedy airport, the same airport Pooja and I had passed through more than four years ago.

I watched them drive into the white winter curtain. Looking around the house, I realized this was the first time in my life that I ever had total and complete privacy. I took full advantage of this on the first day. No sleep schedules, no cleaning, no cooking. Just total relaxation.

The Indian mind is not trained to be alone; by my second day of solitude,

I was already growing restless. As patients, West Virginians were easy to get along with. As friends, I had none. I tried calling Joanne, but her husband told me she was out of town visiting her parents. I tried watching television. American programs never held my interest. The weather was terrible, or I would have gone to the library. Having nothing to do and no one to talk to, I feel asleep on the couch.

I was startled awake a few hours later by snow that fell from a tree onto the roof. For a split second, I thought the snow had fallen straight through the house. A few moments later, I made the uneasy discovery that my pants were wet. My water had broken.

An OB/GYN was by my side soon after I entered the hospital. My brain spiraled back in time to the extremes of my life. I saw flashes of Alpa dying on the stark, white steps of the hospital building, of seeing Pooja playing happily in the parks of Philadelphia, of the gaping hole that was once my father's wise mind. With a final jolt of pain, I squeezed the nurse's hand, and emerged in a parallel time.

"Aaammmmaa!" I screamed at the top of my lungs.

One of the other nurses asked what I was saying, which returned me back to reality. I looked around and rediscovered the painful truth that merely a room full of strangers surrounded me.

Chapter 28

"WHAT SHALL WE name her?" baby sister asked.

"Lucy," Pooja shouted.

Amma looked radiant as she gazed down at her elder granddaughter; she was so proud Pooja could understand Telugu. Pooja proposing a name from her favorite cartoon series, *Peanuts*, was all the more endearing.

"You must decide before you leave the hospital," the nurse told us.

"Chee. Such an important decision," Shankar ticked.

"Who's a woman you admire? Someone you owe?" the nurse prompted.

I translated what the nurse said to amma. She leaned back with the knowledge of what our past had entailed. Other than amma herself—who was not an option, as she was thankfully still with us on earth—there was but one name my life could truly offer. We left the hospital with baby Alpa an hour later. Pooja was elated to have a little sister.

HAVING AMMA AND baby sister with me was the exact relief I needed from an emotionally draining journey. Pooja and baby sister spent the entire year playing. Amma looked after baby Alpa during the day so I could tend to the office. Every evening, we would have an excellent south Indian dinner and spend the night swapping stories, discussing the latest films, and simply enjoying each other's company.

The six of us saw all of the attractions in the state. The Smokey Mountains, the famous coal mines, the University of West Virginia campus. We even made a trip to Senator Byrd's West Virginia office in the capital. Shankar and I closed the office for a week to take amma and baby sister to Washington and New York. After the emotional trauma it had inflicted, we decided to skip Philadelphia.

We bought amma and baby sister brand new suitcases to fill with toys and gifts for the villagers in Chennai. Amma loved spending hours going through discount stores and buying four of everything—toilet paper, key chains, fly swatters, crayons, chewing gum. A new Penney's opened that year, and Pooja was thrilled to finally have someone to chase around the maze of aisles. Baby sister became a huge fan of socks and bought at least forty pairs to take home.

Saying goodbye to amma and baby sister was so difficult. Only the heart is superior to the brain, and my love for Chennai grew exponentially as I knew I would not be joining them on the return journey. But seeing the two of them looking happy and healthy, holding new suitcases and the equivalent of a year of Chennai wages reassured me that Shankar and I had made the right decision to come to America.

The idea of being the woman to change India still roared in my soul. In another life, I swore to make it happen. In this life, I knew Chennai had not let me progress. It was not a place to raise a daughter. It was not a place to be a woman.

Chapter 29

IN THE FALL of 1966, Pooja started the first standard, and Shankar and I decided to have a family outing to celebrate. We went to the only Italian restaurant in town and split a giant bowl of spaghetti and a pitcher of Coke. Alpa made a huge mess of her food; she was too independent to let either of us help her eat.

"Not hungry, beta?" I asked Pooja, who had barely touched her food.

Pooja shook her head, on the verge of tears.

"Is there something wrong?" Shankar gently asked.

"Nana, amma, I'm scared about school."

"What's the matter?" Shankar asked.

"What if the kids don't like me?"

I smiled at Pooja, thinking of all the friends she would make and all the happiness she would find in knowledge. America would let her learn with the same passion as I had and with the same happiness in life as my dear friend, Alpa.

"You are a good, kind person, and many people will want to be your friend."

She was not convinced. I knew it would simply take time for her to get used to going away every morning. With an ease that still made me quiver with excitement, Shankar and I immediately offered to see a fun film after dinner. She brought her head up to our gazes and told us that would make her very happy.

"Four, please," Shankar said to the ticket salesman.

The salesman glanced up from his newspaper and looked at Shankar and over to the rest of us. I recognized that look immediately. It was the same look of lower class hatred I had seen many times in Chennai. Before the salesman said anything, I walked to Shankar and said in Telugu that we should leave.

The salesman overheard me speaking. "What the fuck is that?"

"Nothing. We are leaving," I replied

"But, amma. I wanted to see the movie," Pooja cried.

The salesman looked down at my precious daughter with a disgust that made me enraged enough to kill.

"What did she just say? What the hell is amma?"

Never having lived a life of poverty, Shankar showed his anger for treating his daughter that way and walked as close as he could to the glass window. His India had not taught him the necessity in simply walking away.

"Four tickets."

"I ain't giving you no tickets. We don't sell to your kind."

Before I could stop him, Shankar started screaming at the top of his lungs. The rage in his voice shook little Alpa into hysterics, which in turn made Pooja upset. Seeing the frightened looks on my children's faces, I finally grabbed Shankar's shirt and pulled him back to the car. After strapping in Alpa and Pooja, I got into the passenger's seat and tried to collect myself before turning around.

"Why was he so mean to us, amma?"

"I don't know, *beta*. Some people are just bad seeds. Shall we go get ice cream?"

Pooja hiccupped a few times as she caught her breath. I turned around to wipe the last of the tears from her eyes. She grabbed my hand and brought it against her warm, scared face as she pulled herself together from her first battle of discrimination.

"No, amma, I just want to go home."

POOJA BECAME INCREASINGLY distant as she grew up. Her early years of school were marked with constant teasing and insults from the other children. They did not understand the food she brought for lunch, the language we spoke at home, or the reason we did not celebrate Christmas. Eventually, she turned on us as the cause for her pain and suffering. Even when she agreed with the bullies, they would not let her live in peace.

"Why do we have to be different?" she would scream.

"It is who we are, Pooja."

"I hate who we are."

"You hate how they treat us for being who we are."

"The effect is still the same."

Everything we did was different, and different was bad.

The constant teasing lowered Pooja's self-esteem. She told us the reasons she had few friends was because most of the people were "idiots," and those who weren't wanted to go out to parties, take weekend trips to the countryside, and go on dates with boys. Of course, I would not let her do these things. I did not trust American boys with my precious daughter.

The loneliness took its toll on her, and Pooja's grades suffered as a result. She barely placed in the top ten percent of her school. I constantly warned her that this would affect her future. She merely rolled her eyes.

"Stop being paranoid, *Mom*," she said.

The idea of competition did not mean much to her, but my life had been shaped by both the destructive and miraculous nature of its power. Though the life Shankar and I had built in West Virginia was better than anything I could have provided in Chennai, it still lacked the opportunity and the fairness I needed for my girls.

When Pooja was eighteen, she came home with her final report card of the fall term. Half As and half B+'s. I knew she was proud of what she had achieved. As a mother, I was scared. Shankar and I discussed the situation in private. By the end of the night, I knew what I had to do for my precious Pooja.

Chapter 30

"YOU HAVEN'T EXPLAINED why you are *ruining my life*," Pooja screamed at me.

I was upset at this statement coming from her mouth. I had felt confident she would understand.

"Pooja, we are—"

"Save it, Mom. There's no justification."

The shadow the lamp cast across our skin confirmed the dark feelings brewing inside my daughter. She stood up with such force she knocked over her heavy wood chair and caused a crash so loud I was sure the foundation of our lives had crumbled. I hesitated at the look of pure anger that washed over her face, which reminded of the rage that fueled so many of the evil forces in my life—Sahana, Govind, teacher. Pooja stormed out of the room without another word.

Shankar stopped me from running after her.

"Why doesn't she understand?"

"She will. Just give her time."

I waited a few minutes before going upstairs to try again. In between sobs, I could hear her talking on the phone and describing what had just happened.

"They want to destroy my life, Sally. My mom thinks I'm some stupid idiot who can't take care of herself. What did I do to deserve this?"

I was heartbroken to know I was the cause of such a deep pain my child felt. That was certainly not my objective in the matter, though it was something that was unavoidable. I could not risk gambling with my daughter's future, knowing how close my life choices almost ended the very existence of the people I sought to protect, and how close I came to destroying my own future. I could not let Pooja make the same mistakes I had made.

Pooja needed to start on a path with someone who could work with her to find the opportunities Shankar and I had failed to provide. Pooja needed to marry for a better life, just as I had done twenty years prior.

Part II

Pooja

Chapter 31

EVEN AT ITS worst points, never once during my childhood did I consider my life would devolve from an undying hopefulness to bitter hopelessness. As soon as mom uttered the word, "marriage," I saw my innocence leak with each staggered breath in an emotionally charged retreat to my room.

"It's not fair. My mom is trying to ruin my life. What am I going to do?" I screamed.

"Don't worry, Pooja. Me and Bobby got a plan. We'll get you out of this."

In that little town in the middle of nowhere, I could count every friend I had ever made on one hand. At the age of ten, it was our neighbor, Sam, who led me on his top secret missions in the West Virginia outback. That lasted until I found out his top secret missions consisted of burning ants to a crisp using a magnifying glass. We stopped talking soon after. Sam became quarterback of the football team last year, and now dated the homecoming queen—Peggy—who enjoyed cheerleading and telling me how ugly I was. Sam never stopped her.

When I was fifteen, it was dark-haired Nicole, who quickly became my friend after she realized I was the only one not making fun of her foreign food, foreign looks, or foreign family. Less than a year after moving here, her parents packed up the family and moved to Chicago to join the growing Greek community there. I asked her to write me a letter. It still hasn't arrived.

When I turned seventeen, I met Sally. Her mom was divorced, and Sally had to deal with a lot of whispering behind her back; Sally understood what it meant to be different in a place that hated different people. Her boyfriend Bobby was stupid.

"But he has a truck," Sally said.

She immediately offered to drive the hour with Bobby and me to the Greyhound Station. Though cumbersome, the roads from there led to a path to anywhere in the country, a path away from marriage.

The only trips outside of the area my parents permitted were straight to India, so I surveyed my closet as though looking at the contents for the first time. I had no idea what to pack. All I knew was that I hated hot weather. The gross pieces of garbage Mom bought for me at the local consignment store—sweaters with tassels, bell bottoms big enough to envelop me whole—most certainly did not make the cut.

Twenty minutes later, I dressed myself in a gray shirt with one low-hanging shoulder, a pair of tastefully cut jeans and a black blazer. Jennifer Beals wore something similar four years later in *Flashdance*. I always had a great sense of style. I belonged in New York, I decided.

After carefully hoisting my bag off the ground, I walked around the edge of my hardwood room floor, praying the creaking wouldn't wake up my insomniac of a father or blabbermouth sister. I wished I had time to write Dad a note, but wrestling over the right words wouldn't be a quick task. He shared my love of postcards, though. I knew he'd be excited to receive one from his own daughter.

I wouldn't have to pass by Mom and Dad's room if I took the kitchen staircase. The screen on the front door always slammed so quickly. Just a few more steps and . . . *Crash*!

"Aaah," I screamed.

"Shit."

"Dad?" I asked to the dark blob across the room.

"Pooja? What are you doing?"

He flipped on the light. When the scene came into focus, I saw a broken glass and a pool of milk on the floor just inches away from Dad's fuzzy whale slippers Mom had gotten as a deal with my tasseled sweater. Between the slippers and his milk moustache, Dad looked like a little kid. He stared at me fully dressed, complete with a big bag slung over my shoulder. I stuttered a few words trying to find an excuse. Dad put his hands up.

"Can we talk before you go?"

I bit my lip, mulling over the options. If Mom had been the one in the kitchen, we would have been knee-deep in an excessively loud argument by now. I decided to let Dad say his piece before heading off, knowing he'd give me more of a head start if I did. He had always been the peacekeeper of the family.

"Okay, only for a few minutes."

"Just leave the bags by the door."

"Here, put this over the milk," I said to him as I handed over a few paper towels.

He did the infamous Indian head nod in response. I assumed this nod meant, "thanks."

"Come, we'll go sit in the living room," he said.

There was no way Mom could listen in if we talked there. Good.

He motioned for me to sit down, using his patting gesture. It was the same kind of paw-thumping a dog did when you scratched behind its ears. I wanted a dog when I was a kid. Mom always said that "those beasts" would be too much of a distraction to my studies.

In the corner of my eye, I saw the headlights of Bobby's car as he and Sally pulled into the driveway. What they possessed in brawn they lacked in brains, leaving the headlights on full blast as though blaring yellow beams wouldn't attract attention at two on a Sunday night.

As usual, no sooner had Bobby put the truck into park did they start making out behind the glare. I had never even kissed a guy—my brown skin and aggressive mother made sure of that. But I knew greater things lay ahead in New York. Dad started talking in the midst of my thoughts . . .

"Look, beta," he said.

There was that old Indian word again, "beta," which my family used to mean "dear." I had to admit, it was better than the Southern convention of describing each other as food. "Honey, sugar, sweet pea, dumpling." When I was in first grade, I thought you could use any food to describe someone. I got into my first fight when I called a kid in my class "marshmallow." Dad had to come and pick me up that day.

"Do you want to run away?" he asked (again).

The short answer was yes. The real answer was let me live my own life and go to college. Then no. I might even come home for the holidays.

"Dad, I don't want to get married to some greasy Indian guy."

A small smile crept over Dad's face before his famous eye sparkle emerged in disarming force.

"Hey, be careful, I was a greasy Indian guy once."

I rolled my eyes. Every time I complained about Mom and Dad's head nods, Dad told me the American equivalent was an eye roll. At least our eye rolls weren't ambiguous.

"Your mother is one of the strongest people I have ever met. I could have never done half as well without her."

"I know, but I want to do so many things with my life."

He told me he understood, and so did Mom. I doubted the second part. Mom had treated me like a helpless, blind infant since I was born. My guess was she was tired of taking care of me and too arrogant to let me do anything for myself. One time-honored Indian tradition was the need to feel irreplaceable.

"We want you to have a successful career *and* do all of the wonderful things we know you are capable of doing."

"Thanks," I muttered back.

A compliment was rare in that house. Sally complimented me more on my new blazer than Mom had my entire life.

"The reason we want you get married is to *help* you be who you are, Pooja."

"Marriage ties you down, Dad."

"Pooja, we don't want to force you into anything. Do you think you can just give it a try . . . for me?"

Usually when he asked for a favor, he pouted. This time he looked dead serious. I turned to look away, trying to block his expressive face from my mind as I figured out the quickest way to end this conversation and climb into Bobby's truck.

"Dad, this is a really big deal."

"It is, which is why you must be okay with the decision."

"Does this really mean a lot to you?"

He nodded again, but this time in a very American, somber way. A clump of snow fell on top of the truck, startling Bobby and Sally out of their make out session. That time of year was so cold. New York was expensive. What if I couldn't afford an apartment with heating? What if the public schools there were worse than they were in West Virginia? I questioned if I even had what it took to survive out there all alone.

"And you really want me to have a successful career?"

"Of course."

"And so does Mom?"

"Especially your mother. She just doesn't know how to tell you. What do you say, beta? If it doesn't work out, I won't argue."

"What if I say no?"

Dad dropped his head. A few tears streamed down his face. The only time I had seen him cry was when his mother died. The disappointment on his face was enough to make me walk to the front without my things. I couldn't believe I was doing this.

I pulled open the doors. "Go home. It's okay," I called to Sally.

My hand felt like a dead weight as I waved to her. I reached out to close the wood door, but forgot to catch the screen. *Bam!* It went.

Within seconds, Mom rushed downstairs. In a half-English, half-Telugu panic, she screamed to call the police. "Burglar. Robbery. Get the jewelry! Where are the girls?"

Talk about priorities.

"Mom. It's fine, go back to bed."

After one look at Dad, she immediately calmed down. They exchanged head nods that seemed to communicate the entirety of the situation.

I returned to the kitchen to clean up the milk and retrieve my suitcase, half expecting it would ask for an explanation as to why we weren't going somewhere other than India.

All I could muster in response were four disappointing words.

"We were so close."

Chapter 32

AS EXPECTED, I graduated at nearly the top of my high school class with stellar recommendations from all of my teachers. Ever since grade school I had imagined the regalia of high school graduation and all of the praise for my hard work that would follow. Instead, the last few weeks consisted of listening to my classmates comparing notes about required classes, college boys, and how they would decorate their dorm rooms.

Sally summed up the situation best, in her own benign way. "But Pooja, you're so smart and stuff. You should go to college too."

I couldn't pretend there was a logical explanation for letting everyone who I knew was of an inferior intellect move forward in life while I resigned myself as a married woman. Every time I tried to muster enough courage to have a serious conversation about backing out, Dad would appear with his world-class smile, complimenting me on how well I had done and how proud he and Mom were.

For the many difficult moments they caused in my childhood, deep down, I still wanted to please my parents, especially Dad. He constantly assured me I would still get the chance to do everything I wanted. I believed him; I had to.

All I wanted as a graduation gift was a new bike. I imagined peddling around a gorgeous, expansive campus with my dark hair whipping around in the wind. The scene wasn't exactly out of *The Mod Squad*, but for once the thickness of my mane would work in my favor. Instead of a bike, mom bestowed a different "gift"—a trip to JFK airport in New York. Not New York City, mind you, just the airport.

Five previous times in my life, I had been dragged to JFK to go to India. To me, JFK was a place to jealously look onward at the lucky kids who got to go to one of those amazing destinations I learned about in school. Paris, Rio de Janeiro, the Pyramids in Egypt, or even California. I hadn't been to any of those.

While growing up, I stood in the security line to help Mom count our suitcases full of toilet paper and plastic bags and I would stare into the distance at the husbands happily pointing at the packet of information the Trip Advisors at the local AAA had put together on all of the exciting landmarks they'd see. The kids would excitedly gather around their parents.

"Let's go to the Eifel Tower first, or the Champs Elysées."

The moms couldn't wait to expose their children to all of the interesting foods and cultures.

"Think of all the French croissants, the Brazilian steaks, and the California oranges you'll get to eat, Johnny."

For us, going to JFK always meant the same thing. Drive two hours to the closest regional airport, fly to New York, spend a night in the cheapest motel close by, then come back to the airport and start the forty-eight-hour trip to either Bangalore or Chennai. Our suffering would have been a lot better if we actually *did* something while in India. In my five trips, I had never even seen the Taj Mahal. Neither had Mom.

We'd always spend a few days in Bangalore seeing Dad's family. They'd use the entire time to comment on how fat I had gotten, even the relatives that were big enough to blend in with the cows walking through the crowded streets. No trip to Bangalore was ever complete without Dad's family making snide comments about Mom. Bangalore always made us both miserable—it was one of the few things we agreed on.

The rest of the time was spent in Chennai. Mom's family was incredibly nice, but spending three-to-seven weeks in a slum and using a wooden box as a bathroom was not exactly an American teenager's version of an ideal summer. Overall, I hated our trips to India even more than I hated West Virginia.

"Pooja, your stupid wedding is ruining my summer. I wanted to go band camp," Alpa cried out at me.

"How do you think *I* feel? At least you don't have to get married to some gross Indian guy."

In the distance, I saw Dad shaking his head, as though the marriage prospects in India planted little microphones around the airport and were listening to my every word. Knowing India, there were forties spies packed on each bus, and the surveillance equipment was from the 1950s.

Trips to India were so tiring since Mom and Dad insisted on taking Indian Air. All of the other airline check-ins went smoothly because the passengers understood that wearing every piece of jewelry they own slows down getting through the metal detector. On other airlines, people waited their turn in line, refrained from spitting in the hallways, knew how to use the bathroom, knew how to eat with utensils, and to cover up the awful stench of their own body odor. On other airlines, the staff actually answered you instead of replying the same way to every question.

"Yes, madam." He gave an Indian head nod.

Indian Air was a gross slice of actual India. We *always* flew Indian Air. Never drink the orange juice.

I looked down at the elegant flower watch I had Sally buy for me on her last trip back to visit her father in Nashville. Having such a stylish accessory on my person had made every painstaking minute of babysitting the previous year worthwhile. Still, even the shiny black face couldn't quell my headache; we still had another five hours to London. Then we'd have a twelve-hour layover, and another nine-hour flight, four hours in the Bombay airport, where we'd have to go through immigration, get our luggage, ride an overstuffed bus across the city to the regional airport, and finally fly to the tiny Bangalore airport.

Every exhausting landing in the Chennai or Bangalore regional airport was met with Mom and Dad forcing us to change into Indian clothes so our family could start their two-hundred-point inspection. Just thinking about the next two days made my head spin. I closed my eyes and painfully slid back into the plastic seat that stuck to my skin.

"So are you nervous?" Alpa asked.

"Why? You don't care."

"You're my sister. You should get a nice guy. I'll help you find him, okay?"

I laughed at the thought of skinny Alpa sitting on a throne with reading glasses, a clipboard, and giant pencil in hand, interviewing a long line of Indian guys to make sure the important questions were asked.

"What are your thoughts on The Brady Bunch*? Marsha or Jan?"*

We landed in Bangalore nearly thirty-four hours after taking off in New York. Our blurred vision gave the entire airport that same surreal look of when a negative is overexposed to light—everything is fuzzy and outlined in red lines. Even in the wee hours of the night, the area around the airport was always abuzz. Thousands and thousands of people would pack as close as possible fighting for space to greet family, friends, and random rich Indian-Americans who had just landed.

Mom loved this part of the trip. She'd wave to the crowd as though they were the audience and she was Miss Universe.

"Thank you, thank you. You are all too kind. I dedicate this to world peace."

Within seconds of walking outside, five young men jumped over the gate and offered to carry our bags. I had never paid attention to them before. This time, I looked at them with a strange mix of anxiety and curiosity. I knew Mom would only allow really well-educated people to be considered, but all Indians looked the same to me. What if the guy trying to make extra cash carrying my luggage would be my future husband?

Chapter 33

MOM MADE FINDING marriage prospects like the hiring process at a competitive company. The quantity of candidates wasn't met with comparable quality. After placing an ad in the local newspaper, nearly five hundred guys responded within a week. I would have loved to see the look on racist Melissa Barker's face.

"You can't run for homecoming queen, Pooja. Brown people aren't meant to be beautiful," she once said.

Mom placed the ad in English and immediately discarded all of the replies that were written in anything else. From those, she tossed out all of the "applicants" who didn't have at least a Masters or professional degree in business, technology, medicine, or law. Of the 124 left, she had me go through and pick out the top fifty. From the stupid responses, my judging criteria weren't very selective.

1. Did he spell the "United States of America" correctly?
2. Is he older than seventeen and younger than forty?
3. Did he avoid calling himself "the most greatest" man?

After vetting the top fifty, we realized only twenty could actually speak English. They each came over for an interview.

Number 13 was talking. His number was worthy of its unluckiness. Even if I overlooked the *Saturday Night Fever* suit, the crumbs in his Burt Reynolds-esque moustache danced like lice as he moved his arrogant mouth up and down to praise himself. He hadn't said a nice thing about anyone else since he had arrived. Who walked in through the door demanding to know how much the dowry will be, because, "The house looks quite run-down."

Within two minutes I knew I couldn't listen to Number 13 any longer. Certainly this meant I couldn't marry him. Deciding I deserved a break, I looked at the other side of the room and saw Alpa stick her finger in her throat. Those were my sentiments exactly. Before I made it halfway across the room, bad-body-odor-Number 13 decided to leave. Mom made me stay inside for the next Prince Charming.

Number 14 was way worse than 13. After mistakenly going to the neighbors' house, he terrorized an old woman in the midst of her afternoon nap. Realizing there was no food, he then squeezed his three-hundred-and-fifty-pound self through the door of Dad's family's place, where we were staying. He looked like a rogue Mr. Potato Head.

Before I could ask how on earth he had made the final cut, Mom rushed in between the two of us and demanded he leave. He finally understood what she said when she made a weird motion as though to hit him in the head with a bat.

"Mom, this isn't working. That guy looked like he wanted to eat me."

"You're right."

I soaked in her rare act of a concession. We had been at the application process for nearly two weeks, and the only thing to show for our efforts were pounding headaches.

Alpa and I managed to let our foul moods melt away by sitting in the garden. Bangalore was so peaceful—it was known as the Garden City for good reason. The street Dad's family lived on was quiet and centrally located. Trees lined both sides, kids had a ton of park space to play in, and people in the neighborhood even had small yards.

"Hey," someone next door shouted.

A guy peered at us through a few trees. He was speaking in Telugu. At one point, Alpa and I had spoken the language at home, but Mom and Dad never knew when to stop in public. The staring and pointing from the locals of West Virginia eventually got to us, so we tuned out everything except English.

Alpa and I stood up and gave the guy a blank look. He shook his head at us. We shook our heads back.

"Sorry, I thought you were from here, you're wearing Indian clothes," he said. "Do you know if the owners of the house are home? I borrowed this book from them and I want to make sure they get it back."

Alpa and I were taken by surprise. Any of the applicants we had seen so far would have phrased the same point completely differently.

"Hey. Vhy dooon't you speak Telugu? Vhy pretend be Indian? Give this book to uncle. Bring me tea. I most greatest man."

We both perked up at the thought of an ally who could actually communicate without insulting us. I joked to myself that if this guy had a car, I'd marry him.

"The owners are my Dad's parents. I can give it back to them," I offered.

"Great, thanks," he said back, giving me a big smile.

His perfect white teeth and intense eyes matched those of Dad. I glanced down at the thick book he handed me. The cover said *US Medical Residency Directory*. My usual shyness around strangers decided to make an exit.

"Are you a doctor in the States?" I asked.

"Not yet. I just got accepted to a program in Brooklyn. I leave next month."

"Congratulations."

"Thanks, I'm really excited. Are you two visiting?"

"Yeah, to find me a husband."

My heart pounded at my unnecessarily candid answer. Surely he thought I was crazy. I didn't feel otherwise, describing my ridiculous situation out loud. What kind of American girl lets herself have an arranged marriage? He echoed my thoughts precisely.

"Ah, I see. I thought Americans have love marriages though?"

Love marriage, what a funny term. In America, marriage implied love. In India, there was only one synonym for love—gold.

"My parents are special . . . but at the rate we're going, I'll be going home single."

"Give it time, it'll work out. Thanks for returning the book."

I smiled, suddenly aware I hadn't been to the dentist in two years.

"I'm Anand, by the way."

"Pooja. Nice to meet you."

The bright sun of the Bangalore afternoon cast a long, deep shadow on his retreating figure. I silently praised India for demonstrating the caliber of man we had been searching for.

Chapter 34

THE FINAL SIX suitors showed no sign of promise. Mom was dying to get down to Chennai to see her family.

"Shall we continue the search down there?" Dad asked.

"Absolutely not, it is out of the question," Mom shouted back.

Her intense negative reaction was odd, considering how prideful she was of her culture. She merely played it off by claiming that continuing the search without a break was too exhausting. I didn't argue. Finding a life partner was becoming less annoying and more terrifying by the minute.

After the sweltering two-and-a-half-hour train ride, we found an autorickshaw and let Mom direct the driver into the thicket of the Chennai slums. Avva, Mom's mom, greeted us with her usual smiles and cheek pinching before telling Alpa and I we had grown so tall and pretty. It was hard to imagine how a woman so animated could produce a person as stoic as Mom.

Chennai brought out a relaxed and happy side of Mom that we rarely saw. In Chennai, she was always doing something fun—shopping, going to temples, playing games with her sister, or catching up at the neighbors' houses. It was a nice departure from her "work now, work more later" attitude in West Virginia.

Soon after Mom and Dad started making decent money, Mom remitted a small portion every month back to Avva. The money went to good use—building a new house. Though a welcomed move, the new house still qualified as the slums by my standards. I never got used to the lizards and spiders that shared the space.

For a few weeks every other year, Dad, Alpa, and I would be left to fend for ourselves while Mom went off into the streets of Chennai. As the anxiety of finding a husband continued to build, I encouraged Mom to take all the time she needed. By the look of her reaction to Dad's suggestion, no Chennai man would ever be my husband. I prayed I could convince Mom to spend the rest of trip in her childhood city, and I could return back to the States uncommitted to anything except myself.

Like the calculated machine she was, Mom put an abrupt stop to her pleasure at the end of July, precisely as planned. We soon found our way back on a train through the sweltering heat straight to the Garden City. Avva was famous for her dramatic goodbyes. This time, she calmly hugged me and smiled, as though she knew she would be seeing me soon. I loathed the sensation.

BACK IN BANGALORE, we interviewed another hoard of guys. All of them made a concerted effort to point out their precious gender roles had been swapped.

"It is usually the man who decides who to marry, not the woman," number 22 said.

"I passed the US citizenship test on my own. *I* should demand a dowry," I snapped.

"Pooja," Mom spat at me.

There were no arguments on her side when I decided to sit out the interviews of numbers 23 through 27. I returned in time to see Number 28 enter the room. He was tall, light-skinned, and handsome. Mom started out the meeting as usual.

"What are your qualifications?"

He was an electrical engineer, loved the actor, Amitabh Bachchan, and wanted to have three boys. To sum up: unequivocally boring. Mom was smitten, though, due to his graduating first rank from both pre-university college and engineering school. The conversation quickly started repeating itself like a broken record.

"I graduated first rank from engineering university."

"I graduated first rank from accounting university."

I was half tempted to demonstrate the country line dancing I had learned the previous year in school. That would have certainly made Mom happy.

"Look at my daughter. First rank in cowgirl school."

Alpa was sitting outside in our usual spot, making up one of her new card games. She swore she was going to get rich by inventing the new Gin Rummy. What aspirations my little sister had.

"What's he like?"

"Mom loves him because he graduated at the top of his class."

Before she had the chance to respond, we heard someone laugh.

"Who's there?" we asked at the same time.

"It's me. Sorry, I couldn't help but overhear you," the voice said.

I stood up and peered over a clothesline full of laundry that separated the two properties. Anand was sitting outside, reading a textbook.

"Why did you laugh?"

"That chump. My father and his father used to do business together."

"Yeah, so?"

"He went to one of those private colleges."

Anand looked at me, waiting for a reaction with the same force as the tone of his voice, the same look as when Christian missionaries informed me that I was going to hell for not believing in Jesus. Their obvious point was met with my indifferent reaction.

"That guy is an idiot."

"No way, our Mom got first rank. She worked non-stop for her grades."

"Your mom and I both went to a government university, which are based on merit . . . mostly. Many of the private schools are worthless. They appeared after your parents left India."

That time I gave Anand an incredulous look. I landed on a very valuable playing card out of this marriage mess. Gin rummy.

Chapter 35

"BUT MOM. I don't like that guy."

"Pooja. He is coming from a good family only."

Mom using Indian sentence structures meant she was dead serious.

"Did he ask a single question about me?"

"That will come later, Pooja. He will get to know you once you are married."

I wasn't surprised to hear Mom's decision to go with Number 28. In her mind, "first rank" trumped all other characteristics short of criminal. Even so, I saved my powerful information for one more round of argument.

"I don't want to marry that guy."

Mom threw her hands in the air in her typical "why doesn't she listen?" way and looked over at Dad. "Talk some sense into your daughter."

Dad closed his eyes and scratched his head. Alpa and I joked he was trying to shake the right words loose from his brain.

"Pooja. Raj . . . number 28, is coming from a good family. He graduated first rank . . ."

"Enough with the first rank. He bribed his way to the top."

"What? Who told you that?" Mom asked.

"Anand, the neighbor's son. He told me India now allows non-merit private schools. Anand said Raj is an idiot."

"You have been talking to our next door neighbor?" Dad asked.

I thought about lying. It was a valuable piece of information though. Anand was the most normal Indian guy I had ever met. In a dream world, I thought he might even be able to talk Mom and Dad out of the preposterous idea I should get married by the age of nineteen.

"Yeah, he's really nice. He's moving to the States in a few weeks."

Their faces fell. Dad mumbled something to Mom in Telugu. They finished their conversation in a series of Indian head nods and words I couldn't understand. Before I could interject, they walked out of the front door and left me in a total pile of confusion.

WITHOUT MOM AND Dad to act as our normal buffers against our criticizing relatives, Alpa and I decided to eat dinner that night in our room. Apart from India, where else would cookies and a bag of chips be acceptable as a meal? A few hours after drifting off in a diabetic semicoma, I awoke to loud whispering coming from the first floor. I grabbed my sandals and wandered down the dusty red staircase out of half curiosity and half fear.

Mom and Dad were sitting in the living room with Anand. He didn't look physically harmed, thank God. Dad opened his mouth as though he wanted to say something. He wasn't used to taking the lead when Mom was around.

"Pooja, could you go out with Anand? Maybe sit in the park or get an ice cream?"

"Why . . . What's going on, Dad?"

On their behalf, Anand cut in and said he'd explain. We agreed to take his car to Cubbon Hill. I had been stuck in the house all night and desperately needed some fresh air, anyway.

I couldn't have asked for a more gorgeous night. The humidity and heat had disappeared. The kind of car Anand drove would have prompted me to demand a state inspection in America. In India, all I wanted to do was take advantage of the precious privacy of the moment.

We drove for twenty minutes through the main streets before veering off the side dirt path that led up to the Hill. At the top, we found a peaceful vantage point overlooking the entire city. Not many people in Bangalore had electricity. Tiny specs of light dotted our view.

Neither of us knew what to say. I didn't mind not talking. Anand seemed uncomfortable. Sometimes silence is a good thing in the States. Silence in India is an invitation for someone to start yelling. The agony of the quiet got to him.

"How many times have you been to Bangalore?" he wanted to know.

"Five. We usually spend most of our time in Chennai. Have you lived here your entire life?"

Anand leaned back in his seat, clearly more relaxed without the vacant sound space. "Yes, I've lived in the same house my entire life."

"Me too."

"Really?"

"Well, I don't remember anything except West Virginia."

"What's it like? The States?"

"It's hard to describe. It's really diverse, you know?"

"Just like India?"

"Even more so."

Seeing as I had grown up with two types of people—uneducated white coal miners and uneducated black coal miners—referring to the United States as diverse was an ironic thing for me to say. I knew the vast possibilities America could offer.

"What's it like where you grew up?" he asked.

"It sucks."

I blurted out the word before I could stop myself. There was one strict order for every trip to India: "No cursing." Having thoughts or opinions about my own life was also unofficially banned.

"Sucks?"

"It's terrible. The people are really closed-minded. They secretly hate anyone who is different. What are the people like here?"

Anand turned to stare into the distance. He was one of the few Indians I had met that measured his thoughts before deciding what to say. I liked that.

"The people here are also closed-minded, and they also hate people who are different. But they don't keep it a secret, they tell you straight to your face."

We both laughed. It was so true.

"Are you excited about moving to Brooklyn?"

"That's actually why your parents asked me to take you out."

"Oh no, what did they do?"

"Don't worry, it wasn't bad. They wanted to know . . . well . . . if I'd be interested in marrying you."

If I had been in a TV show, that would have been the shot where I spat out my drink. I never had a soda when I needed one.

"What did you say to them?"

"I told them we needed to talk first. It's not a decision I can make alone."

His was the perfect answer. Despite the fact that the most promising Indian man I'd ever met was entertaining the thought of filling the role of my arranged husband, I still wanted to leave India single. My valuable information card had completely backfired.

"What about New York?"

As desperate as Mom was to see me married, I knew hell would freeze over before she'd consent to me moving to Brooklyn. There wouldn't even be enough time to have a ceremony before Anand was due to start working. An elaborate wedding was non-negotiable to Mom.

"It's a great opportunity that I'd have to give up, but I can start another program later. It'll be easier being married to a citizen."

I hadn't considered Anand could find another job after getting married.

"Look, Pooja, I think we'd get along well. If it doesn't work . . . divorce is more common in America. I'd have a job. We'd both continue on with our lives."

My thoughts narrowed in on the last words of his explanation. At eighteen, I didn't feel like I had started a life to be continued. What if Mom forced me to marry number 28, or number 14, or any of those other jerks?

What if I refused to marry anyone and disappointed Dad to the extent of losing the one relationship in my life that gave me strength?

I felt my every ounce of energy seep into making a decision. I barely had enough left to give Anand his answer.

"Okay. Let's get married."

Not once did it occur to me to ask why he agreed.

Chapter 36

WE WENT OUT several times after that crisp first night to get to know each other better. Anand was an amazingly articulate person, and more importantly, a great listener. He was never patronizing, always interesting, and possessed the same worldly spirit as me, despite only having left India for a week to take an exam in Hong Kong. His relatively privileged childhood was something he did not take for granted, and the fact that women were treated as second-class citizens was a huge motivation for leaving the only country he had called home.

On our third "date," we went for a walk and a coffee in Gandhi Bazaar, one of the oldest neighborhoods of the city. As we rounded a street corner at the footsteps of a massive temple, I felt a tug at my shoulder and realized my purse had just been stolen.

"Hey you, stop," Anand shouted.

Anand chased after the thief with the speed of a tiger. For three years, I had been in love with our high school track star, Ken Johnson, and had found recurring excuses to stay after school to catch glimpses of his gazelle-like body running as though there were no tomorrow. Anand's gallops through the flickers of light that dotted the dark night had that same butterfly-like effect. He took mere seconds to chase down my belongings.

Between his general hygiene, good looks, first rank in medical school, and wealth, Anand had been one of most eligible bachelors in Bangalore. As he gave me my purse and grabbed my hand out of concern, I couldn't help but relish the herd of girls in the background swooning with jealousy at the sight of us. I had my first kiss that night. It was as memorable as I had hoped it would be.

Dad was truly elated with Anand being a part of the family. There was an ease in his body and voice that none of us had ever seen before.

"He's from my city. I'm so happy he'll be my son-in-law," Dad exclaimed.

Mom and Dad spoke the same language, but they were from different parts of the country. Living in an American town of twenty-five thousand for all of those years had clearly had an effect on my parents. The idea of a local Bangalore boy being a quick phone call away was music to Dad's ears.

A woman of very few words but predictable sentiment, I knew Mom was happy with Anand as well. I took her approval as an added bonus to the situation. Nevertheless, it was bittersweet seeing her sing words of praise for a man she barely knew when she rarely complimented her own daughter.

I had come to India that summer of 1979 in the hopes the country would fail to produce any man good enough to be my life partner. Anand easily disproved that suspicion. Though agreeing to marry him was the least of the evils, I genuinely felt that a man like Anand meant Dad was right—it would be within my power to reach my life goals. It would not be a love marriage, at least not in its true sense. Love, however, would come later down the path, down the path of marriage.

Chapter 37

SINCE ALPA HAD school, the marriage ceremony couldn't take place until the winter holidays. In typical fashion, Mom found a way to besmirch the contentment I had found by turning a lovely fall season into Basic Training: Indian Bride edition. She spent the four months until Christmas spouting unsolicited lessons of how to cook south Indian food, how to wrap a sari, how to celebrate Hindu holidays, and the "art" of entertaining Indian guests.

She didn't understand her aggression only made me question everything all over again. Marrying Anand would unfortunately rule out meeting boys at parties, but surely all other aspects of college life would be there. The fascinating classes, long discussions in coffee shops, lounging around on campus . . . Every time Mom spoke about my "duties as an Indian wife," those simple scenes mutated into a list of lofty fantasies.

"NOT LIKE THAT. You'll ruin the chapatti."

"Stop reaching over me."

I had to step back to swat Mom's arms away. She was going to make me burn myself, I swore. Her boot camp sessions had gotten worse; this last one involved me waking up at six in the morning to prepare a mountain of food on an ordinary Tuesday. Who eats all of this food so early in the morning? Who takes three hours to cook? I announced I was taking a break.

"Where are you going?"

"To rob a bank and get some ice cream."

"Pooja, wait. You must learn how to properly roll chapatti."

Not bothering to reply before walking out the door, I let the screen slam shut. One silver lining to the situation was being able to talk back to Mom since she got what she wanted. Her typical threat of, "Do this or I will send you to India," didn't make sense anymore, not with an Indian man who agreed to marry me on the condition he moves to America.

I walked out the door and headed for the small corner store at the end of the neighborhood. Even though it was really close to our house, I was twelve the first time I went. Mom refused to enter, always muttering about how its white-and-yellow exterior reminded her of a store she knew back in Youngstown. Since she told me, I had been going there whenever I needed to get away from her. The store got a lot of my business over the years.

The streets were quieter than usual. Everyone was at work or school. I was sure the rest of the town assumed the same was true for me. I still hadn't decided if I liked the near anonymity of my situation.

My teachers all tried their best to convince me to go straight to college; they couldn't grasp the cultural implications that it was not my choice. Imagine going to college with no money, no help, and against the wishes of your family? There was no way my classmates would understand, so I told few people outside of Sally.

I was lonely not having anyone to talk to. Sally and I tried speaking a few times. The wonders of West Virginia University quickly made that too much of a commitment for her to continue.

Inside the convenience store, I decided on a peanut drumstick ice cream. Normally flashing the item in my hand and tossing a quarter on the checkout counter was one fluid motion. This time, a shout knocked me out of rhythm.

"Pooja. What are you doing here? Don't you have classes?"

I realized a few seconds later it was Bobby who had called out to me. Sally had dumped him her first week away when she found out he had failed summer school.

"Hi, Bobby. How are you?" I asked.

"Everything's fucked up. I can't believe Sally's gone. I was going to marry her."

"Yeah, I miss her too."

"Why are you here, Pooja?"

He hit every nerve in three lines. I did my best to calmly respond.

"I had a change of plans, Bobby. I'm—"

"Oh yeah. *You're* getting married. Now *that* is fucked up. Didn't you get into Duke?"

I couldn't believe he remembered. Mom and Dad had never given me permission to apply, so I only told a handful of people I got in. The acceptance letter was the very definition of bittersweet.

"Why are your parents so dumb? It makes me laugh," he continued.

"Shut up, it's not funny, Bobby."

"I bet you'd be good at doing wife shit. Are you good at folding laundry?"

My head burst at that moment. I could see tiny specs of red straight ahead, as though the store were on fire, burning into ash. Bobby, one of the dumbest people I had ever met, was making fun of *me*. The worst part was I had nothing to say back.

How could I defend what Mom and Dad were doing? How could I

explain I had picked the best choice? Or did I pick the best choice? Maybe I should have gone to Duke against their will, taken out loans, moved myself to the campus, and prepared myself to never talk to my family again? Maybe this was a result of me being weak and scared?

Somewhere in my fit of thoughts I caught another glimpse of Bobby doubled over in laughter. It tapped a rage in me I didn't know I had. Before I knew what was happening, I shouted with the force of a lifetime of frustration, "Shut the fuck up! You're a worthless piece of white trash!"

The other five customers in the store immediately scattered, sending the manager out in a fury. Bobby was fired and I was officially banned from the store. I couldn't have cared less. I didn't leave the house much after that day.

Chapter 38

MOM WAS PERFECTLY satisfied to plan the entirety of the wedding on her own, which gave me solace from her basic training. With nothing else to fill my days, I took to hiding in the local library as I had done so many times during high school. One of the librarians noticed the constant sullen expression on my face and became a great ally in providing me with quality reading material. Though I never asked, she always hand delivered any new brochures on college campuses. I didn't bother to pay them attention as I had before.

Time became a blur until Christmas. The days were so indistinguishable that it was Alpa who had to remind me to pack for my wedding.

"Pooja. We're leaving in three days, dummy. Listen to Mom, go get your suitcase."

My lack of purpose in the previous few months gave me a numbing effect. I was the bride, yet I seemed to be the last thing on everyone's mind. Mom was vicariously living her dream wedding by executing everything for me. Dad was preoccupied with welcoming Anand to the family, and Alpa did nothing but remind me how my wedding had ruined her summer and now her Christmas.

Anand came to greet us when we landed. Dad ran up to him to shake his hand, and Anand bent down to touch Mom's feet as a sign of respect. As he stood up, he caught my eye. His sparkle that had charmed me a few months ago now made me feel uneasy.

"Hi, Pooja, how was the journey?" he asked.

"Your suit is really ugly," I replied, referring to the polyester ensemble he had on.

Mom looked like she was about to kill me. He simply smiled back and assured me this was the best 1970s India could produce.

"You have great style, Pooja. You need to take me shopping in the States."

I was taken aback. No one in my family had ever made that observation. "Yes, of course. Sorry."

"No problem. How are you?"

I had no response. He was the first person in months to ask me how I was doing.

THE NIGHT BEFORE the wedding was like watching a state fair being coordinated on a stage meant for a ballet. Thousands of strangers poured into the house. Most of the women came to find the answer to one key question.

"Who is the woman that finally landed Anand?"

Mom and Avva covered me from head to toe in impossibly ornate saris, jewelry, and makeup. Some of the strangers nodded approvingly; others flapped their mouths in bewilderment that their daughters weren't judged as lucrative.

One concession everyone must make is that Indian weddings are truly beautiful, and mine was no exception. A giant tent was pitched and lined on two sides with black onyx statues of Hindu deities. Workers painstakingly hung garlands of exotic-looking flowers through the entire roof of the tent. In the center of the seating area, a small fountain served as a monochromatic break in the sea of colors the thousand-plus guests at my wedding showcased.

I managed to smile for the pictures, act happy to see distant relatives I had never met, and pretend that pleasing my new husband had already become the number one priority in my life. The truth was that I was numb throughout the entire three-day ceremony. My feelings of emptiness were occasionally interrupted by my feelings of sadness at the sight of Mom's unequivocal happiness. She had met none of my accomplishments in life with pure joy—there was always room for improvement, always something more I could have done, always an extra effort she felt I should have made. My wedding was the first time there was nothing that could make the way she perceived the situation better. In her eyes, Anand was the first perfect thing about my life. He was the first perfect thing about me.

"POOJA?" SOMEONE CALLED out.

I already recognized the sound of his voice. I chose not to turn around. Anand waited a few seconds before timidly taking a seat by my side.

"You look beautiful," he complimented.

"Thanks," I muttered.

He made a few more attempts at starting a conversation, all of which I shut down with one word responses.

"You've been very quiet since you got back," he concluded.

"This is me, I'm a quiet person."

"That's not true. We talked so much last summer."

"Now it's different. Now I'm quiet."

"I don't understand. What happened?"

Approximately thirty-seven minutes before Anand sat next to me, I officially became a married woman and was expected to build a life with this man. But I felt like I had no life to build off of.

"I feel the same way," he offered.

"You do?"

"Absolutely."

"So what do we do now?"

"I suppose we have to figure it out together."

I had never thought of it like that. Anand confessed his life had been prescriptive. His best scores were in science, so his family told him to be a doctor. Everything else, including this wedding, had gone precisely as his parents had planned. Anand just happened to be good at what Indian society told him to do.

"But it hasn't made me happy. I need something different."

His uncertainty put me more at ease. While my parents and wedding guests assumed that Anand and I locked the door to the bedroom that night to consummate as a married couple, we spent the hours devising a plan for the future.

I took comfort in knowing we had both figured out how to be firsts in our lives. I was the first one to grow up in the States; Anand was the first in his family to get an education. Anand wholeheartedly supported me in making my own decisions, so I would be the first woman in our family to have a job outside of the family business. He would be the first in his family to live in a foreign country.

We knew they were accomplishments many others had made before, and some of them were accomplishments we had yet to actually make, but they were ours. We had to start somewhere to build something out of nothing.

Chapter 39

ANAND HAD TO wait three extra weeks to get his initial visa to come to the States. I used that time to repeatedly return to the library to execute my part of our plan. I found my trusty librarian crouched in the depths of the catalog cards and her vast collection of college materials.

Anand had already sacrificed residency in New York. I had already sacrificed Duke. We now had to figure out a place that would satisfy both of our needs. By the time he landed on January 4, 1980, I had a list of schools across the country that I wanted to attend and had the credentials for admission. His first point of order after stepping off the plane was to help me talk to Mom and Dad.

"Pooja, my wife, has the right to apply to all of the schools," he said.

"I have the right to apply to all of the schools," I repeated.

This time no one argued.

Our first weeks as a married couple were less than exciting. There was no honeymoon, no celebratory parties, or mingling with other couples. Anand spent most of his time by the phone or at the local hospital trying to set up as many appointments as possible to interview for the next round of residency openings.

I didn't mind. While he tracked down leads, I worked diligently to compose perfect college entrance essays. Duke had admitted me based on a paper about the generational journey it took for me to be able to approach a serious academic institution as a young Indian woman. Somehow that journey seemed disingenuous after conceding to marry. Talking about building my life with a near stranger eight years my senior would never transcend cultural boundaries.

February 1980 ushered in two months of Anand's residency travels. He had managed to schedule twelve interviews in nine cities, most of which were within easy commuting distance of the schools I had chosen. Two of the interviews were in cities that had no decent school options for me. He had been approached by the hospitals, and was questioning whether to even make the trips.

On the last day of the month, I mailed out my applications for entrance into the following semester. Instead of returning home, I made my sixth trip in three weeks to the Roanoke regional airport to pick up my . . . husband. The first few returns, he described everything—the buildings, the cars, the people, the hospitals. Novelty wears off quickly, and I figured his increasing quietness with each trip was a sign he was growing accustomed to his new environment. This time, the silence was laden with pessimism.

"What did you think?" I prompted him.

"There were many tall buildings."

"That's Atlanta."

"It wasn't my favorite."

"There is also a lot of history to the region. And good schools."

Including a school that would receive my application in a few days. He knew I had posted my work, and I expected he'd ask about my admissions essay topic. Instead, he retreated back to his silence. For the first time since we had met, I got a sense he wasn't sure of himself. That made me nervous.

"Are you okay?" It was my turn to ask.

"Pooja . . ." he said softly.

He asked me to pull to the side of the road so we could talk for a few minutes. By the tone of his voice, I knew our plan was just a plan. Our plan would not be reality.

Chapter 40

EVERY INTERVIEW ANAND went to started out the same way. They'd be impressed with his perfect American accent, charm, and good looks, swearing that a new era had begun and doctors from overseas were welcome with open arms.

"Our Swiss, Japanese, and Argentinean colleagues have contributed a lot to the local medical community," they all assured.

My childhood had taught me that India was still an unknown, even in bigger American cities. Despite all the passion and knowledge he possessed, once the interviewers understood how poor India still was, they dismissed Anand and his education. The names of the cities where he did his field work were too long, the techniques he had memorized were too antiquated, and his professor's credentials were deemed unworthy.

Like a dog whittled in shame, Anand told me with his tail between his legs that all of the interviews so far had ended in an unequivocal rejection. The good ole' Southern boys of Atlanta had practically laughed him out of the room when he told them the name of his medical school: Medical College of Basavanagudi.

"What are our options?" I asked.

"I could wait a year and apply again."

"I don't want to get stuck here for another eighteen months."

"Or I could go to these last two interviews even though they're in cities that weren't part of our plan."

Detroit and Orlando. Those were the choices—different manifestations of hell. Detroit was a city riddled with crime and drug use; they were willing to hire anyone who resembled a doctor. Anand would get a residency position because they were desperate; the city had little amenities or safety to offer.

Nearly a decade before, Orlando had solidified its status as a theme park destination, effectively doubling the city's population overnight. An announcement had been recently made about a second theme park to be opened within the next few years, and everyone—hospitals included—were anticipating a major spike in demand for just about everything. It was a boon for last minute applicants like Anand.

The gravity of the situation hit me like a boulder, forcing me out of the car in a stammering heap of hysteria. Anand gave me a few minutes to let out my tears before walking over to apologize what must have been a hundred times.

Words like, "I'm so sorry" had long lost their meaning and did little more than to enrage me. Everyone was so sorry for me all of the time. No one did anything to make it better or to get out of my way and let me make it better for myself.

"How the *fuck* did you get into a residency program in Brooklyn last year?"

He took a deep sigh, trying his best to stay calm. "I asked the same question after my interview last week. How could I get into New York and not Boston?"

A native New Yorker who was sitting in the room took one look at the address of the hospital that initially extended Anand the offer, and snickered. "Son, that hospital is in Crown Heights."

Anand found out later that the neighborhood of Crown Heights was infamous for gang-related violence, hardcore drug addicts, extreme poverty, and murders. It would have been infinitely worse than anything Detroit had to offer.

Guilt washed over me because I had no way to hide my total disgust for Anand not being able to secure a position in any of the cities we had agreed on, where I had school options. Anger took over as I once again replayed the list of empty promises Mom and Dad had made in forcing me to get married. Shame for America wove its way through my body for not producing people who were able to see how brilliant and deserving Anand was. The three combined to form a thick layer of immobility. Much like I had made the decision to marry Anand, I would again be forced to pick the least of all evils.

A tiny whisper of defeat escaped Anand's lips, and I saw he too was crying. The last time he grabbed my hand, he was the hero. This time, he was the victim.

"Pooja, I'm so sorry. If you move with me to Detroit or Orlando, I promise you the next place we go will be for your career."

I brushed away his tears and fought back another round of mine. "It's okay, Anand. We'll make it work somehow."

Anand received his official offer from Memorial Hospital in downtown Orlando a month later. In April 1980, we packed our moving van and left West Virginia. I got into all ten schools I applied to.

Chapter 41

WITH EVERY MILE we drove south, I felt myself sinking further into depression. At a pit stop somewhere in the middle of Georgia, a woman called me out in front of thirty people while I was waiting in line for the bathroom.

"My lord," she said, pointing at my ring. "Aren't you way too young to be married?"

Before he started work in the summer, Anand tried his best to cheer me up. We'd take day trips to the closest beach, he'd coax me to go to Disney World, and even offered to go dancing at a flamenco bar a few blocks away. Most importantly, he shielded me from Mom.

She was infamous for starting every conversation with the same sentence. "Pooja, I have had a very difficult life . . ." With the same conclusion. "You must not be lazy."

As though my life situation had resulted from my lack of will to make things happen. I quickly became adverse to telling her anything about Orlando. Anand, still feeling guilty for not following through on his end of the bargain, made an excellent filter in those first few months.

"Pooja is very busy; she cannot talk right now," he'd lie.

Once Anand had to start work, I had to deal with the phone. I approached it with many trepidations, until I finally figured out Mom would let it ring precisely four times and then hang up, deciding it wasn't worth the effort to wait any longer. On its sixth or seventh ring, I'd pick up and promptly tell Dad or Alpa I had to go or the caller had the wrong number. My system worked for a while. We never got any other calls.

One week in July, I heard the phone ring. My heart would usually pound with brute force until the ringing made it over the fourth hump. Ring number seven was approaching. I picked up the receiver, mentally rehearsing my routine.

"Hello, you've got the wrong num—"

"Hello? Hello? *Hello*?" a thick Indian voice shouted. I heard Anand's mother. His dad usually directly called the hospital for her.

"*Yekka da* Anand?" she demanded.

I took a deep sigh. I hadn't heard Telugu in months. I was starting to have a visceral reaction to the sound.

"He's not here. Can I take a message?"

"*Yekka da* Anand?"

"He's not here. No. Not here."

"Anand *letha*?"

"No."

I heard some shuffling on the other side.

"Hello? Anand not there?" his father asked.

"No, can I take a message?"

"You don't speak Telugu? Vhhhy don't you speak Telugu?"

On hearing that primeval question, I slammed down the receiver with such force that the apartment rumbled with pity.

After that day, I decided the best solution to the phone was not to be there when it rang. Since Anand was still making peanuts as his salary, going to Disney World and flamenco bars quickly became too expensive. The entertainment of Orlando was tacky, anyway.

Soon, I exhausted the very limited public library resources of central Florida. The region was known for its rollercoasters; people didn't go there to study. Instead, I began visiting Anand in the hospital for lunch. With the commute on the bus, the round trip took an upwards of four hours, the only four hours a day I did anything.

"Would you like pudding?" he asked one Thursday.

"That's apple sauce."

"How about French fries?"

"You mean onion rings?"

"Pooja."

He was getting frustrated. We had an unsaid agreement that given the situation he had no right to ask me to cook, maintain the house a certain way, or fulfill any of those stupid lessons from Mom's basic training. We never discussed how long that agreement would last. The impatience in his voice implied that he felt it would not be much longer.

I never asked about his work even though I could tell he really liked it. The other residents were friendly, the staff was supportive, and administration was grateful to have filled every slot. My presence was a dark cloud over the literal and figurative sun Orlando brought for my husband.

That day, one of the Department Heads of Surgery decided to join us. Like a lion celebrating his newly killed prey, Anand puffed out his chest in victory at the gesture. He told me it was rare for someone so high ranking to pay any heed to a resident. The Head made one feeble attempt to engage me in conversation.

"How do you like Orlando?"

"I hate it."

Anand was mortified. I decided to skip the hospital tour he said he'd give me. He decided to skip coming home that night.

Chapter 42

"POOJA, ARE YOU ready?" Anand shouted down the hall to me.

I thumped my foot against the floor, staring at my closet. Putting yourself together is always easier when the outing is a welcomed occasion. After deliberating for a few minutes, I landed on a blue dress that draped nicely around my waist and landed tastefully at the calf to show off my legs in the heat of the Florida summer. Bold colors were in that year, and I picked out a bright green bag to do the talking for me. Everyone assumed those who sport color were happy people. I needed that assumption made tonight.

Anand and I had our first real argument when he came home a few days after I told the Head I hated Florida.

"Why can't you make any effort? When are you going to stop punishing me? Why do you refuse to be happy?"

Our life together was very new, but that man was one of the few people I had ever truly started to get to know. Anand was my only advocate and friend in an isolating city. You can't just pull yourself out of depression, though I had learned how to feign interest many times in my life. When he nervously asked if I would accompany him to the Chief of Medicine's house party, I had no choice but to go, and I had to make a good impression.

During the car ride, we sat in the same strained silence as when I had picked up Anand from the airport six months prior. This time, our roles were reversed. Topics for an interesting conversation evaded my head, as I hadn't picked up a newspaper, turned on the television, or had a real conversation in weeks.

"Should we go home?" he asked, interrupting my thoughts of nothingness.

"Yes."

His shoulders slumped. "I was being sarcastic."

"So was I."

"No you weren't."

"No. I wasn't."

"For what it's worth, I think you'll like her."

"Her?"

Anand told me the Chief of Medicine was a woman. She had grown up in Washington DC, attended medical school in Virginia, and eventually decided to move to Florida to be closer to her Trinidadian grandparents.

Finding out the Chief was a female gave me an unexpected spurt of energy that even Anand noticed.

By the time we pulled up to the hostess's driveway, he was happily describing all the fascinating things the Chief had done in her life. His humming in the backdrop drowned out to the sight of the massive house that contained a grand foyer straight out of a Humphrey Bogart movie. A gold tint shimmered over the entire space as though someone had taken a giant paintbrush and turned everyone into a Sepia photograph. Anand caught a glimpse of the expression on my face.

"We'll have something like this one day, you know," he said to me.

"Maybe if I go unconscious and dream this place alive."

"I'll give you everything you've ever wanted, I promise."

I knew he wanted to believe it. The problem was that all I wanted was to leave the one thing that he needed.

For the next hour, I dutifully followed Anand around while he mingled with various hospital personnel. Growing up in an environment familiar to medicine gave me enough substance to know when to nod, smile, or tick my tongue in sympathy for a struggling patient or frustrated doctor.

Anand was aware that I had not even the slightest interest in going into medicine myself. On the way to the fifth set of conversing people, he flashed me a quick side smile of gratitude and said he'd understand if I wanted to step outside.

Grateful to make it to the fresh air, I had a chance to sit back and take in the beauty of the garden. Mom and Dad were hoarders of any wealth they had accumulated and never spent money on aesthetics.

"Money is meant to be saved," Mom would always dramatically declare.

Seeing someone make investments into what they owned was something I appreciated.

"Would you care for a glass of white wine?" a woman standing next to me asked.

"Are you saving it for someone else?"

"I grabbed an extra by mistake. It's all yours."

I turned to face her. She was an impressive-looking person, exuding confidence that was both calming and unnerving. At nineteen, I could count the number of times I had drunk alcohol on one finger. Desperate to not come off unhinged, I brought the cup up to my lips without letting a drop in.

"How is it?" she asked.

"Bitter."

"Bitter? I thought it was a Riesling?"

I had no clue what that meant, so I changed the subject. "This place is enormous."

"Enormous is a relative term."

"My guess would be nine thousand square feet. That's enormous to me."

She pursed her lips as if to consider what I had just said, then asked me how I came to that estimate.

"Well, the land in this part of the country is generally very flat and soft, so any hidden or underground basement is unlikely. It's easy enough to guess the length and width of the exterior. Assuming there are no major enclosures, multiply by three floors, and I get about nine thousand square feet."

I barely had time to react to the expression on her face; I was equally stunned I had just said that.

She paused, then asked what I did as a profession. I felt myself blushing beneath the thankful haven of my dark skin. It was obvious I was young. I'm sure she knew as soon as she handed me that glass of wine.

"I'm . . . uh . . . between . . . I . . ." I stammered.

"Follow me," she replied.

We walked a few paces to a man I hadn't yet met. Without hesitation, she broke between his sentences.

"Jonathan, I'd like to introduce you to . . ." She glanced in my direction.

"Pooja," I finished, voice shaking, beyond nervous.

"Pooja just made the most brilliant observation about our house. I think she would make a fine addition to your program."

Our house? I thought. My only goal that night was to make a good impression. How could I not know I was talking to the Chief?

"My wife doesn't say these kinds of things often, you know," Jonathan said to me.

"I must be serious," she asserted.

Without further warning, she spun on her heel and walked back into the house, her silver dress catching the moonlight as though the sky purposely configured itself in her favor.

Jonathan didn't let me take an extra moment to process what was happening. He gave me the next half hour to describe a million thoughts on building facades, landscapes, and open spaces. They came so naturally; I found an autopilot of thinking I didn't even realize I had.

"Pooja, I'd be thrilled if you came in for an interview," he said.

"I've never had a job . . ."

"No no, don't be silly. Allow me to introduce myself properly . . ." Jonathan said—Dean of Architecture at the University of Florida, Orlando.

He gave me his card, making sure to write down his direct line on the back.

"I'll have my secretary schedule you in first thing Monday morning."

Back inside the house, I found Anand by the drink table. I still had the glass of wine in my hand.

"Found a friend to sneak you alcohol?" he playfully asked.

"You'll never believe who," I replied.

"You'll have to tell me all about it during the car ride home."

I nodded, surveying my scenery. The faint glow that persisted throughout the halls of the house had ignited something brilliant within me.

Chapter 43

JONATHAN HAD EMIGRATED from his native Nigeria to the States as a student at Virginia Tech to be "something practical"—as his parents put it—like an engineer or a doctor.

"I was less compelled by people as individuals than people as communities," he said.

Despite his parents' wishes, he accepted admission to the School of Architecture, and landed a job in DC after, which is where he met the Chief, Christine.

"Marrying a doctor was still not out of the question."

He built an impressive career over the next twenty years. When Christine decided she needed to be closer to Trinidad, Jonathan took the unanticipated move to create something new—a Department of Architecture at a school few had heard of. Within a year, it became accredited; within five years, it became one of the top twenty in the country.

"What made you think of those observations about our house?" was his first question of the interview.

"I don't know. It came naturally."

Of course the sole architect behind its design was its owner, and Jonathan took kindly to the implicit flattery behind my attention to his work. We talked about the history of American and African architecture, principles of negative and positive space, and how elements from our everyday lives can influence how a building is designed.

"I noticed you're into fashion, that can play an important role in inspiring one's work," he continued.

"Thanks for noticing, it's something I've always taken to heart."

In high school, my classmates knew me as the weird brown girl who always did her homework. Everything else about me was unappreciated; my classmates didn't know the difference between chic and shit. Jonathan could relate as an immigrant African at a college in rural Virginia.

"Pooja, I won't pretend Orlando is the metropolis you've been searching for."

"I've come to that conclusion."

"Despite its location, we've been able to create a great program. I'd love for you to be a part of it."

Jonathan told me that for him, architecture was about creating spaces for bettered human interaction. What he said made total sense. There was a distinct feeling of comfort in using my life to plan how people interact, and how a family functions and communicates.

Time flew by as we spoke, and two hours after I had first stepped foot in his office, I left with an official invitation for automatic enrollment into the Department of Architecture. Classes started the week after.

"HI, MOM," I said.

"Where are you?"

"At home, where else would I be?"

"How would I know? You never pick up the phone."

That era was over, I knew. I finally had good news to share.

"Guess what? I am starting architecture school."

"Is Anand home? Are you making proper Indian dinner?"

"I'm starting architecture school next week."

"The key to chapatti is to let the dough—"

"*Mom!*" I screamed with such intensity I thought I would have a brain aneurism. This was the most significant thing that had happened to me in a year. I was furious she didn't care to listen.

"What is it?" she finally conceded.

"I'm starting architecture school next week. I'm really excited."

"Architecture? I thought you were going to be an accountant?"

She always had a way of projecting her desires as mine. Her odd obsession with accounting was one of them. I knew this conversation was over before it had even started. With my newfound insight into buildings, I blamed our terrible West Virginia house for never creating the space for proper interaction. I had her pass the phone to Dad before my mood was completely soiled.

He, of course, was thrilled at me finding a new passion, and for making the most out of a bad situation.

"I'm so proud of you for figuring this out on your own."

His words of gratitude were all I needed to hear to refuel my excitement. "She will realize very quickly we all got what we wanted."

Fortunately, I didn't have time to dwell further. There was less than one week before classes started, which meant I needed to get a hundred things in order. The mental block of doing mundane tasks like applying for a Florida driver's license disappeared when it was part of a greater process to register for school.

On August 23, 1980, I finally lived out one of the recurring dreams of my life—I entered my first college class. Though it hadn't happened as I had hoped, the time I had invested in my higher education already had me thinking that this was the beginning of something truly amazing.

Chapter 44

"AND THAT IS why buildings in Washington DC and Paris have such similar façade structures," I concluded.

"Bravo," Anand shouted, clapping his hands with emphatic gestures.

"Thanks for listening."

"Are you sure you don't want another student's opinion?"

I let the question hang in the air just long enough until I was sure it was safe to change the subject. Classes had gone really well my first year in Orlando, and I was genuinely looking forward to the next day when my Intro to European Architecture section began. Jonathan was a guest lecturer and had asked me to make a special presentation. I was thrilled, until he told me the reason.

"Pooja, I'm afraid that our students have trouble finding connections to foreign things in their own lives."

"I second."

"Could you put together something to bring a European city closer to home?"

Because I was one of the few people in the university who owned a passport, Jonathan needed my help relating to students who refused to pick up a book that was not required.

"I'm going to be a lot busier as a second year resident—" Anand started.

"I understand," I assured, not wanting to get into this conversation again.

Anand, Dad, Alpa, and even Mom on occasion had no shortage of praise for my academic performance. I made the Dean's List both semesters, and I was easily one of the most recognized faces among the Architecture Department professors. Everyone knew I was going to go far in this field.

Socially, things were different. Thankfully, I wasn't still considered that weird brown girl who did all her homework; I was just married. At its core, UF Orlando was still a party school. My peers were more concerned with drinking and Greek life than they were about excelling at their work. That intimate circle of friends I was hoping to cultivate through coffee shops and dinner parties didn't exist in a place like that. My one attempt to assimilate in the popular culture of the school was a disaster.

"What's your name?"

"Pooja. You?"

"Poo-WHAT?"

"Poo-JA."

The guy smelled of stale beer and stupidity. But he was the first person who came over to talk to me, and I was still trying to salvage the night.

"Want to make out?"

"I'm married."

"Knocked up?"

"NO. It's cultural."

"How many kids you got?"

"Zero. It was arranged."

"That's a fucked-up arrangement," he said, before stumbling away.

Statements like those put me in a limbo. "That's a fucked up arrangement" was a line I would have thrown in Mom's face two years ago. At the start of my second year of college, I didn't know what to think. I was neither Indian nor American. I was a student without a student's life. I was a wife without a wife's life. But I loved the content of my classes and the professors that came with them. Secondary to my academic fulfillment was that the only thing outside of my school life was my husband.

I looked back at Anand and offered a few pacifying words to end the conversation.

"Don't worry, I love what I do, I'll be fine."

"THANKS FOR STOPPING by, Pooja," Jonathan said.

"My pleasure."

I looked around his office. The family photos were updated regularly, and they always looked gorgeous. In my mind, equal in beauty was his overstuffed drawer of contacts.

"Thanks to a few professors in the department, we have come across some funding," he continued.

"Congratulations. What will it buy?"

"Mostly new supplies. And a paid research assistant."

Doing my best not to be conspicuous, I shifted by body slightly forward, desperate to not miss a word of what was coming.

"If you would be amenable, we'd love to take you on three days a week."

The smile on my face must have stretched a mile wide. There were five hundred students in the architecture program. Being hand picked as a research assistant meant that I was the best; great things were indeed yet to come.

"I would be honored," I screamed, still not sure if I had conveyed the depths of my happiness.

"Excellent. I know Orlando wasn't where you saw your . . ."

I waved my hand, dismissing the thought. Landing an opportunity like this was enough to quell the last waves of bitterness that sometimes surged through me on particularly stressful days. After nearly two years, I finally understood that Orlando not being forever didn't mean Orlando shouldn't be as good as possible. Such an offer meant I was making that happen.

"I'm glad to see things are getting better. This position would be contingent on your commitment to complete the program."

"Absolutely. When do I start? I'd be ready early next week."

Jonathan chuckled with an air of experience. Funding in academic institutions was rarely quick moving. The position would start in three months. He was intent on making sure the role would fit both the needs of the program and give me solid experience. We discussed a few topics that would bolster the profile of the school. Everything French was in style.

"Please keep the following information quiet," he said at the end of our meeting.

"I can keep a secret."

"Some of the faculty would like to visit a field site this summer. We'd of course bring the Research Assistant."

The whole campus must have felt the atomic reaction that caused my heart to explode. My first work trip would be to Paris.

Chapter 45

THAT AFTERNOON WAS the first time in more than a year that I skipped a class. As soon as I left Jonathan's office, my mind began playing out beautiful scenes of what lay ahead. Working side-by-side professors, finally having my days filled with intellectual conversations in coffee shops, only in *France*. Thirty minutes in Jonathan's office had given me more inspiration than the rest of my life combined. How quickly I had been able to work my way up in Orlando was impressive. I had to celebrate.

None of my classmates would appreciate how much of an honor this offer was. Alpa was too young and Mom and Dad turned every conversation about school into a cultural tug of war.

"These American universities do not make sense."

The one person in the world I wanted to tell was Anand. I knew he never meant for me to end up here, and I knew he wanted me to do well. This news was a way to move past those nasty first months and to finally congratulate ourselves for doing so well despite what we had been given.

After tracking him down at the hospital, I told him to be home by eight. Being such big news, I wanted to reveal the surprise over dinner, not quickly tell him in between patients.

I swore to never tell Mom that I was actually grateful for her boot camp sessions. I borrowed the car for the afternoon and ran around the central Florida region tracking down ingredients for a proper south Indian meal. Timed perfectly, by seven-thirty, all I needed to do was let the *idli* cool and set the table. The setup was beautiful; Anand would love it.

I sat by the phone the first twenty minutes he was late. By eighth-thirty I was pacing. By nine I was crying. By ten I was angry. He pushed through the door around ten-thirty, clearly exhausted.

"Where the hell were you?"

"The head of internal medicine called me in, I couldn't get away."

"I spent four hours cooking you dinner."

My voice was shaking; I was so livid. He followed the direction of my pointed finger and saw the feast I had prepared sitting on the table. The steam that had gracefully risen from the dishes was now replaced with cold food that had a grayish appearance.

"I'm so sorry, Pooja. I had no idea, you never cook."

I flinched at the last part, a reminder I was a bad wife, exactly what I had been hoping this dinner would lay to rest.

"I'll go wash my face and we'll sit and eat together," he decided.

There was no better solution. I nodded, and told him I'd wait on the couch. ten, fifteen, twenty minutes later and he still hadn't emerged from the bedroom. The noise of the hand on the clock behind me grew with each second until I was sure my eardrums would explode.

"Anand," I said, trying to wake him from our bed, where he had passed out.

"Anand."

"Anand!"

He stirred enough to rub his face with his hand. "Pooja, I'm so tired. It was a sixteen-hour shift."

I didn't care. The most exciting news of my life was supposed to be celebrated over that dinner I had taken such trouble in preparing. How were we supposed to start over if he couldn't even find two hours to spend with his wife at dinner?

A moment of quiet was all it took for him to fall back asleep. Dejected, I closed the bedroom door with me on the other side and spent the night on the couch, falling asleep to the sounds of late night TV. He was gone by the time I woke up the next morning. The untouched food was still on the table, as though it were an exhibit in a museum.

Chapter 46

WE TRIED WORKING on our communication skills. Anand made the case that had I been clearer with the effort I intended to put into that dinner, he would never have agreed to go into the meeting. Regardless, he said he should have called and let me know how late he would be.

Using very direct statements, unambiguous instructions, and a lot of phone calls, we managed to schedule times to see each other over the next few weeks. Inevitably, one of us would cancel at the last minute, realize we had unfinished work that needed to be done and either leave or simply fail to show up at all.

All the open communication in the world could not change how busy he was and how little I was willing to compromise on school to accommodate his erratic schedule. I realized in mid-October that I still hadn't told him I had been awarded the Research Assistantship.

The drift apart was slow and steady. One day I woke up and realized how far from each other we were. We were both new to our careers and grew each day. The more we grew as individuals, the farther apart we grew as husband and wife.

I GOT A call from the pushy owner of our apartment complex in November that year. Construction of the new theme park addition was near completion and investors were hoping to start welcoming guests within six months. Because of the proximity of our complex to the parks, our owner had gotten a lucrative offer.

"I'm getting three times what I paid. I need you out by Christmas."

"We signed a lease, you can't kick us out. We don't have time to find a new place."

"Ain't my problem. Your lease is nullified if I sell. Read the fine print."

He slammed the phone down before I could argue further. Annoyed but not panicked, I dug out the lease and read the masses of pages I had neglected to look over before Anand and I had co-signed. Our aggressive owner was right, he could sell and we'd have no option but to move.

I sighed and looked up at the calendar. In less than a month, I had finals. Then I had a lot of research to get through before the start of the next semester. How was I supposed to find a new apartment before Christmas?

With only a few minutes before I had to catch the bus to campus, I left Anand a note, telling him to keep the weekend open so we could start looking. I had no desire to become homeless.

We caught each other the next Saturday afternoon.

"I saw your note," he said.

"We should start looking today. When will you be ready?"

"We need to talk."

"Okay, I'll get the keys. I found some listings already."

"Pooja, we need to talk."

"Grab the newspaper for me, would you?"

"Now."

I finally realized what he was asking in between my lines. We were becoming progressively worse at listening to each other.

"You know residency is only a two year program, right?" he asked.

"Then a few years of fellowship, I know."

"I decided on what my specialty will be."

"What is it?"

"Neurology . . ."

His voice trailed off as though that word held some hidden meaning. I thought neurology was an impressive specialty. Beyond that I had no opinions.

"Why are you silent?" I prompted.

He gave me a few more seconds to make the connection myself.

"Orlando doesn't have any hospitals with a neurology fellowship," I finished.

"We're moving in May, Pooja."

The way he said that word—*we*—brought back all the same emotions from when we first got married. Why was it okay his needs were prioritized over mine?

"*We* are not moving anywhere, Anand."

"We have no choice."

You have a choice, Anand. *We* do not. I am not moving again."

"You hate it here."

"Not anymore."

A small look of recognition crossed his face and I knew he finally saw the considerable rift between us.

I told him about the Research Assistant position and all of its glory. The position was a fantastic opportunity that had not existed until now. My timing was impeccable.

"And it's contingent on me finishing the program here."

"I had no idea, congratulations."

"So you see I have to stay here. Now let's go find an apartment."

I found it so ironic the conversation had evolved to me wanting to stay in a city that I had once violently hated.

"Pooja, no."

"No?" I asked, visibly insulted.

"Your Research Assistant position is a great opportunity—"

"But?"

"But this is not up for discussion. This is my career, our financial security."

"What does that mean? That I don't get to be a part of the decisions?"

"You are always a part of my decisions."

"*Your* decisions, Anand. What about what I want?"

"Pooja, you're just a kid . . ."

I saw myself shrivel down to a puppet, the marionette strings sprouting from my shoulders. Anand grabbed the wooden handles attached and whipped me around for the pleasure of the audience. *My first act will be Dance of the Pooja. She'll serve coffee after the show.*

I couldn't bear to see his face anymore. Fifteen minutes after jumping in the car and leaving him bewildered in the apartment, I found myself driving in the direction of Jonathan and Christine's house.

Chapter 47

"POOJA? WHAT ARE you doing here? Is everything okay?" Christine asked.

I pushed past, forcing my way into her house as though we had been close friends for decades. The fact that she was Anand's boss and her husband was my boss didn't even cross my mind. If she noticed, she didn't mind.

"Is everything okay?" she repeated.

I tried to speak and instead felt my throat melt in anger. As though she knew there was a fiery war waging beneath the surface, she walked to the kitchen and poured me a glass of water. There was no air of hurriedness that usually covered my apartment in a dense fog. One of the busiest doctors in the entire Orlando area had more time to talk about my feelings than my own damn husband.

Her kindness was overwhelming; I told her everything. The lonely little girl who passed her days conducting the orchestras in her head, building cities out of paper, befriending plastic dolls, and dreaming of a time when life would be much better. The hardworking student who prioritized studying over breathing, yet still developed a voice and a style. The now young adult who constantly felt the only options in life were her happiness *or* the happiness of everyone else.

Of all the reactions possible, I was not prepared for the one thing I had yearned to hear for so long.

"Pooja, you're absolutely right."

Christine told me about her and Jonathan's experience being decades deep into their marriage. Having two people who are passionate about their career can be very difficult to balance.

"The hospitals I needed were not located in places conducive to Jonathan's work."

"He chose you over what was best in his profession?"

"Often, yes. But he still built an incredible career."

She stopped short of saying it was something I could do too. Neither of us knew if that was true. And both of us knew there was an inherently different motivation behind what Jonathan did and what my relationship with Anand entailed. Anand and I did not marry because we fell in love.

"All I can say is that Anand believes in you," she offered.

"That's doubtful."

"It isn't. How do you think I knew to introduce you to Jonathan?"

My mind reeled. The whimsical child in me had written off the encounter as fate. Christine told me in his first few months of work, Anand was fascinated with the possibilities of careers in America. He wanted to know more about everything.

"He saw that the kind of observation involved in architecture was something you have."

"Why didn't he tell me?"

"Maybe he wanted you to make the decision on your own."

Christine walked to me and gently put her hand on my shoulder. She told me that for all of the brilliance Anand possessed, he still had some growing up to do.

"He is smart beyond his years, but you are wise beyond your years."

"You're saying having me will benefit him?"

"Absolutely, and he knows that."

"What about me?"

"Maybe you would have found architecture without his support. Maybe something even better."

But that was a hypothetical question no one could answer. All that was certain was everything I had built in less than two years and Anand's role in enabling that to happen.

Christine called Jonathan into the room. Jonathan was empathetic to my situation even though it meant he'd be losing his Research Assistant. They assured me that they'd take the next few days to think about cities that had both the fellowship program Anand needed and an architecture program for me.

"Pooja," Jonathan said, "you will make it to Paris. You will make it anywhere you want."

Jonathan's words gave me calmness about the sacrifice I was about to make. I gave him my verbal resignation of the Research Assistant offer, praying with every ounce of will that I had not made the biggest mistake of my life.

Chapter 48

I DECIDED I needed time to organize my thoughts before approaching the same topics with Anand. In the meantime, I simply said I would move with him to a city that had a good architecture program. He decided on a last minute trip to India for the winter holidays; I was so grateful we didn't have enough money for two tickets. Like the unfamiliar roommates we were, we said an apathetic goodbye and parted for the month. For once in my life, I couldn't wait to get to West Virginia.

Alpa and I spent most of the last two weeks of December sitting on the couch and watching TV. Letting my mind atrophy with the mundane entertainment of daytime television was exactly what I needed to balance out an intense eighteen months of self-reflection and evaluation.

Mom always had a belittling way of dismissing my problems when I was growing up. Everything had always been in comparison to her traumatic life events—her father being murdered, her best friend committing suicide, nearly getting deported for something that was not Dad's fault.

"*Those* are reasons to be depressed, Pooja."

This trip, she was thankfully easy on me. I didn't know what had prompted the change, but the few details I had shared with her about my life in recent months actually seemed to register. She knew I was passionate about my work, and a part of me wanted to believe she was remorseful for letting Anand take away the opportunities I had been able to create.

Dad was his in usual good mood and even participated in Alpa's and my cookie-baking marathon, movie watching with hot apple cider, and pillow wars. Being out of the house had given my parents a chance to see that I could be my own person. As much as Mom must have thought our uncharacteristic fun was nonsense, she let Dad, Alpa, and I have carefree moments. I needed a stress relief, and I was grateful I could finally turn to my childhood home for that comfort. Together, the four of us rang in New Year's 1983 with the comfort I had wished for so many nights as a kid.

Chapter 49

A FEW DAYS after the New Year, I decided to resume my old habit of getting the mail. Running to the little black box was one of my favorite things to do as a child; it was one of the only connections I felt I had to the outside world.

As I walked back to the house, I flipped through the contents even though I knew there would be nothing for me. It was a typical stack—a few bills, two Christmas catalogues, a flyer for the new Piggly Wiggly store, and one large envelope from Georgetown University . . . for Alpa.

The envelope was ornately covered in fine ribbons of black and white against a blue inset. I remembered getting promotional materials featuring smiling students outside on a grassy campus or raising their hands to be called on by a professor. When I was in high school, I was so taken with the atmosphere they created. Looking back on the quality of some of the schools that were advertised now only made me cynically smile.

"College you've never heard of: We have students. Some of them can read."

Taking a second look at the envelope, I realized it looked nothing like promotional material. It was a letter. Even though it was a total invasion of privacy, I couldn't help myself. In slow motion, my hands ripped wildly at the seam while the other pieces of mail crashed to the snow and left gaping holes in the smooth surface. I couldn't believe what I saw inside.

> Dear Ms. Alpa Deva,
> We are pleased to inform you that your early admission application has been successful for the Fall 1983 semester. Please find your admission packet enclosed. Congratulations on your hard work. We look forward to seeing you this September.

Not bothering to pick up the rest of the mail, I ran back to the house without the slightest care of the commotion I made. This time there was no Mom running downstairs in a panic. This time it was me who pounded heavily on the staircase, demanding to know answers. Alpa was sitting in her robe, brushing her hair.

"What the fuck is this? Mom and Dad let you apply to college?"

From my past secret applications, I knew that if Alpa had done the same, the letter would have gone to a friend's house. Receiving a response at home meant Mom and Dad knew what was happening.

"Pooja, I was going to tell you."

"To hell you were. I've been home for three weeks."

Her tiny body shook; her hand flapped like a bird trying to escape its captor.

"Why didn't you call and tell me?" I demanded.

"What could I say? Mom and Dad are letting me apply when they forced you to get married?" she could barely whisper.

"Yes. No. Fuck!"

I collapsed into a heap on the floor. In the background, Alpa cried, saying she was so sorry. Everyone was always so sorry.

"Pooja, I love you so much, I'm always on your side."

"I know," I whispered.

"I don't know why they changed their mind for me. When I found out I'd be skipping tenth grade, I guess we had to talk about it sooner."

"What did they say?"

"You should talk to Dad. All I know is that I got lucky."

I knew she was right. My sixteen-year old sister getting married wouldn't do anything to change my situation. We sat in silence for nearly an hour before she had the nerve to ask to see the letter. Her glee of getting in was clearly marred with the sadness and anger my presence brought. Mom and Dad would be home from the grocery store any minute. Despite my instincts to punch a hole through the wall, I slowly stood up and locked myself in my room.

For two days, I stared at the white wall that defined my childhood existence. No photos of friends, no happy drawings of ponies . . . no real sign of life reflected the sad state of the first eighteen years of my life. The only toy Mom would have permitted was a jack-in-the-box shouting her favorite word, "Competition competition competition."

Yet despite everything I did to adhere to her principles of hard work over pleasure, all she wanted was for me to get married. She never listened to what I wanted, about what growing up in America meant, or what I had learned it took to be successful. She was never willing to listen to anything that went against what worked for her and Dad, until now, until Alpa. Why did Alpa get that chance and not me? What was wrong with me?

On Monday night, I heard a faint knock. I knew by the sound of the breathing that it was Dad on the other side of the door.

"I brought sandwiches. I thought you might be hungry."

He was right. I hadn't prioritized eating in the last forty-eight hours. I told him to set it by the door and waited until I knew I wouldn't have to see anyone before carefully pulling the tray inside. Dad anticipated as such. Folded under the plate was a note. Against my first instincts, I saw what it said inside.

"Write 'yes' if you want me to get rid of Mom and Alpa so we can talk. Write 'no' if you don't want to talk before you leave on Wednesday."

I deliberated for a few minutes, trying to imagine how I'd feel returning to Orlando knowing what I did without getting any answers. Before depositing the empty tray back in its place, I returned the slip of paper with one word written on the other side.

Yes.

"HOW DID YOU get rid of Mom and Alpa?" I asked Dad.

"I tried to convince your mom to let me talk to you alone."

"Big mistake."

"Yes, big mistake. Then I gave Alpa ten dollars to ask Mom to take her to the Smokey Mountains."

"But she just kept the money?"

"But she just kept the money."

"Finally, I told your mom she doesn't have to go with me to Bangalore on our next trip to India. That worked."

We let out a chuckle before returning to the awkward silence. Apparently neither of us knew how to start the real conversation. I took to compulsively checking my watch—as if I had anywhere to go—and Dad kept scratching his chest.

"Are you okay?" I asked.

"Maybe it's gas. I have indigestion."

"Ew."

"Sorry."

The scene was reminiscent of every visit to India I had taken during childhood. We'd travel eight-thousand miles to spend two months sitting on a couch and trying to figure out how to relate to our own flesh and blood. We were rarely successful. Dad must have been on the same wavelength, which scared him. No one was especially bothered if we did not know how to talk to a cousin we saw once every two years. Not knowing how to talk to your own daughter was a far greater problem.

"Pooja, I'm sorry you found out about your sister going to Georgetown like that. I know that can't be easy for you," Dad started.

"No, it wasn't. Is she your favorite child?"

I wasn't there to mince words. Dad cried out in surprise as though it was a ridiculous proposition.

"How could you say that?"

"What am I supposed to think?"

"You and your sister are three grades apart. We have learned a lot in that time."

"You guys changed your life philosophy in less than three years?" I could tell I had hit a nerve. I was surprised to find out the reason why.

"It was not my philosophy," he cried out.

"Then why did you get me married off?"

"Pooja, your mother has had a really hard life—"

"Enough. That isn't a justification for everything."

I was so tired of that reasoning. My parents had been in the States for more than twenty years at that point. How dare Dad suggest the first eighteen had made no impact, that they had an epiphany in the last three.

"You're right," Dad conceded.

"What changed?"

"Nothing. Your mother wanted Alpa to get married as you did."

"And you stepped in this time?"

He hung his head in shame. The guilt his tired body stirred in me was not enough to make me regret the accusation.

"Pooja, I'm so sorry."

So sorry, all the time.

"Your mother and I came to this country with very different expectations than what ultimately happened. We wanted to move to a place that would offer much opportunity for you to flourish, for you to be anything you wanted to be *regardless* of whether you got married. We thought . . . your mom still thinks . . . that the only way for you to have a better life is to get married."

"Dad, this is America. It doesn't work the same way as in India."

"I know. I knew that a long time ago. You worked hard in high school. People still tell me how talented you are. But we forced you . . ."

He said that when he heard people speaking of Alpa in the same way, he finally found the courage to stand up to Mom. Alpa and I didn't need to get married to become successful. That was clear after how well I had done with what little I was given in Orlando.

Dad stood up to give me a hug. As soon as his warmth enveloped my body, I felt myself start to quiver as I began the long process of expelling a lifetime of remorse. Dad held me close, apologizing through the embrace.

"I'm so sorry, Pooja. We should not have forced you to get married."

As he uttered the words I had waited so long to hear, I saw the stars in the night sky shining down on me with the sympathy of the entire universe. Dad's apology brought a mix of validation and disappointment my body could barely allow. For two years, I had been trying to swallow my feelings towards school, towards Florida, toward Mom, towards Anand . . . toward myself. Hearing Dad say those words out loud meant that I was not selfish for being angry. My life had become someone else's life against my will.

We spent the rest of the night talking about my situation. Dad offered his own experience—medical residency was one of the hardest periods of his life, and Anand was probably going through something similar. His American resident colleagues were worked to the bone for very little money or respect. As an immigrant, it was ten times worse.

"As immigrants, we don't know what food to eat, what things to say, what clothes to wear, or who to turn to. It can't be easy for Anand, either."

Dad offered to help by calling Anand to help convince him to pick a residency program that had options for me.

"I can't give you the last two years back, but I will do everything I can to make sure the rest of the years are as good as possible."

In the end, Dad and I both decided that two years was not enough time to see if a marriage would work. Things were currently not going well between Anand and me, but I knew that hadn't always been the case. The fact that Dad gave me his full support regardless of what I did made my decision to keep trying with Anand more empowering.

Mom and Alpa returned a few hours later. I knew Mom's instincts were to offer her input on each point of my conversation with Dad. She knew better. Like any good little sister, Alpa simply hugged me, saying how much she loved me.

Before I left for Florida, Dad brought me two belated Christmas gifts—the first time I had received a present from anyone. He bought me two books on Parisian architecture. Mom gave me an old green-and-gold brooch. I left it on their kitchen table.

Chapter 50

MY FLIGHT AND Anand's got in an hour apart, so I killed the extra time by sifting through the limited selection of the one airport store.

"Thought I'd find you here," I heard Anand say.

I turned around to face him, not quite sure if it was a happy occasion.

"How was West Virginia?"

"It was . . . interesting. How was India?"

"Also . . . interesting."

The tiredness in Anand's eyes told me to wait to bring up anything serious. We chatted about mundane things like the weather while collecting his bags and stopped to grab a pizza on the way home.

His time with his family was mediocre as expected. He had been dying to see his friends, and told me that despite everything that had happened, he still felt like a kid when he was around his old buddies.

"Some things never change," he finished.

"Some things constantly change."

He agreed and stood up to clear the dishes.

I caught his wrist and gently grabbed the plate out of his hand. "I'll take care of it. You have a long week ahead of you."

"Yes, thank you."

There was a brief moment of hesitation before he turned back one step to squeeze my hand and give me a kiss on the cheek. It was the first time in months I could remember an entirely positive interaction between the two of us.

We waited a full two weeks to finally say aloud what was on our minds. I recapped the conversation with Dad, first admitting that I knew I had never taken an interest in Anand's work or asked him how he was faring in a foreign country.

"It hasn't been easy," Anand replied.

"I should have been there for you."

Anand told me Christine had approached him with a list of cities that had what we both needed. He assured me the fellowship programs he'd apply to over the next few weeks would all be for programs located in those places.

"I appreciate the effort," I assured.

"I appreciate the patience."

We researched our top destinations and compiled a short list. With our credentials and references, we had no reason to believe it wouldn't work out in both of our favors. Together, we drove to the post office and wished our applications farewell. I told myself I'd see one of the following destinations in the fall: Ithaca, New Haven, Baltimore, Chicago, New Orleans, or New York. This time I was so confident it would happen.

Chapter 51

WE AGREED ON New Orleans. Jonathan was elated at the move, personally calling and telling me all of the wonderful things Tulane's architecture and urban planning department had to offer.

"A city as diverse as NOLA will be very much to your liking."

He was right. Soon after Anand and I settled into our tiny little apartment in the Upper Garden District, I received my course list. The classes covered subjects I hadn't realized existed. Maybe it was the charm of the St. Charles streetcar, maybe it was the infectious energy of the city, or maybe it was the idea of being somewhere I had chosen. Regardless of the reason, starting over in a new city quickly went from a burden to a blessing.

"HI EVERYONE, MY name is Jeff, and I am your new instructor this semester. I know, groan, a TA teaching a 300 level course. On the bright side, cultural references to anything before 1965 are now permitted."

We all laughed heartedly. Though a highly respected scholar, Professor Chang was rumored to have zero tolerance to references to anything before the year he immigrated to the States. Even so, a TA teaching a 300 level course was usually undesirable. With Jeff, I doubted that would be the case.

After living in NOLA for more than a year, I finally felt like I had found a home. Words had always come naturally to me, so I added a second major—English Literature. It showed how much I enjoyed where I was, electing to tack on another year until I completed my degree. The last visit back to West Virginia had been exhilarating; people seemed genuinely jealous of my life. I knew that I was finally living the dream.

Jeff instructed us to write our names on the blank cards he passed out so we could address each other directly. I wrote my name in big block letters, adding a small explanation underneath (it's pronounced like it's written).

He officially welcomed us to the course English Theory of the East. Professor Chang assigned Edward Saïd's *Orientalism*, which was by far one of the most interesting pieces I had ever read. I couldn't wait to give my perspective, though I wanted to wait for the perfect moment.

"So, what are some initial reactions?" Jeff asked.

A guy on the other side of the class raised his hand.

"Yes, Scott?"

"I think Saïd is really bitter about his childhood."

"Can you expand on that?"

"It's very obvious that colonialism scarred him as a kid. He writes about Western perceptions of the East as though they are invalid."

I contained myself from shouting my reaction to that gross misinterpretation and instead raised my hand.

"Yes," Jeff said, staring at my card.

"Pooja."

"Just like the Hindu religious ceremony?"

I was impressed, never having met a non-Indian who knew that. "Well, that form is usually spelled with a 'u,' but yes, exactly."

"So what are your thoughts, Pooja?"

Jeff shifted to give me his full attention. I had to allot myself a few seconds to catch my breath before starting. I couldn't help but notice how attractive he was.

"I agree that colonialism has deeply affected Saïd, though not how Scott claims."

"Can you elaborate?"

"I think what Saïd is saying is that we apply our cultural norms to foreign environments. In the case of European colonialism, colonists didn't recognize non-European advances in society and instead focused on what they thought was lacking."

I looked around the class to make sure they were not lost in the discussion as the student body of UF Orlando surely would have been. Everyone was intently listening.

"Resulting in?" Jeff prompted.

"Resulting in colonists who thought they better understood and were superior to the societies they invaded."

A few of the students in the class turned to say they agreed with me. I peered over at Scott, who was busy weaving his web of grievance at being stood up by my commentary. He crawled back and forth like a spider, waiting for someone stupid enough to get lost in the discussion and find they were caught in his trap. Jeff made eye contact with me and followed my gaze to Scott spider.

"Black widow?" Jeff asked.

"Tarantula," I replied.

The class stared at us like we were insane.

"Very astute observations, Pooja," Jeff said.

I felt my heart catch in my throat.

THE FIRST WEEK of classes was always a mad rush of people on one side of campus trying to get to the other. After half an hour of waiting behind a guy who wasn't sure if he was actually enrolled at Tulane, I finished straightening issues with my student loans just in time to see the last bus that could take me across campus to the streetcar drive away.

"Shit," I cried out.

The first assignments I had for architecture classes required me to take home nearly all of my drafting supplies for the weekend. Trying to balance the metal instruments, the drawing materials, and the giant slabs of paper made me crumble under the weight.

"Pooja."

I looked up to see Jeff running toward me. He moved gracefully for being so tall, displaying a curious level of athleticism compared to the average bookworm Ph.D. student. Briefly forgetting not to openly gawk in public, I regained control of my brain as he padded up to me.

He offered to give me a hand with my clunky materials, which were now spread out over a wide expanse.

"What's with all the stuff? Are you a targeted kleptomaniac?"

"Worse, double major. Architecture."

"I want to again compliment you for your astute observations on Tuesday."

The eye contact worked like a weight against my arm, and I once again spilled the supplies we had just collected. One relief in being a brown girl who grew up in West Virginia was the powerful mask of dark skin. It was the ultimate weapon against embarrassment.

"Where are you headed?" he asked.

"I just missed the bus to take me back to the streetcar."

"Let me give you a ride. That's on my way home. My car is just over there," he said, pointing to the adjacent lot.

A breeze fluttered his partially unbuttoned shirt, briefly exposing a muscular frame underneath.

"I'm married," I blurted out.

"Okay . . . Do you want a ride?"

"I . . . uh . . ."

"I'm a nice guy, Pooja."

Against my marital judgment, I accepted his offer and followed him back to his red Mustang.

"It has an automatic retractable roof," he said.

"Don't put it down."

"You sure?"

"Yes. My hair."

In the open air, my hair would have quickly morphed into a giant ball of weeds. Retractable roofs are not meant for Indian girls. The top closed with a satisfying *click*, commencing what I could already feel would be many moments like this together. I saw Jeff work with a delay, trying to comb through the palpable tension that was enclosed by the intimate space of his car.

"When did you move to NOLA?"

"Fourteen months ago with my husband, Anand. You?"

"Three years ago without a husband, Anand."

I silently told him he was lucky to move here unattached.

"I know I was," he answered my unspoken thought.

"Where are you from?"

"Mississippi."

"Why did you leave?"

"A lot of reasons. The people there are superficially welcoming to strangers, but close-minded with locals, you know?"

Our time must have been cut short with a wrinkle. A normal fifteen-minute ride was reduced to a few seconds. Jeff pulled up outside of my apartment complex, jumped out, and helped me carry my things to the door. The faint scent of cologne tickled my nose with the subtlety of a feather.

He gently kissed my hand to say goodbye. Before we had even made full contact, an electric bolt surged straight through my arm, bestowing me with a shiny new coat of confidence. By the way we had already connected, I knew that armor would only grow stronger with time.

Chapter 52

PARTIALLY DUE TO my workload but mostly in the hopes of encounters with Jeff outside of class, I spent increasingly more time on campus. Soon, I had memorized his entire teaching schedule. Our synergy was so apparent that I took my newfound confidence as opportunities to often "accidentally" bump into him. When the five-minute exchanges became insufficient, I asked him out to lunch.

"Where would you like to go?" I asked him.

"I'm actually kind of busy . . ."

"I won't take no for an answer." I made no effort to hide my disappointment at his initial response.

"Okay, you win. Do you like Creole food?" he conceded.

"I've never actually tried it."

"You live in NOLA and you've never had Creole food? You must try it; it's imperative."

The beauty of New Orleans is that it took mere minutes to reach a completely different atmosphere. We pulled up to a small hole-in-the-wall restaurant on the east side of the French Quarter. Health inspections weren't standard in the city.

"Everything is deep fried. You don't have to worry about getting sick from spoiled food," he assured.

"Oh, so that's why they do it."

"Indians too?"

The walls of the place were plastered with photos, memorabilia, and old jazz records. I imagined someone had tired of keeping the contents of their life on a bookshelf and decided to staple gun everything for public viewing.

"It's the owner's collection. He was in one of the most famous Louisiana jazz ensembles back in the 60s," Jeff explained.

"What happened to the group?"

Normally confident, never-at-a-loss-for-words Jeff hesitated in his response. "There were some internal disagreements."

Before I had the chance to ask for elaboration, the waiter came over and Jeff jumped up to give him a hug. My body quivered at the thought of Jeff being so comfortable with physical affection. When I first married Anand, I thought he was a gentleman in his restraint. Over the last year, I had begun to realize that Anand was just a prude.

"Edward. You're still waiting tables at your own place," Jeff exclaimed.

"Jeff, my boy, how are you?"

"Doing well, still . . . um, living with Charles. You?"

"Glad to hear. I'm still with Tracey. Who's this pretty lady?"

Edward held my eye contact for a second too long before letting his gaze wander down my torso to my legs. The idea of the old man checking me out gave me the creeps.

"Pooja and I are colleagues."

I loved the sound of those words and felt a pang of nostalgia for the Department of Architecture back in Orlando. Working my way up to the same status at Tulane in either of my majors would take more time than before. The students were smarter and the school was better here.

"Sorry for that long sidebar," Jeff apologized as he sat back down.

"That guy was gross; he was staring at me."

"You look lovely, but I doubt that was the case."

The comment was equally offending as it was flattering. Jeff stared down at his silverware, which somehow kept his features in perfect proportion. I couldn't read what he was thinking.

"He is really committed to Tracey."

"His wife?"

A round of beers came out to interrupt the conversation. Grateful to change the subject, Jeff made good use of my still obvious ignorance of alcohol.

"This is one of the best the Bayou has to offer," he explained.

I took my first swig and nearly spit it out.

"Beer isn't for everyone. We'll find you your drink."

Anything implying future social interaction was all I needed to reorient myself. The food was absolutely delicious and helped set the mood back to what I had intended for this lunch.

"How did you decide on an English, Architecture double major?"

"Well, Anand, my husband, had to—"

"I asked how *you* decided, Pooja."

He emphasized it in such a way that I immediately noticed how often I structured my answers to questions in the context of Anand. I decided framing my life this way was antithetical to my deep-seated desire to assert my independence in our marriage and immediately began correcting the wording.

Careful to express my opinions in a way that fit only me, we spent the next hour talking about Louisiana culture, life in the South, and what I thought of Tulane. As we got up to leave the restaurant, I realized that was the longest conversation I had ever had about my thoughts and opinions.

Jeff paid for both of our meals.

"You get the next one." "I'll get the next one." We spoke at the same time.

On the way out, he told me about a new bar that had just opened up near campus and asked if I'd like to get a drink with him that Friday night? Until then, the sweaty, swarthy imbeciles of Orlando nightlife had swayed me away from trying the NOLA bar scene. I completely threw those thoughts in the trash as soon as Jeff asked me out.

"I would love to," I replied.

THE WRINKLE BROUGHT our friendship to a point that normally takes years to reach. Time flowed like water with Jeff. Within weeks, I thanked the world on a continual basis for bringing me someone so intelligent who could relate to growing up in a small, isolated town.

"Ironically, Americans perceive India as backwards. Really, your husband and parents grew up in environments that could be considered more cosmopolitan than where we are from," he once observed.

"That sounds like something Saïd would say."

"You read my mind."

Together, we explored the depths of New Orleans with the same avid curiosity of someone who had never laid foot on its beautiful steps. We painted ourselves into French Creole murals. We tamed the wild alligators of the bayou swamps. We explored bookstores that contained the writings of languages long lost. We picked the brains of culinary avant-gardes. We stayed up late, we rose early, we appreciated the conversations, and we relished the comfortable silences.

With a simple graze of a touch, Jeff conveyed more intensity of emotion than I had ever felt from anyone in my life. My conflicted reality reminded me that I was a married woman, and therefore Jeff had to stay a friend. His loyalty and patience were unyielding, and he never demanded more. We understood the humor in the pain and the pain in the humor of the life we had to live. Our minds were at a convergence, and with each passing moment we spent together, I could feel my intense and profound attraction to him growing.

Chapter 53

JEFF AND I made it a habit to give a unique occasion to our frequent outings. In a tribute to exploring my drinking preferences, we planned one night to go to a bar named Brigista to test Jeff's theory was that I was a martini girl.

Though we had both passed it on our own without a second thought, together, we discovered the sophisticated beauty of a black-lacquered bench by the English building. For its odd and convenient presence, it became our usual Wednesday meeting spot.

He was a few minutes late that night, finally emerging and looking distracted by a disappointing sight—another person. Not wanting to lose his attention even a second longer than necessary, I called out. He slowly turned his chiseled face, the moonlight giving a haloed effect to his person. Two months of seeing him nearly every day had only elongated the breath he stole from my lips.

"Hi Pooja."

The man by Jeff's side trotted up to me. "So this is the famous Pooja. I'm Charles, Jeff's—"

"Roommate," Jeff finished.

My disappointment grew at the thought of Jeff finishing someone else's sentences.

"Hi, nice to meet you," I replied.

"Is it okay if Charles comes with us?" Jeff asked.

I was afraid this would happen. Jeff and my time alone had become semi-sacred, though it was the kind of sacredness that could be easily broken at the behest of either party. As much as I wanted to scream at Charles to go away, I only had one option about what to say.

"Sure, no problem."

Fighting off my discontent, I turned to eye the roommate. Charles had on the same style jumpsuit Michael Jackson wore in the "Thriller" video. Draped over the suit was a sparkling black sweater. A bowler hat sat on his head to round off the outfit.

"Isn't he the unequivocally most stylish person you've ever met?" Jeff asked me.

"Unequivocally," I had to agree.

Charles thanked us by doing a quick spin in Mr. Jackson's honor.

"How does it feel to have this bozo as your instructor?" Charles asked.

"It's hard to get through to that initial layer of stupidity, but once you do, there's no going back."

"Oh sassy. I can see why you like this one."

Jeff looked elated to see the three of us getting along so quickly. Jeff was happy. That made me happy.

Charles, dance instructor extraordinaire, played the perfect balance off Jeff and my serious conversations into the meanings of life. The harmony the three of us quickly struck was infectious, and soon, I was surprisingly grateful to have a regular third to complete our solid triangle of outings.

Jeff's alcohol knowledge paled in comparison to Charles's, who was also an ex-Miami bartender extraordinaire. Within a month, I had learned much about the fine art of red wine and could make the perfect Bloody Mary, which turned out to be my drink. On one particularly crazy night, Charles even showed me the dangers of Long Island Iced Teas.

The two of them were avid jazz fans, and brought me along to their various extravaganzas. Excited to finally have a dance partner, Charles taught me the finer points of swing. Together, we flapped our hands and threw our legs in the air like every moment was worth celebrating.

With his two left feet, Jeff stood in the corner, admiring the courtship practices his best friend used to lift me off the ground. As Charles and I danced the night away, the three of us were elevated into a heavenly ecstasy. Night after night, Jeff stole glances in my direction of a pained and beautiful attraction. I couldn't remember another time in my life that I had been that confident, that happy to be alive.

Chapter 54

"WHAT DO YOU mean you're not coming?" Anand shouted at me.

"Calm down," I replied.

"Just answer the question."

Two years ago, I would have given a long explanation right away. Jeff and New Orleans had taught me how to be assertive in my personal life. I now had the confidence to deal with Anand more directly.

"I'm not having this conversation until you calm down, Anand."

He had booked two tickets to India for the winter holidays without asking; I had already signed up for a January session course, and Alpa was coming to visit in between classes.

"I already went to India once by myself. Everyone will think we're having marital problems if you don't come," he tried to reason.

It wasn't as though that was entirely inaccurate. Anand's neurology program wasn't what he had expected. For the first year in New Orleans, I tried reaching out to him and supporting him in a way I never offered in Orlando. He'd always mutter something about how I didn't understand. Soon after I met Jeff, I stopped caring.

Instead of progressing in our relationship, my limited interactions with Anand were mostly reduced to arguing. Since moving, I could count the number of times we had made love on one hand. Anand had become more repulsive than desired.

"Since when do you care about what people in India think of you?"

"You're such an ungrateful bitch," he shouted.

It was a line he used often. The words rolled off me. Jeff and I had plans that night, so instead of engaging Anand further, I did what I had learned worked best—I left.

"Get back here. We're not finished," I heard in the distance.

ALPA FLEW DOWN to NOLA the day before Anand left for India. I took Alpa out for some sightseeing the morning after she arrived. Anand didn't bother to stick around to say goodbye. He didn't even leave a note. The only sign of his departure was a missing suitcase.

The fact that Anand and I were apart for our anniversary and my birthday didn't register in my thoughts. His absence was completely dwarfed by the scenes I played out in my head of Jeff meeting my little sister.

Jeff joined us for a day of sightseeing, and that night the three of us had plans to go to the newest and most exclusive restaurant in the city for dinner. Jeff must have apologized a thousand times for Charles being out of town. Secretly, we both knew how exciting it would be to spend the night alone with the company of family.

"Oh my God, you weren't kidding, he's so hot," Alpa squealed at me.

Jeff had wandered a few steps ahead to take a picture of a new statue of a street performer the city had just unveiled.

"I know. It's so hard to control myself sometimes."

"You guys haven't . . . you know?"

"I would never cheat on Anand."

The words sounded insincere even though I knew they needed to be true. I was having an increasingly difficult time reconciling the gloomy state of my marriage with the growing strength of the idea that Jeff was my soul mate. Even though Jeff and I had never technically discussed the nature of our relationship, I knew being married to Anand was the one thing holding us back from moving beyond something platonic.

Jeff beckoned us to him. "This statue is amazing. The clothes represent the perfect symbiosis of Bayou culture and Aquitaine troubadour."

"I don't know what that means, but it sounds wonderful," Alpa dreamily muttered.

Jeff smiled at her and playfully grabbed my hand. "Well, this one understood."

Alpa let out another squeal of jealousy. Her response perfectly juxtaposed to the much deeper nature of my reaction.

THE RESTAURANT JEFF picked out for my birthday dinner turned out to be an old manor house set far back in the Marigny district. The establishment was so exclusive that it was not even listed in the phone book. Only people who were well connected could get a table. Jeff had known the owner for a long time, who was a dignified older man with a peculiar resemblance to Rock Hudson.

"That's not the only thing we have in common," the owner said.

Jeff swatted the owner's arm away, complete with an embarrassed smile. "Pay no attention, he's just—"

"Drunk," Alpa finished.

"Exactly."

I was surprised Alpa of all people had a better sense of what was going on than me. I joined in on their laughter nonetheless, not wanting to ruin a single moment of this perfect night. Jeff topped off the occasion with a toast in front of the entire restaurant in my honor.

"To Pooja, my love, my darling. Happy birthday to the best friend a man could ever wish for."

My birthday gift to myself was inwardly making a simple word substitution in his toast. *To Pooja, my love, my darling. Happy birthday to the best wife a man could ever wish for*.

Another wrinkle in time concluded Alpa's visit just minutes after she arrived. Jeff had vaguely mentioned that he did not get along with his family and decided to spend Christmas with Charles in New Orleans. When he arrived at my apartment to drive us to the airport for our flight to West Virginia, I asked him to join us, stopping just short of offering to pay for the ticket.

"I love your humor. Imagine the look on Charles's face when he finds a note saying I left him for West Virginia."

"He'll understand you left him for me," I exclaimed.

"That would take a *lot* of explaining," Jeff replied.

Alpa and Jeff burst out into laughter, leaving me behind in the dust. Without further mention, the two of them loaded our things into Jeff's car and ushered me inside. The interior felt constraining for the first time.

"Don't be a sour puss about going home. Your parents will be happy to see you," he told me.

I realized he thought me soon seeing Mom was the source of my sudden quietness.

"Besides, I got you a present. Open it on the plane."

Determined to honor his request, I practically pushed everyone who stepped in front of me out of the way to get to my seat.

"What is it?" Alpa asked once we were settled.

I clutched the small gift to my heart, letting its subtle power absorb into my blood stream. Jeff had given me a mini replica of the St. Charles streetcar.

Chapter 55

AFTER TEN DAYS of arguing with Mom about how I needed to make choices that suited my needs instead of Anand's, I returned to New Orleans for my winter class. Basking in the peace of a husband-free apartment, Jeff came over several times for late nights of feisty debating over red wine.

We made plans to go out to our favorite jazz club to ring in the New Year, but Charles came down with a cold at the last minute. He insisted and I quickly agreed to go out without him. Jeff was not convinced and persuaded me to come over to their apartment instead. Though I was highly disappointed, curiosity got the best of me.

"I can't believe this is the first time you've been to our place," Jeff exclaimed.

He bent down to swallow me up in his famous bear hug, which this time was shorter than usual. I was beginning to think all of our affection was getting to be a bit uncomfortable for Charles.

"How do you like the place?" he asked, sounding nervous.

"It's great. Minus that pea-color wallpaper."

"Thank God, that means a lot. What color do you think is better?"

Charles came out in a slow march at the sound of our voices. His normally high-pitched sing-songy voice had been reduced to the sound of something grating against sandpaper. Jeff reached out to rub Charles' shoulders before turning to get him a bowl of chicken noodle soup. I dug into my first glass of the many planned wine tastings for the night.

"How was your Christmas?" Charles scratchily asked.

"Mom spent the entire time screaming at me for not supporting Anand."

"Just because you didn't go to India?"

"And because, 'I'm ruining my life wasting time on English studies.'"

Charles rolled in a fit laughter at my mom imitation, telling me about the heart attack he nearly caused his dad when he declared he was going to be a professional dancer.

"It was almost as bad as when—"

"Here's your soup," Jeff announced, walking in from the kitchen.

We watched as poor Charles managed to get down a few bites before being overtaken by a fit of sneezes. He lumbered back into his bedroom shortly after, leaving Jeff and I alone with more than three hours to count down to midnight.

"Was it really that bad?" Jeff asked me about West Virginia.

"I feel like what I need and what's expected of me is always mutually exclusive."

"I know the feeling, trust me."

Jeff didn't offer many details about his life back in Mississippi, but I knew he was talking about how his parents hated his decision to do a Ph.D. instead of a career that involved hard manual labor. He came from a long line of construction workers. His parents thought a Ph.D. in English was a worthless, lofty pursuit he couldn't afford. We had that in common, though for very different reasons.

"What if you went into medicine or law?" Jeff asked me.

"It doesn't matter. The English degree is just another excuse to criticize. My mother wants me to blindly follow Anand around, regardless."

Jeff pulled me to him, letting my head lay against his chest. The sound of his heartbeat was always so calming. I called it my reflection spot; epiphanies about life always came naturally when I was in that position.

"You said you got in to all the schools you applied to out of high school?" he asked.

"I did."

"What was your application essay about the second time around?"

No one had ever asked me that before. I had shuffled away the tear-ridden words to the back of my brain long ago. Dusting them off and showing them was not something I was sure I wanted to do, even with Jeff.

"It's not important."

"It is to me," he assured.

"It was . . . It was about gender equality."

I had written about Mom and how she was my biggest adversary in me finding equality as a woman. All of Anand's smooth talk about progressive ideas convinced the teenager me to marry him. My passionate essay was about the cultural irony of my mother needing a man to tell her that her daughter should be allowed to be independent.

In four years of marriage, I had never told Anand what I wrote. Despite all of his promises about us having equal roles in our marriage, I had come to realize Anand loathed the idea of having to answer to his wife before making big life decisions.

"I know now Anand hates that."

"But not then?"

"No."

"And you think your mom knew that then?"

"Yes."

"I don't think you should be with Anand."

"*What?*"

Of all the things we advised each other about, relationships were never included. It was out of character for Jeff to be so frank.

"Where did that come from?"

"Oh my God, I shouldn't have said that."

I was more upset he didn't follow with what I wanted to hear. *"You should be with me."*

He tried explaining that the holidays always made him think of his family. "I can't imagine giving up your dreams for someone you don't even love."

"What makes you say that?"

"It's just . . ." His voiced trailed off as his gaze settled in the direction of Charles's bedroom.

I peered up to see he was staring at a clock. For once I had no idea what he was thinking.

"Forget I said anything. Just promise you won't give up on you."

"I promise."

I settled back into my thinking spot. Jeff's heartbeat was a steady reminder I was resting against the person I felt closer to more than anyone else in the world. We fell asleep just moments after watching the hands on the clock make it to midnight.

Chapter 56

"WAKE UP, DUMMY."

"What happened?"

"You fell asleep on the couch."

Jeff gently nudged me to get up. I groaned, complaining that I couldn't move. Satisfied when he swooped down to pick me up, I let him carry me outside to give me a ride home.

"Pooja, I'm really sorry for blurting out you shouldn't be with Anand. I had no right to say that."

"It's okay. We were just—"

"Drunk."

"Exactly."

We managed to laugh off the very serious conversation that could have easily transpired. Despite avoiding the potential debacle, something shifted in that moment. As he drove away, I felt the elasticity of our bond had been compromised, and I lingered with a great apprehension for the final snap that would separate our connection.

Unsure whether it had happened, I stepped inside and nearly fainted when I saw Anand quietly staring at me from across the room.

"What are you doing here? You're not due back for another two weeks."

"You sound disappointed," Anand replied.

"I'm surprised. What are you doing here?" I repeated.

He started pacing violently, shaking his finger, and spewing incoherent sentences in a mix of Telugu and English. All I was able to catch was that he had come back to surprise me with great news, but now he wasn't sure what to do.

"What are you talking about?" I asked.

"Don't give me that. Don't think I don't know."

"Don't know what?"

"Here I was, ready to surprise my wife with the news of great riches."

I immediately knew what he meant. We had spoken so infrequently that I didn't know the details, but the words "great riches" coming from an Indian could only mean he landed a high paying job.

"Anand, congratulations," I said with genuine appreciation.

One thing we did still have in common was our work ethic, and I knew that he deserved the successes he received. My warmth in the response calmed him down enough to speak properly. He was as relieved as I was that this didn't turn into another taxing argument.

"I can't wait to get out of this tiny apartment," he said.

I wholeheartedly agreed. We had been living like paupers for nearly four years.

"I was thinking of getting a place over the bay."

"You mean river?" I called back from the bathroom.

"The starting salary is a hundred and fifty thousand dollars," he continued.

That was an impressive number. I was sure his chest was puffed out like a mountain at the thought of commanding that kind of money.

"Imagine all the things we can buy."

"Another car for sure. I'm surprised the hospitals around here could offer that much."

"They can't."

My heart started to race. I prayed that I had misheard the very possible nightmare instead of the impossible ideal. Anand saw the moment of confusion on my face as the opportunity to clarify what I was most afraid of learning.

"The job is in San Francisco. We're moving at the end of the April."

The words came out in slow motion, each hitting me like a rock against my body. One more stone surely would have killed me.

"I have school."

"Berkeley is accessible by train and they have an architecture school. Besides, I already accepted the offer. We're going to be rich."

In all the ways I had grown since we first met, not being preoccupied with material possessions was the most obvious. His glaring negligence of that fact sent me into tyrannical rage. How dare he use money as an excuse to not consult me?

"I don't fucking care about the money."

He was taken aback by the force of my words, but his combative nature didn't stop to appease my anger. Instead he hurled a series of insults that he had clearly been saving for years. As progressive as he sounded when we first married, I knew he still measured his success in wealth. My apathy about dollars stirred an equal fury in him.

"You're lying, all you care about is money," he accused me.

"Have you even met me?"

"Don't pretend it's not true."

"Don't pretend you know me."

"You think I don't know you? You think I don't know what's going on with you and your fucking David Hasselhoff look alike?"

I wasn't cheating, and the implication that I had sent me further into the maniacal rage. How dare Anand accuse me being unfaithful? Every ounce of my being went to staying loyal, and for what? Four years of marriage and all he thought that mattered was the material possessions.

"It's all you ever talked about when we first met each other," he claimed.

"I was lonely. And is that all you recall about me, your wife?"

"You're just like all the other Indian girls."

"Why did you marry me, Anand?"

"No matter what I do for you, you want more."

"Why did you marry me, Anand?

"I was the one who turned you to architecture—"

"Why did we get married?"

"I came to this disgusting city so you could be happy—"

"Why are we still married?"

"I never say anything about you going out alone."

"Why did you marry me, Anand?" I shouted.

He swayed at the turbulence of my question. He tried finding his orientation by sitting down. His hand was lying limply on the table, his face looked pale.

"Pooja, this is a great opportunity for my career. I will be able to take care of you for the rest of your life."

"Anand, please just answer the question. This is a conversation we should have had a long time ago."

Since the day he had arrived in the States, a part of me wanted him to feel guilty. Finally seeing him in that state didn't bring the satisfaction I had hoped for. This was not the way he thought his announcement of self worth would go. Seeing him so dejected made me feel like a monster.

"I don't know," he finally answered.

A few tears streamed down his cheek. It was a humbling moment for both of us.

"You know I was all set to go to Brooklyn for my residency." I felt like it was yesterday and a lifetime ago at the same time.

"When your parents came to my house, they made sure my parents were also present."

"I didn't know that."

"Marriage in India, it's like, it's like . . ."

"Buying a pair of shoes?"

Anand snorted. I had always been good with analogies . . . It was the product of a boring childhood.

"Yes, like buying a pair of shoes. Those girls in India, they just care about money, caste, status."

"And you didn't?"

"Not like they did. I cared about doing well in school. Money clouds knowledge."

I stopped to let him understand the irony of the words he had just spoken. The moment passed without a conclusion.

"Even though marriage wasn't a priority to me, I knew those girls were out of the question. They just didn't . . . fit. But *you*, Pooja. You grew up here. I thought you would be different than those girls."

"Thanks."

Catching my sarcasm, he assured me he meant it as a compliment. Anand was proud of his accomplishments. He was ready to come to the States on his own and figure everything out alone. His mother, however, was scared for her son. She never said anything positive about him leaving the country. When his father suggested the two of us get married, for the first time, Anand's mother seemed happy about him going to America.

"Do you have any idea how it felt to have my own mother ignore all of my accomplishments in life, only to congratulate me on a marriage proposal?"

The words were expelled with such a deep-seated bitterness that I was not sure who had put them out into the open. I looked into the eyes of the smart, successful, honest man I had married and was appalled to see my own reflection.

I could tell by the way he continued that the morbid discovery was completely one-sided. He started talking about his desires to start a family, to build a distinguished career for his sake and for mine. His success meant my success, he thought. I know he didn't see it the other way around.

"This job is a huge step in my career."

He sounded so mechanical. When I failed to concede, he asked if I would consider staying in New Orleans on my own until I finished school and then join him later.

"Pooja? Do you think that could work?"

I thought about if we had been exactly the same people, only he had been born the female and I the male. Would I have done things differently for Anand if I were the one in control? Would Anand's happiness have factored into my steadfast, tunnel-vision desire to conquer the world and reap the praise of a thousand generations? For Jeff, the answer would have been yes. For Anand, the answer was,

"No."

"What do you mean, no?"

"Do you love me, Anand?"

"What? Of course I—"

"Be honest. Do you love me?"

He paused. We both knew what his silence meant.

"The love will come later. It did for my parents; it did for my sister and her husband. Right now, you need to join me in San Francisco so we can build our future together. Will you do that, Pooja?"

I knew then why he asked the same questions over and over again. I softly stroked his face. The sparkle in those gorgeous Bangalore eyes was dying. I wanted that sparkle to come back, but that sparkle had already cost too much of my life.

Chapter 57

OUR DIVORCE HAPPENED quicker than our marriage. When it became apparent that staying together would mean sacrificing his dream job, Anand stopped begging me to reconsider. Because we split on mutual terms and we had no children, it only took a few months to get the paperwork finalized. Without hesitation, he evenly split everything we had in the bank, and even offered to support me after the divorce. I decided it was time to be my own person and politely declined.

Staying true to his word, Dad did not protest when I told him the news. He demanded no explanation and kept his promise to not question my judgment. I had given the marriage four years of mental exhaustion; Dad understood if I could give no more.

Mom's silence conveyed more disappointment than any words she had ever spoken. To her, Anand held the key to my future, and giving up on my marriage was synonymous to giving up on my life. She had not been captured by Anand for the same reasons as me. She could not understand why I had to let him go.

I decided not to talk to Jeff during the divorce process, knowing that if Jeff were at the front of my thoughts it would seem as though he were the reason I wanted a new life. He wasn't the reason I wanted to divorce Anand. I wanted to divorce Anand because we were not meant to be together. Whether I was meant to be with Jeff was another question altogether.

With the emotional distance that had grown between Anand and me, I did not have to wait long to mentally move on to the next stage. Until I had met Jeff, I had been forced down a path of marriage that left me as a half-human. A few weeks after the divorce went through, I retrieved the shelved bond of friendship with my soul mate. I was so certain Jeff and I would soon walk down our own path of marriage to utopia.

Chapter 58

JEFF STEPPED THROUGH the door of *my* apartment like a dignified prince about to escort his bride into the kingdom of an unknown, yet perfect future. His compliment of me in my dress caused me to curtsy like a townswoman admiring her majesty. He was wearing a sharp pair of pleated khakis and a navy blue polo shirt. His clothes always perfectly framed his strong body. His mind always perfectly framed his strong body.

"What's the occasion?" he asked, eyeing the dinner spread.

I had to chuckle at his attempted nonchalance. We had had coffee breaks that were more glorified than my invitation on the phone for me to have him over. I playfully clinked my glass against his to keep up the charade. I was dying of anxiety inside.

"I was surprised to hear from you. It has been a while," he started, back on the serious path.

I explained the reason he hadn't seen me on campus was because I deferred for the semester. Going back to being single after four years was harder than I had thought. I had to figure out how to operate as an individual person for the first time in my life.

As I described the convoluted process of finding my own footing in New Orleans, I sensed an unusual and unwelcome agitation growing in the atmosphere. Three months apart had clearly put some distance between Jeff and me. In the midst of the complicated silence, I could barely make out the thought bubble floating above Jeff's head.

"I made the right decision," I replied.

"It was the right decision."

"*I* made the right decision," I reiterated.

I told him to take the timing of his New Year's outburst and Anand's announcement as coincidence. Jeff wasn't entirely convinced. I did my best to recapture the feeling of euphoria Jeff had brought into my life so many times in the past year. Rechanneling strength from his cherished birthday toast, I started the speech I had rehearsed a thousand times.

"I wanted to talk to you about something, Jeff."

"Of course. More wine?"

"Sure, thanks. It's about us."

"I'm glad to have you back. Do you want to eat?"

Him changing the subject was not a good sign. But I had come this far. I had finally made the bold choice to divorce a man for whom I felt nothing, despite the inevitable repercussions. Stating my obvious love for Jeff was supposed to be the easy part.

"Okay, let's eat. I love you Jeff."

I had said I love him more times than I could count. Why did he look so frail?

"I love you too, Pooja. You know I do. More salad?"

"I really love you, Jeff."

The leagues of distress in my voice echoed in the clangs of his fork hitting the ornate china plate I had picked out precisely for this occasion. Now my effort at the details sounded an intense harshness through the neglected big picture. I could have stopped. I should have stopped.

"Pooja," he quietly whispered.

"I love you, Jeff," I continued.

"Pooja, stop."

"I'm *in love* with you, Jeff."

"I *know* . . ."

All matters of love were applicable to Jeff. I loved him in every way that was possible and acceptable. His violent emphasis of the word *know* told me that the depths of his love could easily be measured in finite containers. I was too scared to make eye contact; I was afraid my dreams would crumble and bludgeon me to death with the pieces that used to form the basis of my existence.

He got up and walked to my side of the table. He put his warm hand on top of my leg and uttered the words I never thought to dread. "I love you like a sister, Pooja. You just got divorced; you're lonely."

"No, Jeff, I know you feel the same way I do."

He told me that even if we could be together, now was not the time. I had just gotten out of a four-year marriage. I needed some time to be single.

I neglected to hear the conditional form—could.

"So you'll wait for me to be single for a while. Then we can be together, right?"

My newfound assertiveness was not only for Anand. "Answer me, Jeff."

"We can't be together."

"Can't" rung in my ears, threatening to shatter me from inside. "Why don't you want to be with me?"

I could see tears brimming in his eyes. He had the most pained look of regret saturated deep into his face. It cut straight through my soul and burned my heart to ashes.

"Why?" I screamed with all of God's fury.

"Pooja, I thought it was obvious."

"You thought *what* was obvious?"

"You didn't pick up on any of the signs? Our one bedroom apartment, spending Christmas by ourselves—"

"What the fuck are you talking about?"

My shining knight let his sword collapse to the ground, claiming he did not have the power to bring me back to his castle. The muddled incoherent apology finally ended in one sentence I never expected.

"Pooja, Charles is my boyfriend. I'm gay."

Chapter 59

LOSING JEFF WAS harder than losing Anand. A part of me died the day Jeff picked up his keys and walked out of the door forever. Losing Jeff was more than I could handle. I went insane, ransacking my own apartment, throwing dishes, breaking the TV, destroying clothes. I prayed to the Gods I never believed in, prayed to the spirits that had danced in my soul for the feeling of self-destruction to go away.

After a week of drowning in my own misery, I knew that Tulane, the entire city of New Orleans, would forever remind me of the one person I had dared to love. At the end of April, the same week Anand moved without me to San Francisco, Alpa flew down to New Orleans to help me leave the city for good. I couldn't stand to be there anymore.

"DO YOU WANT to come out tonight?" Alpa asked.

I shook my head. It hurt to speak.

"Pooja, just come out for one drink. The bar is very close."

"I don't want to."

"Geez, okay. Let me know if you change your mind."

I didn't bother to respond.

I knew better than to tell Mom the reason why I ultimately left NOLA. Instead, once I gathered my composure well enough to go two minutes without crying, I made up a list of excuses about how Tulane was never a good fit for what I wanted. I claimed I moved there primarily for Anand's benefit. Had Mom known a man other than my husband had played such a central role in my life, the blame that would ensue on the cause of my divorce would last a lifetime. Being reduced to an impulsive child who acted on a little schoolgirl crush would have broken me.

Dad didn't ask for an explanation, nor did he suggest I return to West Virginia. Mom probably forbade him to offer. With nowhere else to go, Alpa offered to let me stay in her dorm. At eighteen, living in a dorm room was a dream. Now it was an absolute nightmare.

Alpa did her best to include me with her adolescent friends. Somewhere in the back cellar of my damaged spirit, I appreciated the gesture. But the realities of being in my mid-twenties weighed down by a lifetime of emotions made even basic conversation taxing. Being around someone even a few years my junior brought a constant reminder of how quickly I was forced to reckon with the battles of adulthood.

"Divorced at her age? What a failure," they all thought.

"How much pain they've yet to endure," I mentally replied.

Alpa's friends were three calendar years and one lifetime younger than me.

"OH MY GOD, are you alright?" Alpa asked me.

I could barely lift my head away from the toilet bowl. Half of the time since I landed in DC had been spent vomiting. I thought I was reacting to the trauma of everything that had happened, as though my emotions needed to be physically purged from my body.

I asked Alpa to run to the local deli and buy me a bottle of lemonade. Before she made it half way to the door, I felt my knees give out and a distant thump of my head hitting the floor. By the time I awoke, I realized I was in a stark white room connected only to other stark white walls. At first I thought I was dead. I hoped it was true.

"Nurse," I heard Alpa scream.

"What happened?" I asked.

"You passed out from dehydration."

"You had quite a fall," the nurse said.

The first sip of water she nudged down my throat felt like glass. It seemed a cruel punishment considering the necessity of the act to gain my strength back. Giving me a few seconds of mercy, the nurse quietly asked Alpa to give us some privacy.

"Am I dying?" I asked.

"Quite the opposite."

"What's the opposite of death?"

"Birth."

By May 1984, I was in my second trimester of pregnancy. The extreme stresses life had recently dealt me ensured that the normal symptoms— weight gain, fatigue, dizziness—had gone entirely unnoticed.

My connection to Anand and our marriage's end was mediocre, unattached, and unemotional. Yet the overwhelming feeling that came over me when the nurse broke the news of my pregnancy was happiness. I knew I might never again fall in love as I had with Jeff, but at that moment, I knew I would never again be alone.

Chapter 60

DAD'S EFFORTS TO acquiesce Mom were immediately dropped after I phoned them with the news. Within a day, he had made arrangements to indefinitely shut down his practice and drove the four hours to DC to personally escort me back to West Virginia.

Somehow, in the chaos of completely reorganizing his life, he convinced Mom to respect my wishes not to tell Anand the news. We slept together so infrequently during our marriage that I had stopped birth control soon after moving to NOLA. One fleeting moment of Anand's sexual desires did not warrant him being brought into the conversation before I had decided what role I wanted him to play.

Dad caught me in the kitchen during one of my long nights of mental planning. Unlike our last chance encounter, he did not try to convince me to listen to his advice.

"Look at what our choices for your life has made happen."

Instead, he assured me that he would financially support me and my baby as best as possible for as long as possible.

"Does Mom know you offered?" I had to ask.

"It doesn't matter, beta. I don't need her permission to help my daughter."

I was relieved at those words. Dad would give me money without Mom attached, and without Anand attached.

Though the practice was shut down, Mom spent all of her time crouched over the office accounting books crunching phantom numbers to avoid having a real conversation with me. Any flicker of hope I had that my pregnancy would bring her closer to her firstborn daughter remained a fantasy.

I PEERED AT my alarm clock and saw it was past midnight. All attempts to fall asleep the past two hours had failed, so I threw my legs over the side of the bed with surprising grace for being in my third trimester. My baby was a good kicker, but my baby was surely small. I wasn't showing much.

Eating whatever I wanted whenever I wanted was a pregnancy luxury I was quick to cash in. After serving myself a huge portion of chocolate ice cream, I settled in the family room to a repeat of *Saturday Night Live*. Billy Crystal was hosting. He was funny sometimes, funny enough for the middle of the night at least.

I put the TV on mute and walked back to the kitchen to replenish my bowl. Behind the buzzing of the freezer, I heard shouting coming from upstairs. Quietly approaching Mom and Dad's room, I made out Mom screaming something in Telugu. Not surprisingly, a few key words told me she was complaining about money. As though she knew I was outside and wanted me to understand what was going on, she switched the conversation to English in the midst of violent paper shaking.

"What about these loans she took out? Who is going to pay back twenty-thousand dollars?"

"I will go back to work after the baby comes."

"That barely covers Alpa's tuition. It will take our life savings to pay off these debts."

"You don't charge a third of our patients."

He said the last part with a distinct undertone of bitterness, a feeling I had long come to recognize. They entered familiar territory of whether Dad's poorest patients should be denied service because they couldn't afford to pay. I had heard the same argument before my stupidly extravagant wedding. At the time, I was rooting for Mom not charging patients in the hopes they would decide against marrying me off. Now I could only sympathize with Dad. I knew how it felt to be underappreciated for hard work.

"You would rather give them free service than support our own daughter."

"You do not understand what it is like to grow up in poverty."

"That's the same reason you have given for every important decision we have ever made."

Mom muttered something in Tamil so Dad wouldn't understand. It was a sure-fire way to know she was angry. I imagined what she was saying. "Now this is all my fault? I am the one who told Pooja to take out loans to pay for an expensive school? I am the one who told her to get pregnant and then divorce the father who is now making a huge salary?"

Dad stammered in the background, trying to find a line of reasoning against the words he couldn't understand coming from Mom's mouth.

"We forced her to get married. This is her child—"

"That she can't afford."

"In her own time, she must decide with Anand what to do with the baby."

"She must go back to Anand, Shankar."

"All we have done so far is tell her what to do. Look where that got us."

Mom's rattled breathing heightened as she started again. I slid to the floor with a revolting sense of awareness. Though delivered in her hallmark insensitive manner, Mom jolted me to the reality that I was young, hadn't finished school, and didn't have a job. Dad's money would only buy me limited time before Mom called for Anand's reinforcement.

Chapter 61

THE NEXT MORNING, I took the car keys from Dad's jacket and went out to buy baby clothes and a crib. I decided that flashing tangible objects in Mom's face would be a more salient way to drive home the point that I was prepared to raise my baby on my own and figure out how to get my life together. I cashed in all the money I had left to my name for the outing—a whopping hundred-and-twenty dollars.

The other car was gone by the time I got back to the house. For the first time in months, I had space to myself, and took advantage of the privacy to map out my argument. I would have gone straight through the day had the phone not rung an hour later.

"Hello?"

"Pooja. It's Mom." Her normally monotone voice sounded alarmed.

"Mom, it's fine, I just went out to get some baby clothes."

"Pooja, come to the hospital now."

"Did you hear me? I went to go get baby clothes. I've decided to raise this child on my own."

I had just sunk two-hundred minutes into planning how to break the news, and I accidentally slipped three seconds into a phone conversation. Mom didn't notice.

"Just come, Pooja."

I expected anger to bubble after such a dismissive reaction, but her tone told me not to question and to simply listen. A nurse directed me to the fourth floor. Dad's shifts of hospital duty immediately came to the forefront of my mind; the fourth floor was the ICU. Completely panicked, I thudded up the stairs to save time, and saw Mom waiting. She was alone.

"Mom."

"Pooja." She ran over to give me a hug, a rare occurrence throughout my entire life.

"Mom, what happened?"

"He had a heart attack."

"What? Is he okay?"

The next five words changed my life forever.

"He died ten minutes ago."

Chapter 62

THE SPOT ON dad's chest that had been bothering him wasn't indigestion; it was a sign of heart problems. Dad suffered a massive heart attack that the doctors could not explain given his diet and lifestyle.

"Our technology is not good enough. There's nothing we could have done."

Alpa called us a few hours later to tell us that a friend was giving her a ride home the next day. Mom's usual emotionless voice cracked throughout the five-minute conversation. That day her tears came down so hard we left the hospital in one car because she couldn't steady herself enough to control the wheel.

Having already lost the one other man who had made a positive impact on my life, losing Dad effectively shut down my brain. I barely registered as I watched Mom, a usual steadfast being, fall apart under the loss of her life partner of twenty-five years. Dad had been with Mom for more than half of her life. Dad knew Mom better than Mom knew herself. With Dad gone, I lost my interpreter to Mom.

Thankfully, just hours after the obituary in the newspaper was distributed, hundreds of Dad's loyal patients rushed to our support. One sweet old woman even came over to do our laundry.

I took the opportunity for a confession. "I don't remember people around here being so nice."

"He was a good man. No one took care of us like your dad did."

"No one took care of me like Dad did."

With all of the help around the house, Alpa and I made arrangements for dad's memorial service. More than seven-hundred people in a town of twenty-five thousand came. My OB/GYN told me it was unsafe to fly at my late stages of pregnancy, so I offered to go to the travel agent and book tickets for Mom and Alpa to take Dad's ashes back to India.

Mom refused, speaking her first words in days. "This country was his home. He would want to rest here."

In the summer of 1984, Mom, Alpa, and I drove to the heart of the Appalachian Mountains and spread Dad's ashes in a tiny creek overlooking one of the largest valleys in West Virginia that went just beyond the reach of society. The serenity of the mountains was a perfect representation of the calm, solid, soothing person Dad was.

Staring out into the abyss of the mountain range, I knew that the pain I had suffered during the course of my pregnancy would take years to truly sort out. A tiny creek carried the remnants of my father away from me, and I prayed, as I am sure he had done for me. I prayed that my baby would have a better life than I had. In a final bid to the strongest man I ever knew, I closed my eyes tight and whispered the words I should have told him when I had the chance.

"Your belief in me will make me a better mother."

Chapter 63

I TRIPLE CHECKED the number before turning the phone dial to the last digit. He answered on the third ring.

"Hello?"

"It's me."

"Pooja. I'm so sorry about your father. Are you okay?"

"Yes . . . I will be. I miss him so much."

He could not empathize. His father was not a good man. "I miss you, Pooja."

"I need you to come here, to my parents' place. We have to talk."

"I'll be on the first flight."

He was there within eight hours.

I stepped back to let him inside. A bottle of wine he brought as a token of appreciation made a hollow clang as it found its resting place on the table. Thinking the visitor was another patient who had come to pay respects, Alpa walked over to say thanks.

"Anand. What are you doing here?"

"It's okay, Alpa," I told her.

Anand held up the wine bottle, suggesting we talk over drinks. He sounded so unnatural, speaking of anything recreational.

"I brought some wine. I know you love red wine."

"It's all for you," I replied.

"Not drinking?"

"I can't."

He thought it was out of caution for Dad passing. Being Indian, he was accustomed to clandestine alcohol to deal with emotions.

"I'm so sorry, Pooja. Shankar was a better father than I ever had."

He was genuine in those words. Dad's elation in me marrying the boy next door was mutual with the boy next door.

"Anand, I need to talk to you."

"I still want to make this work."

"It will work in a different way. I'm pregnant."

The glass in his hand soared out, splattering blood-colored spots over the patchy carpet that outlined the room.

"Is it mine?"

"Yes. I'm positive."

"I can't even tell."

"I haven't gained much weight."

Before he misinterpreted the situation as a concession to annul the divorce, I made it clear I wanted him only as a part of my baby's life. The look of defeat was unmistakable; a part of me had realized in our time apart that he had begun to love me, despite our conversations. But having this child together didn't mean that we were meant to be together.

"I don't want to be your wife as much for your sake as for mine."

"I don't understand."

"It doesn't matter if you do."

He told me he needed me to know he was truly sorry. His first years in America had been really lonely, and he felt more lost than ever after the divorce. He came to this country to build a life, and to have a family.

"Please know that I will do everything I can to support him."

"Or her."

"Or her. Having a child means more than anything else to me in the world."

We had that in common. Though Anand had not made me happy, with this baby he had given me happiness. I knew that I would give my baby the love I had never had. And I knew he would give her the money he had intended to use to buy my love.

Chapter 64

MY DAUGHTER, DEEPA, was born on September 3, 1984. At just over seven pounds, she was the smallest, fully gestated baby the hospital had seen all year. Jeff was the first person who could send a shiver straight to my heart. Deepa was the second.

Though the kindness of West Virginia after Dad's death was unprecedented, the kindness was not enough to equalize the lack of opportunity of the area. I wanted my Deepa to have the world at her fingertips. Less than a year after Dad's death, Mom and I packed up our lukewarm lives and bought a house just outside of DC to be close to Alpa.

Deepa quickly became my guiding light in the aftermath of chaos that had wrecked everything good in my life. Together, we explored every interest that struck her fancy, steadily decorating her room and turning our new house into what I knew Deepa most needed—a home. My hesitation in facing the world outside of the comforts of our brick walls, fireplace, and kitchen felt inconsequential when I held Deepa's hand in my own.

My personal situation continued to grate on my confidence as Deepa hit her teenage years, and I made it a point to disengage from other parents in her class whenever possible. I was the mother of the constant model student of the neighborhood, however, and could only dodge so much of the other parents' endless bickering. From their complaints, I knew it was "normal" to be at odds with one's own child once they hit the age of thirteen. Deepa and I never suffered through such a period. Our connection had only grown.

One rainy day in March when Deepa was fifteen, she bounced through our front door, waving a wet piece of paper.

"Mom. Look at what I got today."

"What is it?"

"They want you to come to the school early next week."

I read the paper she had brought home and felt an instant jolt of shock and admiration. After a few meetings with Deepa's school counselors, I had agreed to let my incredible daughter follow in the footsteps of my sister. Deepa would skip the tenth grade and go straight to being a high school junior. Deepa was going to be so successful. Deepa and I would have one less year together.

MOM, ALPA, AND I stood on the sidewalk at the southwest corner of Washington Square Park in New York City. I turned to my mother and sister and asked they give me a few minutes alone with my daughter. Time had once again wrinkled to bring me to my last few protected moments with Deepa.

"You be good, you be safe, you be kind, you be—"

"Me," Deepa finished.

"Always."

I wrapped her in a tight hug and told her to hurry home the moment she had a reprieve from her first semester of college. My job the last seventeen years had been to make Deepa's environment as open and supportive as I had wished for myself growing up. I knew then while holding my daughter that she had returned the effort. I was so scared to let her, to let that, go.

"Mom, I'll be okay. We'll see each other soon."

"It won't be the same."

"Maybe that's the point."

I rubbed my eyes, debating whether to bid her off in one final piece of guidance. As a mother, it was my duty to ensure she made the right choices, and that she grew into a moral, upstanding version of the person she was. She gave me one last hug and I saw her flash a smile brimmed with tears.

Before I had made my decision, she turned and slowly walked up the stairs to the building of her dorm room. I knew it took every bit of her courage to not declare defeat and run straight back to my arms. The window of opportunity to impart my advice passed. Instead, I whispered the same words I had said the first time I had held her, praying the thought would lead her to the correct decisions.

"You are my angel, Deepa. I will always respect your choices, your thoughts, and your opinions. I will never make you get married before you are ready, before you have found the right man."

Part III

Deepa

Chapter 65

THE THICKET OF swaying drones that populated the bar were closing in on me. I tried to refocus my thoughts on the girl I was convinced needed to hear an explanation of the trait we had in common.

"That's one theory why some people are born gay," I shouted.

"Okay. Hey, I gotta go," she replied.

Unmoved by the incredible information I had just offered, she trotted away in a skipping gallop that accentuated the extra baggage hanging over her overly stylized Japanese jeans. Her muffin top that bounced over the strained material mirrored my reverberating brain. How had brands so successfully passed a cut of fabric clearly meant for a meatless East Asian body off to fat Americans tourists that fainted at the sight vegetables? *"Can it at least be deep fried?"*

I trembled with both excitement and fear at the power of persuasion from such a thought. A quick glance around confirmed my suspicion that the reason I had been dragged out to this miserable club was not within earshot to hear my new revelation. I spotted Gloria through the barrage of social media statuses bragging about "an awesome night in New York City." Very few people who came out were actually concerned with having an awesome night.

"There you are. I thought you left," she said.

"I came to get a drink."

Gloria narrowed her eyes—I could tell she was trying to figure out how many "a drink" I had had so far. From previous experience, I knew it was straightforward calculation that factored in the hours by the bar and how closely my face resembled a French bulldog. I hated this examination.

"You were talking about your little stress theory, weren't you?" she asked.

"How did you know?"

"You always look stressed afterwards. Come on, dance with me."

Gloria pulled me to the center of the dance floor and swayed in exaggerated movements to the thumping reggaethon music. She was doing it in mockery of the scantily clad women in the accompanying music videos, but I knew she was also contorting her body that way because her moves really did turn me on. It was an odd position to be in as a feminist.

The "Happy New Year 2008!" sign behind Gloria was distracting. I always had to stop and think about whether those kinds of signs were referring to the year about to end or the year about to begin. The sign really should have had a line of explanation at the bottom.

"Hey, I'm down here," Gloria shouted.

"Sorry, I was just thinking."

"What's wrong with you tonight?"

Gloria said that line so often it implied that something being wrong with me was the norm, not the exception. I hadn't replied to that question in over a year.

A woman across the bar stared me down with daggers in her eyes. She had approached me during "Happy New Year 2007" with an aggravating sense of entitlement.

"How about a kiss?"

"Sorry, do I know you?"

"No, but I'm Indian, you're Indian . . ."

I told her to shoo. She told me to fuck off. Before I could perfectly formulate my rebuttal—there are more than one billion Indians in the world; we all can't be expected to live out one another's fantasies—Gloria grabbed hold of my shirt in final countdown excitement.

"Five. Four. Three. Two. One. Happy New Year!" everyone cheered.

Gloria jumped into my arms, blocking my angry Indian counterpart from view. The five "a drink" I had had made the catch a near fall.

"Happy New Year, baby," Gloria whisper shouted in my ear.

"Jesus, it's 2008."

"You're supposed to say Happy New Year, back."

"I'm going to take off."

Gloria stomped her foot three times before brushing aside a stray lock of my hair. Then she complained about how "it would be no fun without me," all in the hopes I would stay and she could complain about how it was no fun with me. Her usual whining ritual was exhausting.

"Everybody acts like an idiot at lesbian bars on New Years," I countered.

"That's every bar, ever."

"Which is why I wanted to stay in."

"Fine. I'm coming," she said in an exasperated tone.

I had never understood why my concessions to go home for the night so often resulted in her need to accompany me. I had no desire of the sort.

"No, stay."

My futile effort was drowned out by the blasting music. She had taken three hours to apply makeup and pick out a pair of shoes, yet Gloria's speed in cutting through club traffic was unparalleled. I gave the poor soul manning the coat check my last two dollars. Gloria looked at my wallet and dramatically sighed—it was a reaction she had conditioned soon after we first started dating. Personally, I didn't see any problems with its bright red *Snoopy* aesthetic. It was my thing.

Gloria took my cold-induced shivers as a cue to cuddle-walk. I wasn't in the mood to be touched and shirked away at her advances.

"What's wrong with you tonight? Thinking about your dad?"

She could read me like a book.

"No," I lied.

"Then what is it? Your bitter bitch of a mom?"

"Watch it. My mother is a good person."

Gloria's father claimed he was one-thirty-second Native American and found the whole tradition of the American Thanksgiving "utterly despicable." Out of pity, rather than forcing her to hear his stupid manifesto again, I had made the tragic mistake of letting Gloria come down with me to Maryland for the holiday. I explained to Mom and Avva that Gloria was my cool Dominican friend.

I thought with adequate preparation, Gloria could get along with Mom. For days, we studied the nuts and bolts of Mom's inner thinking: from the pauses, the sighs, and the hand waves, to the deep yearnings. Gloria was an excellent student and a thorough note taker who mastered several case studies. Even so, a lifetime of sarcastic remarks could not be tamed for a straight seventy-two hours.

"Gloria, that is quite a short skirt you have on for the dinner table," Mom remarked the last evening.

"Sorry, Ms. Deva. Would it be better if I changed?"

"The damage is done. Too bad life does not come with a CTRL+Z command."

"Buy a Mac."

Mom immediately placed Gloria on the top of her block list. I estimated the statute of expiration was two-hundred years.

"So what's wrong?" Gloria asked again.

"Nothing. I just think it's interesting that—"

"That studies have suggested excessive stress during pregnancy can lead to a hormonal shift causing the unborn fetus to mature into a person of a minority sexual orientation. You've said that a hundred times."

"It's worth repeating."

Had it not been the opening credits to Gloria's favorite show—*As Deepa Turns*—I would have been very welcoming toward our current physical distance.

"You have a problem with homosexuality," she said.

"That's ridiculous. I work for an organization that advocates LGBTQ rights."

"I'm not saying you have a problem with gay people. You have a problem with being gay yourself."

"You're being a bitch."

"Baby, I call it like I see it."

She ended all hurtful exchanges with that line, as though her brutal honesty was like declaring an Italian shirt on a customs card. It should not have been allowed just because it was publicly stated.

We stopped in front of the Christopher Street 1 train stop. Centered perfectly such that no one could descend into the station, a young couple was making out like they had mere hours to live. Across the street was an Original Sal's Pizza. I lived three blocks from another one. So did Gloria.

"You go ahead. I'm gonna get a slice and head home."

"Why the fuck did I leave the club?"

"I told you to stay."

Not giving Gloria the time to let the conversation devolve into another unnecessary argument, I popped the collar of my pea coat and dug my hands deep into my pockets. I silently screamed at myself for forgetting gloves on such a miserably cold night. As I ran across the street, I heard Gloria commence her anger ritual—four stomps of the left foot, right hand on hip, and a long string of Spanish curse words she claimed doubled as a list of my inadequacies. I spoke French, not Spanish.

"That your girl?" the guy behind the counter asked.

"Indeed. One pepperoni, please."

"She's hot."

"And smart."

"And crazy?" he asked.

He hit the nail on the head. Anyone who had ever dated in New York knew that of the three—hot, intelligent, sane—only two were possible in a potential partner. Partials existed, though an unequivocal whole in all three did not. Whenever one of my friends thought they had found the exception, inevitably, news of an impending federal indictment or evidence of a psychotic break would soon surface.

I stole a quick glance out of the window and saw that Gloria had entered her post-ritual phase of unabated waiting. A slight flicker of guilt crossed my thoughts for watching her suffer through the bitter chill, though I knew she would concede quickly. The low that night was ten degrees. Even her heart froze below twenty-five.

"That'll be three-seventy-five."

"You take cards? I'm out of cash."

"Minimum is fifteen dollars. ATM is across the street."

The cashier followed my gaze straight to my darling girlfriend and her instinct to kill. All that separated me from doom was Gloria's undying sense of pride, which kept her from following me inside the restaurant.

"It's on the house," the cashier said.

"Thanks, man, you saved me."

"No worries. Happy New Year."

"Happy New Year, back."

My normal method of pizza eating consisted of stuffing the slice down my gullet in the fewest possible bites. I knew that night would not break any records. I instead meticulously sprinkled each of the condiments, selected precisely three napkins, and examined each table before making my seating selection. In the midst of my fourth tiny nibble, Gloria finally forfeited.

"Puta," she shouted as she stormed off.

I waited a few minutes to confirm the rattling train underground safely contained her person. On my way to the F train, I passed the usual assortment of New York New Year-ers—the grad school student who was devastated because she thought she'd be married by then, the middle aged guy who realized his life had no meaning, the drunken frat boy having anonymous gay sex by the dumpster, and the angry suburbanites who finally understood that five-hundred dollars in the City on that night only bought a tiny corner table in an overrated bar.

"Hey, Deepa, back already?" Julie said.

"Yeah, it's miserable outside."

"Oh no. I'm about to go to a party."

If Julie was prepared to wander into the frozen abyss, the apartment must have been nice and warm. My disappointment at a squandered cozy night in was obvious, and it took Julie all of ten seconds to realize Gloria and I had gotten into another fight.

"Gloria is not good for you, Deepa."

"Gloria gets me."

"You think Gloria is attractive."

I could not deny that fact. Fortunately, Julie chose New Year's sympathy over her typical life lecture.

"Hey. You never read me the piece you want to submit to the paper for the anonymous contributor column."

I realized I must have looked suicidal. Julie abhorred my writing, but I was not above capitalizing on the moment. After pulling out my prized essay, I launched into my best narration voice.

> One of the most common questions we queers get is, 'So when did you know you were gay?' My answer: Birth. I knew I was gay before I knew what gay was. When I was eight, I went to

my first sleepover. My friend told everyone to close their eyes and think of the guy in our class they thought was the cutest. Truth be told, I thought red-haired Amy, who sat two rows up from me, who loved butterflies and wanted to sing in her church choir was the cutest person I'd ever seen. As the girls at the sleepover began to name the boys, I realized that perhaps thinking of another girl isn't so normal. As I grew older, I learned to fill my life with made-up crushes, fake fantasies, and the pronoun game. "Yes, I have a crush on *someone*, but I'm not telling you who *it* is."

Somewhere in between that first realization of "abnormality" and the pronoun game came a moment of self-realization, which presented itself in the form of an article about the movie remake of *The Brady Bunch*. (I'm sure Robert Reed would have endorsed a gay equality episode in the original series.)

My mother gave me the article, only half-glancing at its contents before cutting it out. Apparently in the first version of the script, Marsha is way too receptive of her best friend, Maureen, who is clearly in love with Marsha. In the first version, Marsha seemed like a *lesbian*. "What's a lesbian?" I shouted to my mom. "What?" "They said Marsha seemed like a lesbian." "Uhhhh . . . A lesbian is someone *who doesn't like men*."

Wholly unsatisfied with my mom's vague definition, I finally thanked the world for being an Indian nerd with a giant dictionary. I flipped to the correct page as my mom nervously called out she didn't want me to know that word at such a young age. "Lesbian" was on page 317. It read: "lesbian, *n.*—of or relating to sexual relationships between two females or female homosexuality."

I almost fainted. There's a *word* for this. I must not be the only one. Judging by my mother's reaction, I could tell she was not fond of the word or the persuasion, so I kept quiet. Two weeks later, I turned twelve.

Julie twiddled her thumbs with such fervor you'd have thought the motion held the earth in orbit to the sun.

"What do you think?"

"It's . . ." she trailed.

I reminded myself to take Julie off of my list of people to call in case I needed someone to talk me out of jumping off a bridge.

"It's what?" I prompted.

"Distant. You need to make it more personal."

"It's just supposed to be a light piece."

"Deepa, if you want to get an article published about something as common as being gay, you have to be more exposed."

She emphasized the word *common*. Being gay was too common. I did my best to hide my disappointment to her reaction, though I could tell by her body language she had just witnessed my mood tumble from bad to worse. All she offered in consolation was a kiss on the cheek and pat on the shoulder before she left me alone in our apartment.

"Happy New Year, back," I said to myself.

Chapter 66

EVEN WHEN I didn't feel particularly social, I was still a slave to an electronic technology-laden daily regime. The last thing I did before going to bed that night was to check my phone, yet somehow I had six missed calls by the time I woke up the next morning. Three were from Mom and three were from Gloria. Mom probably thought I was dead and Gloria probably thought I went home with someone else.

Gloria's last attempt at communication was a text message.

Brunch at 12? Same place as usual?

I knew by the amount of time I spent staring at the phone that I didn't want to see her. Our relationship had been one long compromise, however, so I answered with a message that would simultaneously comply with her wishes and piss her off.

Ok.

She hated those replies.

"Can't you vary the damn message? How about an 'I gotcha,' or a 'Great, that sounds good.'"

Mom made her fourth phone call appearance soon after I stepped out of my building.

"Hi, Mom, Happy New Year."

"What happened?"

I let her start off our first conversation of the year with a scolding on my "poor communication." Reading between criticisms, I took this to mean she did not have a good night.

After ten years, the neighbors had finally found the courage to invite her over for their annual celebration. Mom had accepted and promptly used the rest of the week to complain about commitments. She cancelled on them at eight on New Year's Eve.

"Grace was being childish," Mom said of the neighbor.

"Childish how?"

"She wanted to go dancing. Deepa?"

"Still here."

Judging from Mom's pattern of breathing, the time of year, and the emphasis on my name (dee-PAH), I detected the ensuing pause was of the second persuasion. "Ask me about what I am doing." This pause was one of the earliest varieties–originating in the mid-nineties and second only to pause of the first persuasion. "I want to talk about how your father ruined my life."

I first spotted pause of a second persuasion after Mom took up a hobby of a rather bizarre nature. She would sigh and mutter, drop newspaper articles, and leave the TV running to showcase subject matter of relevance. Her methods were entirely to draw me into her latest obsession.

1995: "I simply do not understand why you are not as passionate about saving the manatees as I am, Deepa."

2000: "I simply do not understand why you are not as passionate as getting Dr. Brown elected as city comptroller, Deepa."

2005: "I simply do not understand why you are not as passionate about scrapbooking as I am, Deepa."

Mom was almost at her fifteenth breath of this pause of a second persuasion. I interjected before we passed into dangerous territory that no one should ever enter.

"How is your Foucault book club going?" I gingerly asked.

"Terrible. They're all Neanderthals reading like he's from the Stone Age."

I had no idea what that meant. Mom had a tendency to express her discontents with life in seemingly random combinations of words. I knew this conversation could last indefinitely if I left Mom continue unabated.

"I gotta go. Say hi to Avva for me. Love you."

"You know, Deepa, you really don't give me enough time to express my thoughts . . ."

I hung up before Mom finished. Gloria was a few paces ahead of me, and I saw she had just flipped on the X-ray eyes she used to inspect the contents of my brain.

"Was that your Mom?" Gloria asked.

"It was my grandmother."

"Bullshit."

Gloria's instinct was too strong for my feeble lie. Over Thanksgiving, Mom had told me at least ten times in front of Gloria to give her time to express to her thoughts. Mom thought she was being assertive. Gloria thought Mom was being immature.

Whatever chord Mom struck in Gloria's nerves had not quelled in the six weeks since. Gloria used any trigger as an excuse to list out her top grievances.

"Your mom is codependent, has low self-esteem, is homophobic—"

"My mom is not homophobic."

"Then why haven't you come out to her?"

We had this conversation so often that my points were already numbered. The Indian community had not yet embraced the idea of homosexuality–it was not an easy concept for South Asians to understand.

"Like it's easy for *any* community. You think my Dominican parents were happy to hear their precious little girl dates other precious little girls?"

"At least Dominicans *talk* about sexuality."

I had learned from my own family history that marriage in Indian society wasn't predicated on love or attraction. Mom never failed to mention that a woman's feelings for her future husband were not a primary consideration in the world of arranged marriages. Ironically, it was this absence of martial love in Mom's past that made it so difficult for me to explain what it meant for me to want to build a life with another woman.

Gloria had the enraging habit of mistaking this impasse in understanding for homophobia.

"Your excuses for that woman are eating you alive," Gloria shouted in conclusion.

The five vodka sodas from last night were beating a hole in my head. I knew this would be followed by cannons shooting in my stomach, and a round of grenades detonating in undisclosed locations. My ideal surrender flat was a toilet. I found out the previous year that Gloria was a double agent for the enemy.

"This was a bad idea. I'm leaving," I told her.

"Fine, run away."

"That's affirmative."

Chapter 67

THE NEW YORK City landscape the first day back to work after New Year's was always filled with emotionally conflicted people. I was no exception. As I pushed my way from the subway platform onto the street, I saw seas of faces that reflected my own internal debate—was this concrete jungle of endless possibilities really worth another year of grime-covered insults?

On one hand, we New Yorkers reflected on our holiday trip back to the respective corner of the world we once called home. Most of us quickly realized that the nostalgia we had built up over the course of an endless December was largely fabricated. Every year, a mass of New Yorkers returned to the City after a week of reminders that it was impossible to function outside of the five boroughs (if you counted Staten Island). My situation was a perfect example. Where else but New York City could a gay Indian-American woman with a penchant for German pop music and a divorced arranged-marriage mother be so easily accepted?

Yet every year, the first walk back to work was met with an annoyance that only New York City could produce. My challenge came in the form of Brian—part best friend, part sadistic cat. I barely made it out of the elevator before he pounced on his favorite awkward conversation.

"Deepa. Thinking about your dad abandoning you? How was your mother's annual horrid phone ca—"

"Hey, Brian," I said to cut him off.

Brian stared at me as though I were about to combust. "Your dad?"

"What about your dad?" some guy asked.

Judging by his standard college white guy uniform of khaki pants, a light blue dress shirt, brown loafers, and a tan belt, I could tell the person who had wandered into Brian and my conversation was a new intern. He introduced himself as Garrett.

"What about your dad?" Garrett asked again.

"He moved to an ashram in India three years ago," Brian clarified.

"What's an ashram?"

Garrett had a distinct aura of Ben Stein. I could only laugh at how slowly he spoke. Unable to subdue my expression of pity, Garrett shifted uneasily before lumbering off.

"Deepa's dad left after she told him she's gay," Brian called after him.

Brian let his eyes wander to Garrett's ass. I sighed with an air of grievance as to how 2008 had started.

"Did your mom call for her usual pity party?" Brian asked.

Brian was the president of the Pooja Deva-haters club; not even Gloria could take his reign. In fact, it was Brian who fed Gloria's choice answer to my stock defense of Mom.

"She's a good mother."

"Just a highly temperamental person."

Our freshman year of college, Brian had just escaped the gay detention center of Kansas, and made no concessions in unleashing the suppressed effeminate in full force. I hadn't yet solidified the syllabus for my crash course on Mom. He greeted her for the first time, wearing an ensemble of short shorts, a pin-striped shirt, and a beret. Mom commented on Brian's "howler monkey" voice and choice of clothing ever since.

By now, Brian knew his complaints about Mom would not be addressed. His effeminate ways did not die after graduation. I turned to leave, and Brian waved me off with a cat claw and an order he had given me every day the past three years. "Transfer to the LGBTQ division. Fight the straight power."

Working at The Justice Coalition, I had grown accustom to the litany of non-profit trademarks that decorated the office—overworked staff, squeaky orange felt chairs, a carpet that had been last replaced the year I was born, and of course, paper-covered faux wood desks. I looked up and saw a sign above the entrance to our division unit doors that did not fit in with the rest of the jaded atmosphere.

"Welcome back, fighters of immigration justice!"

Out on the street, The Justice Coalition staffers were a socially aware, often extreme, progressive contingent fighting for people who could not fight for themselves. The opposition, the pressure, and the backlash were equally frustrating as they were motivating. In the office, however, we were all more or less of the same opinions and spent our time fighting over details that would never become part of the real mainstream dialogue. Our drive was thus killed soon after joining. The uncharacteristically emphatic sign hanging over our division's entrance was not put up by a veteran staffer.

"Hello," someone said behind me.

She introduced herself as Carrie, the new junior associate for the Immigration Division, and very obviously the source of the sign.

"Hi, I'm Deepa, one of the senior associate researchers."

"Great to meet you. Barbara told me I'll be reporting to you."

"How long are you here?"

"Six months to start."

Barbara was a great boss and the reason I continued to trudge through the monotony of The Justice Coalition. The one thing I couldn't stand about her supervision style was her tendency to hire new junior associates and list me as the immediate supervisor without first consulting me. Four times last year, I found myself responsible for writing recommendations, giving professional advice, and delegating assignments. It added to the monotony of my work without paying any real returns.

"I didn't sign up to be a career counselor. I signed up to be a researcher," I muttered to myself.

I asked Carrie to edit a lengthy background guide and a few memos I had written on a series of illegal deportation cases in Florida. Our neo-conservative president did not bode well for the many Hispanic immigrants simply trying to better their lives. Carrie seemed content with the assignment even though I knew it was garbage.

After a day of sorting through e-mails, I heard the same voice pipe up, this time timidly in the background.

"It's time for me to go. Thanks for your help, Deepa."

Carrie thanked me in such a way that I immediately realized how frugal I was already being with my time. This city did that to you. Not needing to contribute to the problem of destroyed enthusiasm, I asked her to stay back for a few minutes and give me a summary of what she was interested in doing while here. Within minutes, I had a detailed, well-organized list of actual topics and cases. To my pleasant surprise, I could tell I finally had a junior associate who would be an asset to my life.

I GLANCED DOWN at my watched and saw it was nearly seven. We were supposed to meet at six-thirty. The hostess had refused to seat me at a table in the nearly empty restaurant, which I knew was a tactic to drum up sales at the bar. It worked.

"Another vodka soda," I told the bartender.

"Make that two," I heard her say.

"Hi, Pinni."

"Please, call me Aunt Alpa."

She had been using that as a running joke ever since we figured out fifteen years earlier that the only two Telugu words I ever said were "avva" and "pinni." Somehow "mom" made it through the list of familial references I employed.

Pinni had on her usual corporate boss regalia. That night's ensemble featured three-inch stilettos, a perfectly tailored light gray suit, and a black dress shirt that likely cost more than my entire outfit. The hostess immediately noticed Pinni standing table-less at the bar, and apologized profusely for not seating her earlier. I guessed delay tactic was reserved for the less affluent-looking clientele of the restaurant. Pinni was worth much more in command of a menu.

"How was your New Year's?" I asked.

"Great. We had the nanny watch the kids so we could go to a party."

"Where?"

"Just a few blocks down from us on 8th Ave."

Pinni and her husband, Amir's, current enormous loft was located in Chelsea. They decided to upgrade from Brooklyn Heights after selling their second start-up for an ungodly profit. Normally I found such grandiose lifestyles a total turnoff, though Pinni and Amir had given so much of their wealth to the less fortunate that I knew they would leave the world a better place.

"How many college funds have you guys set up so far?" I asked.

"As of last count, more than two-hundred full rides to residents of West Virginia and Iran."

Both Pinni and Amir were determined to focus their payments forward to the children of their respective homelands. When Pinni announced the first set of scholarships, the local West Virginia newspapers answered her generosity with a media craze. One article featured the plaque in a high school computer lab she set up. A close-up photo detailed her dedication quote:

"Through the depths of time, education remains the portal to my success."

Mom hated that plaque. "My God, did Alpa's education fail to teach her time does not have depth?"

Pinni reached into her bag and pulled out her credit card. I saw a stack of her expensive, embossed business cards underneath. She told the waiter to keep the drinks and food flowing on her tab. After selling the start-up, she tried the stay-at-home mom thing for all of five minutes, but quickly took a Senior Managing Director position at McKinsey. Amir, on the other hand, loved being at home with the kids.

"And how was your New Year's?" she followed.

"Stressful."

"Gloria is not good for you, Deepa."

Her assertion was not unfounded. Every time I had seen Pinni in the past two years was either just after or just before an argument with Gloria. What could I say? I found it was hard to find someone through the dating chaos of New York City. Crazy was better than boring.

"Wait until marriage to be in the midst of a constant battle," Pinni offered with a wink.

"Except it's not allowed."

"It doesn't matter if it's not legal."

Though Pinni fully supported the idea of marriage equality, my determination in its necessity was not met with equal passion on her end. She and Amir were afforded all legal benefits and privileges when they were married. Pinni did not understand the prospect of not being able to visit Amir in the hospital past visiting hours if he got sick. She didn't have to adopt her own child, or mark "single" on her work HR forms. I faced that prospect; every queer person faced that prospect. Of course the law mattered.

"How's the rest of life going?" I asked to change the subject.

"A special gift from God."

Pinni picked up that expression from Avva. I felt its profound nature was too pronounced for me, though Pinni insisted our family had amassed enough good fortune to use it without hesitation.

"How is Pooja?" Pinni asked.

"Mom is mom."

"Is her new book club going well?"

"Yep."

I lied about Mom at least once per conversation. As a topic of discussion, anything related to my parents usually died quickly. They represented subjects that were either superficial or too mentally consuming–there was no in between.

Two hours and a mountain of food and drink later, Pinni and I stood up to say our goodbyes. I made my usual half-hearted attempt to pay for any portion of our meal. Pinni simply smiled before assuring me there would never be that expectation.

"There are plenty of years to make piles of meaningless money," she said.

Chapter 68

GLORIA CALLED ME the next afternoon. Her apology consisted of a standard set of sound bytes, though I could tell by the tone that she did genuinely believe what she was saying. I agreed to meet her over the weekend, insisting we go to a new performance art-inspired exhibit in SoHo. I knew it would be best to meet in broad, public daylight where the sympathetic queers abounded.

Gloria's genuine apologetic tone disappeared by the time we saw each other at the show.

"So nice of you to drag me out in this cold."

Somehow she was allowed to force me out in the insanity of New Year's Eve, but I was chastised for wanting to leave my apartment on a sunny Saturday afternoon. I used my own passive-aggressive skills to remind her art galleries are typically indoors.

"You couldn't have waited inside?"

"I'm not going in alone with those eightiess-era heroine addicts," she replied.

"It's a performance art-*inspired* exhibit. They're *nineties*-era heroine addicts."

My quip softened the mood, and she threw her head back in a slight laugh. The position of her head made me imagine her as a life-sized *Pez* candy dispenser. I think she would have been strawberry flavored. I was allergic to strawberries.

We walked into the room and saw that as with most SoHo exhibits, the one before our eyes had been set up in a half-intentional, half-neglectful way. The entire scene made a desperate attempt to straddle the lines of chic and shit.

"I love the raw emotion the asymmetry of this piece captures," someone observed.

Gloria leaned in to whisper, "Honey, that isn't the product of raw emotion. That's the product of a stroke."

I laughed a little too loudly. Thirty people in tight black shirts and gaudy Italian-framed glasses turned and glared. I knew it meant our twenty-dollar entrance covers would be blown, but we couldn't pass up the opportunity to mock this ridiculous scene of pretentiousness. I rolled my eyes, looked at my watch, and brought my gaze to a completely empty corner.

"The cultural dynamism of warfare is so eloquently captured," I mocked.

"Thisss is thSoHo aaart. Thhhiisss is a thsseerious placthe of bussinnesstth," she spat with false purpose.

My snort reaction was so loud, it echoed through the entire gallery. Before the walking stereotypes had the satisfaction of kicking us out, we excused ourselves from the gallery in hysterics.

"Oh baby, when we're good, we're terrible," Gloria said.

"Indeed," we said at the same time.

"So we're okay?" she asked.

I wasn't sure whether a joint heckling session was enough to sooth our constant bickering.

"Sure," I finally decided.

"I know this time of year is hard for you. I didn't make it easier."

An acknowledgement of the fact was the closest she would come to an actual apology. I managed to at least wrangle a free brunch from her in exchange for last time. Our usual spot was just a quick train ride away.

We were seated almost immediately. The unforgiving cold must have been keeping the City inside.

"Yet here we are," Gloria said.

I let the comment slide. Another round of passive-aggressiveness would not sit well on an empty stomach.

"I don't know why you dragged me out today," she followed.

I continued to sit in silence.

"Only a masochist would want to go out in this weather."

Everything was so difficult with this woman.

"Why do you like me? You complain seventy-five percent of the time we're together," I finally replied.

"Because the other twenty-five percent of the time is fucking fantastic sex."

"Geez. Keep it down, Gloria."

"This is New York City. Lesbians are allowed to say the word sex."

Fortunately, a very well-timed waiter appeared. He asked for our drink orders, and I responded in automatic pilot. Gloria always had an apple juice and coffee. My drink of choice was a Bloody Mary with extra Tabasco.

Gloria caught my gaze as he walked away. "*This* is why I like you."

"Because I remember your drink order?"

The first girl I had ever dated told me she like me because of a weird hair growth pattern on my head. Until now, that was the worst explanation for why someone wanted to date me. Fortunately, Gloria used her X-Ray eyes and saw my brain wanted further reasoning.

"You're a good listener, you're kind, you're smart. All of that."

"There are a ton of people who are all of that in this city."

"True. But you're one of the most unique."

I had my doubts. Already, I had established there were more than one-billion Indians on the planet, and Julie said that being gay was too common in New York. Ergo, I was a common subset of a common population.

"What do you like about me?" Gloria asked.

I hesitated way too long on the timeline of appropriate responses. By now, there was no alternative to making a joke. "Fucking fantastic sex."

Gloria and I both realized in my inopportunely timed pregnant pause that I couldn't think of one good reason why we were together. My free brunch came with a strained silence. As with every one of my previous girlfriends, there was no formal relationship termination agreement. We merely stopped contacting each other. Within a few weeks, we had effectively broken up.

Chapter 69

BARBARA CALLED ME into her office a few weeks later. She was the only person I knew who had both a regular drip coffee maker and an espresso machine side-by-side. Her office aesthetic was completed with her own personal industrial copier that she used to create a massive pool of paper.

"We have a predicament in the Florida case," she told me.

I didn't have to ask which case. Barbara spoke in the same outlined format as a formal research memorandum.

She told me it was the case in Orlando. Apparently the green card we had thought was illegally disregarded was indeed invalid.

"What? That throws out our entire argument," I cried out.

"We found out the two defendants are not brothers. They're long-time partners. I'm sending you and Carrie down to help."

"You're sending me because I'm gay?"

One thing I absolutely hated was being pigeon holed because of my sexual orientation. Brian's efforts to have me transfer to the LGBTQ division were met with my stubborn refusals for a reason. I was more than queer.

"Deepa, we're so progressive we'd like to *not* send you down because you're gay. You're going because this was already your case, and you'll need Carrie's help."

"How long will we be gone?"

"As long as it takes, kid."

Before I had a chance to protest further, Barbara dove off to add another four-hundred-page document to the pool.

"AISLE OR WINDOW seat?" I asked Carrie.

"Window. I hate flying."

I found that ironic given her interest in immigration rights, though few of our cases fought for people who had found their way to America on a jet plane.

"Do you travel a lot?" she asked.

Conversations on this subject made me happy. I had made up in international excursions what I lacked in material possessions. My most prized memories were India, South Africa, and a year in France. I lingered on the last bit, hoping Carrie followed with my all time favorite question.

"Do you speak French?"

Flaunting my French skills was the one arrogant thing I embraced, especially after coming out of Gloria's slurred commentary in Spanish.

I offered a few sentences in a very verbose response to say, "Yes."

"Very cool. I bet you get all the ladies with that," Carrie replied.

The moment of glory quickly faded as I felt my face turn to stone. As the façade of a house, it was an attractive shade; as my visage, I looked like a demon.

"How do you know I'm gay?"

"I guess it's obvious? It's not a big deal . . ." she trailed off.

Being obvious wasn't something I aimed to achieve. I wore women's clothes, went through the charade of donning makeup on my face, and even sometimes caved into wearing heels. I thought I did a great job in finding a comfortable balance between who I was and remaining ambiguous to an assumption-prone society.

I cooked in my annoyance for the duration of the flight. My bubbles rose high enough to block Carrie's attempts from having us go over the case. By the time the flight landed, I was undoubtedly angry. Part of working at The Justice Coalition, however, required setting aside one's own existential crises to focus on the people who truly needed our help. I had no choice but to put off my feelings.

Chapter 70

WE WERE GREETED at the airport by a man named Carlos Hernandez, who was a field investigator and Spanish interpreter from the Miami affiliate office. He was grateful to have the extra research capacity on the case, which was turning out to be much more complicated than anyone had initially anticipated.

"What's the general sentiment?" I asked.

"Mixed. This could go either way," he replied.

Carlos drove us to the offices of Patricia Sanders, an Orlando-based lawyer who had agreed to take on the case when it was an open-and-shut matter of US Immigration and Customs Enforcement—ICE—bias against Hispanic immigrants. The Justice Coalition got her call a few months ago to make sure the media was on the sides of the defendants—Jorge and Pedro Ramirez. Now that call for media attention might backfire considering the still pervasive homophobic attitude of most Americans.

Carrie and I arrived to the office, which was decorated in expensive, modern furniture and accessories—lavish enough to remind us non-profiters that Patricia had taken the Ramirez's as her pro bono contribution to the world. Normally, I felt conflicted about such arrangements, though even I had to admit the prospect of unlimited corporate funding at our disposal would be invaluable in this highly controversial case.

Instead of poring through banal notes, Patricia had asked her IT department to set up a video of Pedro and Jorge to refresh the assigned team on the new developments. The screen flickered for a few seconds before revealing the two men. Pedro was tall, light-skinned, and had grey streaks running through his thinning brown hair. To his left was Jorge, who was much shorter, darker, with wild-and-thick black hair, and likely a strong Native American ancestry. I had never before seen a photo or video of either of them. Their stark difference in appearance left me bewildered that anyone had believed they were biological brothers.

One of The Justice Coalition senior staff attorneys sat in the room with Pedro and Jorge and began the line of questioning with Pedro.

"How did you meet Jorge?"

One boiling hot summer day during his second year of university, Pedro took his car to the local mechanic's shop where Jorge worked. Though he was relatively affluent, Pedro's jalopy of a car had a tendency to overheat.

"When I looked at the engine, I thought I had been electrocuted. But then I realized the shock was because I had accidentally touched Pedro's hand," Jorge offered.

I saw Pedro steal a quick glance of appreciation in Jorge's direction. The power of his gaze drew everyone watching the video closer to the screen. We could all tell how deeply these two men cared for one another. I stifled my breath so as to not miss a single word, wishing the staff attorney and I could have switched places. At that moment, I wanted nothing more than to sit in the presence of this remarkable couple.

"The two of you then began a sexual relationship?" the attorney continued.

"Si, but we learned quickly how to keep it a secret," Pedro replied.

To keep their cover, both Pedro and Jorge began publicly "dating" two closeted lesbians. The plan worked, enabling them to continue their relationship all the way through the completion of Pedro's academic career.

"When did you first come to the United States, Pedro?" asked the attorney.

"In 1978."

"And for what reason did you come?"

Pedro earned his Ph.D. in Mexican Literature from the University de Santa Fe, Mexico in the 1977. The University of Florida, Orlando offered him a position as a Spanish professor a few months later, after their Dean of Foreign Languages heard Pedro speak at a conference. The university quickly recognized Pedro's talent and fast-tracked him through the department. He was offered a full-tenured position in 1983.

"I accepted the tenure on one condition—that they bring Jorge over to the States as a permanent resident."

Under the Immigration Act of 1965, the National Origins Formula was abolished, making immigrants' skills and family relationships with citizens or residents the primary criteria by which residencies were granted. Same-sex relationships did not qualify under the law.

"Jorge had come a few times before under a visitor's visa," Pedro said.

"Did you tell the UF Orlando the true nature of your relationship?"

"No, our life in Mexico taught us to never reveal the real details."

Unaware Jorge might have qualified for asylum after first entering the United States, Pedro and Jorge lied to the then-existing INS, saying Jorge was Pedro's brother by birth. They spent several years creating a fake paper trail to "prove" Jorge and Pedro were born to the same parents. Jorge finally applied for a green card in 1986.

"It took ten years for Jorge's application to be approved," Pedro said.

"We lived in peace for eleven years, until . . ." Jorge trailed.

"Until ICE found out you two are lovers?" the attorney finished.

I cringed at that word. An attorney would not refer to a wife's husband as simply her "lover." The law fell short in adequately describing Pedro and Jorge's relationship.

The attorney went on to draw out how ICE flagged Jorge's green card after misplacing their copy of what turned out to be a falsified birth certificate. The then Governor of Florida immediately saw the case as a prime example to support his anti-immigration policy platform. Using much more time and capacity than warranted, he ordered a state investigator to follow both Pedro and Jorge for nearly two months. Speaking with former students and friends, and with the help of a legally contested entry into their residence, the State of Florida was shocked to learn Jorge and Pedro were actually long-time partners.

"It didn't take long for our entire life to come crumbling down," Pedro said with tears in his eyes.

Within days, Jorge was hauled into a detention center, where ICE had the authority to hold him until a formal hearing. Luckily, Pedro had become a US citizen three years earlier and could immediately take an indefinite leave from his job to spend as much time by his partner's side as the system would allow through bars.

Patricia motioned for her IT guy to turn off the video and flick the lights back on. As the spots in my eyes cleared from the sudden change, I heard echoes from the past generations of my family. Avva's immigration battle had had a huge impact on my decisions as an adult. Seeing these two men carry this same weight plus my own familiar burden—the stigma of the LGBTQ community—made for a pronounced clash that shook my heart.

I stood up to grab a glass of water, when Patricia caught my gaze.

"What's your name?" she asked.

"Deepa."

"Deepa, hold on a minute."

The grimness of her voice told us our emotional rollercoaster had one final loop to complete.

"I have the great displeasure to share a critical update. Our office received a fax this morning from Central Florida Oncology. Jorge has lung cancer."

Chapter 71

THE GRAVITY OF the Ramirez's situation immediately filled the entire room. Carrie and I purposely neglected our prior awkward altercation from the plane. We knew to prioritize the mountain of research we would need to help the team of lawyers properly formulate a defense. Finding a way to establish precedence for the Ramirez's required understanding how the overlap of two communities produced one result. In that realization, I saluted Barbara's wisdom in sending me down to work on this case. I understood what it meant to live in the intersection of two cultures.

Weeks into our research, weeks into Carlos's field investigations, and weeks into the lawyers hashing out different strategies, Carrie and I already understood how much was stacked against our defendants. To make matters far worse, the few visits to the oncologists the detention center allowed Jorge showed the tumors on his lungs had metastasized several times. Ours throes of carefully composed memorandums were not working fast enough to argue for the care Jorge needed to combat the cancer.

By mid-March, the perpetual insurmountable mountain had worn down Carrie and my spirits. For a straight twenty days, we had forced our brains into a constant onslaught of information searching and cataloging. That day, I hit a wall. I knew I needed a recreational pause.

"Want to get a drink?" I asked Carrie.

She hesitated, unsure whether I was serious. Our neglect of the plane confrontation had not produced closure, and it was unclear whether our relationship would ever extend past the confines of work.

"Sure," she timidly responded.

I hadn't bothered to ask Mom if she had any favorite places to go out in Orlando. I could only imagine what her response would have been.

"Nightlife in Orlando? You mean a boom box playing Jimmy Buffet and a case of cheap beer?"

I opened a new browser window on my computer to cover the thirty tabs on immigration cases, did a quick search, and found out a highly rated bar just a few blocks from the office.

We walked inside and found the reviews pleasantly accurate. A few people in suits were enjoying martinis at the far table, a group of students were intently discussing something over a bottle of wine, and a few lone individuals were quietly getting lost in themselves at the bar. The vibe was chill. I needed to frequent more places like this.

"A vodka soda and . . ."

"Your house white wine," Carrie finished.

Carrie offered to get the first round. She used it as an opener to immediately address the lingering irritation. "I want to apologize for what I said on the plane."

In that moment, I decided it was too forgone and too petty to blow into bigger proportion. "It's fine."

"No, it's not. We barely know each other. I should not have made an assumption. I hate when people do that to me."

"Like your favorite show is *Friends* and you only shop at *American Apparel*?"

I involuntarily blurted out the last line. An awkward moment of silence immediately erupted, in which the two parties involved were silently debating whether the playing field was now level, or whether this would evolve into a "friendship" of backhanded insults.

Carrie managed to sidestep her offense at my "white person" assessment. Her chuckle a few seconds later told me our relationship would thankfully be the former.

"So what do you think about all this?" she asked.

"Please, let's change the subject. It's all we talk about."

"I want to know *your* opinion, not what our work is saying."

There were a thousand thoughts I had on each aspect of the case. Determining where to begin and who to tell what were overwhelming tasks.

"Fine, I'll start. It's bullshit same-sex partnerships aren't recognized," she offered.

"Agreed. That needs to change now."

"Our immigration laws are worthless."

"Don't say that."

Carrie looked down at my tightly clenched fists. I sensed sets of bar patron eyes on my back in response to my loud outburst.

"Sorry. Why so sensitive?" she quietly asked.

"It's just family stuff."

I had always been one of those people who could dance while totally sober. Talking was another issue. Carrie answered that call by buying another round of drinks. I took a sip out of the second glass and immediately felt the alcohol loosen the vault of my mouth.

"Why should I tell you?" I teased.

"I'll tell you my family history. Four hundred years ago, a big boat carried a bunch of pale British people over to North America. The end."

"Nice try."

"If you tell me your family history, I'll set you up with one of my friends."

"Pass."

I gagged at the thought of my friends' previous attempts to set me up. On the hot-intelligent-crazy system, few even placed in the "decent human being" category. My last blind date was with a woman who took indescribable amounts of Prozac and literally tried to push me off the subway tracks. After that night, I had laid the blind dating option to rest.

Still, as I took bigger and bigger sips from my drink, the lock on my mouth gave way, and I soon found myself volunteering the intimate details of Avva's struggle to Carrie.

"India is an amazing country," I started.

"I bet."

"*But.* It was so fucking cruel to my grandmother. She got married to escape, but since she and my grandfather were different castes, my grandfather's family didn't talk to them for yeeeaaaarrsssh."

The harrowing tales Avva told me of her childhood still made me break down in tears. Even though she was willing to work her entire life, India did not allow her, a poor woman, to progress.

"She knew if she stayed that she would die in the same place she was born into."

"What does this have to do with our immigration laws?"

I told Carrie how Avva got married to my grandfather in 1959. How they initially had to lie to get Avva and Mom into the country. How the Immigration Act of 1965, how the immigration laws of today, would have helped them so much.

"My grandfather, the *immigrant*, was blamed for something that was not his fault."

"There was an investigation?"

"Yeah, if INS had discovered their lie, they would have been deported back to India."

"Here we are again, fifty years later."

I nodded. The faces, names, and places were different, but the struggle was still the same. Recalling so vividly the layers of pain and humiliation on Avva's face was the exact same harsh mix I saw in the Ramirez's.

"Nothing shook me more profoundly than the thought of my baby Pooja returning to the desperation of poverty I promised my amma I would escape," Avva once said.

Avva's struggles inspired me to dedicate my life to immigrant rights. I thought I could help bring justice and hope to the lives of people who were simply trying to break a cycle of despair. Yet somehow, my life's passion and work was failing for people like me—for gay people.

"Did it work out?" Carrie asked.

"Perhaps an English major would declare the story complete."

But I knew the suffering to get the conclusion and the characters that remained made the idea of a happy ending a delusion.

"For my mom, it ended in a profoundly unfulfilled life."

"But I thought arranged marriages are common?"

"In *South Asia*. I was so close to my mom when I was a kid. Now . . . not at all."

I decided that was more than enough of a life confession and turned the conversation back to Carrie.

"Tell me more about what you think," I said.

"Excuse me, are you gals talking about that UF Orlando professor?"

I peered over Carrie and saw a young, white couple staring back at us. Their body language reflected kindness.

"Yes," I shouted.

"We couldn't help overhearing you. Your grandmother's story is so remarkable," the woman exclaimed.

As steadfast as I was in my conviction to be a strong brown woman, I admitted it could be satisfying to hear positive affirmation from the majority population.

"The Ramirez case is an insult to hard-working immigrants," the man offered.

"Absolutely," Carrie and I agreed.

We learned the couple had married a few years ago. Both were locals and had many close friends of Hispanic origin. Some of their friends were even brought over illegally by their parents.

"Their parents were just trying to give their children what they deserved," the woman asserted.

"I couldn't agree more," I replied.

"Yet here are the Ramirez's turning the issue into a blasphemous joke. Fucking faggots," the woman finished.

Carrie and I froze in shock. I felt the atmosphere of hope and warmness dissolve as though someone had shot a bullet at the red balloon in which the bar was contained. Had I been in a more sober state, I would have lashed back at the sacks of ignorance. I didn't have the mental stamina to make that happen in my current inebriated dimension.

"Let's go," Carrie whispered to me.

She grabbed her purse with one hand and my arm with the other. In a disappointment that only came from realizing what we thought we had was for naught, we slammed the door in the faces of bigotry calling out behind us.

"Fags don't belong in America!"

Chapter 72

PATRICIA ENTERED THE room our team shared in her office. She announced that our request to free Jorge due to his worsening lung cancer had failed. After the episode at the bar, Carrie and my general feelings of dejection increased logarithmically with Patricia's announcement. Orlando lacked the mental and emotional comforts of New York, and we were feeling its effects grow with each defeat.

Patricia had been paying out of pocket all of the expenses to keep Carrie and me in Orlando. When we approached her to go home, she was happy to convince Barbara that neither of us had much else to contribute to the case. Our work couldn't continue indefinitely; the Florida The Justice Coalition offices needed to take over. A few days before Carrie and I were set to leave, Patricia asked us to perform one last task.

"Would you be willing to visit the Ramirez's in person?" she asked.

"You want us to speak directly to Pedro and Jorge?" Carrie asked.

"We're not lawyers," I added.

Patricia thought a fresh perspective would help reveal new details. She assured us we'd only be asking questions that had been previously thoroughly documented. I hardly felt fresh after the mental gymnastics we had done. Still, a part of me reminisced back to the first video we had watched of the couple, and I felt a twinge of that same desire to sit in Pedro and Jorge's physical presence.

"We'll do it," I agreed.

WE ENTERED THE detention center, which was advertised like a hotel on the owner's website. The bottom line of turning a profit took precedence, however, as evidenced by the bareness of the real-life facility. A state-of-the-art electronic system was the one luxury the company pulled out, and our passes worked without hindrance. At the end of a long corridor sat the questioning room. I knew by then that because Pedro was not considered a legal spouse, he had jumped through countless hoops to be continually included in Jorge's proceedings. Carrie and I took an extra second of appreciation when we walked in and saw both men sitting together for our interview.

Pedro and Jorge looked incredibly calm despite having had their lives turned upside down. Even so, the turmoil of the past few months had greatly aged both of them. Their spirit was not reflected in the aging process, and they greeted Carrie and me with lively handshakes and a kiss on the cheek.

I gave myself a moment to organize my thoughts before launching into my first question. Three years as a glorified paper writer was not adequate preparation for looking this powerful story in the eyes.

Pedro noticed my nerves and calmed me down. "It's okay, take your time."

I knew then why he was such a popular professor. Summoning my normal confidence, I launched into the slate of questions the legal team had prepared for us. Pedro and Jorge answered almost verbatim to what we already had recorded. An hour in, we had not uncovered any new points. Carrie stood up and thanked the Ramirez's for their time. She didn't realize I hadn't moved from my seat until she was at the exit to leave.

"Coming?" she asked me.

"Could I ask you a few questions in private?" I asked Pedro and Jorge.

Such a request was unconventional and probably not allowed, but Carrie and I had grown close in our time together, and she knew how much the fate of these two men meant to me. She excused herself from the room without protest.

"Why didn't you apply for asylum when you first came the States?" I asked Jorge.

He smiled, thinking I had lost track of our conversation. We had already covered that question.

"As we said, we didn't know that was possible," Jorge replied.

"Right . . . I know. I mean . . . why didn't you ask anyone when you got here? Why didn't you ask what options you had?" I clarified.

I saw I caught them off guard. No one had yet bothered to ask this very obvious question. For the first time in months, Pedro and Jorge conferred with each other on how best to phrase their response.

"We were scared," Jorge finally replied.

"Why?" I asked, though I knew the answer.

"When I got the job in the States, I thought Jorge and I could finally live openly as a couple. I soon realized hatred of gay people was not limited to Mexico," Pedro said.

Homophobic rhetoric, blatant acts of violence, little legal protection, and a generally intolerant society quickly told Pedro and Jorge that the United States was not the progressive paradise they had been hoping for when they decided to uproot their lives.

"Then why not move back to Mexico or break up?" I continued.

"Being apart from *mi amor* was like not having the left side of my body. Other people were just crutches; it wasn't the same," Pedro replied.

For Jorge, it went further. He wasn't just a gay man in Mexico. He was a poor man, an uneducated man, and a dark-skinned man.

"Some people treated me worst than their dogs."

The way Jorge's body rocked to the sadness of his life story reminded me precisely of Avva whenever she talked about her experience growing up. Through the many times I had seen Avva recount her struggles to others, I knew the emotion that stems from a life of poverty was enough to melt the coldest spirit.

"America gave me a new start in some ways," Jorge said.

"Yes, in the thirty years I have been here, the law came very far. It just did not come far enough," Pedro offered.

"Was it worth the risk?" I pressed.

I knew it was unfair question. Had I asked them the same a few months prior, their candid answer most certainly would have been yes. Facing the turmoil before them, hindsight was not a luxury to evaluate their choices.

"How did you know to take that risk?"

I asked yet another impossible question. Pedro and Jorge did not have another option even though the opposition argued they did. Neither of them had intended to be the poster children to call attention to inadequacies of our immigration system. All they knew was their time together on this earth was limited, and that their love was not a crime.

"Submitting to the wills of society when society is so inherently wrong is not something many people must face," Pedro explained.

Pedro and Jorge had not chosen this risk; this risk had chosen them.

Chapter 73

BACK IN NEW York, Carrie and I parted ways at Penn Station. Wading through the herds of people desperate to beat fellow passengers to their platform, I was quickly reminded of the pace at which this City moved. Despite the dynamism of home, I felt like I grew so much in its absence.

In the cab ride home, I passed hallmark neighborhoods central to the gay rights movement. The main LGBTQ center had specialized seminars for every imaginable expression of sexuality. The South Asian LGBTQ members had their own queer alliances, book clubs, film screenings, and parties. The South Americans, the East Asians, the Africans, and the African-Americans did, too.

Yet somehow through the complicated rhetoric, we all forgot the basic truth—it was hard be gay. It was hard to come out. We each had our own reasons, but those reasons often extended beyond our control. For years, New York City had made me feel like a coward for being only partially out. Shame was why I told Dad prematurely. Feeling the complexities of Jorge and Pedro's story reassured me I was not unreasonable for still being in the closet to Mom. I just needed to know when to take that risk since that risk had not been forced on me.

"CAN I HAVE a hug?" Carrie asked me.

"Yeah, of course," I replied, standing up.

Our embrace lasted minutes. I felt like a lifetime would have more adequate. Patricia had called us directly to tell us news we all knew was both inevitable and dreadful. Maintaining they had fulfilled all federal and state requirements, the private detention center facility's systematic denial of proper care finally killed Jorge. A formal autopsy would be conducted in the next few days, and we had no doubt it would come back saying Jorge died from preventable complications caused by the cancer. Unable to withstand the guilt, Pedro committed suicide just hours after seeing his late-husband's body.

Carrie and I walked out of the building. I looked up at the dark evening skyline of midtown east. A few beads of sweat dotted my forehead on the abnormally hot spring night. The timing of the sunset hadn't yet caught up to the temperature change. Carrie spotted a lone cab with its letters illuminated and hailed it down to take us to the site.

"You going to that thing for the Florida chicos?" the driver guessed.

"How did you hear?" I asked.

"From my gringo heffe, of all people. Who'da think they fucking let the guy die? They don't treat us right."

The driver peered at me through the reflection of his rear-view mirror. I shifted uncomfortably, trying to determine whether to correct him. He was on our side; I didn't want to lose that connection.

"I'm not . . ." I started.

"I know you ain't queer. Me neither. I didn't like queer people when I first got here, but you see everything as a driver . . . I dunno. It opens your eyes. It ain't right he was left to die like that."

Carrie continued on the conversation, and we found out the driver was from Mexico City. He told us he couldn't even imagine how hard it must have been for Jorge and Pedro in south Mexico back in the seventies.

"What brought you over here?" Carrie asked.

"Shit, where I come from, you got two choices to make money—deal drugs or join a gang and deal drugs. My sister brought me here, bless her."

We pulled up a few blocks away from the vigil in Jorge and Pedro's honor. I handed the driver enough money for a twenty-dollar tip. Morose occasions always made me feel generous.

"Light candle for me?" he asked.

"For sure, I promise," I replied.

Until the autopsy report came back, there was not much The Justice Center or any other non-profit could do to draw attention to the case. Instead, we took a step back and organized the vigil. Invites went out to nearly every organization working for immigration and/or LGBTQ rights, but it didn't take long for Carrie and me to realize that the event had been hijacked. Surveying the scene, we saw legions of buses from mega churches as far away as South Carolina. Hundreds of people were rallied behind hate signs I had been privileged to never see in the City.

"God hates fags!"

"Gays killed our troops!"

"Mexico is not America's 51st State!"

Their unrelenting buzzing maligned any feelings of positivity that was associated with Jorge and Pedro's struggles.

"Jorge and Pedro are symbols of bravery!"

"God agrees, the President agrees, gays don't deserve rights!"

I did what I could to concentrate on the messages of hope and realism.

"Pedro loyally served *thousands* of students throughout his career!"

"May God strike down the sinners and disobeyers of Jesus Christ, our Lord!"

When the dialogue turned to election calls, Carrie and I conceded and decided to leave. This was supposed to be a vigil to remember two men who lost a battle for their human rights and dignity. After extinguishing our candles, we shuffled off in a disappointing lack of closure.

Chapter 74

"I'M GOING TO head home," I told Carrie.

"No. Let's go get a drink."

Alcohol was the last thing I wanted. It would only amplify my sorrows. Carrie was convinced it was what we needed.

"There are better ways to honor Jorge and Pedro," I argued.

"Please? I don't want to be alone right now."

She had a point. Julie was out of town, I also did not want to be alone, and the thought of chasing down another friend to keep me company was less than appealing. The heat of the night would make sitting in either of our apartments miserable, anyway.

"A drink in their honor?" Carrie pleaded.

"Okay, you win."

We decided on a speakeasy that was a short walk away. Carrie ordered her usual house white wine, and I let the bartender convince me to try a new vodka jalapeno drink she had just perfected. The bar was thankfully quiet, and we settled into a set of overstuffed couches. Taking an extra moment, we reflected on the conflicted scene we had just witnessed. I felt like the bigotry of the Orlando couple had been cloned a thousand times.

Carrie's concentration in her work was not met in her personal life. As I had seen so many times, she quickly buried herself deep in text messages from her friends.

"Hey. I'm talking to you," I said, annoyed.

"What? Oh, sorry. It's Odri."

"What's an Odri?"

"No, Audrey. That Parisian friend I wanted to hook you up with."

I was surprised to learn that had actually happened. I was so inebriated by then that I thought I had invented that part of the conversation. Carrie assured me it was in fact true.

"She's on her way," Carrie said.

"Here?"

"Yep. Get ready, she's as close as you'll get to perfect on your stupid dating system."

Before I had a chance to mentally prepare, Carrie jumped up off the couch and ran with her arms outstretched toward a stunning-looking woman. They did a dramatic ten-minute song and dance number akin to

"Any Crappy Hindi Movie X." I stayed back on the couch so as not to intrude on their mini-reunion or be exposed to the Bollywood Invasion.

Observing from my safe corner, I saw Carrie had not lied. Audrey was beautiful—her long chestnut hair hung freely over shoulders and her black dress tastefully formed a perfectly curved body. Even from a distance, I could tell her brilliant blue eyes could both cut through steel or warm an entire ocean. She was incredibly intimidating.

I lacked the courage to walk over, so Carrie ushered Audrey to our couch and practically pushed me in front to say hi.

"*Bonjour, ça va?*" I managed to ask.

"*Ah, vous parlez français? C'est formidable quoi,*" she said, leaning in quiet close.

Being one of the most coveted cities in the world, New York always had a brilliant equalizing effect. I learned early in my college career that if you lived here, people tended to stop caring about where you were from. Still, I was shocked this beautiful Parisian woman had so quickly taken an interest in me—someone from the suburbs of Maryland. I already felt Audrey transmitting a new energy, and I wasn't sure whether to absorb or deflect it.

"How was the vigil?" Audrey asked in perfect English.

"A disaster. It was hijacked by hate and politics," I replied.

"I spent a summer in New Orleans after hurricane Katrina. So many vigils there were the same way," Audrey offered.

Mom's loathing of New Orleans was far more intense than for Orlando. Somehow, her loathing had only piqued my interest in the former.

"I love New Orleans. My mom lived there right before I was born."

I told Audrey I had also volunteered there after Hurricane Katrina. New Orleans was such as fascinating city—a unique cultural experience in the United States. I had never understood why Mom left.

"Have you been to that bar under the bridge . . . What's it called?" Audrey asked.

"Brigista, yes."

"Okay, kids, I'm going to get another drink," Carrie interjected.

I caught Audrey's eye in an apologetic laughter. We hadn't intended to so swiftly cut Carrie out of the conversation. I took Carrie's absence as an opportunity to do something I certainly hadn't thought I was capable of when first seeing Audrey.

"Have you ever been to Comfort?" I asked.

"No, what's that?"

"It's the best Cajun restaurant in Manhattan. Maybe we could go sometime?"

My breath caught in my throat as I questioned what I had just done.

Between the emotional and drunken turmoil of Orlando and today, maybe I had misheard Carrie both times. Maybe Audrey wasn't gay after all. Maybe I had already forgotten everything about French body language and misread Audrey's non-verbal cues. Maybe I could take back what I had said . . .

"It's a date," she replied.

AUDREY WAS STANDING across the street. The seconds I had to wait for the cars to clear a path to let me through to her felt like years. The spaces in between us seeing each other were dragging on with no mercy, yet I felt like time had flown since we first met. I smiled to myself at the thought tonight was already our fifth date.

"Time is going quickly? Is that a bad thing?" she pretended to scoff.

"Eet ees so aaard tooo spend-uh tiiime wiz youuu."

"Great-T madam, I vill go zen."

We congratulated each other for being such stellar pupils in mastering the other culture's stereotypical accent. I think we could have allotted an entire series of dates for that very purpose. We were hysterical together, I decided.

Turning to a more serious note, I picked up our last conversation precisely where we had left off last time. I had a question that had gotten lost in the wind of a post-dinner kiss that left me completely breathless.

"When you said your mother is a doctor, you used a feminine article with the word *médecin*. Isn't that a masculine noun?" I asked.

She complimented me on being so observant. I was right, but some people in our generation in France were making it feminine to reclaim the word when speaking of women.

"It's like a gender revolution with words. My mother actually did it when she was young before it was as common," Audrey explained.

"That's amazing."

"Yes, my family is really forward-thinking with gender equality."

I managed to avoid offering any information on my own family's take on the subject. I myself didn't completely understand Mom's situation and never felt apt to describe to the outside world the exact path that led her to where she was now.

Audrey and I decided to take a stroll by the Williamsburg Bridge before our dinner reservation. A perfect sunset cast a warm glow over the shimmering water. Gloria had always complained that my romantic appreciation was limited to a few candles and a drunken Karaoke song dedication. Stealing a quick glance at Audrey, I knew my inner passion just needed to be unleashed in perfect company. I had seen that view of the Bridge at least a hundred times. I appreciated its serenity for the first time that day.

My prudishness in physical affection for anyone of a platonic or familial nature was usually countered with moving too fast in a relationship. I thought back to my previous three girlfriends; I had slept with each one on the second date, and within a week we were spending nearly every night together. Audrey and I had only kissed a few times. I was strangely settled going so slow with someone I found so complete.

"I love the ease of our discovery," Audrey suddenly said.

"Discovery of what?"

"Of each other. Usually I rush through this part and go straight to the end."

Our hands reached for each other at the same time, sending a jolt to my heart exactly as Jorge had described a few months ago. The first time I heard him say those words, I could only sympathize with the feeling. Now I could truly empathize.

Audrey had mentioned during date number four that she might be returning to France within the year. She liked her Masters program in psychology at The New School, but the way the discipline was practiced in France wasn't considered psychology in the States.

"It's therapy," she had said.

"Have you made a decision yet?" I asked.

"Why? Do you want me to stay another three years in New York for my doctorate?" she teased.

"Of course. Is that a question?"

By the way her face relaxed, I saw that she had half held her breath. I realized my affirmation was obvious, but something that still needed to be stated.

Audrey didn't believe in using pills as the cure for most patients. She aimed to help people through talking and assisting them in analyzing their problems. In France, medicines were used as the last resort, not the first solution. As she described her opinions, I felt her hand getting increasingly warmer. The subject tapped anger. Not being able to offer a lighter topic from my own work, I kept quiet until she blew off enough steam.

"How are you doing otherwise?" she asked.

I knew she was asking about Jorge and Pedro. The Justice Coalition lawyers were forming an argument against the private detention center so we could formally bring the owners to trial. Since then, I had been slammed with a huge human trafficking case involving Chinese tradesmen who had smuggled in Vietnamese immigrants as slaves.

"I haven't had much time to process everything," I answered.

"It's such a tragedy to lose your partner like that."

"I know. They were fueled by such a deep . . ."

"Passion?"

"And commitment."

Part of me was relieved Pedro had committed suicide. The American and Mexican media would have surely been ruthless.

"There is so much homophobia in this country," I finished.

"That's crazy, it's 2008."

Audrey had only lived in New York City; she hadn't seen the backlash the LGBTQ community experienced in the rest of the country.

"Perhaps Africa and . . ."

"Asia, you can say it."

"Yes, okay. Perhaps Africa and Asia are still homophobic, but not America."

I wanted nothing more than to agree. But I knew her quick valuation of the States was too narrow in scope to see the true picture.

"America is still filled with a lot of animosity," I argued.

"There are always the extremists."

"These are not the extremists."

My mind flashed back to the last presidential election. Along with the rest of the LGBTQ community, I vividly remembered the hatred the Republican Party used to mobilize their base of anti-gay supporters. They spun the issues such that suddenly, American debates were not about the economy, war, the Constitution, or world affairs. We, the LGBTQ community, became the scapegoat for all problems of society.

"They made sure we couldn't marry, openly serve in the military, or adopt a homeless child. That hatred won the election. That hatred still exists in most of this country."

"You are too negative about this, Deepa. You must focus on the positive."

Her face showed worry lines I did not yet want to discover. The sourness of our first fight created tension inside my stomach. Whatever point I would win in continuing on was not worth souring the perhaps limited time we had together.

"Did I tell you that you look incredible?" I said.

"That is nice of you to say," she stoically replied.

I squeezed her hand, hoping it was the valve on which to put pressure to dispel the bad vibes. The effects were minimal at best.

"Audrey, I'm so fortunate to live in a world where we can be together."

I felt the burn of insincerity swell my mouth as I pushed out the sentence. Pedro had been right in saying America had not come far enough.

Chapter 75

BRIAN, CARRIE, AND I sat down at a table in the most expensive sushi restaurant midtown had to offer. I regretted promising Carrie I'd treat her to a lunch of her choice on her last day in the office. The Justice Coalition funds had run very short of keeping her on full-time any longer. She decided to use the bad news as a chance to conquer her fear of flying.

"Are you nervous about going to Ghana?" I asked her.

She nodded, still unsure about the final terms of her English teaching contract there.

"What are you doing for your birthday?" she asked to change the subject.

Mom had always said how my birthday was the first day in her life she knew everything would work out in the end.

"This day is symbolic of our freedom, Deepa."

Her emphatic declaration meant I had to spend every birthday with her. As an adult, I saw the love behind the gesture. I just wished it were an *option*. The past two years, my birthday had been on a workday, and Mom made sure I took a vacation day to spend it with her. I counted one other time she had ever come to visit me in New York—my college graduation.

"She spent the entire day alone on the opposite side of Washington Square Park," Brian recounted.

"She didn't want to see my dad and his obnoxious new wife."

"I thought your dad is single?" Carrie asked.

"He remarried for a few months."

"What happened?"

I told Carrie about Dad's sudden departure from my life, our lives. He divorced his second wife, sold his condo, donated half of his money to charity and gave the rest to Mom, all within a span of a few weeks. The timing was too coincidental to me coming out to him.

"He moved to an ashram New Year's Day 2005."

I was sure he took one look at his life scorecard and left after tallying the total.

Work: +5
Wife: +2
Salary: +10
<u>Deepa: -100</u>
Total: failure

Result: Do not pass go. Do not collect two perfect grandchildren.

"Do you really think that's the reason he left?" Carrie pressed.

I had no idea how to answer that question. In the back of my mind, I knew Dad was a doctor who understood the basic biology and physiology behind homosexuality. Whether he was still disappointed at having a gay daughter was not something I had ever determined. I preemptively answered the question that always followed.

"And yes, him leaving is another reason I haven't come out to my mom."

"Also, because she's crazy," Brian screamed.

"All this charm, and yet you're still single," I shot back.

"So what about your birthday?" Carrie asked again.

I still had a few months to figure something out.

TO TAKE ADVANTAGE of my favorite time of year and to remain calm during a surely stressful phone call, I approached the birthday situation while seated outdoors at the local biergarten. The end of August always ushered out the masses of tourists and ushered in the rightful residents of the City. Watching Manhattanites come out of hiding from their obscure connection to a summer beach house in the Hamptons was a nice backdrop for my call with Mom.

The phone rang precisely five times before Mom answered. She loved to keep people waiting just so.

"Hey, Mom."

"Hi, Deepa. How are you, dear?"

"Good. I wanted to talk to you about my birthday."

"Don't worry, I already made a reservation at our favorite Greek restaurant."

"Actually, I was wondering if you'd want to come up the following weekend instead?"

I recognized a pattern of two short breaths and one long sigh. Mom had officially entered pause of the third persuasion. "I'm waiting for you to reconsider." Said pause made its first appearance around 1998 when that same cute, red-haired Amy invited me over to her party. Unfortunately, this conflicted with the Emily Dickenson speaker's panel for which Mom had already purchased tickets.

Being a hormone-crazed teenager, I accepted Amy's invitation without consulting Mom, exposing me to my first pause of a third persuasion. Mom stared me down while using the pause until I finally caved and cancelled on the party. Pauses of a third persuasion were certainly persuading.

"You don't want to spend time with your own mother anymore," Mom lambasted.

"Of course I do. It'll just be hard to get that day off of work."

"Why is it suddenly so hard to make the arrangements?"

I felt bad for bending the truth in my favor. Barbara vaguely mentioned a day seminar she'd need me to help prep that day. The real reason I didn't want to make the arrangements was because Audrey already promised a special evening. Saving up my vacation days would also be smart in case Audrey asked me to come back with her to France for Christmas. Spending my birthday with her was a great step in that direction.

"We'd get more time if you came the weekend after," I reasoned.

"Honestly Deepa, I'd strongly suggest you reconsider."

"There's nothing to reconsider. It's out of my control."

"This is very disappointing. I'm very disappointed with this situation."

Repetition was not a good sign.

"Please just come the weekend after."

"I'd strongly suggest you recon—"

I hung up before she finished. Audrey was the first healthy relationship I had been in, and my devout adherence to Mom's impossible demands was fading.

Chapter 76

CARRIE'S BAD FORTUNE turned out to be my good luck. The sum of money that was too small to keep on her staff had to be allocated, so Barbara decided to give me a raise and a promotion in title. The prospect of not going broke to go to Paris lifted me out of my post-Carrie work slump.

Mom reacted to the news with an unusually indifferent tone. The disappointment of my birthday request had clearly not worn off.

Barbara, on the other hand, took my promotion as an excuse to work me even harder. She made no exception on my birthday. I called Audrey three times to apologize for the delay. Audrey feigned an air of understanding and told me to not get fired.

"Deepa, I have an important assignment for you."

"Seriously? It's seven pm."

"I want you to assign each of these two-hundred case files an arbitrary color and use the colors to file the cases. Then put the cases back in their original order."

"Okay, I'm leaving. Night, Barbara."

"As you wish."

"Am I fired?"

"Not at all. Happy birthday."

"SURPRISE!" A ROOM full of people shouted.

I jumped back a few steps before realizing my apartment was full of an assortment of friends from every stage of my New York life. Audrey was standing in the center, holding a huge chocolate cake.

"*Joyeux anniversaire ma chérie*," Audrey cooed at me through the crowd.

I looked over to Audrey's right and saw Sonia, one of my department colleagues. Sonia told me Audrey had called to keep me at the office longer than usual to give guests time to come over after work. Barbara was all too willing to invent nonsensical assignments to keep me occupied.

"Are you ready for your surprise?" Audrey asked me.

"I see it. This is the first surprise party anyone has even thrown for me."

Brian rolled his eyes. I knew he wanted to call attention to the fact he tried several times to throw me a surprise party, but had always been thwarted by Mom's appearance. Instead, he leaned over and offered kinder words.

"This one's a keeper." He nodded in Audrey's direction.

Audrey grabbed my hand and led me up to the roof of my building, where I saw heaps of Cajun chicken, collard greens, and mini po'boys staring back at me. The word "Comfort" was written on the enormous takeout bags, in perfect testament to how I felt at that moment. The woman that brought this all together was clearly a natural entertainer and a master at creating the perfect environment. There was just one thing she wished she could have done to complete the scene.

"I wanted to call your mother and invite her to the party," Audrey told me.

I silently choked on my food at the thought of her calling. Audrey still did not know I wasn't out to Mom. Mom did not know Audrey existed. Julie later told me that when Audrey asked for Mom's number, Julie had to pretend to unsuccessfully search for an entry that was clearly on her phone as "Deepa's mom."

"Audrey, do you like ponies?" Brian asked, coming out of nowhere.

For all of his dramatics, Brian was brilliant at reading body language. He ran over as soon as he saw the look of shock on my face. His tactics involved a brand of repetition and convoluted statements not far off of Mom's. I knew by the end of the conversation that Audrey would be so disoriented, she'd forget what she had been trying to say.

With the company of twenty of my closest friends, I spent the evening eating and drinking on the roof against the brilliant backdrop of an East Village sunset. Audrey had negotiated an excellent deal on the food, and by the time we had all finished, there was a ton left over. We divvied the remainder to distribute to the homeless people in the neighborhood. Julie found a few recruits to help with the cleaning.

"Go enjoy your time with Audrey," she encouraged.

I didn't need to be told twice. The universe was on my side and sent us a cab just seconds after we landed on the street.

"I still have to give you your gift," Audrey said once we were inside.

She was amazing. I leaned over to give her a kiss, which prompted the driver to cough a sound of homophobia.

"Save it for the hotel, ladies."

"Oh my God. It's two girls kissing," I mockingly shouted.

"I've never seen you so . . ." Audrey started.

"Happy?"

"Exactly."

She planted another kiss on my mouth. The driver looked like he was going to vomit with our continual displays of affection. As we stepped out, I made sure to hand him a large tip, though this time not out of moroseness.

"Why would you do that?" Audrey asked.

"So he feels conflicted about hating us."

She chuckled and handed me my gift once we were in her studio. She had wrapped everything in a neat box. The first girl who had ever broken my heart was that infamous red-haired Amy. After I missed her party, I made sure to schedule my own birthday party so she could come. I was so excited to see what Amy had given me, I tore open the package with all of the world's passion.

"I spent an hour wrapping that," Amy cried.

"I'm sorry, I was so excited."

Traumatized by gift-wrapping love aches, I took care to open Audrey's gift without ripping the paper.

"It's a gift, not a weapon," Audrey said.

Happy to once again employ all of the world's passion, I was elated to reveal the contents of the gift. On top laid a choice of great thought.

"A Barack Obama shirt."

I tried on the top, which was a dark hunter green with Obama's face in relief. Beneath the portrait, the word "Progress" was written. The subtly of the design was paired with a precise fit around my chest.

"It's tasteful, it's elegant, it's perfect," I declared.

Just like its buyer.

She handed me the second object that fell from the box—a compilation CD by one of the greatest French singers of all time, and certified icon of Francophone lesbian culture. Audrey had it shipped from France months ago, as my favorite track was in the collection. The title translated to "The Battle of My Other."

Chapter 77

"THIS IS PRECISELY the image of luxury France associates with America," Audrey said.

As the elevator carried us up through the floors of the Harlem building, the air thickened with an unmistakable rise in anticipation. We both knew this would be a night that would live in either inspiration or sorrow by the time the elevator doors opened straight into the apartment.

Dan perfectly timed his arrival and ushered us into the massive kitchen lined with every possible home cooking utensil. His boyfriend waved at us from his perch by the custom icemaker. A woman was finishing her pesto in the smaller of the two food processors.

I stood back for a moment and watched in amusement as Audrey took in the excess of what New York life could offer. Behind me, Dan explained a few of the highlights. He finished his introduction and gave me a compliment I hoped to be hearing all night.

"Nice shirt."

"Thanks. My girlfriend gave it to me."

"They've already tallied the votes from twelve states," Julie said, coming up from behind.

"I still don't understand the American election process," Audrey said.

I had tried to explain it to Audrey in English, but even her impeccable language skills didn't make up for the fact that no other government in the world had such a convoluted system.

"So practice your French and explain *en français*. You must tell everyone if you come to France this Christmas."

I desperately prayed no signs of reconsideration polluted the feeling of euphoria her voice brought me. She was suggesting I come for the first time.

"Obama leads by fifteen," someone shouted from the TV room.

Audrey smiled at my brain being completely overtaken in election and Parisian victories. "You are obsessed with this race."

"Obama will do a lot for gay rights. It will bring security and happiness to so many."

"Just don't mention gay rights to your mooom," Brian hissed, entering the room.

By now, Brian's constant criticism of Mom was also getting on Audrey's nerves. She called out his Mom bashing.

"I don't hate Deepa's mom, just her homophobic ways."

"Perhaps it is just you. She loves Deepa very much," Audrey said.

In the sixth grade, I dedicated my spring break to the wonders of watching movies frame by frame. At that moment, time slowed down to the same speed, and I watched in horror as Brian prepared to defend his gay honor. Before I could catch his eye and silently beg him to keep quiet, I heard the truth I had been avoiding for months.

"Deepa's mom doesn't know she's gay."

Audrey usually shimmering face took on a ghastly shade, as though she had suffered a brush with death. The color drained out like she was an open faucet. She whispered she must use the toilet and rushed off to avoid the impending disaster.

"Idiot," I screamed at Brian.

"You didn't *tell her?*"

"I couldn't find the words . . . It always gets too close to an argument."

Audrey's cultured parents lived in the heart of Paris. Her mother had been a gender equality fighter from a very young age. She had a sister who was happily married to offset the parental dreams of a stereotypical family. Audrey was born into an easy coming out situation. So easy, she viewed the issue with unnecessary inflexibility. I had avoided the coming out conversation because it was the one aspect of our relationship I had come to despise.

"Audrey?" I quietly asked, tapping on the bathroom door.

"Leave me alone."

"Audrey, please come out."

"*Laisses-moi.*"

Her violent shouting scared me into backing away. I waited for nearly twenty minutes in half fear, half hope. She pressed her hands to the door, repeating for me to leave.

Brian escorted me back to the kitchen full of an uncommon shame. He had no idea. He was so sorry. She emerged half-an-hour later, still reminiscent of a ghost, and told me she would go home. Alone.

"I'll come with you."

"No. You stay and be a part of this."

"Please don't go Audrey. Please don't do this."

"You do not know what I am doing. I do not know either. Just stay."

She walked over to be swallowed by the piece of American luxury.

On any other night, on any other occasion, I would have unquestionably followed her departure. And I thus debated the tone, the intonation, the speed, and the body language that accompanied her words to decide what to do. But the anxiety in the air was quickly becoming optimism, and I found myself torn by the idea of leaving this remarkable moment.

"He's up by forty. Now fifty."

What if she left me?

"Sixty-five. We're making history."

I couldn't lose her.

"Oh my God, he got Ohio!"

At the sound of that announcement, I rushed into the TV room and stared at the screen in total amazement. Every candidate who had won the US presidential election in modern history had won the state of Ohio. Though thoughts of Audrey continued to rip apart my mind, I recognized the power of this inspiring scene.

Looking around the room, I saw the liberal, the progressive, the jaded, and the tired. After eight years of torment by a neo-conservative administration, they held onto a prospect that tonight would usher in a new era that used "freedom" as muse, not an empty show of patriotism. Outside, we heard the calls of joy in this important neighborhood. As the night progressed and the lead in our favor grew wider, I was swept up in the historic Progress.

When Obama hit the almighty count of two-hundred-and-seventy electoral votes, I found myself in a flash flood toward the streets of New York City. Two jumbo screens and the hope of a collected nation lit up the corners of 125th Street and Adam Clayton Boulevard with a display of final victory. A young man lifted his little daughter in the air, and both jumped up and down with an uncontainable excitement.

He leaned over to his wife and shouted. "Our baby is gonna look ev'rybody straight in the eye. It ain't a curse to be black no more. You hear me, baby girl?"

"I hear you, Daddy," his daughter shouted.

Somehow I felt my phone vibrate in my pocket through all of the motion.

"We did it," I shouted.

"I've lived so long to see this moment."

"It's a celebration of an impossible victory."

"I can't wait to see you. I love you."

"I love you too. I love you, Mom."

I relished in no pauses, no sighs, no criticisms or lies. That was the best conversation I had had with my mother in years. The unifying power, the new era had begun.

We celebrated in the streets until the early morning. I downed six shots of tequila in keeping with my past bad habits, and by the end of the night, could barely hold myself upright from the extreme bitter-happiness coursing through my bloodstream. A still guilty Brian hailed a cab and accompanied me home.

"She won't let this stop you two," Brian said.

"I dunnn . . . she'sss gotss suppor-ive fam bily. She'sss not understand . . ."

"Well said, madam drunkard."

"Fuck you. The room ishh spinning, why is so fassstss?"

"We're here."

"Oh, rights . . . cab."

He paid the driver and took my keys from my hand. He carried me up to the apartment and laid me down in bed. I had the strangest feeling of déjà vu.

"Deeepaaa . . ."

"Yesh?"

"We won!" he shouted.

I threw my fist in the air and fell asleep with a drooling smile on my face.

I CALLED BARBARA the next morning as soon as my stomach had stopped shaking. Apologizing profusely, I lied about a particularly incapacitating case of food poisoning.

"Too much to drink or too high?" she asked.

"The first."

"The office is practically empty today. Get some rest, see you tomorrow."

I counted my blessings to have the best boss ever. Staring at my phone, I saw the best girlfriend ever had not called or texted since we last saw each other. Audrey's phone went straight to voicemail. I left a long detailed message.

"Our relationship is the only thing that has ever caused me to be grateful for my orientation. I need you Audrey. I . . . value your opinion."

I couldn't bear to utter my first confession of love through a receiver. I spent the next hour trying to map out the response to the cavernous questions that were surely to follow.

"Why haven't you come out to her? Why didn't you tell me before? Why are you so scared?"

I stopped at the corner deli to pick up flowers and a copy of the only newspaper left—a tabloid. Her studio building was thickly coated in foreboding warnings. As I raised my fist to knock on her door, I saw the giant pulsating bulge that was my heart beneath my shirt. I couldn't tell whether the persistent feeling of queasiness was from alcohol or nerves.

She quietly whispered for me to step in. I tried to make contact as I handed her the flowers, praying even the softest graze would convey the care my inner core breathed for that woman. She was too skilled in the art of persuasion and took the flowers with caution to avoid any physical touch.

"They only had roses. I'll bring you lilies later."

My silent plea for her to confirm there would be a later went unanswered. In a halfway assurance, she asked me about the rest of the night. I told her of the awesome power of the hope and the promise. This was something that so many people had been waiting for after centuries of discrimination in a country that prided itself as a land of opportunity. Now that promise had taken a great leap forward.

"It is really remarkable," she agreed.

"For immigrants."

"And black people."

"And women."

"And children."

"And gays."

We discussed the Progress for a full hour before bringing ourselves to the sensitive issue at hand.

"Are you mad?"

"Not mad. Just sad."

I felt an intense guilt for causing her pain—that was the last thing I wanted to do. I tried to explain how much of an emotional toll an arranged marriage took on Mom. Mom was deeply committed to shielding me away from the judgments and constant queries of society. Before I even knew what it meant, I had learned her ultimate conclusion, which however disappointing, was not ambiguous.

"Be yourself, find who you are. Don't get married, Deepa, not until you have found the right *man*."

I told Audrey about the contradictions of my mother, about how Mom never got along with much of anyone. She never went back to school or started a career. She never took up any hobbies or found peace with her past.

"But she raised me with undying love and care."

A nostalgic smile crept over my face as I described Mom, who guided me past the monsters and demons to my first steps of kindergarten. Mom volunteered for the role of sound master when I rocked to the beats of my techno music. She strolled with me in a gorgeous kimono through the Japanese gardens we created in our minds when I chose a year in France over a summer in Tokyo. She never questioned when I asked to take a trip to New York over prom.

"She built me the highest pedestal when I accepted a job that paid less than thirty-thousand dollars."

I was sadly aware that our convergent minds had split ways through the years. But the immature gestures, the dramatic motions, and the continuous need for positive reinforcement were the small prices I paid to look at my mother, to hold her hand, and to thank her for always being strong enough to let me be who I was.

"My only condition to rewrite is this—her view of my orientation."

Through her pauses of various persuasions, in her sighs of inner reflection, and her visible disappointment with the world's grand operations, Mom had never wavered on her disapproval of queer people. My vagueness in appearance, my disinterest in dating, and my successful employ of pronouns successfully carried me until I moved away.

"She doesn't know, and I am terrified to tell her. I am terrified to lose her."

"Deepa, you will not lose her if you tell her you are gay."

"I don't know, Audrey, who is to say?"

"What about your mother's sister? She doesn't care, and she grew up with your mother."

I explained to Audrey the fundamental difference that graced Pinni's life in being the second-born. Pinni was allowed to choose her own path, to define her own future, and find her way to happiness. Pinni lived her life as an open book, and as a result, had many diverse people write themselves into her story.

"My mother did not have that choice. She can't relate to me on this," I said.

"There will always be something your parents do not understand about you."

"How would you know? With Paris, your sister, a revolutionary mother?"

"Deepa, I know you think that it was easy for me to tell my parents." Audrey argued that her mother was progressive on female equality issues. For Audrey's mother, homosexuality was not the same. Audrey had to tell her parents she was gay just like everybody else. "It was hard and I was scared. But I did it, and it worked out."

"It won't for me. Look at my dad."

"Maybe it was one thing that made him upset. But, Deepa, your mother is not your father."

Audrey was the first person who disambiguated Dad's actions from Mom's potential reaction. Treating the two separately did nothing more than to further confuse me. My breath began to rattle, and Audrey finally gave way to our physical distance and wrapped me in a protective embrace.

"Do not let fear dictate your life," she said.

"Life has dictated my fear," I replied.

"If your mother wants you to be who you are, she must accept who you are."

"Audrey, I can't take that risk."

Tears formed in the corners of Audrey's gorgeous blue eyes. This conversation struck a chord that upset the very tenets of her being.

"Deepa, I can work out so many things, but I cannot live a half lie. If you can't take this risk—"

"I couldn't handle the world if I had let you go," I whispered.

"Please, for you, for me, you must come out to your mother."

Her tears hit the ground like bombs in an ocean.

"I love you," I barely uttered.

"I love you too."

"I do this or I lose you?"

"Or we lose each other."

Chapter 78

"OVER HERE." I waved at Pinni.

"Not our typical venue," she commented.

She stammered that the place was cute, though the fact that her visual evaluation followed her words told me that she felt obligated to say as much. The walls were covered in random pictures of France and Belgium—not typical touristy shots. They were intimate scenes of a nineteenth-century family, recognizable only through the landmarks that stood centuries' test of time. Our tiny round table was met with two mismatched chairs that could be described as either vintage or garbage.

I had called yesterday and asked her to meet me at my favorite hole-in-the-wall crêpe shop in the City. After I had returned from my life-changing experience of studying abroad in France, I found myself in mental limbo between two continents. This crêperie was the perfect resolve, as it had always been an excellent place to talk and to think. Pinni sat with an unusual self-doubt and waited for me to speak. She was out of her normal pristine corporate environment.

"What do you remember about the few years my parents were married?"

I was not there to mince questions. She was not there to mince answers and recounted the vague details she knew of Mom's existence in Orlando. Just when Mom sourced what she had been looking for in life, Dad forced her to uproot and move.

"Your mom restarted in New Orleans and ended with a deep hatred that could only mean a great happiness in between."

"What did she love about New Orleans?"

Pinni let out a rush of air. No one had ever asked that question before. No one else would. I was my mother's only child.

"In particular, she loved her friend, Jeff."

I had never heard of a Jeff.

"He was really great. Smart, good looking, charming, kind, supportive. Your mom had a crush on him."

"Did anything ever happen?"

"No, I don't think he was interested. Your mom thought he was, though."

"Where is he now?"

"I don't know. They lost contact after the divorce. She was a mess by the time she moved."

I found that detail surprising. Mom spoke more emotionally of her smartphone than she did of my father. Even with the anticipated turmoil of ending a four-year marriage, Mom being so traumatized with her New Orleans departure made no sense.

"Why do you want to know all of this?" Pinni asked.

"Audrey wants me to come out to Mom."

"When?"

There was no explicit deadline. It went without saying that Audrey would not let our relationship progress until I took the risk.

"What do I do?"

Nearly four years ago, I had asked the same question. Without hesitation, Pinni told me to come out to Dad.

"He's a doctor, he'll understand," she had said.

This time, she chose her words carefully.

"I can't tell you whether to come out. This isn't anything I've experienced before."

Her concession was a strong departure from our last similar conversation, when she had said she could easily relate. She had met Amir back in grad school, and they dated in secret for nearly two years. After listening to the meaning behind Avva's words, Pinni decided to take her risk and announce to the world—Avva included—that she was in love with an Iranian and they wanted to get married.

With years of Avva's confessions of guilt and devastation at her older daughter's life, Pinni had became confident Avva would accept the idea her younger daughter had found someone she truly loved. Pinni was equally surprised as me when Dad did little more than disappear after I came out. Until then, my father had been a distant presence in my life, but not a negative one.

"How do you think Mom will react?"

"Honestly, I have no clue."

The once close relationship Pinni had to Mom had died long ago. Mom was not the same person Pinni knew growing up. She was not the same person Pinni visited in New Orleans. That spirit had died slowly.

"She has never reacted well to these topics," I reasoned.

"Obama's support of gay rights will set a positive tone."

"And Avva?"

"One battle at a time. Your grandmother's priorities are much different than they were with your mother."

Pinni saw the doubt seeping out of my pores and reminded me I had a strong support system regardless of Mom's reaction.

"This is so difficult," I said.

"Love always is. Relationships and marriages involve more than the commitment."

"I know. It's not just the marriage. It's the paths of marriage."

"HOW WAS DINNER with your aunt last night?" Audrey asked me.

"It gave me a lot of answers. Now I have even more questions."

"You can never have the complete information."

"I at least want some indication."

"You know you have to tell her."

I shot Audrey a look of bitter annoyance, which were sadly becoming commonplace in our daily lives. She wrung her hands a few times and apologized for being pushy. Rewriting the inner workings that had been hardwired in Mom's brain would not happen overnight.

For a week, I listed out reasons why this was a bad time to have the coming out conversation with Mom. Audrey always shook her head, arguing Mom would always have something to blame. Ultimately, Audrey was convinced of one winning factor.

"Your mother would want to know that you are loved."

The naïve part of me had always wished that were the case. I knew instead that the role love played in my family's life shifted greatly in definition and execution from generation to generation. I could never find the words—in English or in French—to articulate what this meant for me.

Audrey settled into bed and pulled the covers to her chin. Her worry lines left traces of resentment that I couldn't stand to watch expand through the night. I fell asleep on the couch, letting my brain slip into the unencumbered world I created as a child. The next morning, I promised Audrey that Mom would know by The New Year.

Chapter 79

I REACHED OUT to adjust Audrey's scarf so it completely covered her neck. She had the habit of placing it so that it served the sole purpose of decoration underneath her pea coat.

"Passport, boarding pass, camera, both phones. Got everything?" I asked.

"*Oui, tous.*"

"This is going to be the longest two weeks of my life."

"I will call you twice a day and tell you everything."

A pile of snow I kicked splattered into a million pieces and left a dark mark on my shoe. I wished I had a camera attached directly to my eye that would have allowed me to zoom to microscopic levels. I would have loved to see the individual flakes burst into freedom and descend to their new environment.

"I'm gonna start the meter, ladies," the cab driver shouted, honking his horn.

I wrapped Audrey in a giant hug and held her there for a solid minute, forcing my brain to make a copy of the feeling in case I got lonely without her presence. She held my gaze as though trying to sort through the disorganized files that made up my thoughts and feelings. The file she was searching for was password protected.

"If it goes very badly, remember to come to me in Paris."

"I'll come next year, I promise."

"I have already told my parents."

"*Je t'aime.*"

"I love you too."

"God, I hate Christmas," said the driver.

I DECIDED TO take the train to Maryland after three consecutive years of experiencing the brattiness of New York City children at the airport Christmas week. Every year, it was the same story. At Gate 12, I'd see little Johnny complaining to his mother about being dragged away from presents for the sake of her African adventure.

"Mom, I don't want to see a damn lion."

At gate 15, the father of an already elitist ten-year-old girl tried to convince her how much fun it would be to visit the rest of the family in Central Michigan.

"It's a really lovely area."

"Really, Dad, nicer than our duplex on the Upper East Side?"

The train had its own issues, though the sheer amount of time I had to lose myself in my own thoughts was a calming effect before facing the next eight days. Mom greeted me at the station with her usual blend of welcome and dramatics.

"I'm so happy to see you. It's nice you've finally made an appearance."

She scolded me for missing a birthday Avva was not sure of and never celebrated, my own day of birth, Thanksgiving, and a smattering of weekends she had planned for mother-daughter exploration of her newfound hobbies. I smiled in return with my usual charades of regret.

We only had to drive ten minutes to pull into the driveway of the house Avva and Mom bought less than a year after I was born. Though West Virginia had provided a dearth of opportunities, a large serving of blatant racism, and unspeakable amounts of snow, Avva said it was surprisingly difficult to leave that tiny town she had longed to escape for so many years. She said after my grandfather's funeral, she experienced a sense of community she had only felt in India.

"In India, we relied on the community to take care of us, because it is all we had. West Virginia showed us that community when Shankar died," Avva said.

With my grandfather gone, and with Pinni at Georgetown, even a newly demonstrated community was not enough to keep Avva and Mom in West Virginia. Mom especially wanted to move to give me a better environment to grow up in as a brown woman. Avva cashed in every asset to her name for the down payment on this house and gladly let Dad help with the mortgage after.

A master investor, Avva knew our two-story brick house just five miles outside of DC proper would skyrocket in value. Soon after moving, she took a job at a local bank as an accountant and worked there for fifteen years. Between what Avva earned, the excessive amount of money Dad sent to support me, and the appreciating value of the house, the three of us lived very well without ever needing Mom to make money.

I padded upstairs to the familiar room that I had called home the first seventeen years of my life. Mom wouldn't let Avva change a single thing inside the square box interior that was heartedly decorated with memorabilia of every interest I had growing up.

"My daughter will always have her own space in this house," Mom proclaimed.

Before going downstairs to my alternate reality, I called Audrey for a quick taste of her soothing voice. She was somewhere over the Atlantic

Ocean, so I had to settle for a very old voicemail message of broken English.

"You have reach me, Audrey. Thanks to please left your message after the sound. I will to return this from as soon as possible."

From the center of my bed, I could still see the outline of the celestial sticker packet I found in a box of my favorite childhood cereal. After sucking down two bowls of the sugary cubes, I spent an afternoon using my bed as a catapult to build "Constellation Deepa."

Most mothers would have dragged their kids straight down. Mine climbed right up and helped me determine the newest astronomical phenomenon. I spent six years staring up at the sky we created together, foiled only by a necessary paint job after the stickers were recalled for Mercury poisoning.

"Deepa. How are you, beta?" Avva asked me, once I returned downstairs.

I smiled at the word, "beta." The few non-Indian software engineer friends I had always thought my grandmother was speaking of a highly classified Android robot in beta testing. I found that reason far easier and far more amusing to let flourish, rather than explaining the education system that taught a Hindi language word to my Kannada and Telugu speaking grandfather, who then passed the word on to my Tamil and Telugu speaking grandmother.

"Hi, Avva. I'm doing well, you?"

"Still a tired old lady, but much to thank God for."

Avva sat me down to hear all of the latest updates with my work. Mom and I managed to lie to the accounting queen about my starting salary. Thinking I earned much more, Avva was elated to hear that I had chosen to work in immigration rights.

Pinni appeared in tow with Amir and their kids, Sahra and Malak. I felt it strange to see her outside of her impressive professional state. Amir and I chatted politely for a few minutes. Growing up with a gay older brother, he loved to use his eyes to indicate when he was using a euphemism for anything "queer talk."

"How is the *personal life*?" He glanced at the French painting.

With Avva in the room, I didn't want to bring up subjects related to relationships, and steered the conversation to innocuous New York topics—the vending machine ate my metro card, an interesting movie just opened, I discovered a new candy store, and, "I'm hating the transition back to winter."

"It's better than being stuck in a perpetual oven like I was at your age," Mom called out.

Mom's avid vocal support of me usually paired with avid vocal detestation of her past. She launched into a pause of the first persuasion before reminding us of the situation into which I was born.

"I was pregnant and alone, my life was in shambles, and—"

"Time for dinner," Avva shouted.

"You always interrupt my story. It wouldn't have happened if—"

"Enough," Avva shouted, again interrupting Mom.

The passive-aggressive battles of the two generations of women thus commenced. I used to play out battle scenarios in my head as a kid at the dinner table.

"In the right corner, we have Mom weighing in at 125 pounds. She will be testing out her new custom-made guilt rays flown in directly from West Virginia. And in the left corner, we have Avva weighing in at 115 pounds. We expect to see another appearance from the poverty cloak and competition sword."

To make up for a Thanksgiving spent apart, Avva insisted we go around the table and give a word of appreciation before eating. Rejoining reality, I heard Amir was already in the middle of his list. Pinni then gave her thanks for her promotion as a Director at McKinsey, a great family, and a niece who forced her to go to restaurants that had more character than attitude.

"So you *did* like the place?" I teased.

"What place?" Mom asked alarmed.

Mom was upset at the idea that Pinni and I had dinner together on occasion. She used the opportunity to cut Pinni off and start in on her list. Mom's mockery of the "Giving Thanks" ritual went without criticism because she always ended on a note no one could question.

"Thanks for getting me out of that God forsaken marriage, thanks for my headphones that drown out stupid comments, thank you for peanut butter cookies, and thank you for the most wonderful daughter a mother could ever ask for."

We left the honor of finishing to Avva. She included her usual list of always having food on the table, having a healthy family, and enough wealth to last several lifetimes.

"Amen," Avva concluded, standing up and cheering with the steel tumbler she had managed to save from the slums of Chennai.

We all stifled our laughs at her complete clash of cultures. She had picked up the word "amen" from an American movie she saw as a child and carried its use around as a testament to the humility in American thinking.

"They were so sophisticated, yet they thanked God no matter what their wealth."

She was elated when she found the perfect occasion to showcase the word.

We had covered the table with our usual mix of Indian food and American side dishes. I smiled in a brief flashback to my grade school days, when I had to describe how my family celebrated the holidays. The round of snickers back then were traumatizing, though now I found the memory hilarious.

"What does your family have for Thanksgiving, Deepa?" my teacher asked.

"Chapatti, vegetable korma, and mashed potatoes, Ms. Brown."

Mom was the first to break into the comfortable silence as we ate through our first round of food. "Thank God you didn't bring that horrid friend of yours this year."

"Gloria? We don't talk anymore."

"She was very unpleasant."

"Deepa, congratulations on getting that promotion," Pinni called out, trying to control the conversation.

Grateful for the diversion, Avva and Amir chimed in their sounds of encouragement.

"What's a promotion?" Sahra asked Pinni.

"It's the thing Mom got, dummy. It means you are more important at work," Malak told his sister.

"Alpa didn't really get a promotion. Deepa did, not Alpa," Mom heatedly said.

I saw Pinni speed her proverbial car faster down "The Mom Pacify Highway" by reiterating her elation at my promotion. I mouthed a quick "thank you" before staring down at my plate in embarrassment for Mom. This was certainly not Progress.

"Deepa, what happened to Pedro Ramirez?" Avva asked.

"Unfortunately, he died not long after his partner."

I cursed myself for blurting out that word in front of Avva and Mom. Pinni and I held our breaths in unison, waiting for Mom to comment on the nature of Jorge's and Pedro's relationship. Thankfully, Mom pretended to be engrossed in her string beans.

"Immigrants never deserve to be treated like this," Avva continued.

"But they broke the law," Mom finally shouted.

"What choice did they have?" I asked her.

"To not break the law. They violated the law doing what they did."

I shifted anxiously as the ides of repetition made their way. Mom took out her frustration by stabbing her macaroni and cheese with a fork. Sahra and Malak liked the looks of it and followed in motion. Thanksgiving '08 now consisted of three people stabbing macaroni and cheese and one unbearably rough discussion.

Avva did not understand how much or why the rest of us wanted to skip ahead to the next topic of conversation.

"The law isn't always what is should be," Avva concluded.

"Your case was different," Mom exclaimed.

"How? Pedro thought he had to lie to keep Jorge in the country. That's exactly what happened to Mom, Dad, and *you*," Pinni pointed out.

Mom waived her hands in a very predictable two-part argument sequence.

Part One: "It's just different!" "It's just different!" "It's just different!"

Part Two: "It's just different, dissimilar, unalike, atypical, *unnatural*."

My mind flashed back to all the signs of Mom's homophobia— the disgusted stares at the happy same-sex couples in DC, the negative commentary on TV shows with gay characters, and the clear revulsion of the word *lesbian*.

"Why don't you approve? Because they were gay?" I heard myself say.

"Just drop the subject. Gay is not a happy word," Mom said, sardonically chuckling.

Avva sat with a confused expression on her face. The rest of us adults were too shocked at how fast the conversation went from bad to terrible to respond.

"Geez, no one got my joke."

"We got your joke, Mom. It wasn't funny," I replied.

Mom looked aghast that I would dare take that tone. "What has gotten into you? You are so short-tempered with everybody."

"Not with everybody, just with you. Someone pass me the mashed potatoes."

Happy holidays, amen.

Chapter 80

DEAD OAK TREES lined the street. I was sure Tim Burton used something in this scene's vein as inspiration for his life's work. Even in broad daylight, the giant arching branches, the large knots on the trunks, and ghastly gray overtones gave the appearance of a soul-sucking world.

"How's it going?" Audrey asked me.

"Mom is stressed out having my aunt around all week."

"Why?"

"Seeing a slice of my aunt's perfect life is always tough for her."

Audrey was eager to meet Mom for this reason. When Audrey's perfect older sister announced she was getting married to a tall, handsome, stable guy, the look her parents bestowed on the world was one Audrey never forgot.

"We have two daughters—one successful, one gay."

Even though Audrey still had options, her parents had been dismissive of the idea of her ever starting a family.

"I told them I could still enter into *Pacte*. You know this term?"

"Yeah, it's the civil u--baaa--nion."

"Why are you breathing like that?" Audrey asked.

"It's nothing, keep going."

"I think my parents are just sad sometimes—"

Clang clang clang clang clang. My teeth involuntarily became a percussion instrument.

"Deepa, are you outside?"

"I just wanted to take a walk."

"It's minus four Celsius."

"Maybe in Paris, but here it's real-aaaahhh-ly nice."

"That's the temperature for DC today. Are you hiding from your mother?"

She caught me so easily. After the debacle from last year, I knew I couldn't pass off the same excuse with Audrey. *I'm just talking to my cool French friend.*

No else but a significant other would call three times in the first forty-eight hours of a vacation to visit family. The simple solution would have been to ignore Audrey's incoming calls. My heart did not allow me to execute the simple solution.

"Deepa, this makes me so sad. Why should you freeze outside just to have a conversation with your girlfriend?"

"I would do the same thing if you were my boyfriend."

"That's bullshit."

She was right. That was total bullshit.

I did my best to control my loose teeth and vibrating body to prove my failing argument. She babbled about wholly unimportant things, like shoes, her tiny rodent dog, and the declining quality of Parisian chestnuts. To be sure I stayed to listen, she dropped in an occasional, "I love you. I miss you."

Her cooing was just enough to keep me from throwing down my phone in a shivering defeat. The formula she used to estimate my stamina left out one key variable—I hadn't been to the gym in months and had a layer of fat to keep me insulated. I finally conceded to the antics of my clever girlfriend when I realized my hand was completely immobile over my phone.

"I should go inside or I'll freeze to death."

"That was mean to keep you on the phone like that."

"Where's the sorry?"

"It was just a statement."

I knew I shouldn't have used that line when describing her "euro trash" Halloween costume as more prostitute than satire. We exchanged our melodramatic proclamations of love before parting with our lines of communication for the day of Christmas. I hated the time difference. The blackout period was a straight thirty hours.

"MERRY CHRISTMAS, MOM," I exclaimed as she opened my gift.

She was very careful to remove the paper without ripping a single shred. Perhaps I wasn't the only person traumatized by dear Amy. I retrieved my best stupid grin as she revealed a two-foot long frame containing my one extra copy of the November 5, 2008 Obama victory edition of the *New York Times*.

"This is beautiful, Deepa. Thank you. How did you get a copy? I thought you were out late that night?"

"I had to go all the way out to the end of Queens."

I deserved zero credit for this gift. In my veiled queer identity, producing credible sounding lies had become second nature.

"Why do you think there are so many closeted gays on Capitol Hill?" Brian always said.

Despite her severe sadness on election night, Audrey woke up early the next morning and got me a few copies of the paper while I slept in a drunken stupor. I had two copies professionally framed—one for Mom and one for myself. A pay raise and no real plans for Paris had some advantages.

Sahra opened my gift to her—a fifty-piece set of oil pastels. I figured she could use half the colors to draw and half to throw at her brother. She absolutely loved the idea. I congratulated myself for reminding a kid who had everything that there was still something to look forward to.

"Are you going to draw me a picture?" I asked her.

"Yeah. I'll draw one of you in Paris."

"No, dear, Deepa studied abroad in Lyon," Mom told her.

"I knoooow, but she's going to Paris with Au—"

"I might go to Paris next year with a friend," I told Mom.

Mom gave me a strange look for cutting off my ten-year-old cousin, and continued distributing gifts. "Santa's aide" (Mom hated the word "elf") was her favorite role of the year.

Pinni offered to make everyone hot chocolate, and I seized the opportunity to both help and chew her out for telling my ultimate secret to a child. Sahra had a mouth the size of Mount Everest that was as equally poorly regulated as the Nepalese climbing authorities.

"Why did you tell the kids?"

"We live in Manhattan. These days kids know what gay means before they know what sexuality means."

Pinni tried to pass her gross error as further incentive to actually come out to Mom before going back to New York.

"I can't believe you told Sahra. What if Avva finds out?"

Pinni met my worried question with an inappropriately amused expression. Somehow the gravity of the situation had not impacted her the way I had expected.

"It's not funny Pinni, this is my life."

"I know, Deepa. I do take this seriously. That's why I threatened to take away the kids' ski trip this January if they tell."

I felt like running off signs that prominently displayed our new family status.

"Rich people problems in progress."

Mom wandered into the kitchen and asked if I wanted to open her gift. All I really wanted for Christmas was a note on pleasantly scented paper that proudly proclaimed her unconditional love for her gay daughter.

Instead, I followed her back to the giant tree she had hauled in from the neighbor's yard. Mom took on Christmas decorations like a finely trained soldier. Navigating through the train set and floor ornaments, she found my gift in the back. It was a large envelope. In the background of my naively pulsating heart, she said it was a combination Christmas/birthday gift. I would never again expect a gift from anyone if it were the note I prayed for.

I tore open the top portion of the envelope and slowly looked down into its depths.

"This is a ticket to New Delhi," I said.

"You, your avva, and I are finally going to see the Taj Mahal in March," Mom replied.

Mom had a radiant glow evenly coating every inch of her normally defeated face. I couldn't remember the last time I had seen her so excited. Her wanting to get out of the house and return to India was a good sign of her Progress.

"We're finally going after all of those worthless visits to India," Mom continued.

Avva shifted uneasily at the word "worthless" and launched into one of her long explanations about how it was her duty and honor to visit her mother and sister until they passed away.

Mom's energy was so infectious. I let the usual serious demeanor I had developed as an adult melt away and switched back to playful childhood mode. We did our happy dance that helped make growing up with a single parent a (mostly) pleasure.

Pinni came rushing in at the sound of the commotion and asked what had happened. Mom grabbed the ticket from my hand and waved it in victory.

"We're going to Agra to see the Taj Mahal," she bragged.

"That's great. When?" Pinni asked.

"March seventeenth," Mom shouted.

I felt myself crash down from my last leap, as though the word "seventeen" was a secret code to engage lead shoes. Audrey's birthday was March twenty-first, which meant there would be no way to both make the trip to Agra and be in New York for her birthday. I couldn't miss the first of her birthdays we were together.

"I can't go the third week of March."

"What? Why?" Mom said, whipping her body to face me.

The turnaround time on this lie was too short. I knew this was the perfect entry into the conversation I had avoided for twelve years. I should have asked Mom to step into the other room so I could calmly explain my reason.

"It's just . . . I have a conference for work."

I was both impressed and ashamed at how quickly I formulated a cover story.

"We will reschedule. When would be good for you, beta?" Avva asked.

"No. You'll have to miss it, Deepa. This is too important," Mom said.

"Chee. Too important for whom, Pooja? This is her job, she must go to the conference," Avva argued.

Pinni took the tension as a cue to usher the kids and Amir back upstairs to give us air. The way Mom and Avva were shouting, they would use the entire supply of oxygen within minutes.

Sahra's and Malak's scared steps checked Mom back to reality. She managed a measured enough tone so we could discuss other options. I knew I couldn't get off of work before mid-March, and the weather from April—August could render the visit worthless.

"What about October?" I suggested.

"I am doing a seminar series in October and November," Avva quietly said.

"Great. There goes the entire year," Mom screamed.

"What about my birthday?" I offered.

Avva did a head nod in agreement. I thought Mom might pull out another pause of the third persuasion, but changed her mind at the last minute.

"It's disappointing to miss another birthday in the City, but I suppose that's the only solution."

"Cheer up, Mom. We're still going to the Taj Mahal," I encouraged.

Guilt overtook me in my last sentence. Mom managed to give me a weak smile, but the look of defeat was already creeping back into her system. She stalked off without replying. Avva mistook my guilt for sadness in Mom's reaction.

"Don't worry. You go to that conference and make us proud, beta."

Chapter 81

BRIAN EMITTED A few dramatic sighs and quips before finally bringing his phone up to his ear.

"Deepa, darling, you're obsessed with me."

"Very funny. Merry Christmas. How's it going?"

"I hate it here. Don't ever let me make the mistake of coming back. What's up?"

Somewhere in his subconscious, I knew that my coming out ordeal with Audrey and Mom made Brian reevaluate his relationship with his mother and stepdad-zilla. He had decided for the first time since moving to New York to visit them for the holidays.

I told him about the trip to the Taj Mahal and how I blew the perfect entryway into *the* conversation.

"Just tell her the truth," Brian said.

"I can't let her down again."

"Your mom has serious issues if she's upset about a six-month delay on a trip she has waited forty years to take."

I wished Audrey weren't deep in the lairs of Parisian Christmasland. Also in mode of reevaluation, Audrey had decided to have serious conversations with her parents about her life as a gay woman and her future professional plans. We agreed the majestic nature of Christmas Day in France was the perfect occasion, hence the strict thirty-hour moratorium on our communication.

Brian was offended at the notion Audrey knew me better after eight months of dating than he did after seven years of being my emotional rock.

"I've heard more about your relationship with your mother than any human being should ever have to suffer through."

"Thanks for the sensitive discussion."

"Please. We both know your mom wants everything that involves you to be perfect, but her idea of perfect is so out of touch with reality that the world will never live up."

Gloria had said the same thing to me before. She even went so far as to write out a few examples in a flow chart. It was a work of genius, if not extremely offensive and slightly disturbing.

"What do you like about Audrey?" Brian asked.

"Everything . . . most things. I like the way she always picks out the perfect wine—"

"No. Not that small mushy shit. What did you think of the guy I brought to Kelly's going away party?"

"Even during my existential crisis you turn the subject back to your dating life."

"Just answer the question, Deepa."

"I dunno. I liked the way he described his work and the way he dressed."

"See?"

"See what?"

Brian told me that a year ago, I would have said the guy's skinny jeans made him look like a drag version of the *Little Mermaid* and asked him what it was like to work in a company devoid of personality or emotions.

"You're right," I admitted.

"Audrey has made you relate to the world in a more positive way. She's not going to change her mind and you have to come out eventually, Deepa. Audrey is just the catalyst you need."

I TOOK A deep breath and did my best to steady my head, which was swaying like a buoy in turbulent water.

"Hey, Mom, can I come in?"

She sat at the enormous mahogany desk she had three burly movers drag in during one of the hottest days of that summer. The significance of birthdays in American culture never registered in Dad's mind, and he had just sent her a giant check for her forty-second; he never learned when her birthday actually was. She used the money to set up the giant wooden edifice to designate her place in the world.

Seeing Mom at her perch, I made the connection that the reason Barbara's ever-growing pool of papers gave me comfort was because her style was the same as Mom's. Mom printed off hundreds of academic studies related to urban design and architecture, always speaking of the "fallacy of paper being an unsustainable renewable resource." She never told me what she was planning on doing with all of the printed knowledge.

"What are you reading?" I asked.

"It's about the advent of the traffic circle in 1850s Paris."

"That's interesting. Is that . . . ?"

Your latest random obsession? I decided to fill in the substantive part of the question from the safety of my own head. She smiled and looked past me out the window.

"It's hard to believe there are only four days left in the year," she said into space.

"Can I talk to you about something, Mom?"

"I'm sorry, Deepa."

"That's okay, we can talk later."

I turned to leave, partially upset, but mostly relieved.

"No, Deepa, I'm apologizing for acting so crazy lately."

I didn't know if I was more surprised by the apology or the "lately."

"December is a hard time for me. The next one will be the thirtieth anniversary of your father and me getting married."

My "Mom Feelings Geiger" was giving me mixed signals. I wanted to ask if this was a happy conversation of her personal life Progress or a regretful conversation on the lack of her life Progress.

Her gaze softened as she refocused her attention on me. "What did you want to talk about, dear?"

My heart warmed at her eye contact. I often forgot how pretty she was beneath her dark-circled eyes and furrowed brows of analysis. Rare moments like this brought out glimmers of the mother of my happy childhood.

"Tell me about New Orleans. What was it like to go to school there?" I asked.

"Well, the fundamentally unfair circumstances under which I had to move . . ." she trailed off, noticing my immediate sadness at the once again sour tone. "It was a great city in which to study. It was the south geographically, but the people were progressive."

"Progressive people are important," I agreed.

"Did I ever tell you I studied about France, about Lyon?"

"Really? That's awesome. What did you study?"

Mom walked over to her accompanying massive shelf of papers and pulled out four from a seemingly unordered stack. I realized then that she had her own system to sort through what I had perceived was haphazardly grouped.

From the placement of key statues, to the historical significance of districting, to the class warfare of street layouts, we covered nearly everything I remembered about the physical aspects of the Rhône-Alps region of France. I had no idea everything was laid down with so much purpose. I had no idea Mom *knew* all of this was laid down with so much purpose. She beamed with the knowledge that she had imparted new context to my understanding.

"The level of development in the European continent—the history, the stories—it's fascinating to see how they play out in the end product," she said.

Her entire body became animated as she waved her arms to conduct the intricacies of her field. With every new street, with every new passage, the ornate hall began to take shape. The lights shone down as though directed from the Heavens, the curtains fluttered at each breath of enlightenment, the instruments bellowed out their music with passion. As the performance came to a close, she beckoned me to join in as a co-conductor.

"Deepa, you wanted to talk to me about something?"

She held her baton in midair, waiting for my cue on which direction to move the ensemble. I looked out into the audience waiting patiently for the completion of our song. They had been anticipating this for many long years.

"Don't keep us waiting. Let us know the ending."

I held my breath as I marched to the dignified podium that looked upon the intense spectators. Raising my arm to match her poised level, I said the words that completed her work of genius.

"We should stop in Paris for a few days on our way over to Agra. I know you've never been."

The audience gasped at my twist ending. I saw the lead violinist frantically search for a pencil to scribble down the final notes I had directed. Mom turned to face me to confirm the conclusion, to forever etch into the stone the grand finale.

"I thought you were going with your friend?"

"No, Mom, I want to go with you."

I left Maryland a few days later without telling Mom what I had planned to discuss before our co-conducted orchestra.

Chapter 82

THE DAY AFTER Christmas, Julie had written me an e-mail saying she decided to stay with her family in Boston for New Year's Eve. At the time, I forwarded the message to Audrey with domestic elation. Now I regretted that move. I, least of all, would have guessed last year that I'd prefer to spend this New Year's Eve in a crowded, impersonal club instead of being at home alone with my girlfriend.

I kept myself busy the last day of 2008 by pulling out all the stops to create a romantic atmosphere in the hopes that it would soften the blow that I was a lying coward. Audrey called from the airport as I was making the wine reduction for the pasta.

"I'm coming straight to your apartment," she said.

I had drenched the pasta in a giant pool of my sweat by the time I hung up the phone. I managed to finish cooking dinner without burning my hands, though the thought of purposely hurting myself did cross my mind. The girlfriend who had turned me on to vodka sodas made for a particularly tumultuous relationship, and during one of our fights, I had first entertained such a move. Brian made a comment to dissuade me from the crazy notion.

"If you are willing to inflict bodily harm on yourself, it's time to break up."

I heard the door buzzer just forty-five minutes after Audrey called. Without fail, the New York City taxi system brought her to Lower Manhattan from the outskirts of Queens in record time the one occasion I would have relished an extended delay.

"Wow, you didn't have to go to all of this trouble, Deepa."

I didn't have time to clean up the counter, the sink was piled high with dishes, the soap dispenser was nearly empty, and the mystery sweater from our last party was still on the couch. Even so, Audrey eyed everything with such appreciation as though the room was the very definition of perfection.

I told her to take her time getting ready. She took advantage of the one free thing Manhattan offered—water—and emerged later flushed from the heat and wrapped in an oversized bathrobe.

"*Alors, je suis vrai canon?*" she asked, playing on the French-English translation to ask if she looked "hot."

She wore her fuzzy dolphin slippers and strutted down a fake catwalk the length of the apartment.

"Bah, *oui*. Youuu hhhare zoooo beeyoutifffull."

"Great-T. Zank you wery much."

Her constant smiling helped me relax, and we caught up on the mundane details of the past few days without me slipping in and out of consciousness. I had called her only once after our Burton-esque oak tree chat, and said that I wanted to recap *the* conversation with her in person. She agreed, thinking Mom and I had actually had *the* conversation. I still hadn't figured how to break the news there was no Progress on that front. Audrey was clearly dying to bring up the subject, but we both knew how quickly that could sour the mood.

After dinner, we settled onto the couch with glasses of wine in our hands. I looked down at Audrey resting her head comfortably on my shoulder. Her legs were crossed over mine. Despite the difference in our skin tone, the point at which she ended and I began was indistinguishable.

My mind flashed back to this precise day one year ago. I spent the last few hours of 2007 explaining to a stranger why I thought I was born gay. Gloria was right. I did have a problem with my sexuality. I was comfortable enough to not suppress it, but not enough to embrace it. Denial had made me a bitter person. Audrey was the first person to cause that bitterness to evaporate. All my previous girlfriends had only played to my intellectual and carnal needs. Audrey went much further in stimulating a part of my heart that had previously been dormant.

"Five, four, three, two, one . . . *Bonne Année!*" she yelled.

The TV screen flashed over to president-elect Obama.

"My fellow Americans, from the great city of Chicago, I extend my warmest wishes of gratitude for your support this past year. As we look forward into 2009, I want to reach out to every one of you—black, white, Democrat, Republican, Christian, Muslim, straight or gay . . ."

Audrey squeezed my hand as Obama said the word "gay." I felt the Progress. Her warmth and the emphatic release of our new president supporting our right to live honestly enveloped my entire body. I gently guided Audrey's chin to look into the depths of her stunning blue eyes. In their reflection, I saw the black of my own eyes poised for a confession.

Chapter 83

"YOU LIED TO Audrey's face," Brian screamed at me.

"I panicked, I didn't know what else to do."

"What exactly did you say?"

"That Mom needs to keep some distance while she figures things out in her head."

Brian congratulated me for regurgitating his mother's exact response from eight years ago. I remembered him standing up at the only LGBTQ Alliance meeting I ever went to and telling everyone his step-dadzilla was too stupid to figure out basic concepts like evolution or homosexuality.

Step-dadzilla had a complete breakdown and accused Brian of being a pedophile and practicing bestiality. Since I had skipped a grade, Brian was a year older than me and of legal age when the horrendous episode happened. After calling the cops, step dad-zilla was nearly successful in having Brian hauled away to the county jail. Brian's mother defaulted as the negotiator.

Brian and I became instant best friends after I heard his story. Unfortunately, I didn't have a balance of a second parent to calm the other down.

"What about your grandmother?" Brian asked.

"She doesn't share our concept of sexuality."

"She's asexual?"

"No, not exactly."

I always loathed the Westerner narrative of associating bravery with coming out at an early age. Mom's life had taught me Indians did not view their children as the autonomous beings Americans did. I knew the lack of sexual desire that went with Indian arranged marriages confounded my ability to have a conversation about homosexuality with Avva. How was I supposed to use the typical Western emotional reasoning?

"My love and desire for my life partner is simply for someone of the same sex."

I knew Avva hadn't married my grandfather because she was in love. Avva had married my grandfather because she knew he was kind, trustworthy and they had compatible views. I could only assume love had come later.

I saw the coffee shop empty out with morose and conflicted faces. Brian and I were already late for the first day back to work. Before parting ways on our familiar landing spot, Brian warned me of introducing any more stupid decisions.

"And remember to cover all of your bases," he said.

AS I HAD expected, the first few weeks of 2009 went by in a blur of computer, train, and bed. The only weekend I managed to stay away from the office was met with a bowl of chicken noodle soup and a treacherous landscape of dirty tissues.

Audrey's studio, my office, and my apartment formed a giant triangle of inconvenience. To spend any time together, one of us either committed three nights away from home or we had to be satisfied with a mere drink like common colleagues. My immune system could not handle the pressure when our schedules were combined with the nasty winter season.

"Deepa, you look terrible. Where's Audrey?" Julie said one week in mid-February.

"Dealing with her place."

"Great amenities?"

"The works."

I had spent the last Saturday helping her contain the perks of her rent-controlled studio—including broken pipes, mice, and a possible case of bed bugs. We spent a fantastic day playing detective, exterminator, laundry washer, and paranoid repellent sprayer.

"Why don't you move in together?" Julie suggested.

"Am I that bad of a roommate?"

Julie tapped her foot in annoyance. It was too late in the day, too late in the week to go fishing for compliments. We had established that activity was best done Monday through Wednesday, from ten a.m. to four p.m.

"You know what I mean. I can find someone to take over your room."

"Am I that easily replaceable?"

"Still off hours. You're a fish out of water."

I thanked her for the offer, and declined by saying how stupid it would be to give up such a great apartment to move into Audrey's dump.

"She could stay here until you two find somewhere else," Julie pressed.

"Thanks for the offer, it's just—"

Julie gave me a look of annoyance now turned anger. I had spilled my inner turmoil to her two weeks earlier in a coughing, sneezing, dazed three a.m. confession.

"You still haven't told her?" Julie guessed.

"No, I'm afraid to move in together."

I knew the conversation I had been carefully avoiding would soon surface if Audrey and I saw each other every day. I told Julie that conversation was literally the only thing keeping me from suggesting the move.

"Dummy, then tell Audrey."

"I want it to be clear I lied out of the genuine fear of losing Mom."

"You'll lose your mother regardless if you don't have a visa to go to India."

I had tried every day for a week to fill out the visa application form, as my past experience with the process told me there was never enough time when dealing with the Indian government. Whenever I sat down to fill the application out, Barbara came rushing to my desk to tell me to find a solution to a seemingly impossible immigration problem.

"I haven't even printed off the thing," I said.

"I'm an incredible friend, right?"

"Hey. No phishing."

Julie walked over to her gigantic purse, which engulfed her whole as she rummaged around the basement level. I heard a few crashes of overstuffed file cabinets. She reappeared and waved a gigantic envelope as though I were her puppy and the envelope were a bone.

"I took the liberty of filling out all of the parts I knew."

"Oh my God, thank you so much," I exclaimed.

Julie had correctly filled out most of the application, and attached extra copies of my passport photo left over from our trip to China.

"Deepa, in exchange, you have to promise me something."

Julie walked to the door of my room and peered around, flipping through her mental memory book of us being roommates for five years. Together in that apartment we had battled the all-nighters of school, the mistakes of young love, and the realities of transitioning into adulthood in an overpriced yet tantalizing city.

"You have to tell Audrey. Coming out to your mom is your decision, but lying about it is a whole other issue."

This was a memory I hoped would get tucked away in the archives. I promised to take care of everything. Julie looked truly undecided about whether my honesty would prevail.

Chapter 84

AUDREY'S HOUSING SITUATION deteriorated further when her landlord announced her building had significant pipe damage and would be shut down by April. Residents had four weeks to figure out alternate arrangements. On the upside, security deposits would be returned. On the downside, lives would be ruined.

With no credit score in the States, Audrey had moved into her studio under a sublet instead of a lease. To her credit, her studio was rent-controlled at a price established around 1975. When I found out what her budget was for a new apartment, I knew immediately her only options would be to move to the ends of the City to retain the level of privacy we had come to enjoy, or have roommates.

"These arrangements were too good to last forever." I sighed.

"If only there was a way for us to live together."

We had benefitted greatly from the process of "discovering each other," and she had dropped many lines to suggest we were ready for cohabitation. I loved the idea of coming home to her, but my secret followed me around like a grenade. If I took my thumb off the pin, our entire world would be blown to pieces.

"I can come to Queens on the weekends. Roommates are an option; it's nice to have company," I told her.

"We'll make it work," she agreed with disappointment, unsure why I didn't agree to the ideal move.

For two weeks, I helped her search through every nook and cranny of Manhattan, Brooklyn, and Queens. The best options we found were still pathetic.

> Apartment 1: Lower Manhattan, two roommates, practically condemned, room about the size of my head.
> Apartment 2: Brooklyn, three roommates, one of whom may be a serial killer.
> Apartment 3: Queens, no roommates; we'd essentially be a long-distance couple.
> Apartment 4: Hoboken, New Jersey, one roommate with the following kitchen requirements: no dairy, no meat, no gluten, no sugar.
> Apartment 5: Brooklyn, four roommates, two live-in partners, one bathroom.

Audrey agreed to take the one bedroom apartment in Queens, and was set to sign the paperwork just a few days after her birthday. She spent a few nights with me, though the noise of my neighborhood kept her in her broken studio most of the week.

"We can make this work, right?" we both questioned.

"AH, I AM so 'appy to get out of that fucking apartment," Audrey exclaimed.

Up until we started dating, I had hated the way French people drop the beginning "h" in English words. I looked at her face and could now see how deaf I had been for all of those years. What else could describe her total elation?

"Appy."

My gaze was fixed straight ahead at the road. I silently debated whether I should have indeed skipped out on Audrey's birthday for India to avoid the hanging doubt that had been so hard to stuff in this motorized vehicle. The previous week, I took a timed ride out to Audrey's new apartment from my supposedly conveniently located office building. At the end of the run, the timer read 112 minutes. Rides two and three came in at 117 and 124 minutes, respectively.

"What are you thinking?" she asked.

"Maybe if I had taken the bus . . ."

Her *'appy* expression eased the suffocating pressure of the remaining doubt. Over the years, I had charted the thoughts, feelings, and emotions that populated my being against my needed reaction from other people. As my relationship with someone progressed, the lines moved in a direction of divergence or convergence. My whimsical childhood had awarded the only true case of convergence in my life. Audrey had just accepted to do a year of independent research in New York; I was confident she would become the second case in that time.

"Really, what are you thinking?" she asked again.

"Just be careful, it's not permanent."

"I have no idea what you are saying. Where the hell are you taking me?"

Dan's father died when were in college with two explicit directions:

1. Marry a beautiful woman
2. Clean up the God damn beach house

Queer as the West Village during Pride, Dan failed miserably on the first account. The previous week I offered to help with the second direction in exchange for exclusive weekend usage rights. I knew the beach would be freezing, the town would be dead, and the surroundings would be as quiet as the French countryside. I knew it would the perfect setting for my surprise. As we entered, Audrey let out the gasp for which I had very much hoped.

I had reopened my toolbox of graphic design skills on images from our well-documented journey. With the help of a thick curtain, I blocked out all of the light in the main room, save the warm strokes of a few jasmine-scented candles. The black-and-white chronicle of our lives thus far was washed in a stunning sepia-like glow.

"It's beautiful, Deepa."

"I have another present. It's very small."

In between my Long Island house cleaning, I took a day trip down to Maryland to see Mom. We started the conversation by outlining the forthcoming memory blocks of all things Parisian, of all things north Indian. She as the architect, and me as the builder, our voyage would be a lifetime of happiness on which to reinforce our foundation.

"I'm hopefully moving in with someone," I then told her.

"Is it a friend from school?"

"I met her through a friend. We're moving into a one-bedroom apartment."

An earthquake erupted, shaking Mom so violently she spilled half of her tea on the kitchen table.

"Rent is expensive in New York. Many friends split one-bedroom apartments."

"Mom. I'm moving into the apartment with Audrey, my—"

"Friend. Yes, I heard you, Deepa."

I finally saw that our foundation on this topic was too damaged to even plan for construction. Mom would not entertain blueprints of discussion; the conversation itself would not happen. Mom's decision was swift, and it was final.

"Yeah. My friend. Audrey."

"We'd better get you back to the train station, Deepa."

Audrey was staring into my eyes, waiting for her small gift. I had tried to replace my deception to her with the truth, but it was like molding steel as clay. My only other option, the one I knew would work was to move forward with my soul mate and explain the verity of the matter when the opportune moment came. I knew with time I could make Audrey understand, and my falsity would become a distant, inconsequential memory.

"Audrey, I know I didn't ask before, so if you hate the idea, I completely understand."

She looked down at my hand and gasped at the sight of a small gold box. I steadied myself as she carefully removed the cover.

"It's a key to your apartment?" she asked with distinct disappointment.

"No, it's the key to an apartment in Brooklyn."

"I don't understand."

"I signed a lease two weeks ago . . . for us. I want us to move in together."

I held my breath to tread the approval water.

"I love it," she screamed.

Treading was not necessary. The water was at waist level.

"Where is the apartment? What does it look like? When can we move in? Can we get a *téléphone fixe*?"

"Right off of the Bergen F train stop, modern and sleek, and yes, I think a fixed landline phone is a splendid idea."

A picture of Audrey, Brian, and me faced us as we let our minds escape to a perfect future.

Chapter 85

I HAD LIVED in the East Village for five years, and had thoroughly enjoyed my time in a neighborhood of a city whose change outpaced the most frequently changing people. The boxes to move my life to Brooklyn signified a new era in my life, however, and I couldn't wait to move forward with Audrey.

We only took two days to distribute our collective belongings into a perfect symbiosis. The gimmicky appeal of the modern-style stainless steel appliances and shiny hardwood floor said that we had become sell-outs, but that was a compromise we were very willing to make. On our first decorating adventure, we discovered black furniture that contrasted perfectly with the apartment design, and we finished off the look with a few splashes of color that showcased our respective personalities.

"We make a great team," Audrey said.

"Indeed we do. I love that shelf we bought."

It was an asymmetrical unit that a certain ex would have said was the product of a stroke.

"Oh, I forgot. I bought a *fixe*."

"A landline phone."

"Yes, a landline. This will make it much easier for me to call France."

Audrey's two years in the States was enough time to justify not carrying a computer around as a phone for cheap Internet calls. Unfortunately, I was a dud at operating the antiquated system.

"How do we record a voicemail message?" I asked.

"Are you joking? Remind me to teach you before September," she said.

"Why?"

"Because my parents only use a landline . . . I was thinking we could go to Paris for your birthday."

My brain split in two. We had been in the apartment for less than forty-eight hours and the conversation had already surfaced.

"I forgot to tell you though. I'm going to India for my birthday," I replied.

That part was indeed true.

"Ah that's too bad about Paris, but India will be great. For work?"

"Yeah, Barbara is sending me to a human rights conference in Delhi. I'm sorry I didn't tell you sooner, it just got crazy with the move—"

"No problem, I know I can trust you."

OUR SCHEDULES WERE polar opposites:

"Student v. Professional"

We read each other's minds and knew how to make it work. The luxury of Brooklyn-sized apartments gave her enough room to carry on raging debates of psychology well into the night without disturbing me, so I could wake up on time the next morning to ponder the all-important question, "Bagel or toast?"

One of the reasons most of my friends were straight is because lesbians had a tendency to disappear when dating. Audrey and I both lived in the City to enjoy the City, however, and we made our own "Pacte" not to bring each other down. Some nights were surely spent alone in the comfort of each other's arms, though mostly one or both of us were out to live our lives in the vast expanse of the urban paradise.

We had a housewarming party a few weeks after we moved in. To compliment my Chelsea Market cheese excursion, Audrey paired my favorites to three types of wine, and the finest meats and bread my credit card would allow me to purchase. We stood back in proud wonder as Audrey's international friends blended effortlessly with my artsy, progressive New York companions. The verdict was in—our life was nearly perfect.

Chapter 86

AUDREY'S PARENTS VISITED the third week of May for her graduation from The New School Masters of Psychology program. After dealing with a stingy customer service, I cashed in all of those overtime nights from the winter. Audrey and I cleaned up our first few months of apartment filth and mapped out a treasure chest of her parents' favorite foods. They were not stubborn people, just French.

"This apartment became so dirty in just two months," Audrey cried on day two of our deep cleaning.

"I once heard the reason New York is so dirty is because it carries the emotional dust of the world."

"I think it's because of poor funding."

"At least people clean up their dog shit here."

Despite a society so concerned with cleanliness and order, I lost track on how many times during my year in France I jumped around on the sidewalk to avoid dog turds. In a country that functioned with poise and grace, they were literally the black dots that maligned the pristine face.

"Ahh, Deepa, don't say things like this in front of my parents. They think France is the best country in the world. It is really important to me that you get along."

She looked at me with an intense expectation that further aggravated the anxiety brewing inside of me. The previous week, I realized that this would be the first time I'd meet a girlfriend's parents in any formal capacity. Gloria once dragged me to one of her father's boozy backyard Bronx barbeques when we first started dating.

"Are you the girl from ER?" he screamed in my face.

I had no idea whether little frame of reference would work in my favor. All I knew was that I couldn't screw this up. First impressions were everything.

We decided to take the subway out to JFK to pick up Audrey's parents. From our neighborhood in Brooklyn, the ride was one of my favorites in New York City. Together we sat on the train, observing the fine details of the New York City masses. There were so many influencing cultures.

"What does my father do for a career?" Audrey quizzed.

"He is a professor of economics at Université Sorbonne Nouvelle, Paris III. Your mom is an orthopedic surgeon at the nearby St. Germain hospital."

"And my sister?"

"Your sister, Cécile, is three years older than you and a marketing executive. She is married to Nicolas, a successful software engineer."

"And the dog?"

I snickered. "Your dog, Pépite, is a bichon."

I couldn't help but fall into hysterical laughter. What better stereotype for this dark-haired, tall French family than a tiny *Bichon* named *Pépite*?

"Don't make fun of *chère* Pépite."

"Sorry, I just think small dogs are lame."

She told me we were getting a small dog eventually, so I'd better find my inner appreciation for them or else it would be an awkward dynamic.

"When do you envision getting this small dog?"

"Perhaps in two or three years. Once we can move to a bigger apartment . . . What's that look on your face?" she asked.

"I'm just excited to think about the future."

Exactly zero times I had been to JFK without an accompanying mad dash through security and to my gate. When we entered Terminal 1, I took an extra moment to recreate my family's stories the airport buildings contained. I imagined the anticipation and fear Avva must have had setting foot here on the other side of the world—her new life—for the first time. I knew Mom must have been so scared bidding farewell to her childhood decades later. Now there I stood, awaiting the beings that bore the reason I was a better person.

I spotted Audrey's parents a mile away. Audrey was clearly her mother's daughter, with the same flowing chestnut hair, a perfectly curved figure, and an identical poised walk. Her father was a tall man with a slight slouch and simple features that formed an unyielding face. Their clothes were impeccably in place and they walked in harmony straight into the arms of their loving daughter. By the way they subtly pointed and found each other's gazes, I could tell they had developed their own mental language for comparing notes.

Back at the apartment, they examined every inch of the space. From my year of living with quintessential French students, I guessed the level of detail at which two older Parisians examined something. Compared to my relaxed American standards, I only hoped my portion of our apartment clean up met Audrey's parents' expectations.

> *American Inspection Point 1:* Is the bathroom clean?
> *French Inspection Point 1:* Precisely how many bathroom tiles have a disagreeable substance between the crevasses?
> *American Inspection Point 2:* Do all of the appliances in the kitchen work properly?

French Inspection Point 2: Are the utensils arranged for maximum efficiency? Are the cheeses, yogurts, and creams stored separately?
American Inspection Point 3: Is the apartment nice?
French Inspection Point 3: How many trains, buses, metros, and trams in the vicinity? How good is the grocery store access? What is the historical significance of the neighborhood?

Audrey's parents completed their detailed inspection and returned to deliver the verdict. Thankfully, there was only one complaint.

"There should be a bidet."

Audrey rolled her eyes, saying that was ridiculous by current French standards. "Even in France it's just for decoration."

"Perhaps you have become Americanized," her father said, eyeing me too coldly.

I WAS FASCINATED with the dynamic between Audrey and her parents. They formed a perfect triangle in debates and discussions.

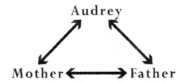

My family had always operated differently. Either Mom or Avva would be a firm other side of my conversation before the other inevitably interjected in the middle.

Most of my friends in Maryland had divorced or single households. I hadn't made it far enough along in the relationship with any of my previous girlfriends to entertain significant time with their parents. No one who lived in New York City dared to drag friends on their obligatory touristy family excursions. This was my first intimate look at how a two-parent family functioned.

Until I met Audrey's parents, the idea of a proper nuclear family seemed so outdated and boring. Audrey's parents were different. They disagreed respectably, they supported each other fervently, they were assertive without being abrasive, and they had most certainly found every type of conversion. Her parents' relationship was an encouraging window to my future.

Unfortunately, Audrey's father hated me. Hate was a strong word. Hate was the Westboro Church on gay rights. Hate was a native New Yorker's feeling toward a Boston-based sports team. Hate was my feeling of the George W. Bush administration. Audrey's father hated me.

Seeing as her father and mother were so close, I took Audrey's father's hatred of me to avoid all one-on-one contact with either parent. Audrey's mother managed to corner me at breakfast one morning as I debated another all-important question.

"Waffles or pancakes?"

A native Parisian, Audrey's mother had lived the bizarre split life of white privilege in the midst of an incredibly diverse city. She was fascinated with my family's story.

"Your parents grew up in India?"

"No, just my father."

I explained my hatred (hate was the right word) of the new Bangalore city developments. "They call it the Garbage City."

"And your parents want you to have an arranged marriage?"

"Not at all, my mother is very against it."

"She is accepting of your sexual orientation?"

My guess was that on the scale of acceptance, the best I could ever hope for would be constant, total denial. "She is getting used to the idea."

"I was the same way. It was not an easy thing to hear my daughter is a lesbian."

Though Audrey had made the claim her mother felt this way, I was still surprised to hear Audrey's mother speak so candidly of her reaction.

She explained that as a straight mother, it was upsetting to know her daughter would go through something very different to find a life partner. Even having a straight older daughter did not lessen the blow. "I found it hard to connect to my own child on as fundamental as love."

"In Indian culture, a partner is found for you. The love may or may not come later."

Audrey's mother scrunched her nose in a moment of negative reminiscence. The first Indian she ever had met was a resident at her hospital. His parents were from one of the last surviving French-speaking villages of the formerly colony of Goa. He was a young fellow, a quiet fellow, and very set in his ways.

"He spoke of his wife as though she were a furniture purchase. 'She must be durable, comfortable, and easily transported.'"

"Wives in India are often treated like a long-term investment purchase. American ideals combined with Indian execution . . ."

"It must have been hard for your mother, then."

This woman was perceptive, just like her daughter. She told me of her fights in gender equality when she was my age.

"As with the using the French feminine article when describing a doctor?" I asked.

She was happy to hear Audrey was spreading the message of the mini revolution. "I demanded people show me respect as a female doctor, even if the French language didn't have the correct words."

"That is very eloquently stated."

"It was Audrey who first described it this way when she came out to us."

Audrey had recognized her mother did not see the link between gender equality and supporting the right of two women to fall in love and build a family.

"Audrey helped me realize that it is very much the same struggle."

Her mother gently laid a hand on my shoulder and thanked me for making her daughter so happy. This visit was the first time since she could remember that Audrey had been at ease with the world.

"I am so grateful you have made her a stronger person."

Chapter 87

UNDER A BRILLIANT blue sky, fluffy white clouds, and a perfect temperature, Audrey decided she did not want to waste another day indoors at the giant University commencement ceremony the next morning. With no need to rush to dinner and back to the apartment for an early bedtime, I awkwardly played the role of third-wheel to Audrey's parents as we patiently waited for her to say a last goodbye to nearly every one of her classmates. I concentrated on the irony of the cutting-edge program graduation ceremony taking place in an old Gothic-style church. At the same time, I tried to block out the relentless looks of disapproval Audrey's father shot at me.

Audrey spent a solid hour finding her classmates—now colleagues— and doling out generous flushed looks of appreciation. She was proud of their collective accomplishments that signified the start of most promising careers.

Audrey's mother turned to me and winked. "You have helped make our daughter so happy."

"It's just the City," Audrey's father snapped.

Finally, Audrey galloped toward us and recapped the feelings of the bittersweet ending. Her father congratulated her on the academic achievement and offered to pay for the most expensive meal New York City had to offer. He adjusted his body so my invitation was in question.

"There is a fantastic Italian restaurant in the East Village." Audrey turned and waited for me to say that was my old neighborhood.

Her father's back was still to my face, and I hesitated at the chance of starting the first true fight of the visit. Reading my hesitation, Audrey declared me available for a tour of the neighborhood. Her father's reaction made me feel as though Audrey and I were a theme park ride. "Please proceed in an orderly fashion. No drinking, no eating, and certainly no screaming. Priority seats available for the vision impaired and disapproving."

I saw Audrey's father stare at our piano keys display of handholding affection. The laser beam that accompanied overprotective fathers burned a hole straight through my right palm. Audrey was unharmed.

"Don't let it bother you, seeing me with my girlfriend is still new to him," she whispered to me in English.

Audrey called the restaurant and took the first available reservation for ten o'clock. With three hours to kill, she decided we should wander west to the Highline in the Meatpacking District before heading back to the East Village. I was embarrassed to show her parents our gross, polluted Hudson River. I knew Audrey's father would take it as my attempt to one-up Paris.

"This is a filthy body of water, nothing like the magnificent Seine," her father immediately commented once seeing the river.

I suggested alcohol might best celebrate Audrey's achievements, thinking a stiff drink might ease the harshness of Audrey's father's remarks. Once settled at a table, he wasted no time in continuing his open disapproval of me, this time questioning my level of French culture exposure.

"Have you been to France?" he asked me.

"Of course. How do you think she can speak French so well," Audrey exclaimed.

"It passes," he answered back.

"I studied abroad for two semesters in Lyon," I offered.

"Ah, Lyon. I grew up near there. How do you find the city?"

I did my best to balance out potential competing interests, surprised he even wanted to know my opinion. "It's a beautiful city, but I prefer Paris."

"Why don't you like Lyon?" he asked.

"It just isn't as open or progressive . . . the people, I mean. There is not the same level of diversity."

I heard Audrey's nervous sigh at my response. I knew no matter what my answer, her sigh would have been the same; there was no pleasing her father.

"The important thing is that Deepa speaks French and she loves Paris," Audrey remarked.

"Yes, Paris is the best city in the world," her father thankfully agreed.

"When will you come to visit, Deepa?" her mother asked me.

"Septem . . . September was our hope, but I have to go to India for work. Perhaps Christmas?"

"We will be in Luxembourg for Christmas. You cannot come," her father snapped.

"No problem, I understand."

"Family is important," he growled.

"Supporting and understanding family is important," Audrey snapped.

"They are all important," Audrey's mother shouted.

Mercifully, the waitress interrupted the conversation. I waited for everyone else to order before requesting the same drink as Audrey's mother, thinking it was the safest move given the situation. She was the only person Audrey's father did not question.

"Would you like to stop in Paris on the way to India?" Audrey's mother suggested.

"Yes. That is a great idea. What do you think, Deepa?" Audrey eagerly asked.

"It's not possible, we have to go back to Lyon to help my brother after his surgery and Deepa hates Lyon," Audrey's father scoffed.

Her mother angrily explained that Audrey's uncle was having minor surgery on his hand, which did not require they be there all month.

"No. Don't rearrange anything for me," I exclaimed.

"Yes, she is actually right," he backhandedly agreed.

The three started in on a triangular fight.

"There is no need to argue," I desperately chimed in.

"Supporting family, remember Audrey?" her father snapped.

Audrey looked at me as if to say I was shooting myself in the foot.

Her mother caught the glance and soothed the storm once more. "Deepa, you are welcome to stay with us when you can come."

Practically slapping him in the face for bad behavior, she demanded her husband repeat the same thing. He looked at Audrey and saw the emerging sadness on her face. This was supposed to be her special day.

"Yes, you are welcome to our home, Deepa," he reluctantly replied.

I sucked down the rest of my drink before excusing myself to the bathroom to send Audrey a text to come join me. Without conferring further, I told her I would leave the solid family triangle less I cause a major breakage.

"You don't have to. My father does not have the right to treat you differently—"

"Stop," I pleaded.

This was the first time that I forcefully challenged her judgment on our relationship. I could count a thousand reasons why her father may not have liked me.

"Why are you assuming his disapproval is because I am a woman?" I asked.

"What else could it be?"

"My race?"

"Is that better?"

"No. Okay . . . Maybe he is just afraid of losing his little girl? I'm the first partner he has met, right?"

She pursed her lips at the thought before confirming I was indeed her first partner her father had met. I was on to something.

"He may not see me as some gay girl with his daughter. Maybe he sees me as that person who took his daughter away from him," I elaborated.

For the first time since we started dating, she gave me credit on something coming out-related. I told her parents I wasn't feeling well and bowed out after paying for the drinks. Her father looked elated to see me go. I didn't care. I had a call to make.

Chapter 88

I WALKED BACK to the Highline and chose one of the last free seats overlooking the Hudson. I saw thousands of happy couples walking, children eating ice cream, and relieved students celebrating the culmination of a lifetime of work. The scene gave me a soothing effect to counter the storm I was about to unleash on my life.

As with most gay people, I had had countless nightmares about the day I came out to my mother. Most TV shows and media recounted tales of catastrophic proportions—children being thrown out on the street, sent away to psychiatric facilities, or completely disowned by their families. In reality, of the many queer people I had met over the years, the only person whose story came close to that extremism was Brian.

When I reasoned with Audrey why her father was being so disrespectful to me, I immediately realized I was no longer speaking of only her father. The pronoun "he" was off, but pronouns had been established as inaccurate in these matters. In a strange epiphany, that angry, jealous, irrational man made me realize the degree of my paranoia.

Since I could remember, everyone had dealt with Mom's actions and words, but I knew then that her actions and words were symptomatic, not the root cause of her discontent. I still had to piece together exactly how to present the information, and how prepare myself for a possible pushback. I had, however, finally figured out one piece of critical information—Mom simply needed to know how much I loved her. She needed to know my life partner would never supersede her place in my life. Mom would never lose me. It was time to take the risk.

Mom picked up on the third ring, just as expected. We exchanged mundane life details—the weather, the television, the work, and the family.

"Deepa, are you okay?"

"Everything is fine. Are you free next weekend?"

"You are always welcome to your own home."

Her words hit the drum of my pounding heart with a new kind of reverberation.

"We can discuss hotels when you get down here."

"You go ahead and book whatever you want. The important thing is that we get to spend my birthday together."

I sounded suspicious. She asked if I needed money, if I was in trouble with the law, or if pressures on the job finally forced me to cave into quitting. I yearned for a return to the days when a few simple words could be read for all its hidden meaning.

"It's nothing bad, I . . . I just love you, Mom."

She assured me she loved me, too. I told her I would forward my itinerary once I booked the ticket down to Maryland.

AUDREY JUMPED UP with excitement for me, though she was too loud in her enthusiasm.

"You're going to see your mother."

"Shh, you'll wake your parents up."

I needed seven months since Audrey's ultimatum to actually find the courage to come out to Mom. I knew one swift look of doubt from Audrey's father would dismantle every bit of bravery I had summoned.

"My mother is just scared to lose me. I called and explained how I miss her."

"This is such a big step."

Audrey thought this step would lead up. My hope was Mom and I would stay level.

"It's two am, you should go to bed," I said.

"Aren't you coming?"

"I have some memos to finish."

"An insomniac consumed by work. Perfect, I live with my father."

She left me as I wondered if she appreciated the irony of her statement. I looked at her angelic silhouette as she arranged her body in her favorite sleep position. In all of the misery and all of the deception this lie had created, my biggest regret was not being able to decipher between my fear of losing Audrey and my need to be wholly honest with Mom.

Well into the night, I researched resources for family members of LGBTQ community members, as I had done three times before. In 1999, my findings included a few text heavy web pages. In 2004, my search led me to websites with online newsletters and event pictures. Now, in 2009, I found blogs, social media groups, smartphone apps, and links to more than twenty organizations in the DC area alone. I was starting to see the benefit of being in the mainstream.

Around six a.m., I finally e-mailed myself the extensive list I had pulled together. I quietly changed into my pajamas, emerged from the bathroom, and crashed into the intimidating relationship enemy I had been so careful to avoid.

"Ow."

I managed to stifle a full scream.

My night vision finally made an appearance, and I saw the angry man covered in a milk moustache. I made my way back to the pullout bed, trying my best to walk around his demonic persona.

"I have a stomach ache from that terrible restaurant. I came to get a glass of milk," he announced, forcing me to come back.

"Good luck. American milk is not nearly as good as French milk."

"You speak the truth."

He appeared to be the kind of person who connected to people through complaining. I wondered how he first won over the affections of Audrey's mother. I told him I was going to bed. He tried to correct my French verb use.

"You mean back to bed."

"No, I mean to bed for the first time."

"Why are you up this late?"

I hesitated to tell him, reasoning that he would say my analytic skills were like that of a monkey, or that I should have first asked Audrey.

"Just research."

"For work?"

"No, on resources for the family members of LGBTQ people."

"For me?" he angrily asked.

"No. For my mother."

My answer calmed him down. He told me he did a lot of research on the subject when Audrey first came out to him.

"Really?" I asked.

"Of course, I'm not an imbecile."

"I didn't . . . Why are you treating me like this? What did I do to make you so mad?"

In the darkness, I saw him lower his head and stare at the floor. He had caused this visit to be so stressful, yet I hadn't considered simply confronting his behavior head-on.

"I'm sorry. I become like this when I am nervous," he apologized.

I was completely unfamiliar with the humble side of this man and did not know whether to trust the apology or move on as though it were a trap. He sounded genuine, though I had little experience in the way of fathers.

"Audrey called me twenty times to tell me how to behave. I see I have failed," he offered, sensing my doubt.

I decided to give him a reprieve, hoping my forgiveness would speak louder than echoing his childlike behavior.

"You researched LGBTQ groups in Paris?" I asked, switching back the subject.

He did quite a lot. Having been in Paris a long time, he had been exposed to many gay people without ever having a problem. He felt having a gay daughter was entirely different.

The temperature of our conversation had cooled considerably, and he took the change as an opportunity to ask me a candid question. I never would have entertained answering him a mere hour before.

"I have many colleagues in human rights and immigration. I looked it up; there is no conference for this in Delhi this fall. Are you cheating on my daughter?"

"No. I would never, ever cheat on Audrey."

"What then? Are you going with your mother?"

I realized too late that the silence I used to formulate a response was the very thing that answered his question.

"Deepa, it's okay. But I thought you are not speaking to your mother?"

My silence and lies were not working.

"Audrey asked me to come out to my mother before I was ready. I didn't know what else to do."

"My daughter has many great qualities, but she is too stubborn. I'm sorry, she should not have pushed you."

"I shouldn't have lied," I said, scolding myself.

He and I awkwardly faced each other for what seemed like an eternity. He feigned a yawn and told me he should get more sleep before the demands of his wife kicked in. Completing his change of character, he patted me on the hand without a hint of negativity.

I finally crawled into our pullout bed. The love of my life was snoring softly by my side.

Chapter 89

BY THE TIME the train pulled into the station, I was going crazy at the three-hour delay. My plan to arrive before it got dark had been foiled.

Mom guessed well and was standing almost directly in front of the door as it sprang open. She greeted me with the kind of warmth that precedes a volcano.

"You should have called. I don't appreciate waiting the extra half hour."

"Sorry, my phone died on the train."

"You didn't pick up when I called. I left a voicemail."

"I forgot my phone charger."

We sat in near silence to cool down from our bad start. The torrential downpour reduced our car ride to a slow jog. Twenty minutes later, we finally pulled in behind Avva's car in the driveway. Avva never understood the concept of a garage. The rain intensity had increased, so I left my bag to collect later.

Fortunately, Mom's phone call related to a most happy occasion—hotels for Paris and Agra. Mom told me she had booked them this afternoon, and they were grand.

She soon lost herself recounting a conversation she had with Dad yesterday. He had forgotten about an investment account he had opened while they were still together, and felt it important we meet him at the ashram to sign off on important documents to transfer the money to her name.

"Honestly, if it's just a ploy to get us to see him . . ."

Her voice became a steady hum in the background as I ascended up to the ceiling to evaluate the situation from afar. I had so carefully organized my thoughts in a way that demonstrated wit, logic, courage, and sharp skills. Still, one comment from my true love floated up beside me as I tried to determine which starting strategy was the strongest.

"Do not prepare as though your mother is a presentation," Audrey had told me.

Images of my whimsical childhood appeared on the four white kitchen walls. The journey to Mom and my convergence was simply beautiful. I saw clearly for the first time the gap that since plagued us could only be mended with our original approach. The new leg of the journey would be impressive, not impossible.

"Deepa. Hello. Come down from outer space," Mom shouted at me.

"Mom, you know how much I love you, right?"

"What's wrong?"

"No matter who comes into my life, I will always love you."

Even though I felt the statement was worth saying, I had yet to actually say it. I had never once questioned my love for Mom in all of the steps that led to my independent lifestyle. Her sharp comprehension of this fact caused her to nearly faint at the sound of my words.

"Deepa, stop. I don't need to hear this."

"We need to have this conversation."

"After everything I've been through—"

"I'm gay," I heard myself say.

Her reaction of panic was instant. She watched in terror as our well-maintained appearance of tranquility gave way to an avalanche of harsh truth.

"I did not raise a gay daughter," she screamed.

Her voice made me panic. Her voice made me lose grip on my strategy. Audrey's advice crashed to the floor, and I felt myself jump back ten paces of understanding. Against my own will, I launched into the academic, impersonal logic.

"Studies have found that undue stress during—"

"Just stop. Stop talking."

"Many famous historical figures are thought to have been gay."

She brought her hands to her ears, as though praying to go deaf. Her first true reaction to my words came in the form of a barely audible whisper.

"Get out."

"What, no. Let's talk about this."

"I want you to take the keys to the car and get out."

"I'll go to the car, but only to get some information on support groups I brought."

"Get out!"

I begged her to reconsider, to sit down and let me explain. I begged her to see me, her child, her Deepa. But centuries of discrimination backed her reasons. She could not handle an uprooting of her expectations. I reached out in a final attempt of a loving gesture.

"Get off me. Don't touch me," she screamed with a terrible fury.

A force far stronger than any physical human power was at her disposal. I had no chance at negotiating a peaceful recess. As she pushed me out the front door back into the pouring rain, she cupped both of her hands over her mouth at the sight of our broken family. The sobs rushed out as though she were mourning the death of her child. I heard her say one lone sentence before slamming the emblazoned door in my face.

"You will never understand the pain the words 'I'm gay' have caused me."

Chapter 90

I FELT SAFE in only one place in the world, given the situation. I was on the first flight back to New York a mere two hours after I had reached Maryland. Shining streaks of travelers flew past me as I pushed my way through LaGuardia airport. I caught the first taxi back to her apartment without bothering to wait my turn in line.

"Oh my God, Deepa. What happened?"

I collapsed in the doorway, unable to hold up the remains of the fraction of the person I had been a mere twelve hours before. Sahra was woken up by the commotion, but immediately retreated after seeing me crumpled on the floor.

In a rush of incoherent explanation, I told Pinni everything—the single blemish that had wrought my perfect relationship, an epiphany borne out of the unlikeliest of places, a miscalculated risk, and a final ending that was delivered in a most offensive fashion.

"I couldn't call you because my phone is dead," I said.

I WOKE UP the next morning to the sound of my own belabored breathing. Every inch of my body ached and I could barely see through the clouded contact lenses that normally made my perfect vision possible. After a long shower and a few pampering tricks straight from Pinni's personal collection, I felt physically capable of making it out of her apartment.

Instead of using Pinni's charger, I decided to take my phone's deadness as a sign to go home and immediately face Audrey. Pinni walked me down to the street, hailed a cab, and handed the driver a hundred dollar bill. She also had the habit of giving large tips in battered situations.

Before summoning up the courage to face my own lies, I cleaned away any stray tears and put on a brave face. I was certain I could not use my emotional turmoil with Mom to win Audrey's affections. Pity would inevitably subside and be reborn into anger.

I stepped inside the apartment and immediately noticed the darkness that enveloped our normally bright home. Audrey was curled up on the couch. She had drawn shut all of the curtains. The apartment looked stripped of life.

"*Salut chérie*, I'm home early. My phone died and I forgot my charger," I managed in a steady voice.

Audrey was coated in a thick substance that repelled close contact. I walked past her without even a hint of a touch.

"Audrey?"

"You have a message on the answering machine."

I let in a tiny sliver of light and slowly brought myself to look at her face. The mascara she was wearing had covered her cheeks in a dark film. Her normally caring eyes were red and puffy. I knew what was coming.

"One new message. Deepa, it's Mom. Your phone went straight to voicemail. I got scared and called Julie. She gave me this number. Why didn't you tell me you got a landline? Anyway, I found a hotel for us in Paris and Agra. I'm so excited, can't believe the trip is only three months away. Okay, hope this message reaches you before you get on the train. If not, I'm sure your new roommate will call and let you know. Her name is Audrey, right? Love you."

I faced the window at the message's completion. A knife had just pierced my heart, and I was sure the remainder of my spirit had splattered over the glass.

"Turn around, Deepa."

"Audrey, please, I was going to tell you."

She buried her face in her hands and started sobbing. Through the corner shadow I saw her rocking back and forth. The movement terrified me.

I was too scared to speak. I was too scared to move. I was too scared to breathe, to feel, or to live. Finally, she started her lines of questioning.

"Your trip to India is not for work?"

"No."

"It is with your mother?"

"Yes."

"When did you plan this?"

"Over Christmas."

"And you are stopping in Paris on the way?"

"Yes."

"You weren't going to ask me to come?"

"No."

"Does your mother think I am your roommate?"

"I'm not sure."

"Did you come out to your mother over Christmas, Deepa?"

"No. I lied."

Audrey clenched her fists and slammed her eyes shut at my last answer. She stood on the edge of a cliff, waiting for me to push her over. "How could you do this to me?"

"It just happened."

I tried explaining the intricacies involved in disappointing one of the two people in my life I couldn't bear to hurt or let go. Lying wasn't the solution, but it was the only thing that could be done given the battle both she and Mom left me to solve on my own.

"You accuse me of forcing you. I am here to support you."

My calm instantly broke as Audrey said "support." My retaliation came out in a waterfall of acid.

"Fuck you. Support me? *You* didn't want me to come out when *I* was ready. *You* wanted me to choose between you and my mother. Well, I am sorry, Audrey, but that is not a decision I could bear to make."

She was taken aback by my sudden aggressiveness and let out a guttural scream that echoed how unreasonable she thought I was. Her training as a therapist wanted to reduce the conversation to a teacher and a student. We both claimed to be the former.

"Deepa, do I . . . Do I make you happy?"

I closed my eyes and willed myself to respond with patience. It would have been all too easy to ruin everything we had built in the last year.

"More than anything."

"When we first met, I could tell there was something that was eating at your soul. I could tell that you were not comfortable with being gay," she said.

"Hiding my sexual orientation to my family does not mean I wasn't comfortable with being gay."

But I knew she was right. I knew Gloria was right. I knew Brian was right. I knew they were all right.

"Deepa, I understood that feeling. It wasn't easy for me in France. Men are more aggressive there, and they never believed me when I said I was a lesbian."

"Why are you telling me this?"

"Because it is the real reason I came to New York. Not being accepted for who I am was destroying me inside."

I knew that feeling, too. I knew that feeling of being criticized, tormented, and shunned by both family and strangers for simply being who you are. That feeling had turned me into an angry, bitter person.

"If we cannot be honest about who we are, it will destroy us," she continued.

Even so, that feeling was not enough to justify the relationship I had just lost.

"Audrey, I was fine with living our life here and having another life there if it meant keeping my relationship with my mother."

Her English was too perfect to not recognize the tenses. "Why are you using the past to explain the present?"

"I came out to my mother last night."

"Oh my God. What happened?"

"It doesn't matter. It wasn't the right decision for me."

"It *was* the right decision."

"You're *wrong*, Audrey. You made me destroy my relationship with my mother."

She became livid at the accusation that anyone but Mom was responsible for Mom's homophobia. Regardless of Mom's reaction, I had still lied to Audrey for six months.

"I wanted to tell you the truth so many times. I'm so sorry."

"One apology is not good enough. I am in New York for *you*."

"Don't act like this is second best."

She argued that the career she wanted to forge, her closest friends, her real life, was in Paris. She thought she could start a second life in New York with me.

"But you are willing to lie about something so important. What happens in five years? In ten years? Will you lie about something bigger?"

"I wasn't sure how you felt about me back in December."

"You're lying again. I was so confident. Not anymore, Deepa. Not after this."

She walked over to the kitchen table and picked up a bag from the floor. It was not the same kind of overstuffed daytime menace that Julie always carried. This one was for the long-term, for departing.

"Audrey, no. Don't do this."

"Let me go, Deepa."

"Where are you going, Audrey? Please talk to me."

"I have tried to talk to you. I can't be here right now."

"When will you be back?"

She stared out the window with an untimely stillness.

"Audrey. *Will* you be back?"

Her silence spoke louder than any words could convey. My lie had finally driven her away.

Chapter 91

AUDREY'S IMPACT ON my life felt large enough to fill the universe, yet all of her New York possessions fit in two suitcases. After only an hour, her friends emptied her material contents from our perfect future. Although her friends seemed sympathetic, their loyalty laid unyielding to my better half.

"She's a wreck, too," is all one of them was able to offer.

In a cruel ending to the happiest story I had ever told, I lost the two women that meant more to me than life itself. They shut the door in a betrayed silence and left me to tread the furious waters alone. I came close to letting myself drown.

Part IV

Narrator

Chapter 92

FROM THE BACK hallway, Lakshmi heard Pooja slam the front door with a deep-seated rage that had been festering for twenty-five years. As she looked at her daughter coated in a mix of tears, panic, and anger, she felt a sadness creep over her body—a sadness that was anticipated, yet impossible to prepare for.

"Pooja?"

"Leave me alone."

"Beta, can we please talk?"

In a deafening quiet, Pooja turned and stormed to her room without so much as acknowledging Lakshmi's trembling body.

After hours of hoping Pooja would change her mind, Lakshmi conceded at five in the morning and retired to her own room. Inside her nightstand sat the green-and-gold brooch she had given to Pooja the Christmas Alpa received acceptance to Georgetown University.

She brought the brooch to her heart, closed her eyes, and allowed her mind to transport her back to the perfect days of Philadelphia, back to the pristine period of her and Shankar's life that had been met with total professional *and* personal satisfaction.

In the years she and Pooja had lived together, Lakshmi's one wish had been to see her daughter enjoy that same perfect balance in this world. She had contemplated for two decades and had many conversations with Alpa to understand her choices had failed Pooja. Seeing the one person who made Pooja happiest—Deepa—cut out from Pooja's life scared Lakshmi in an intense way that only a survivor of extreme cruelty and poverty would understand.

TOO EXHAUSTED TO leave, too unnerved to sleep, Pooja paced around the ten-by-ten space that contained the contents of her existence. Below, she heard Lakshmi's mirrored anxious pacing as though begging Pooja to return downstairs.

Pooja saw a reel of the numerous moments of regret in her life flashing before her eyes; raising her daughter was not contained in any of the clips. Deepa had done well in school, she was popular; she was a strong woman and a good daughter. Deepa had become synonymous with Pooja's pride.

The idea of a perfect daughter had always been enough to convince

Pooja it was normal that Deepa did not want to go to prom, that she never talked about boys, and instead brought home that despicable Gloria, who was otherwise inexplicably close to Deepa. When the signs of Deepa's sexual orientation became obvious, the denial in Pooja's heart had been reborn from her days in New Orleans.

Just weeks after Deepa's graduation from NYU, Anand had flown back to the East Coast to deliver to Pooja what he called a lifetime of reflections.

"It's only a letter?" Pooja had asked.

"Little happened since we split."

"You accomplished all of your goals."

"Only professional."

As she had done so many times before, Pooja walked to the top shelf of her left bookcase where she kept this life reflection of her ex-husband. She pulled it out and reread the words for a wind of assurance.

Anand had met his synthetic doll of a second wife at an Indian fundraiser in San Francisco. The fundraiser was to help the baby seals of Norway, or some equally transparent, fake cause. The doll was one of the event organizers. Anand had used that as a reason to find the woman as one of substance.

Having recently made Chief of Neurosurgery at the preeminent hospital in the country, Anand couldn't help but feel he had already reached the pinnacle of success. He had proposed to her just three months after they met and even had the nerve to bring the doll to Deepa's graduation.

"She's a puppet," Pooja had remarked to Anand upon meeting his new wife.

"Don't be bitter."

"Open your eyes."

"Open your heart."

"I'll be at the other side of the park."

Within a few weeks of being back home, Anand had begun to see the validity in Pooja's assessment of his new life partner. Gradually, he had worked up the courage the approach the plastic person.

"Why did you want to marry me?"

"The luxury, the status, and the parties," she replied.

Anand had moved to America to conquer the world, to leave behind a life dictated by superficial motivations. The person he had chosen to share his life's accomplishments possessed the emotional and mental depth of a puddle.

Before handing her the reflection, Anand had apologized to Pooja one last time.

"Pooja, I'm so sorry. I wanted an equal, a partner."

"That's what you want, not what you wanted."

At the end of his four-page reflection, Anand had written the one line for which Pooja had waited since the divorce.

"I finally understand what you meant."

Every time she read that letter, Pooja knew she had made the right decision to leave Anand. She knew eventually Deepa would also understand Pooja was right about Deepa's sexual orientation.

Chapter 93

ALPA CONVINCED BARBARA to sign Deepa over on a temporary consulting contract under McKinsey. The contract bought Deepa a month of recovery; Deepa was sure it would take a lifetime.

By week two, Deepa was able to emerge from her catatonic state enough to make small trips alone. On her first outing to the pharmacy, she noticed someone had left 9-volt batteries on top of the last package of toilet paper. She remembered the answering machine also used 9-volt batteries, and she found herself slowly sinking to the ground.

During each of her attempts to step outside, Deepa inevitably found a weak or ridiculous connection to associate with Audrey and was set off in another downward spiral. The word "pineapple" sent her into cardiac arrest on command, as the citrus was Audrey's favorite pizza topping.

"Deepa?" a familiar voice called.

"Fuck . . ."

"Girl, I haven't seen you in forever. Why are you on the floor like that?"

"It's nothing, just leave me alone."

Deepa had landed face down in a pile of paper towels. If this had occurred in the subway, passengers would have stepped over her body and let her lie in peace. Since this was an overpriced pharmacy in an overpriced neighborhood of Brooklyn, Deepa was forced to pick herself up to avoid getting arrested. Gloria managed to catch Deepa's arm in the midst of her next crumbling.

"I know nothing. This ain't nothing. *Que pasa?*"

"How much time do you have?"

"All the time in the world, baby. Let's go back to my place."

Gloria was much stronger than Deepa following Deepa's almost muscular atrophy from two weeks of nearly no movement. She guided Deepa through the aisles, down Bergen Street, and stopped in front of a building less than three blocks away from Deepa and Audrey's apartment.

"You live here?" Deepa asked.

"For the last six months. Bad breakup?"

"Have you been stalking me?"

"Don't flatter yourself. I can still read you like a book."

Gloria snatched away the dark sunglasses that had been shielding Deepa's eyes from the world. It was so bright outside. Eventually, the white dots that floated around in her eyes subsided and her vision came into focus. In every corner, she saw pictures of Gloria and an attractive black woman.

"Still think I'm stalking you? What do you have to say?"

"You guys suck at taking pictures."

Gloria caught her mouth in her hands and eventually came up for air in between fits of giggles. Deepa couldn't help but burst into laughter as well; everyone had been exceedingly morose around her.

"What happened?" Gloria asked.

"I never cared about relationships before meeting Audrey."

"Really bitch, that's how you start?"

"Sorry."

Against her initial judgment, Deepa told Gloria everything about the extended lie and losing Pooja and Audrey in less than twenty-four hours.

Gloria listened with a care that she never displayed while she and Deepa were together. In that moment, they both realized how bad of a couple they really did make.

"Why aren't you fighting for them?" Gloria asked.

"Because I'm devastated. Because I feel like dying."

"This is what I hate about you, Deepa."

The last thing Deepa wanted to hear was another one of Gloria's enumeration of all things wrong. Deepa made another attempt to leave, but still lacked any sure footedness. Gloria again caught her in mid-sway and dragged her over to the living room couch. The warmth of Gloria's arms opened up another box of Deepa's emotions, and she couldn't help but babble the melodramatic thoughts that came to her mind.

"I loved the way Audrey spoke of passion with such nonchalance and nonchalance with such passion. I miss how Mom would tell me to follow my dreams instead of following money . . ."

"Deepa, enough. For all of your detailed thinking, you always lacked action to back up emotion."

Failure to acknowledge the good, the choice to remain in a pity party, and no efforts to correct the bad were among the reasons why Gloria had decided to fall out of touch with Deepa.

"How am I supposed to right these wrongs?" Deepa asked.

"Start with your strengths."

"I can barely hold myself up."

"Not literally."

"Figuratively?"

"Baby, you won me with your words. This will be no different."

THOUGH JULIE WAS not a stranger to bad breakups, even she stumbled on words of consolation for Deepa. Julie knew her relationship woes paled in comparison to Deepa's debacle.

"What do you want to do for your birthday tomorrow?" Julie asked.

"Unpack."

No mood could describe Deepa's current state, least of all, fun. The world still felt numb against her fingertips. Her brain was moving on automatic pilot.

"No answer from her?" Julie asked.

"Who?"

"Audrey."

"No."

"And your Mom?"

"No."

Deepa's new strategy to conserve what little energy she had involved other people asking questions such that she could whittle down responses to one word whenever possible.

Within weeks of the breakup, Audrey had discontinued her cell phone service. Gloria's observations of Deepa's normal fluidity with words was not holding true through a shattered heart. Before, Deepa had the ability to string together even a basic sentence, "Please come back to me."

Audrey had virtually vanished. Deepa had taken the disappearance as a sign to find the correct written words before she made any attempts at contact, and thus she spent countless hours searching through the archives of great poets, of Pulitzer novelists, and of world leaders who had used their ideas to inspire generations.

Meeting Jorge and Pedro Ramirez had first alerted her that the intersection of being a common Indian and a common gay woman was infinitely more complicated than the individual groups. Loving a gay French woman made the search for the perfect words still harder. She could not find the way to properly articulate her and Audrey's convergence.

During one particularly long attempt, Deepa had come across an online conversation dated August twenty-eighth.

Audrey à Jessica: Thanks Jessica! I am all settled. How are you?

Jessica à Audrey: I'm good! Started my research program. I miss you!

Audrey à Jessica: I miss you too! Come visit me here in Paris! Bisous !

By September, Deepa and Julie were once again roommates.

Chapter 94

"I'M GOING OUT for my seminar," Lakshmi told Pooja.

"That's the third time this week."

"It is good for me to continue to learn. Will you be going anywhere tonight?"

"I have a lot of work to do," Pooja curtly replied.

Lakshmi lingered by the door in the hopes Pooja would ask her the simplest of questions, "What is the seminar about?"

Lakshmi had not yet found the courage to commence the conversation on her own. The weight of the silence on her aging heart in the four long months since the unofficial ban on communication with her granddaughter was dangerously close to unbearably heavy.

Pooja showed no sign of budging, so Lakshmi pushed herself out the door in a somber march. Only the knowledge she was moving in the correct direction kept her fighting without a timeframe to accompany the motions.

MOST OF POOJA'S days had been marked with alternating cycles of anger and depression. The latest manifestation of this vicious cycle was her total indecision of how to decorate the house. Before Pooja had heard Deepa utter those heinous words, "I'm gay," the walls had been littered with pictures of Deepa, Pooja, Lakshmi, and every combination therein. At this current hour, Pooja decided those displays were entirely inappropriate, and she began removing all signs of a photographic past. When she had made the same effort back in New Orleans, it was permanent. She knew cutting out her daughter would never be as straightforward.

Pooja felt each oscillation of indecision added another layer of volatile misery to the situation. In the back of her mind, she knew she needed to talk to someone, but the vows of silence had taken before Deepa was born made the idea of confessing her soul to a stranger nothing short of terrifying.

Instead, she continued to her escapist reality of the Internet, where new identities were encouraged and rarely verified. Sentences were typed out and reviewed before being sent. No one online criticized her judgment, her choices, her non-choices, or her life. She got more than what she gave to the online world, and at that moment in time, she had very little to give. The Internet reminded her she still had a life to live.

LAKSHMI'S MIND SWIRLED with the disappointment that Pooja had chosen another night alone talking to strangers on the computer. She barely noticed when the tiny phone in her purse vibrated and answered once safely inside her car.

"Hello?" Lakshmi asked.

"Hi, Mom," Alpa replied.

"Hello, beta, how is Deepa?"

"Better, thanks for asking about me."

Alpa was being sarcastic. Sarcasm was the one trait she and her sister had in common. Lakshmi discussed Alpa's tiring work schedule for a few minutes before reminding Alpa to take a vacation. The reminders did not go very far. Lakshmi had been telling Alpa the same thing since Alpa was twenty-five.

"How are the support groups going? Have they covered challenges in the workplace yet?" Alpa asked.

"I find garages very redundant."

"Your car roof is more secure than any you saw until coming to the States."

"Who needs a roof for a roof?"

"I called Pooja yesterday," Alpa said.

"She has not risen from behind that computer in days."

"Hamed is coming for Thanksgiving. You both should come, too."

Lakshmi let the pang in her stomach subside before replying. "I will respect the wishes of my elder daughter."

Both Lakshmi and Alpa knew this meant they would not be seeing each other for the holiday. Hamed, Alpa's brother-in-law, had always been a contentious force with Pooja. Least of all, this year Pooja would not stand for such confrontation.

"Beta, I must go. The Bobby boy will be waiting only," Lakshmi said to break the silence.

Bobby was the session leader who took kindly to Lakshmi once he found out they had lived in the same town in West Virginia for nearly fifteen years. The high school in which the sessions took place was the same size as Lakshmi's university in Chennai. Very unsure of herself at first, Bobby had been invaluable, and Lakshmi did not wish to give the kind soul the impression she was not coming.

"I'm proud of you, Mom," Alpa replied.

"It is for Deepa."

"It will be for you, too."

Chapter 95

ALPA INVITED DEEPA over for Thanksgiving this year.

"I'm staying home," Deepa replied.

"Are you having people over?"

"No, I'm spending it alone."

Alpa ticked her tongue in a Morse code-like way as though trying to send a message.

"Don't do this, Deepa."

"Do what? Be gay?"

"Don't turn into a hermit because life isn't working out the way you want."

Deepa couldn't help but think that was a terrible thing to say to someone who was going through such a difficult time.

"I don't feel like seeing anyone. It has been a hard year—"

"You know who says things like that?"

Alpa's words prompted Deepa to recall the hundreds of moments Pooja had used her difficult past as an excuse for not doing something, for not being nice to someone, or for blaming someone for her own errors. Deepa quickly saw where the conversation was going. Pooja had never talked about the way she had felt after the divorce. Deepa wondered if her pain was similar to what Pooja had endured? Was the retreat from society Deepa had summoned to her Thanksgiving the first step Pooja had taken to a lifetime of loneliness?

"Point taken. I'll be there," Deepa conceded.

DEEPA LOOKED UP from a pile of oil pastels and cousins and saw Hamed peering down at her. Except for the terrible pea-green inseam of his jacket, he looked his usual sharp self in a finely tailored Italian suit.

"Are you free for a tea before dinner?" Hamed asked.

He explained one of his old university "mates" owned a shop a few blocks away.

"Brits refusing to celebrate Thanksgiving," he said.

Sahra and Malak were busy drawing giant orange-and-red circles on sheets of paper. Deepa told Hamed they should go now before the cousins migrated to using her pants as a canvas. The cousins liked to experiment with mixed media, especially media Alpa had explicitly forbidden.

"The shop has a delightful cinnamon-infused black tea. Fancy trying it?"

"Sure," Deepa replied while she suppressed a scrunched nose.

The two orders of tea and biscuits barely reached the table before Deepa blurted out the pressing question on her mind.

"What kind of conference would bring you to New York for a month?"

Deepa couldn't shake the feeling that Alpa had actually flown Hamed over to talk. Alpa's offer to fly Deepa to Paris had been met with Deepa's panicked indecision. The timing was coincidental.

Hamed assured Deepa otherwise. "My pompous colleagues are calling a brainstorming session for a new LGBTQ writing collaborative a conference."

In swift British efficiency, the bill made an appearance a few seconds later. Deepa motioned to throw in five dollars.

"Nope, I got it. This place is a rip-off. Just supporting my friend."

Seventeen-fifty for this?" Deepa exclaimed.

"Better than London."

Deepa diverted her persistent thoughts for one moment to imagine a new city slogan—*New York: Where Londoners go to find a bargain.*

Even Hamed looked dumfounded as he settled down twenty dollars to cover quite possibly the worst tea of all time. His next subject of conversation did not pick the mood back up.

"What happened with the Ramirez case?" he asked.

"It had a tragic ending."

"Gross discrimination?"

"Yeah, it was egregious. They died, and we lost the lawsuit."

"Alpa said the case really made an impression on you."

Deepa stared down at the biscuit that cost more than Lakshmi's father had made in a week.

She had psychoanalyzed every move of every involved person from the past year. Despite the "gross discrimination" involved in their ending, the bravery the Ramirez's had been forced to display had given her a temporary burst of confidence in the face of Audrey's ultimatum.

"When I first met Pedro and Jorge, I couldn't empathize with their need to stay together."

"What happened?"

"I thought that empathy was all I needed to come out to Mom."

"Turns out it wasn't," Hamed finished.

Hamed made a sudden shivering gesture and remarked how unsettled he felt, thinking about the millions of people who had to be completely closeted, even in modern-day. "Jack and I have been together for ten years."

Deepa got the impression that Hamed was no Pedro and Jack was no Jorge. She had no room to judge; she was no Pedro and Audrey was no Jorge.

"Your parents never knew?" Deepa asked.

"The only thing I know is what they didn't want to know. Have you spoken to your mother at all?"

When it came to Pooja, Deepa had followed Gloria's advice to be proactive, to use her strengths.

"As of last count, I've sent twenty e-mails, thirty-three voicemails, and seven letters by post."

"Nothing?"

"Not a word."

"When I see other parents reacting like this, I'm glad I never came out to my parents."

Deepa knew Hamed's situation was much different, though. His parents had come from Iran to England in the eighties. Having met Hamed's mother before she died, Deepa could still recall her flare for the dramatics.

"I was afraid she would kill herself if I came out," Hamed said.

Deepa was confident suicidal tendencies was not a claim she could make about her mother.

"And your father?" Deepa asked Hamed.

"He was quite senile before I told him. I doubt he understood. Yours?"

On the slate of subjects to dance around with caution, why Anand had moved to the ashram had ranked high on Pooja's list. Even now, Deepa still had no information beyond the cryptic explanation Anand offered.

"He moved shortly after I came out to him," Deepa said.

"Because?"

"He became the person he despised. My being gay had nothing to do with it."

"Is that what you believe?"

Deepa thought back to when Audrey had first asked her that question, which had happened right after they saw Audrey's favorite play for the fifth time.

"Imagine revealing only half of your face to those you hold closest?" Audrey had remarked.

Audrey and Deepa had both instantly made the connection to Deepa's father.

"I didn't know then, I don't know now," Deepa finally replied.

"Did it affect your decision to not come out to your mother?"

"How could it not?"

Hamed echoed Deepa's thoughts on how hard it was to balance complex cultures in a world whose views toward homosexuality were constantly evolving.

"Those intersections are poorly defined," Hamed concluded.

"I crashed and burned at the last intersection. Do you think my mom will come around?"

"I do. I can tell she knows the power of love."

Deepa had never considered love was behind the hidden half of Pooja's face.

Chapter 96

"POOJA, CAN YOU please bring me the forks?" Lakshmi called out.

As a child, Pooja had always been coy in letting Lakshmi know she was not paying attention. She decided to employ the same tactics today in her response.

"Aw, they're so cute," Pooja screamed.

The puppies on the computer screen afforded Pooja a thin layer of sanity to coat her increasing frustration. She was supposed to be recounting the details of her dream Paris and Agra vacation to family gathered around a giant table.

"We're going to have to throw out half of this," Pooja said to Lakshmi, walking up from behind.

Pooja had refused to entertain any conversation on the subject of Thanksgiving, leaving Lakshmi to do the food order alone.

"I will not be throwing out this much food," Lakshmi replied.

"Or what? The poor people in Chennai will starve?"

Lakshmi froze in place before tensing up into a stiff board. The words "I'm sorry" hung on the tip of Pooja's tongue before she finally managed to sound them out in audible form. Subjects of disagreements with her mother were endless, though Pooja knew she crossed the line in making a mockery of Lakshmi's impoverished upbringings. She knew there were far better ways to articulate the absurd scene unfolding.

Lakshmi's perpetual grandiose image of America was shown by the black pantsuit she wore. Pooja hadn't found a reason to change clothes after crawling out of bed.

"Thanks for my headphones, thanks for the money, thanks for the Internet." Pooja almost slipped in her usual ending before painfully realizing why she had to abstain from the words.

"Thank you for this day, another special gift from God. Amen," Lakshmi finished.

"This day is far from special."

"We could have gone to visit Alpa."

"There is unwelcome company."

Until recently, Lakshmi had not understood Pooja's relentless disdain of Hamed.

A flash of nausea overtook Pooja as she recalled her most vivid memory of Hamed's "good friend," Jack. When Alpa had called Pooja with the news Hamed would be in town for the holiday, Pooja had instantly spotted the trap.

"What were you watching on the computer?" Lakshmi softly asked.

"A video of cute puppies."

"That's nice."

"You're lying. You hate dogs. You always have."

"Your father helped me li—"

"Don't bring up Dad."

Lakshmi looked taken aback. "Your father died before his time. I miss him dearly."

"You could have showed it more."

"One cannot agree with their spouse about all decisions."

"Or any decisions, especially about your own daughter."

Lakshmi lowered her eyes. They had almost had this argument more times than Pooja cared to count.

"Pooja, I have apologized a thousand times. What else can I do?"

"How dare you throw this back on me."

The leak in the bottle was too wide to withstand the pressure. Thanksgiving and all, Pooja screamed at Lakshmi about the argument the night before had Shankar died.

"You cheated Dad out of his income," Pooja shouted.

"That is not accurate."

"It's not a coincidence he died the next day." Pooja felt an armor of truth build around her body as she stared her mother down.

"The fight was about your mistakes, Pooja. You lived beyond your means."

"You hung me out to dry. You paid for all of Alpa's education."

Pooja knew that her parents had also technically paid for her education, though not with the same guilt-free entitlement Alpa had enjoyed. As she expanded on her argument, Pooja felt her protective barrier strengthen, which made her feel unbeatable.

"I did not cause your father's heart attack," Lakshmi said.

"You destroyed my life, Mom. Look at what you did."

"What about Deepa, Pooja?"

"What *about* Deepa? She's *my* daughter."

"You are pushing away the best part of your life."

Pooja reconciled this effect by justifying she had at least had the strength to acknowledge Deepa's potential. Her job as a mother was to steer her child in the right direction.

"Imagine what would have happened if I had actually run away?" she countered.

The color drained from Lakshmi's face. Pooja saw her mother's orientation of the events that fateful night wash away in the waterfall of color.

"You were going to run away?"

"Yes. Dad is the one who convinced me to stay."

"Pooja, I have had a very difficult life—"

"Enough, Mom, just stop!"

Pooja clenched her fists and held her eyes shut as she had so many nights after Shankar had passed away. Her father was the one to recognize her suffering. Without her father, she felt like she had no hope of conveying her persistent pain to her mother.

"Beta, it is your decision to not speak to Deepa."

"Of course it is. I know that."

"But you must ask yourself *why*. Otherwise, you are doing to Deepa what I did to you."

Lakshmi turned and left the room–her suit perfectly in place. The remnants of her protective armor were dragging on the heel of her mother's shoe.

Chapter 97

THE BRUTAL THANKSGIVING argument marinated for a month before Pooja brought up the topic, which happened just after she saw Lakshmi take a small tumble on the stairs.

"I am getting old," Lakshmi remarked.

"You should be around family, it's Christmas."

Not having many friends to share the experience, Pooja had never used her computer-savvy to join any form of social media. Finally armed with a reason, she took all of ten seconds to find out Jeff was a professor at Emory University. A few clicks flooded her screen with the highlights of his now impressive accomplishments. On a page of selected works, Pooja felt her heart plummet at the sight of his memoir, titled *My Roommate, My Partner, My Husband*.

Jeff was the kind of author who wrote precisely as he spoke, and Pooja was only able to get a few pages in until echoes of his voice took over. Overwhelmed, she came up for air less she lost her courage. Eventually, she settled on the simplest possible e-mail.

> Dear Jeff,
> Remember me? I came across your website and thought I'd say hi. Hope you have been well.
> Pooja Deva (formerly Suresh)

Pooja took an hour to compose the message. As an English professor, she was certain Jeff would notice any grammar mistakes. Then again, she reasoned effective writing was sometimes best harnessed through creative use of punctuation.

e.e. cummings [For Example].

Pooja's attempts at self-sabotage did not prevail; no error or bounce back message appeared in her inbox after more than an adequate period of staring. A botched effort would have been the perfect scenario on some level.

"I tried to make peace," she could have told herself.

He responded several days later with a more detailed reply, and went a step further in inviting future conversation.

The Paths of Marriage

Hi Pooja!

So nice to hear from you! I am doing well, thanks. Where are you living these days? If you ever find your way down to the Atlanta area, I'd love to get coffee sometime.

Sorry for the slow response, been busy with work.

Jeff

They wrote back and forth before Pooja said she'd be down in early February.

"Are you going to be in town?" she asked.

"Sure will. What brings you down?" he responded.

Using her daughter's default work excuse, Pooja lied and said she was coming to Atlanta for a conference. The numbers of her credit card barely made it on to the screen as she steadied her hands enough to type. A brain lapse immediately followed and she almost forwarded the flight confirmation to Jeff as she had done so often with Deepa.

Pooja couldn't help but smile as she used the calendar function of her phone for the first time in ages. A date, place, and time was secured and confirmed. She was amazed at how much it took to get to here.

"ARE YOU READY?" Lakshmi asked Pooja.

"All set."

Pooja's enormous suitcase took up so much room in the car trunk that she failed to notice a tiny overnight bag was already stuffed in the back corner.

"Are you nervous?" Lakshmi asked.

"Why would I be nervous?"

"No reason."

"You don't know what I'm doing."

This much was true. Pooja had not offered and Lakshmi had not asked the nature of Pooja's trip down south. A mother knows, however, when her child makes a transformation. Lakshmi was just not sure whether the transformation had already started or was soon arriving.

"Have a safe journey, beta," Lakshmi wished her daughter at the airport.

"Hey, that brooch."

Pooja was staring at Lakshmi's tiny frame. On top of Lakshmi's black suit of the day sat the same green-and-gold brooch.

"Yes, I am delivering it home."

"I thought it was garbage," Pooja replied.

"Far from it."

Pooja looked surprised that the tin brooch had real significance. On any other day, Lakshmi suspected Pooja would have pried further. Today, she knew other concerns were simply taking all of her daughter's mental bandwidth.

Lakshmi had needed time to realize the significance of the jewelry on her chest had not meant to be shared with her daughter.

"Have a safe journey, beta," Lakshmi repeated.

Pooja looked relieved at the pass, and set off to confront her past.

Lakshmi reached the tranquility of the Appalachian Mountains in less than three hours. The size of the giant formations had served well as a calming effect to the turbulence the area residents had often wrought on Lakshmi's family. Even today, these mountains were her home.

The crisp, fresh air invited Lakshmi outside, and she stretched her feeble legs. Her old memory failed her on occasion—how to turn on the computer, where she put her glasses, what were the neighbors' names. She had no troubles finding Shankar's resting site, though, as she was guided by something far more powerful than the mind.

Pooja had been several months pregnant when she, Lakshmi, and Alpa gave Shankar's ashes to the earth. At the time, Lakshmi was sad they could not go down farther into the thicket to lay Shankar as Lakshmi had laid her nana down. Now she was grateful to only have to walk a few steps.

With a light kiss, Lakshmi bent down and placed the brooch in the riverbed. Just as the blue-and-black water had returned Shankar to the depths of the earth, the water washed over and absorbed the brooch into the delicate landscape. She brought her head down and felt a few tears fall from her normally dry eyes. The eulogy she could not bear to say before came out in soft whispers that were swept away by the wind.

"Oh Shankar, oh nana, even when society publicly shamed you, you had the insight and the audacity to listen to me, to amma, to the women of your life. You are the reasons I survived to raise a beautiful family. I am so thankful I am able to pay my respects before my gratitude dies with my humble body. I carry a piece of each of you in my soul on to the next day, on to another special gift from God."

Chapter 98

"I'D LIKE A small skinny latte with extra reduced fat milk, a shot of hazelnut, and a touch of vegan cream. What about you, Deepa?" Brian asked.

"A small coffee."

Brian squealed as a mother pulled away a hyperactive girl to leave a highly coveted table open. Children in coffee shops were like trucks on the highway—they slowed down ninety-nine percent of traffic and left the road open for one lucky car to skip ahead. Of course the day Deepa felt like leaving, she was the lucky car.

"You seem more listless than usual," Brian said.

The topic of persistent silence from Pooja and Audrey had become stable enough that people automatically assumed Deepa was a depressed half-human. As cool as she had tried to play her efforts, she had told Brian and Julie during a particularly emotional, drunken holiday party how broken she still felt.

"Isn't Audrey's birthday is coming up?" Brian prodded.

"Next month."

Brian offered a moment of silence. "Well, let's get away. Let's take a vacation."

"It's cold."

"San Francisco? The weather is the same there year-around."

"Reminds me of my dad."

"Miami?"

"Reminds me my failed relationship with Gloria."

"Hawaii?"

"Reminds me of a vacation Audrey and I once planned."

"Austin?"

"Reminds me of Mom's preferred type of Tex Mex."

"Jesus, Deepa."

Deepa sensed Brian foresaw a losing battle. Brian walked up to the counter to pick up their lopsided order.

"Hey," Deepa shouted and ran to Brian.

"No. Our table. Damnit, Deepa."

The coffee shop hawks immediately pounced on the in-demand real estate. Deepa barely noticed with a surprising moment of recognition.

"What is that song?" Deepa asked the barista.

"My buddy works in Paris. I promise I didn't steal it. Oh God, are you the police?" the barista asked in a rush and tumble.

For the first time since she could remember, Deepa felt uplifted by a sound. The song playing was a new addition by the same French artist of her birthday CD.

The strung out patrons snapped their heads up to remind Deepa how valuable their paper reading time was. Fortunately, the barista—the person who controlled the coffee—was on her side.

"What's she saying?" the barista asked.

Deepa was only able to make out the basic premise at first. Much to the dismay of the "iced skinny mocha with caramel and vanilla extract" woman a few feet over, the barista stopped making drinks to bring over paper and a pencil on the condition Deepa left him a copy of her translation.

Careful to look up a few key words, Deepa confirmed she did not confuse something critical. When she was in high school, she had had the most comical mistranslation: "My presentation will be on Mozart, the famous *Ostrich* Composer."

Making good on her promise, Deepa scribbled down a copy of the translation for the barista before she jetted outside. A confused Brian still stood in the corner as Deepa shouted out a quick line of explanation, "Last mail collection is in thirty minutes."

New York postal workers were some of the meanest people on the planet, but Deepa managed to dive through the doors with a few seconds to spare, postcard of the Brooklyn Bridge in hand. Her sense of urgency was enough, even by New York standards, to stop the employees from kicking her out.

Audrey had written down the address of her parents' apartment in Paris on a sheet of paper, which she had stuck in Deepa's bag before Christmas '08. At the time, Audrey thought they would write each other while apart for the holiday.

Deepa pulled out this most valuable piece of paper in the world, though she had long ago memorized the contents. She was able to fit the address and her meticulous translation on the postcard by writing in microscopic script.

In the distant horizon
I walk the path towards your shadow.
The soul you carry
Was mine to share.
The soul you left
Cannot bear to move forward.

A river that echoes water,
Does not flow without your presence.
The blue, the black that remains,
This is our battle.
I walk the path towards your shadow,
My love.

With a soft kiss, Deepa dropped her last hope into the blue-and-black mailbox. She knew she would never find better words to say to Audrey than the words that had found her.

THE SUN WAS teeming at the surface of the tall buildings on the opposite side of Houston Street. Deepa glanced up to do a quick survey of the scene, which revealed no one who resembled her impending, admittedly boring date through the crowd of late commuters, hipster explorers, and the occasional lost tourist. Online dating was such a pain.

By the end of her second beer, Deepa realized the girl was not coming. She decided the only thing worse than going on a date with a dull, unappealing person was getting stood up by a dull, unappealing person. The two pints of liquid she had consumed sloshed uncomfortably in her stomach as she brought her feet to the pavement. Just moments after paying the check, her phone went off. The display on the new, flashy screen showed an unrecognized New York number. Of course the stupid date decided to call now.

"Hi. You're like an hour late, so I'm going home," Deepa answered.

Deepa paused after the last word to allow enough time to hear which lame excuse, like a subway delay or a late night at work, was the reasoning. Those excuses were the perfect, uncreative, impossible-to-dispute New York City defenses.

"Deepa?" the woman on the phone said.

Deepa nearly dropped the phone. This time, she did nearly go into cardiac arrest.

"Um . . . How are you? How's the psychology?" Deepa replied.

How's the psychology? Drunk after two beers, Deepa appeared.

"Is this a good time to talk? I can call back later. I'll call back later."

"No, no, no. This is fine. Now is great. Are you in the City?"

"Yes. I arrived a few months ago. Are you still here?"

"Yes. Are you?"

"Yes."

She was living in Astoria now, which Deepa knew to be a good choice for a Parisian. Deepa recalled from her seventh date with Audrey that the bakeries in the neighborhood were the best New York had to offer, restaurants flaunted their al fresco dining, and none of the buildings were massive structures designed to extinguish architectural diversity.

"Are you free tonight? It is no problem if you have plans," Audrey followed.

"No. I don't have plans. I did have plans, but she stood me up." Deepa shook her head at her magnificent showcase of her attractiveness as a girlfriend.

"Can you meet me at that beach place in Queens? What is it called?" Audrey asked.

"I know what you're talking about. See you in an hour?"

"Okay, see you there."

The "beach" was a quaint area of Long Island City, Queens. During the summer, the carved out, sanded area was open to the public for concerts, food festivals, and fundraisers. Deepa found the choice surprising, as Audrey had always preferred less expensive venues. Deepa was not disappointed. The vantage point the "beach" offered was a brilliant sunset of intense rays of color in every direction behind the massive skyline of midtown Manhattan. The effect was so . . . romantic.

Deepa did her best to talk herself out of thinking such a setting meant anything. Audrey was probably dating someone by now. She reasoned it best to assume this meeting was for something insignificant, like getting clothes back or seeing how much money had been returned on the apartment deposit.

"Deepa?" Audrey said, this time not through a phone.

Her efforts at practicing turning around slowly were futile; as soon as Audrey uttered the "D" in her name, Deepa whirled around like a trick pony.

"Hi," Deepa said, a little too eagerly.

"Did you get a drink already?"

"No, I'm just having water."

A dry spell had kicked in toward the middle of March. The two beers from the bar were the most alcohol Deepa had had in nearly a month. A drier Deepa was pleasing to Audrey.

"You used to drink too much."

"Thanks."

"Sorry, I didn't mean . . . I'll go get something and come back."

So she could shift to watch Audrey walk to the bar, Deepa pretended to spot something on the side of the bench facing the other direction. A random guy across the way caught Deepa's gaze at Audrey and flashed an obnoxious wink. Some people never learned lesbians didn't exist for the entertainment of straight men.

"It's pee. I'm moving because there's pee," Deepa lied.

One ignoramus was not enough to spoil the moment, and Deepa's attention snapped back to her favorite Frenchwoman. Audrey looked as radiant as ever in a simple long black t-shirt and a stonewashed pair of jeans. She had gained a little weight, though the effect was to merely accentuate the perfect curves of her waist and chest. As Audrey reached in her bag to pull out money, Deepa caught a whiff of the subtle way Audrey's mouth curved when she was excited. It still turned Deepa's breathing into an enamored rattle.

Audrey and Deepa's mutual admiration for the other didn't manage to translate to the conversation.

"When did you get back to the States?"

"Two months ago."

"Just visiting?"

"No, I said two months ago."

"Oh, right. What brings you back?"

"I will start a Ph.D. at Columbia. I have preliminary research now."

"Wow, congratulations. But I thought you didn't like the programs?"

"Thank you. I changed my mind. Are you still working?"

"Yep."

"Okay."

They turned their attention to the cups in their hands. Audrey seemed as disappointed as Deepa at the awkwardness that had never been present when they were together.

"I got your postcard," Audrey said to break the silence.

"I thought you've been here for two months? I sent that a few weeks ago."

"Yes, well my father actually saw the postcard and called me. The poem was really beautiful."

Deepa explained about the paranoid barista and his contraband demo. Mozart, the Ostrich composer drew out a little laugh from Audrey. Deepa had missed that laugh so much that it hurt her to be happy.

Audrey complimented Deepa on what seemed like a very good translation. Deepa knew Audrey wondered whether she kept up her French language skills for her.

They settled on recapping the past. The conversation had to happen eventually.

"Did you see Paris and the Taj Mahal in September?"

"I got the ticket cancellation soon after . . ." Deepa held back finishing the thought with any of the possible painful endings—

—you broke my heart.
—I broke your heart.
—we lost each other.

Audrey stared at the exact spot where the dangling endings were sitting. Deepa knew Audrey heard the options even if they were not spoken aloud .

"And your mother?" she tepidly asked. "Sorry," she quickly added.

"It's not your fault."

"Yes, it is. I pushed you. I'm sorry."

Deepa was unsure whether she deserved that apology. Audrey had always been honest about her need to not be in the closet to either of their families. Audrey and Deepa were allowed to disagree on coming out; Deepa had not been entitled to question Audrey's reasons.

"And I should not have questioned your reasons, Deepa."

Audrey told her that her father had eventually recounted the conversation Deepa and he had that night in the milky dark. He had told Audrey about his own challenges in accepting a gay daughter. Who was Audrey to question Pooja's process? Who was Audrey to question Deepa's hesitation? An ultimatum was unfair to hang over Deepa's head.

"I thought I was supportive. My father made me realize what that really means."

"There were a lot of cultural factors hanging in the balance."

Lying had not been one of them. Lying had been entirely Deepa's fault. "I am so sorry, Audrey."

"That lie killed me inside."

And the fact that lie had killed Audrey inside had killed Deepa inside. Not having the option to legally marry did not diminish Deepa's implicit vow to support and defend Audrey.

Now almost a year later, Deepa finally told Audrey what happened the last night she had seen her mother. She felt nostalgia of the fantastic, whimsical childhood Pooja had so selflessly helped Deepa create. Even in the years that separated their convergence, she still felt overwhelming moments of Pooja's protection against the world. Nothing, not even Audrey, affected Deepa so deeply.

"In a split second that changed everything. I convinced myself that my understanding would be her understanding."

Pooja's understanding was entirely her own.

"I connected to my parents through their own experiences," Audrey said.

"My mother's path led to her very different circumstances."

"I know that now. Deepa, you found the words to reconnect with me."

"I haven't found the words to reconnect with her."

"Perhaps they are not for you to find."

Chapter 99

POOJA REACHED THE coffee shop first. She sat down among the students half her age before she realized the overpriced espresso did not come with full service tables. The menu was written in impossibly small text as if to signify the hipsters milling around were wearing glasses for purposes other than vision correction.

"What the hell is a chai coffee?" Pooja asked the cashier behind the counter.

"It's—"

"You know 'chai' means tea in Hindi? So that means tea coffee."

The cashier included an evil eye with Pooja's small Americano at no extra charge.

"That'll be three-twenty-five."

"How is this place more expensive than New York?"

"I'll get that for the pretty lady," someone behind Pooja said.

The cashier smirk at her panicked expression. Fortunately, the cashier used the awkward exchange as a cue to leave Pooja and Jeff alone.

Pooja turned around in slow motion to fixate on the eyes that broke her heart so long ago.

"Did you find the place okay?" Jeff asked.

"I have a GPS. I'm very good with computers," Pooja blurted.

"That is one thing I could have never known about you back in NOLA."

"Yes, we are old."

Jeff managed a chuckle in what already appeared to be a tainted atmosphere.

Pooja tried to look into his intense blue eyes for comfort as she had when they were younger. All his eyes offered now were uncertainty.

"What brings you down to Atlanta? What's the conference about?" he asked.

"Immigration human rights," Pooja responded without thinking.

"Decided on a career change from architecture?"

"No, I just find the subject interesting."

Pooja scoffed at herself. She couldn't believe the career she had fought so hard to establish wasn't even her instinctive fallback lie. Thoughts of Deepa permeated her brain.

"You're a professor here at Emory?" she asked.

"Yep. Been here about fifteen years now."

"Where were you before?"

"UCLA for two years, UVA for one, George Mason for five—"

"Oh my God. You were in DC for five years?"

Jeff was alarmed at Pooja's sudden onset of hysterics.

The thought that this man had roamed the streets minutes from her home made Pooja tense. "Why didn't you stay at Tulane?"

The half-finished ceiling suddenly caught Jeff's attention. His eyes stayed fixated upward for an extended break in conversation.

Pooja did not fly all the way down to Atlanta to stare at Jeff's Adam's apple and cleared her throat to get the point across.

"I had some memories I needed to escape," he eventually responded.

"You mean me?" Pooja's voice trailed.

"No." He quickly changed his tone after he saw Pooja's offended jaw was lying on the ground. "Losing you was very hard, Pooja, but I was referring to Charles passing."

"AIDS?"

"Car crash."

Fuck! Pooja's mind screamed. She couldn't have said something more offensive if she had tried. Jeff's Southern chivalrous behavior hadn't worn off, and he assured Pooja hers was a fair guess given the era.

"Would you like another coffee?" he offered.

"No thanks, I think I will save the money to buy a motorcycle."

"Ha. I see you still have that biting sense of humor."

He produced the first real smile since they had sat down. She felt the tension was cut in half and deflated to the ground. Her seat then moved miles across the field that had separated them. Both were sliding back into place as close friends.

"Can I ask why you got back in contact?" he asked.

"I randomly came across your website," Pooja lied.

As she had many times in the past year, Pooja silently thanked the Internet. She was growing confident using the excuse of "randomly" stumbling across something online to bring up in a discussion or to contact someone. It had been much harder to lie in the eighties.

Pooja's feeble excuse was enough to keep Jeff satisfied for the moment. He recapped his life at Emory, how he felt being on a tenure track, and how he felt to once again teach rich kids as a man from a poor background. Chats with Jeff as the main subject were never to his liking, however, and he quickly reverted back to Pooja's (fake) conference.

"There was an interesting immigration case in Orlando. I think his last name was Rodriguez," Jeff said.

"Ramirez," Pooja immediately corrected.

"You've heard of it?"

"Yes . . . My daughter worked on the case."

"Pooja. You have a daughter?"

Pooja's heart raced so fast, as though it were competing for an Olympic gold medal.

"Yes. She's twenty-five, lives in New York and works at The Justice Coalition. I think."

"You don't know?"

"We haven't spoken in nine months. That's the real reason why I wanted to meet."

"Pooja, we never . . . You know she can't be mine . . ."

"Anand is her father, Jeff."

Jeff looked mortified. "Of course. What a stupid thing to say. But why her? Why me?"

"Jeff, you broke my heart, and as a result, I rejected my gay daughter."

Jeff went bug eyed, and she questioned if she was being unreasonable. Her moment of doubt quickly passed.

"Pooja, for me, our connection was just platonic."

"I was in love with you. I went insane when you left."

"I never wanted to let you go."

Jeff gently guided Pooja's face to make eye contact and apologized for something that was never really his fault. Though these kinds of situations had victims, laying blame was not the answer.

"Even platonic, I really loved you, Pooja."

"I can't remember the last time I've seen a true friend."

"Tell me about her."

Pooja always smiled as she described her daughter, her Deepa. Deepa was an amalgamation of so many different people.

"What part of her does she share with you?"

"With me?"

Deepa saw the world with the same curiosity as Pooja did as a child. When Pooja had seen Deepa frolicking through the rivers of chocolate, the cities governed by music, and a globe that shifted at her touch, Pooja had rediscovered excitement in the future.

"Together, we constructed our own world and marched to the beat of a drum no one else could imagine."

"What happened?"

"Our convergence parted."

Fantasies didn't translated to the harshness of the real world.

"Deepa wanted to join the outside, the others. I didn't have the strength to follow."

"What does that have to do with me?"

"Everything and nothing."

"The words 'I'm gay' destroyed your first utopian society?"

"That's everything."

"Deepa made the only real choice to move forward?"

"And nothing."

Pooja had dreaded the thought someone would be with Deepa the way Pooja had dreamt of being with Jeff. Her pain had become her homophobia.

"Her orientation doesn't change your relationship."

"No."

"Her love of someone else is what scares you."

"Yes."

It had everything and nothing to do with Jeff. It had everything and nothing to do with Deepa's sexual orientation.

"You need to talk to her."

"I can't."

"Why not?"

"I did the same thing to her as my mother did to me. We'll never recover."

"One year of no contact will not destroy a lifetime of good will."

Now a domain expert in reconciling with family, Jeff assured Pooja he would get her connected to the right resources. The right resources would help Pooja reconnect to her daughter.

Jeff glanced down at his watch and sighed. He had a class starting in ten minutes. "Do we have time to meet again?"

"The conference was a lie, dummy."

"I know. I was being polite, dummy."

They exchanged every possible form of communication before verifying when they would next meet in person. Before leaving, Jeff swallowed Pooja in a bear hug he seemed to have been saving for this very occasion.

Pooja stood back as he grabbed his keys and walked out the door. She had the ultimate comfort that this time he had not left forever.

Chapter 100

MAKING GOOD ON their original commitment, this time around, Deepa and Audrey decided to take things slowly. Ample time apart had built a kind of excitement that weathered with too much exposure. Even so, they found it strange to go at this pace. Their interactions were rich with a personal history a new relationship did not offer. Both had to make an effort to refrain from saying previously innocuous statements.

"We'll do it tomorrow."

Deepa found a lack of these statements disappointing. A lack of these statements meant they were not where they thought they would be. This was part of the battle.

Audrey had come over tonight to cook dinner with Deepa. A talentless chef before she went back to Paris, she had spent much of her breakup therapy learning how to use the kitchen. The menu for this evening hailed from Scandinavia.

"Did you find the wine?" she called out as Deepa walked through the doorway.

"They didn't have any good Rieslings. I got a rosé instead."

A rosé was not the best for her recipe. The wine store Deepa had been going to for the last four years was always a hit or miss in its selection.

"A great new store just opened in Gramercy. We can go there tomor . . . umm . . . We can go next week," Audrey said.

"What's in the dish?" Deepa asked.

"Sprinkle some flour and sugar over the garlic, and . . ."

Deepa was starting to regret agreeing to this meal. Garlic and sugar sounded similar to the combinations Audrey had thought worked when they first started dating.

A knock at the door interrupted Audrey mid-explanation. Grateful at the timing, Deepa ran over to answer. The peephole was dirty with the years of familiarity. When she finally got a visual, she nearly fell over.

"It's my grandmother," Deepa exclaimed in a panicked whisper.

Deepa felt her good psychologist of a girlfriend rush to her side. In the chaos of coming out to Pooja, Deepa had simply assumed she was not to talk to Lakshmi. When she saw her grandmother at the door, she invited doubt to the few constants of her intricate situation.

"Invite her inside," Audrey suggested.

"And say what?"

"That I am your girlfriend . . . or whatever you want."

Deepa was just starting to reconnect with Audrey. Now was not the time for Audrey to reassert her opinions.

Patience had never been a virtue that graced Lakshmi's being. She was knocking rapidly on the door. "Deepa? Are you there, beta? I can hear voices."

Deepa painted a smile on her face before she opened the portal to reality. "Hi, Avva."

LAKSHMI NOTICED HER granddaughter was sweating as her dear friend Alpa had in the hottest Chennai months. She gingerly took her first steps inside the apartment and recalled how she had calculated the expenses when Deepa had decided to move out of the university dormitories. Deepa's rent was more than any mortgage Lakshmi had ever had.

"There is not much space," Lakshmi commented.

From Deepa's reaction, Lakshmi could tell this was not the best first thing to say. On the other side of the six-meter apartment, she saw a brown-haired woman stirring a pot and staring in her direction.

"Avva, this is Audrey," Deepa introduced.

"It is a pleasure to meet you," Audrey followed.

"What is your accent?" Lakshmi asked.

"It's French, I'm from Paris. Have you been?"

Deepa shot Audrey an expression that to Lakshmi communicated constipation.

"Try a laxative," Lakshmi advised.

Deepa whispered to Audrey in language Lakshmi could not understand.

"Sure, I will give you two some privacy," Audrey agreed.

Following Deepa's cue, Lakshmi waited for Audrey to leave before she offered an explanation of why she had come, and had come alone.

"Audrey appears kind. You have chosen your partner wisely."

"Partner? How do you know that word, Avva?"

The story was still hard for Lakshmi to piece together. It had started two Christmases ago, when she had approached her other granddaughter, Sahra, for a bit of information.

"Pooja was always insistent we never push you to get married," Lakshmi said to Deepa.

"I know. She wanted me to establish myself as a person first."

"Still, I would sometimes press the little ones for updates."

As a New Yorker and a child, Sahra was terrible at keeping secrets. Lakshmi took less than five minutes with Sahra to find out Deepa was in a relationship.

"Sahra's main concern was losing her ski trip," Lakshmi said.

"How did Pinni react?"

"Alpa forced me into a confrontation."

"Confrontation?"

"She phrased it differently. An intervention."

Alpa was first to use a set of words Lakshmi had found highly offensive:

—Gay

—Lesbian

—Sexual orientation

Not wanting to be any part of the discussion, Lakshmi had tried her best to leave the room whenever possible. On her last attempt, Alpa stopped her with one powerful question.

"Do you want to make the same mistake you made with Pooja?"

Lakshmi had never been so caught off guard. She screamed at Alpa for comparing the situations.

"This is different, this is sick," Lakshmi argued.

"This is *no* different. This is you not understanding," Alpa retorted.

"Too much New York has ruined your judgment."

"Mom, you have the chance to accept your granddaughter as you never did with your older daughter."

Lakshmi told Deepa how many times she had cried inside, seeing Pooja cry outside. Pooja had sacrificed everything for Deepa; Pooja felt like no one had sacrificed anything for her.

"That's not true, you did so much for my mother," Deepa countered.

"And she did so much for you."

"She took her empathy for me much further than you did for her."

That was precisely the point Alpa had tried to make to Lakshmi. For all of the battles Lakshmi had conquered for her daughters, she had not taken the initiative to understand her path of marriage should not be the same for Pooja.

"Pooja never found the words to tell me, how could she?"

"And you never found the courage to listen."

Alpa presented to Lakshmi a new choice with Deepa. "Mom, if I connect you to the right resources, will you try to understand? For Deepa?"

Lakshmi relied entirely on faith to respond as Alpa had hoped. "Yes."

Lakshmi brought her hands up to her granddaughter's and gripped with a gentle, but strong assurance. "I am going to sessions about minorities, beta."

"What kind of minorities?"

"They are very informative, talking about challenges in the workplace, at home, why stereotypes are hurtful."

"What kind of minorities, Avva?"

Deepa looked into the eyes of her tired grandmother. Lakshmi knew in that moment that her face communicated the depths of her struggles, triumphs, and losses.

"What kind of minorities, Avva?"

"The LGBTQ community, beta," Lakshmi replied.

A river of emotion seemed to erupt within Deepa. "What finally convinced you to go?"

"I was born into this world a Shudra, a peasant caste."

"You overcame all odds to be here."

"I did, though the costs entailed were pure injustices."

Lakshmi and her family had endured the evils of society in exchange for Lakshmi's progression.

"Deepa, many people in India said I did not deserve an education. Many people said educating a girl was unnatural. Just because there were many people does not mean they were right. I will not be a part of the many against you."

Chapter 101

JEFF TOLD POOJA one of his students had just walked into his office with a question.

"Talk tomorrow?" he asked her.

"I have lunch with the girls. Anytime before one works," she replied.

"Excellent, can't wait."

A happy sigh escaped Pooja's lips as she stared down at her phone, which flashed, "Call ended. Duration: 60:51." She and Jeff had made it a point to talk every day since her trip to Atlanta. His renewed friendship and a newfound openness toward others constituted the resources Pooja needed to move forward. This time the Internet was the facilitator, not the replacement.

Clanging plates grabbed Pooja's attention, and she made her way into the dining room. A confirmation of Lakshmi's old age was on the table.

"Mom, you brought out three plates. Trying to set me up with a husband?"

"Very funny."

Lakshmi continued her place-setting efforts without a further line of explanation.

Pooja walked to the study to her other form of progression. She knew she was getting ahead of herself with the depth of her urban planning research. First she needed to get into the program at the University of Maryland. Then the thesis would come.

Out of the corner of her eye, she saw an unrecognized car pull into the driveway. From her Orlando days, she knew a Florida license plate meant it was likely a rental. The mystery person entered through the back door as if this were their house. Suddenly, Pooja realized this was indeed their house.

"Deepa," Pooja screamed in alarm.

"Hi, Mom," Deepa replied, flowers and forgiveness outstretched.

"What the hell are you doing here?"

The furious reaction from Pooja was involuntary. She immediately regretted not saying something else—the stories, the apologies, the explanations. Any attempt she tried to make at reconciliation was replaced by the same offensive question.

"What are you doing here?"

"Chee. I invited her," Lakshmi interjected.

Pooja felt her body turn into a sack of sand. She grabbed the countertop to avoid crumbling into an amorphous pile.

"You *knew* what happened?" Pooja asked Lakshmi.

"I have come a long way in my understanding."

A tide of betrayal spewed from Pooja's body, nearly knocking down Lakshmi and Pooja. The word "understanding" was understood as irrelevant in the childhood Lakshmi had offered her elder daughter.

"*How* could you do this to *me*?" Pooja screamed at her mother.

"Mom, it's not *against* you, it's *for* me," Deepa offered.

In due time, Pooja knew she would know this. Her younger sister had made the same logical argument when they were kids. But her animosity of the situation had been constantly deflected to the recipient of the understanding—to Alpa.

"What if that happens again?" Pooja argued out loud.

Lakshmi and Deepa exchanged confused looks, telling Pooja she was not understood.

"I can leave you if you want," an already scared Deepa said.

"Yes, that would be best," Pooja whispered.

Lakshmi looked resigned and escorted her granddaughter to the car. Deepa's flowers and forgiveness were lying pathetically at Pooja's feet.

"IT'S TOO SOON, why did you tell me to come here?" Deepa asked Lakshmi.

"Go to the corner of Chester Road and Bridge Place. If we do not call you in an hour, you can go," is all Lakshmi offered.

Lakshmi came back inside and sat on the ground to face her daughter. She knew her daughter did not understand her efforts to properly express her sympathies. She knew Pooja would not understand sitting at eye-to-eye level was her best attempt at trying.

"Pooja, my life in India was extremely fragile."

"I know; that's all I heard growing up."

"I lost my father and my closest friend in the cruelest of ways."

"You've already told me the ending to this story."

"No, I haven't. Because the ending to my story is you and Deepa."

Lakshmi described her and her nana's walk to the decrepit cabin.

"Lakshmi, sometimes we do not live this life for our own opportunities. Sometimes, we live this life for the opportunities we bring to others," Nana had said.

Her father's words sustained Lakshmi through every hardship life had presented.

"I was living for *you*, Pooja."

"You were?"

"Yes. You are the reason I survived."

Lakshmi took a step back in her mind to recall how ill prepared she had felt for so much of her existence. She had raised a family in a foreign land; she had left a life to which she could never really return, and she had faced the reality she would spend half her years without her life partner.

"Pooja, I cannot correct what has already happened. Only what will happen."

"I am still not ready."

Lakshmi had been careful to observe Pooja and her transformation, and had delicately factored Pooja's fear when determining whether she thought Pooja was indeed ready. With a clarity she had never before experienced, she knew the answer before Pooja did. She took this opportunity to bestow a new confidence in her elder daughter.

"Pooja, you are an excellent mother. Deepa is so strong because of what you have done for her. One of my deepest regrets is not including you in your own life dialogue. You had a far greater insight to not repeat this mistake with Deepa."

"Mom, then don't do this to me now."

"Beta, I am not doing this *to* you. I am doing this *for* you. I am doing this *for* Deepa."

COMING FROM LAKSHMI, the line of reasoning had deeper meaning. As a daughter herself, Pooja knew she had a right to retreat. As a mother, her responsibility to include Deepa in their life discussion was an entirely different matter.

"I drove Deepa away. She must hate me," Pooja decided.

"Pooja, do you hate me?"

For many years, the answer to that question had been yes. Through Pooja's depression, anxiety, and anger, Lakshmi had turned a blind eye and had told Pooja to quit complaining.

"Pooja, do you hate me?" Lakshmi repeated.

But Lakshmi was also the reason Pooja grew up with food, a roof, and a steady modicum of safety. Lakshmi was the reason Pooja could focus on being an excellent mother.

"Pooja, do you hate me?"

"No . . . I don't hate you."

"Deepa does not hate you, either."

IN THE MIDST of yoga breathing techniques Audrey had taught her, Deepa jumped at the sound of her phone ringing. True to Lakshmi's prediction, the call came only thirty-five minutes after her second runaway from the house. She pulled into the driveway once more, praying these were the first steps back to a convergence.

"Want to take a walk?" Deepa and Pooja asked each other at the same time.

"Yes, this day should not be wasted," they both replied.

They fell into a rhythmic unison of small talk catch-up and petting dogs to lay a foundation to unfamiliar territory. Deepa took the first round of explanation and apologized for leaving a live bomb without instructions on diffusion.

Much to Deepa's shock, Pooja said the signs of Deepa's orientation had been obvious for a long time. Pooja hadn't been thrown by the shallow elements of how Deepa dressed or her curiosity in certain subjects. Her intimacy with Gloria, her disinterest in the opposite sex, her unease with the milestones that traditionally mark a girl's life had been the true signs that told Pooja.

"I should have approached you a better way," Deepa admitted.

"I should have listened to what you had to say."

Pooja recounted the lifetime of a difference four years between she and her younger sister had entailed. Beyond her education and profession, Alpa had been able to choose a love and happiness that fit her needs.

"I vowed my daughter would have the same opportunity."

"Thank you so much for letting me be who I am."

"I needed time to recognize who you love is part of who you are. It does not matter if your life partner is not a man."

The partner that had been chosen for Pooja was not her soul mate. Her soul mate had not been available to be her partner. Pooja had known that love, commitment, and passion in all its complicated forms were neither predictable nor formulaic. She was finally comfortable applying that same standard to Deepa.

"I wish Dad understood that. I drove Dad away," Deepa said.

"My darling Deepa, your father had his own reconciliation to address. You did nothing wrong; you are not his reason."

Pooja gently touched Deepa's shoulder to make it clear she had just agreed to soon disclose the details of Anand's departure from their lives.

Deepa offered to connect Pooja to resources to help her understand what it meant to have a gay daughter. Pooja merely smiled at the suggestion and told Deepa a former demon now turned angel had already started her along that journey. The process would be as long as it would be cathartic.

"HOW WAS YOUR walk?" Lakshmi asked back at the house.

"Transformative," Pooja replied.

"Reassuring," Deepa said.

Lakshmi gave an uncommon smile to her daughter and her granddaughter. She deeply inhaled the clear air and took a moment to watch in awe as the two women before her so eloquently captured such a remarkable journey.

"Come, let's go outside and watch the sunset," she told her family.

As the shadows the sun cast danced in the distance, they walked on to the patio for a long-deserved gaze of appreciation. Lining up their family from the slums of Chennai to the heart of New York City, they joined hands in the security of each other. Together they directed the giant clouds to part above their heads. Brilliant streaks of color beamed down from the Heavens and revealed the paths of marriage. A generational harmony at last illuminated an intersection at the converging horizon.

Tomorrow starts another special gift from God.

Epilogue
Deepa

IN THE YEARS after Mom and I took our walk, she approached the complex discourse in sexual orientation with the fervor of an academic subject. I was more comforted by her philosophy.

"No matter what, you are still my daughter."

One incredible milestone in our collective paths of understanding happened on my twenty-sixth birthday, when Audrey came down to Maryland with me. Seeing Mom, Avva, and Audrey at ease with each other was the best gift I could have ever imagined. Many LGBTQ people will never experience a comparable moment.

Two years later, Avva, Pinni, Audrey, and I gathered on the main lawn of the University of Maryland campus and cheered with the hope of every woman as Mom accepted her Bachelor of Science in Urban Studies and Planning. Mom enrolled in a Masters program at American University the following year.

A week after Mom completed her first semester as a professor, Avva passed away. Mom, Pinni, and I spread Avva's ashes in the same river as my grandfather.

Barbara eventually promoted me to the head researcher on the immigration unit of the New York The Justice Coalition office. Against the backdrop of one of the most significant eras of gay rights in America, my job increasingly dealt with cases that were as much LGBTQ as immigration issues. I loved it.

New York State legalized gay marriage in June 2011. Audrey and I continued our promise to take our time to grow into each other, less I would have proposed to her at the law passage announcement. During our fourth New Year's in concert, she suggested we move back in together. We decided that the racial and ethnic diversity of Queens best fit our needs. We have been there ever since.

"ARE YOU READY?" I whispered to Audrey.

"I am going to vomit."

"I love you too."

I glanced over at the giant banner that had become a symbol of inspiration. I knew there were many battles left to fight, but the power of that banner made me feel invincible.

"Equality? Check."

The announcement of federally recognized same-sex marriage was made sixty-five days ago. I proposed to Audrey sixty-four days ago. She said yes before I finished my sentence.

We surveyed the crowd—nearly two thousand sets of chattering, ecstatic voices were waiting alongside us to hear the words that honored decades of struggle.

"By the power vested in me by the District of Columbia and the United States government, I now pronounce you wives, and husbands. You may kiss your partner," the judge said.

As we made our way down the steps of the US Capitol, I spotted our amazing support system in the distance. Through the millions of people celebrating in the streets, and the thousands protesting our peace, Pinni gave us each a single flower. Before I had a chance to say anything, I heard someone shout.

"We're from Channel 10 News. Can we get your reaction on the events today?" a reporter said to us.

Audrey let me properly thank Pinni as she explained the significance of today as an immigrant. We had already started the paperwork for both of us to be entitled to live as a married couple in either of our countries of birth.

The reporter and cameraman turned to me. I saw they were mentally debating whether to highlight our obvious different cultures, our different skin tones.

I preemptively responded with a sentiment of universal relevance. "I've known so many who have lost this battle. I'm incredibly lucky to have a family who supports our right to live open and honestly."

"Your family has reacted well?" the reporter followed.

I grabbed Audrey's hand and directed the reporter a few steps over. "I owe everything in my life to this woman!"

"And who is this?" the reporter asked.

"This is my mother, the bravest person I have ever met."

The reporter captured Mom's shining face and shining words before finishing the interview with a final question. "How are you and your wife planning on celebrating?"

I peered over at Audrey who happily motioned for me to continue.

"In lieu of a honeymoon, we're taking a long family vacation."

"Where are you going?" the reporter asked.

"New Orleans, Paris, and Chennai."